Cut Her Out in Little Stars

Daniele Kasper

Chapter One

Present:

Cara ran as fast as she could, but it was too late.

The subway's red taillights vanished into the dark tunnel. One day Cara would make it to work on time. Today was not that day.

Cara slipped through the thick crowd of morning commuters. There was an alternate subway she could take. This line would take her further north than her office building, adding an extra ten-minute walk, but she couldn't afford to be late again. She already had two written warnings in her file. A third would, at best, get her pay docked, or worse, fired. Her colleague, Lauren, had been covering for her for over a year, preventing that third strike from sending Cara to the local job search office.

Cara had fallen in love with New York eight years earlier when she vacationed there with her family. Central Park was her favorite, especially this time of year. She could picture the vast expanse of trees, colored amber and crimson, the leaves tumbling to the ground covering the grass in a blanket of sunset shades. After all this time, the magical beauty of the autumn colors still had her captivated. More like a captive, she thought. Were there any good reasons why she still lived there? She couldn't think of any.

Her phone beeped in her pocket. A text from David. Still on for dinner? David, her boyfriend, was nice enough. He had a good job, and she got along with his family. He wasn't unattractive with his sandy blond hair, dark brown eyes, and boyish jawline that couldn't seem to grow a beard. They had met through friends almost two years prior, and he asked her out on a date that same night. She had reluctantly agreed. She hadn't wanted to start anything serious, but her best friend, Olivia, convinced her to give him a chance.

She slipped the phone back into her pocket. David could wait. She already knew what the evening plans would be. They would meet at 7:00 P.M. on the dot at the little Italian place a few blocks from her apartment. As always, David would order the lasagna then tease Cara for how long it took her to decide on something new. They had the routine down to a science, which felt more like a rut with every passing week.

David was utterly smitten with her. Cara still hadn't developed the deep emotional connection to him that she expected. She mentally shushed herself. She should consider herself lucky to have found a genuinely decent guy. The city's shallow dating pool was something she wanted to avoid at all costs.

Olivia had gotten married last year to one of David's close friends, Greg. Cara envied their relationship. Greg treated her like a queen. They were equally crazy about each other, almost to the point of mushy grossness.

They were inseparable. Traveling, running marathons, and exploring the city, they did it all. Just last week, Olivia had texted her pictures from their weekend hiking trip in the Catskill Mountains.

David was far less bold and daring, preferring a more low-key lifestyle. The most adventurous he ever got was when Cara convinced him to order Chinese takeout. He was safe, which became incredibly boring sometimes. Secretly, she wished he was more like Greg.

Yesterday, she'd spotted a business card from a jewelry shop half-hidden under a pile of unopened mail on his counter. Cara's chest tightened. She checked to see if David had noticed her discovery before quickly shoving the card back under the stack of envelopes. If he was planning on proposing, she was in big trouble. She wasn't sure her answer would be yes.

Couples should click. She longed for the natural, easy-going relationship Olivia and Greg had. It just worked. With David, it was like they were always on their own trajectory. They were like two magnets, pushing away from each other no matter how hard you forced the poles to touch.

Her doubts were even further confirmed when Olivia invited her to a gallery opening last week. David made several excuses, attempting to get out of having to attend with her.

"Just go with Oliva. You can spend some time together. I have too much work to finish."

"Greg will be there too. I don't want to be a third wheel."

"I don't really like art."

"We don't have to stay long. You can have a few beers with Greg. All I have to do is make an appearance, and we can leave."

It had taken a lot of convincing, but he reluctantly agreed. The beautiful abstract art pieces lining the walls captivated her.

"It's so sad." She looked at one of the largest paintings in the room. Roughly brushed streaks of blue crisscrossed over the canvas conveying frustration that only came from a place of immense grief.

"How can a painting be sad? It's just paint slapped on paper." David shrugged, sipping his beer.

"You don't see it? There is so much emotion in all of his work."

"I'm sorry. I don't see the point in all this. It's a bunch of blue paint. Look at it. A three-year-old could do better than this."

Cara was disappointed David couldn't see what she did. The real problem wasn't his inability to see any deeper meaning in the painting. It was more evident now than ever before; David didn't truly understand her. She quietly browsed the rest of the gallery alone while David talked numbers with Greg.

Oliva came over and handed a glass of white wine to her. "Are you avoiding David, or is he avoiding you?"

"I'm not avoiding him. He isn't interested in the whole art scene. You know him. It's not his thing. He'd rather talk to Greg then look at the paintings."

"They always want to talk shop," Olivia joked, trying to lighten the mood. "Just ignore them."

Cara did her best to enjoy the rest of the evening, but a dark cloud cast shadows on her good mood. She couldn't stop herself from questioning the longevity of their relationship. There was an expiration date rapidly approaching.

"Did I do something wrong?" David approached her towards the end of the night. Cara didn't respond right away.

"No, it's fine, really." She dismissed his concerns. An argument was the last thing she needed. "We can leave now."

"I'm sorry if I upset you tonight, but I tried telling you art isn't my thing. You're the creative one, not me." David walked to the corner and hailed a taxi.

"No, David, it's not that. I'm just tired." She hoped to reassure him, but he didn't let it drop.

"I just don't get it. I don't understand you." His mouth set in a hard line, he looked away from her, shaking his head. "You just seem so miserable all the time. Maybe you'd be happier if your head wasn't always stuck in the clouds."

Cara recoiled. Where had that outburst come from? "You think I'm miserable because I like art and talking about my feelings?"

"You know that isn't what I meant."

"Then what did you mean, David? Please, explain it to me." She crossed her arms over her chest.

"You're an optimist. You have a heart of gold, and you always try to see the best in people, but Cara, you're always dreaming. You're trying to live a life that doesn't exist. This," David gestured an outstretched hand towards the busy streets, "is real life."

"Maybe if you spent as much time analyzing art as you did your stupid stock numbers, you might understand how I feel." She hadn't meant to snap, but it slipped out before she could stop it. What was wrong with wanting more, having dreams? David was a realist, grounded in the gloomy truth of the world around him. His idea of dreaming was hoping the stock market closed over a hundred points up.

David's shoulders dropped and his stern expression melted.

"I'm sorry. I didn't mean to say that." Cara reached for him, but he stepped away.

"Yes, you did."

Uncomfortable silence ballooned between them. Fortunately, a taxi pulled up. Always the gentleman, he opened the door for her.

"I know things between us have been strained lately, but I think things would be so much easier if you moved in with me." David reached for her hand, but Cara skillfully moved it away under the pretense of rubbing her nose.

Stuck in the taxi with no way to make a getaway, Cara pretended to laugh, even though she cringed internally.

"David, we've talked about this. You live on the opposite side of the city. Your commute is already over an hour, and it would make mine just as long. It just makes sense for us to stay where we are for right now. It's the smartest choice." She used David's logical tendencies against him. "And you can't move in with me because Rick already said he would double the rent with a second occupant."

David reluctantly agreed she was right, but she could tell he was hurt that she didn't want to discuss it. He slumped in his seat and was quiet for the remainder of the drive back to her apartment. When he walked her to her door, he gave her a soft kiss on the lips. There was no spark, not even a tingle, just an empty indifference that worried her.

She envisioned David sitting across from her holding a ring box, and she had an overwhelming urge to run as far as she could. Why was she still with someone she didn't want to marry? Because it was easy? Because he was nice? Those were not good enough reasons, no matter how much she tried to justify them.

Cara wanted more than khakis and a four-door sedan in her future. She wanted the wind in her hair. She wanted to travel and see the world. So many dreams she wanted to fulfill. Those dreams would never become a reality if she continued to head down the same road she was currently on. Cara could never find an exit, and she definitely couldn't see herself becoming a Goldschmidt.

The screeching of the subway coming into the station jolted her back to reality. She yanked her subway pass from her pocket and slid it into the turnstile slot. It beeped loudly, and she pushed through the barrier. She knew what the plans were for tonight. Plans for the rest of her life? Those were still up in the air.

She ran across the platform and jumped onto the closest car as the doors slid shut. Another close call, but for her, it was the norm. She was always cutting it a little too close. With the subway and her rent also, she was barely making it. When did living become just getting by? She was barely hanging on by her fingertips from paycheck to paycheck, struggling to get through each week. She grabbed a silver handhold above her head and took a deep breath.

In the lobby that morning, her landlord, Rick, had been standing on a ladder, changing a bulb in one of the light fixtures. She'd dropped her head, hoping to avoid him, but he twisted to look at her as she walked by him. Busted.

"You're over a week late on rent, again."

She threw him her biggest smile, hoping to smooth things over. "I'll get it to you by Friday, I promise." She hurried toward the doors.

"You said that last month too!" Rick shook his head, waving a screwdriver at her.

"I'll have it!" she called over her shoulder, making her getaway.

Cara leaned back, letting her head rest against the wall. Never did she imagine she would be on the verge of thirty and working as a telemarketer. Cara remembered when she used to have so many plans for her life. Moving to New York had put a screeching halt on all of them. She had been so young and naive about the world. Despite how things had turned out, she didn't regret her decision. It had opened her eyes to what she truly wanted in life. The allure of the fast-paced life in the Big Apple had drawn her in. She quickly discovered fast-paced and exciting were not synonyms.

She had desperately wanted to get away from her small-town life in Pennsylvania. She jumped on the first opportunity to move. Landing a job as a waitress at a swanky uptown restaurant had been her ticket out. The job was physically demanding, and she worked long hours, but the tip money alone made it worth it. It was also where she met Olivia.

Realtra closed less than a year later, and she desperately needed a job. The telemarketing gig was less than ideal, but it was a paycheck. It paid for her rent and food but not much else.

With her rent nearing $1,600 a month, her salary was barely covering it. By the time she paid all her bills, she had nothing left at the end of the month. Moving would be a costly venture. As much as she wanted to leave, she couldn't afford it with an empty savings account.

Her mother had offered for her to move home for a while until she got things sorted out, but Cara couldn't bring herself to accept the offer. It was more out of pride than anything else. Looking back, she worried she'd made a colossal error in judgement by not using it as her opportunity to get out.

She pulled out her phone and texted Laura that she would be late again just as the subway arrived at her stop.

"Excuse me." Cara squeezed her way through the thick mass of people in the car, slipping between the closing doors. She hurried up the steps to the street. Olivia leaned against a bike rack, waiting for her, coffee cup in hand.

"I got your favorite." Olivia gently shook the cup.

"You are the best!" Cara took a long drink, letting the coffee warm and energize her. She wished she'd had a chance to tell Olivia to add an extra shot of espresso; she had a feeling she would need it today.

"One of those mornings?" Olivia chuckled.

Cara shook her head, blowing out a long breath through her nose. "You have no idea," she groaned. "You didn't have to meet me here."

"I don't have a meeting until ten, so I had a little extra time. Plus, I could use the walk. We won't have many nice days left before the snow arrives."

The brisk chill in the air made Cara even more grateful for the hot latte in her hand. She zipped her jacket and shoved her free hand in her pocket to stay warm. Winter was on its way and would soon dump heaps of snow onto the city. The beautiful layer of pure white wouldn't last long, quickly turning into ugly brown slush.

Cara liked to believe autumn was nature's colorful way of apologizing for what was about to happen next.

Olivia worked as a paralegal in the office building next to Cara's. After they lost their waitressing jobs, she and Olivia applied for a decent paying secretary job at the law firm. Oliva got the job. Cara was happy for her. Olivia was a hard worker, and it was a great company. Her boss had even added on a small stipend to take night classes and get a degree. Cara had never quite been able to get her feet back under her. Despite the differences in their lives, Olivia was loyal. She was the kind of friend every girl needed. If she moved away, leaving Olivia would be the hardest part.

"How does lunch at Lida's sound?" Olivia's question pulled Cara's wandering mind back to the conversation.

"Sure." Cara couldn't afford the high prices at the little bistro across the street, but she didn't want to let on how much she struggled financially. Olivia picked up on the hesitation in her voice.

"We did just eat there a couple of days ago. Let's hit up the food trucks today instead. Is that okay with you?" Olivia smiled over her coffee cup as she took a sip.

The rotating string of food trucks that came by during lunch hours wasn't much cheaper than Lida's, but at least Cara would be able to find the least expensive option available.

"That works for me. See you later." Oliva and Cara parted ways. Cara scanned her work badge, pushed through the turnstile, and got in the elevator. Cara pulled her hair into a ponytail and leaned against the wall until the doors opened on her floor.

Shift changes were always hectic. She made her way down the long rows of cubicles until she arrived at hers. Lauren worked the overnight shift. She was finishing up a phone call. The transition between them would be quick and effortless. Lauren would slip off her headset and hand it to Cara, who would tuck it over her ears and adjust the microphone as she slid into the chair to make the next call without even a second to settle in. Work here was fast-paced, tedious, and mind-numbingly monotonous.

Lauren pressed a button on the earpiece and swiveled in the chair to face Cara. "I logged you on at eight. Curtis hasn't made any rounds yet, so I think you're in the clear."

"You're amazing. I owe you. Again."

"Just add it to the list." Lauren laughed and grabbed her coat. Cara sat in the chair and hit the button to dial. She waved goodbye to Lauren. Lauren returned the gesture with a smile, slung her purse over her shoulder, and was gone.

"Hi, my name is Cara. I'm calling from Impro. Is this a good time to talk for a minute about life insurance?" A shrill, angry voice yelled back at her. Cara pressed a finger to the bridge of her nose. It was going to be a long day.

One call blended into the next. She hated the robotic nature of her work. Maybe David had a point; she was miserable. Her mind kept drifting to images of white sand beaches, towering mountain ranges, and endless stretches of open road that faded away into the horizon. When the lunch break finally arrived, Cara practically ran to the elevator.

"You okay?" Olivia put her sandwich down; her brows pinched together in concern.

Cara shrugged sheepishly, caught not paying attention, but she couldn't stop her mind from wandering to vacations, travel, escape. "Yeah, I'm sorry. I can't seem to stay focused."

Oliva frowned.

"I just feel…" Cara trailed off, not quite sure which word to use. Cara took a few extra seconds to chew while she came up with an answer.

"Restless?" Olivia supplied, crossing her legs casually. "You've been restless since we met."

Cara chewed at the corner of her thumbnail. Olivia knew her way too well. "I just keep feeling like something in my life has to change."

"What kind of change? Job? Apartment?"

"Boyfriend?"

"Have you talked to David about how you've been feeling?" Olivia pressed. "I know he isn't the most exciting guy, but you have to give him a chance to work on things."

"I found a business card for Argento's in his coat pocket."

"The jewelry store?"

"I think he is planning on proposing." It didn't feel right saying it aloud, but as her best friend, Olivia had a right to know.

Olivia's brown eyes widened. "Shut up, are you serious? That's so exciting!" She paused. "Why don't you seem excited about this?" Olivia slumped back in her seat. "Oh no."

"Oh no, what?" Cara feigned offense.

"You're doing it again. You're going to run away." Olivia gave a shake of her head and sipped her coffee.

"I'm not going anywhere."

"I meant mentally," Olivia corrected. "You did the same thing with, um, what's his name? Owen." She waved a hand in the air as she racked her brain for the name. "As soon as someone gets a little too close, you freak out and shut yourself off."

"I do not."

"What about Michael?" Olivia crossed her arms over her chest.

"Hey, that isn't fair. He was still in love with his ex-wife."

"Whatever. It's the same reason you don't even own a pet."

"I can't have cats or dogs in my apartment. You know that. Rick has strict rules against-"

"You could get a fish." Olivia looked smug, knowing she was right.

"Really? A fish?"

"What's wrong with a fish? They don't smell. They don't make a mess. You don't have to walk it. Having one could help you finally commit to settling down."

"I don't need help committing. I've been here for eight years. I think that's pretty settled, don't you?"

"No, I don't. If you were so happy with your life here, you wouldn't constantly be thinking about leaving the city. Don't look at me like that. I saw the travel brochures in your apartment."

"You dirty little snoop."

"I didn't snoop. You didn't even hide them that well."

"Don't you ever think there's more to life than just work and home every single day? You and Greg take trips all the time."

"Yes, but we always come back here. But it's okay. I understand. You just want to move away from me." With an exaggerated sniffle, Olivia dabbed her napkin at the corner of her eyes.

"Okay, drama queen. I don't want to move away from you. I just don't think I'm meant to live here forever."

Cara stared at the busy streets. All the people were in such a rush. Cars honked before lights even turned green. People pushed and shoved, desperate to get to their destinations. She hated the perpetual feeling of impatience that came with living in New York. Why was everyone in such a hurry? No one ever took the time to slow down and relax. The only place she found any reprieve from the endless hamster wheel whirl was deep in Central Park. Nestled under the thick branches of a cluster of huge oak trees was a green, metal bench she had stumbled upon years ago. She would often sit there, watching people pass by on the path and let the world slow down for an hour or two.

Olivia laughed. "You know what you need? A vacation. Spending a week on the beach somewhere might do you some good. You'll come back feeling refreshed. Maybe David will go with you. He's a nice guy." As if reading Cara's mind, Olivia continued. "Okay, so he's a little quiet, but he's good for you."

Cara wasn't sure what Olivia meant by that. Maybe David did keep her grounded. Then why did it feel like she was suffocating around him? Being held down was far different than being kept grounded. Olivia was right about one thing; she did need a vacation.

A week somewhere in the tropics with cocktails that had the little pink umbrellas in them wouldn't hurt. Just a short break to reset, and when she came back, maybe she'd be ready to commit to this life. David could easily pay for it, but she needed to convince him to go with her.

Olivia chattered on for the rest of lunch, and Cara did her best to listen, leaving her even more drained by the time it was over.

The rest of the day was a fuzzy blur, and when Jennifer from the evening shift arrived, Cara wasn't sure exactly what had happened in the last few hours. How could a simple day at work leave her so disoriented?

"I'll see you tomorrow." Cara waved to Olivia as they parted ways at the top of the stairs leading down to the subway.

On her way down to the platform, someone roughly bumped into her, nearly knocking her off her feet.

"Watch it, bitch!" the angry man glared at her over his shoulder. Cara rolled her eyes, rubbing her tender shoulder. Rude.

New York had lost much of its magical charm years before. Once, she had loved the city's endless hustle and energy, but New York had a dark side lurking behind all the bright lights. A rough edge that could cut somebody too soft to handle the sharpness of the people. It hid deep anger that simmered just under the surface that could explode out at unexpected times. It still took her by surprise even after all these years.

She boarded the last car on the subway, ready to go home and relax for a bit before dinner. She wanted to spend as much time as she could in a hot shower before meeting David.

New York was too loud, too crowded, too big. More passengers streamed into the car, squishing her up against the back door. Crammed apartment, crammed cubicle, and crammed subway. One day soon, she would leave.

Cara closed her eyes and dreamed of a vacation somewhere far away, where there was a lot of space. No people, just a whole lot of personal space; a concept New Yorkers were forced to forget.

The subway rocked back and forth. The fluorescent lights overhead flickered. It rocketed past a station and into the tunnel.

Cara daydreamed of her vacation with big fields, open prairies, and plenty of legroom. She dreamed of climbing mountains, hiking across forests all alone. Strange how David was never alongside her in any of her daydreams. She was always alone. It was the most obvious clue that David didn't have a place in her life long-term. Even if she asked him to go with her, would he be willing to leave the city? Chances were good that he would say no. She would be on her own. There was an accompanying sense of overwhelming loneliness, something she was used to.

That was the funny thing about New York City. A person could be surrounded by thousands of people and yet, feel completely alone. And if things didn't change, pretty soon she'd be homeless too. She was lucky Rick hadn't evicted her yet. She would be eating dollar slices from Gino's Pizzeria and two for one hot dogs from Oscar's corner cart for the next month.

No fancy food truck sandwiches or French bistro soup for her for a while. Eventually, she would have to tell Olivia funds were tight. Olivia would end up offering to pay for everything, making her feel even worse about it. To Olivia, money wasn't an issue, especially since marrying Greg. She meant well by it, her heart was in the right place, but it made Cara more insecure and self-conscious. Olivia would tell her to ask David for money, but Cara refused to be indebted to him in any way.

The lights flickered again, momentarily leaving the car dark. In the blackness, Cara could smell ozone, an acrid electric smell, hanging heavily in the air. As the lights came back on, they flashed red momentarily. She frowned. That was unusual.

A loud bang and a harsh grinding noise made Cara jump. She got a whiff of smoke but couldn't determine the source. There was strange shouting faintly in the distance - a man shouting. Someone else yelled back. A woman, possibly? She couldn't make out what they were saying.

No one in the car appeared concerned. They were completely engrossed in their newspapers, smartphones, and idle chit chat; too busy to pay any attention.

Could they not hear that?

The lights went out again, and the subway jerked violently. Cara slammed against the back door of the car. Someone's elbow connected with her ribs, and her lungs emptied. The wind was knocked out of her. She coughed and wheezed, gasping for air. She groped around in the dark for a handhold. An ear-piercing beeping sound chirped, but it was distant as if it was coming from outside the car.

When the lights didn't come back on, the first cries of alarm from the other passengers rang out in the dark. Something was wrong.

Cara fumbled for her phone in her pocket to text Olivia, but someone bumped into her. The phone slipped from her grasp. Shit, no. It was too crowded for her to reach down to get it. The glass had cracked when it hit the floor, just another expense she couldn't afford. As the subway raced around a curve, it slid underneath a seat, the white glow of the screen vanishing.

A sizzle of electricity crackled down her arms, leaving behind a trail of stinging goosebumps. She sucked in a deep breath of air. The charged air had a metallic tinge to it like she was sucking on a penny. The car jerked again, flinging her against the door. Her head and shoulder connected with it, and it flew open. She was inches from being ejected from the car.

A scream welled up in her throat, but she couldn't make a sound: the wind rushed around her stealing the breath from her lungs. She wildly reached out for anything to hold onto and looked over her shoulder at the open door. She could see the tracks flashing below in a dark blur. One misstep or one wrong move, and she was dead.

The subway raced along the tracks and around another corner. The car leaned, and Cara's body momentarily tilted away from the open doorway. Her hand grasped something cold and hard. She clutched at it, pulling herself closer, clinging to it in relief.

There was a flash of blue so bright it left her seeing spots in the blackness. The scream stuck in her throat finally made way to her lips, and it sounded over the thundering air rushing around her. Her fingers slipped from the handhold. Tendrils of blue light snaked around her wrists and up her arms. It coiled around her ankles and up her legs. Electricity crackled through it. Every part of her tingled with the prickly sensation of pins and needles.

Just as she lost her grip, an immense pressure enveloped her. She was being crushed and ripped apart at the same time. It was like she was being torn in two, being pulled in opposite directions by unseen forces and yet contracting into a singular point. She could hear a man yelling again through the commotion, followed by the deep boom of an explosion.

She flew out of the subway car but never hit the tracks. For a brief moment, she hovered, as if time had stopped. The blue light curled around her brightened and exploded into a brilliant flash of white. It cracked like thunder, blinding her, and she blacked out.

Chapter Two

2936:

If his crew were the stars, Commander Nikolas Caine was their sun. He stood motionless in the middle of the Bridge, hands clasped behind his back, deep in thought. He mentally analyzed every moment, picking apart the details of the last few days, no matter how insignificant they may have appeared. His crew was unusually busy - they flowed around him undisrupted, even though he blocked their path.

His presence was like gravity, and they were orbiting him. They hurried to complete their work as he remained undisturbed by the heightened commotion in the room.

The Confederation Council had moved one of his regularly scheduled supply drops ahead a day, and it turned out to be an error on a massive scale. One he and his crew were paying the price for in the aftermath.

Yesterday's Hostile raid on the nearby border planet was an absolute political nightmare. The unexpected attack was the bloodiest in recent years.

Thousands of colonists were dead: women and children murdered in their beds as they slept. The Hostiles came in the night, taking the small, remote border planet, Evid, by surprise.

It had been an uncharacteristically coordinated attack. Raiders from at least three different Clans had attacked village after village. With no means of communication, the villages had little to no warning, and the Raiders swept through each encampment, slaughtering every living soul they were able to hunt down. The numbers of survivors were in the mere hundreds.

Caine's crew was still in the process of analyzing the overwhelming amount of data and evidence to determine which Clan was ultimately responsible for planning the attack. However, it was unlikely they would be able to pinpoint one.

Caine's stomach rolled as he recalled finding the body of a small girl in a hut, still tucked into bed under a thin burlap sheet with a tiny stuffed toy clutched in her cold hands. Her throat had been brutally slit. A black puddle of her congealed blood had dried on the dirt floor.

For some inexplicable reason, he had taken the small trinket with him. He held it in his left hand, inside his pocket, rubbing the soft, worn fuzz with his thumb as if it would bring him some sense of comfort after all the carnage he had seen.

When his crew received the distress signal, he had immediately ordered his ship to turn around. Unfortunately, by the time they arrived, it was too late.

Caine and his crew spent the better part of two days tending to the wounded survivors, and there was still a significant amount of work to be done.

There had been no time to mourn the dead. The crew had piled the bodies, burned them, and returned to the ship. The stink of burning flesh lingered, clinging to him still, despite having scrubbed his skin raw - as if he could wash the memories away too.

Against his better judgment, Caine had several tactical assault ships remain behind to help the survivors with the continued recovery efforts. Although, he didn't think the small number of crew members left behind would make much of a difference. It didn't sit right with him, leaving the survivors there, defenseless, and with no assistance. He should have called in other ships under his command instead of leaving some of his own ship's defenses behind. There was a light cruiser just two days flight time away, but two days was a long time to leave the traumatized villagers on their own.

Caine had ordered his crew to head directly to the Capital planet, Arctus. He wanted to meet with the Council in person to discuss how to proceed with handling the increasing number of Hostile attacks.

Caine's job as Commander of the Confederation Fleet was mainly that of protector. His ship, the Archon, was always on patrol in the system as a preventative measure, deterring the clans from attacking. It was a heavy cruiser, the largest in the entire fleet.

With Hostile attacks growing more frequent and violent, Caine feared his job might soon turn into that of a combatant.

Regrets weighed heavily on his mind. If he hadn't allowed the Council to move the supply drop forward, he and his officers would have been there when the attack happened. At least the villages would have had a fighting chance. Unfortunately, the Archon had been long gone when they received the distress call, too far to turn back in time to help. The raid was over as quickly as it began, and the devastation was immense.

A small part of him was relieved they had missed the attack because it meant all of his crew were safe. He knew he would have lost some of them in the attacks if they were present in the fight against the Hostiles. However, as a leader, he felt the sting of remorse. He knew the number of civilian casualties would have been much lower had he been there. Maybe the Archon's presence would have deterred the attack altogether.

Caine let go of the toy. Regret was not a luxury he could afford in his position. Decisions were made, consequences unfolded, and everyone had to keep going in the aftermath. There was no looking back.

He had to make calculated choices for the greater good of all the Confederation and not second guess himself.

If he did, so would his crew. They looked to him to make those hard calls with unwavering indifference. He was finding remaining indifferent was much more challenging these days.

Lieutenant General Than Theoi, the ship's Flight Engineer, approached carrying a metal mug in each hand. He handed one to Caine.

Amka was a thick, bitter drink derived from ugari roots. It was a hardy plant, one of the few that grew well on the barren Border Planets. The drink was popular in many of the smaller, more remote colonies. It was commonly consumed to increase strength and stamina. Amka was an acquired taste, both in texture and flavor, but on the ship, it was the closest thing they had to the expensive kafei found back on the core planets.

The Confederation wasn't willing to spend thousands of denar in order to supply the crew with an energy boost they could pick up at any of their scheduled stops in the smaller colonies for far less.

"You better be here to give me good news." Caine downed the cup's potent contents in one gulp, preventing a grimace from turning down the corners of his mouth.

Than couldn't suppress a slight shudder as he swallowed down the last of his drink and placed the empty mug on a nearby table. "Disgusting stuff." He slid the mug away from him with the tip of his index finger.

Caine huffed, amused by Than's intolerance. They'd been drinking it for years, but Than still looked like he was about to be sick every time. The earthy flavor and thick, slightly slimy texture was hard to stomach.

Than was more than just a navigator. The two had gone through Confederation Fleet School training together, becoming close friends over the years. Than was his right hand, filling in when he was occupied elsewhere, handling various issues with the crew, and occasionally taking on the role of an unwanted voice of reason.

"We picked up something on the scanners. It's small, which indicates it's most likely a merchant class ship."

Caine placed down his mug. "Show me."

Than walked over to the command station towards the back of the Bridge, and Caine followed.

"Preliminaries showed no heat signatures, so, if it is a ship, it's likely been abandoned." Than tapped on the glass display screen in front of them. He pulled up images of the scan using his fingertips to make the image larger. He leaned closer, squinting as he inspected them.

Caine gripped the back of his chair with his hand. He was never one to sit. He always preferred to be part of the work instead of standing to the side and directing. It was why his crew was irrevocably loyal to him and the reason he was so well respected.

He had handpicked each one of his crew members, and they had stuck with him over the years. He could count the number of new crew assigned to the Archon in the last five years on only one hand.

Caine stared at the display, reviewing the results of the scan. A little blinking red dot indicated the location of the unknown ship. There was still a small, tight knot of tension in the pit of his stomach. He shifted his weight from one foot to the other as if it would help quell some of his unease. Maybe it was just his leftover nerves from yesterday, but something just wasn't right.

"Run the scan again," he directed. Than shot him a quick, questioning glance out of the corner of his eye before following the order.

Caine ignored the look. He knew Hostiles would have fired already, but he still couldn't shake the feeling he needed to double-check.

Hostiles tended to attack in a direct manner, hard and fast. They were brazen, aggressive, and extremely reckless when launching their assaults on Confederation ships.

Hostile ships were usually grossly outgunned, but they were bloodthirsty, irrational, and, frankly, psychotic. They didn't care what kind of disproportionate odds they were facing. As long as they caused mass casualties on the Confederation's side, they viewed it as justification for any lives they lost on their own.

"Xan, can you connect us to their comm system?" Caine asked the ship's Communication Officer.

Gensai Xan looked down at her screens, touching her display to check on the connection status. The green glow from the screen cast strange shadows on her face. "We are still too far out, Sir. We should be close enough shortly to create a stable link."

"I want to know as soon as we are in range."

"Yes, Sir."

Than turned to Caine. "Shields?"

"Not yet."

Than made his way back to the navigation area. Tabak Senn was the ship's Navigator, always keeping an eye out in space for objects and potential threats but during a time like this Than stepped in to assist.

Than slid into his chair next to Senn and checked the scanners. It wasn't long before Caine could see the ship in the distance, a small silver speck floating in the black. They approached as usual, but Caine was still on edge.

"Sir, we're ready," Xan informed him.

"Get us linked to their system."

She nodded curtly to Caine and went to work connecting the two ships' communication signals.

Caine grabbed the hanging transmitter from overhead and pressed the button on the side to speak. "This is Commander Caine of the Confederation Ship the Archon. Please identify yourself."

There was silence, nothing but the soft crackle of space static. The entire deck was silent as everyone waited for a response.

"Please identify yourself. Are you in need of assistance?" he tried again - still, no reply.

Caine replaced the comm on its hook and took a moment to let out a deep breath. Maybe it was just an abandoned merchant ship.

Parts and machinery broke on old ships and were often unfixable in space. Mechanical failures often forced crews to leave their ship behind, especially if they lacked the funds to pay for repairs. A crew would hail for assistance, board another ship and hitch a ride to wherever it was heading. Many crews would split up and take work on whichever planet they landed on. Scuttling was frowned upon, but more common than the Confederation preferred. It wasn't the first time they had run across an abandoned ship, and it wouldn't be the last. Caine needed to relax.

"Mark the location. Take the ship's registration numbers and-"

At that precise moment, just as the last bit of tension slipped away, the scanning screen gave a small ping.

In the quiet, it rang out like a scream. In the middle of the screen was a small red dot. The scanner had picked up a heat signature. The hairs on his neck and arms stood on end. Without warning, the ship in front of them thundered to life and opened fire. Lasers shot toward them from the small ship.

"Shields, now!" Caine roared as the entire Bridge descended into chaos. The vibrations of the first blast caused him to lose his balance. He grabbed the table to remain steady.

The scanner beeped rapidly. The merchant ship had cold start fusion engines and cloaking technology, which prevented the Archon's scanner from recognizing residual heat given off by equipment or people on board.

Top of the line, incredibly high-tech, and extremely expensive, the cold-fusion engines were made exclusively for military ships in the Confederation Fleet. They didn't need the same amount of time to heat up like a standard reactor before full engine ignition. It was a piece of advanced technology the smaller ship shouldn't have had any access to at all.

Caine's entire fleet had only been outfitted with the new engines a year ago, shortly after the technology was perfected for space. The specialty engines, paired with heat shielding technology and sophisticated laser weaponry, were illegal on any civilian ship. If Caine hadn't known any better, he would have sworn he was being attacked by one of the ships in his fleet. He was more in shock at the audacity this little ship had to launch an attack on him at all.

The Archon was the largest battleship in the entire Confederation Fleet and considered the main hub ship, carrying the highest number of personnel. It was designed to withstand most direct attacks: double-hulled with the strongest alloys and outfitted with the most advanced weaponry.

It was one thing for Hostiles to attack defenseless villages, even to attack smaller Confederation combat and assault ships but to attack the largest and most heavily armed and defended Confederation Ship in the fleet? Well, that was a suicide mission.

The only problem was their suicide mission was working.

Caught fully unawares, his ship had been momentarily defenseless. As he locked eyes with Than across the Bridge, Caine knew this was entirely his fault. He should have implemented all protective measures the moment they noticed the ship on their scanners. He should have taken the necessary precautions, despite the apparent lack of danger. Than had even questioned him, given him an opportunity to give the order. Not wanting to appear paranoid in front of his crew, he hadn't given them.

Now his aversion to showing weakness had led to actual weakness in their defenses. He knew there would be severe ramifications for this when the Council found out about it.

"Return fire. Get secondary shields up now!" Caine yelled. "Scramble the assault ships."

The crew on the Bridge was scrambling. Major Danko, the Munitions Officer, was already ordering his officers to fire back.

The primary shields on the Archon were a gravity-based force field. They were always on, protecting the ship from any space debris, particles of rock, or small meteorites; anything which could potentially hit the ship during its travels.

During battle, they repelled most of the smaller and moderate explosions entirely, the concussive shockwaves from the blasts rippling through the gravity field and dispersing out across the entire hull of the ship.

If the primary shields couldn't diffuse the shockwaves effectively, substantial impacts could still damage the ship's interior and injure crew on board. Caine himself had recovered from several concussions, and a broken leg sustained during battle over the years.

In most Hostile encounters, their weaponry was limited to small-scale detonations, ones a ship as large as the Archon could easily handle.

The secondary shields filled in the gaps. Without them, the ship could still sustain significant damage to more vulnerable areas from well-targeted, direct attacks.

The Archon's secondary shielding system was a complex, gridded layer of intertwined laser beams capable of disintegrating most objects that came into contact with them. The two systems working together made the ship nearly impenetrable.

"Kuso." Caine swore in his native language; it slipped out under his breath. The ship rocked from a blast, sending objects flying across the floor. Caine nearly lost his balance. "Kendar, where are my shields!"

Weapons System Officer, Zora Kendar, was struggling at her post.

"The system is malfunctioning," she yelled at him over the commotion. "The first impact was right where the shield control panels are. It overloaded the system. It's jammed. I can try to do a manual override, but it might take a minute." She jabbed frantically at the screen.

"We don't have a minute. I need them now!" Caine snapped at her. Another blast sent the crew stumbling. Caine grabbed onto a nearby desk to keep himself upright. "Dammit, Zora!" he growled.

The explosives launching at his ship were capable of doing more damage than the ones the Hostiles usually used, but there was nothing 'usual' about this attack at all. His display screen lit up with alerts indicating damaged locations.

The outer hull of the Archon was nearly twenty feet of composite metal. Made from a tungsten carbide and iconel alloy, it could withstand the extreme temperatures and lack of pressure in space.

Beyond that ran a secondary layer. Ten feet of solid carbon fiber protected the electronics and piping within the innermost segments of the wall.

The ship was designed for combat, to take a hit. The hull was taking those blasts like a well-trained fighter took a punch. The blows were mainly superficial, as long there wasn't a direct hit to one of the few vulnerable areas.

In this case, the first blast was carefully aimed, targeting the area where the shields were generated, causing a surge in the system that rendered them unable to create either shield.

The Archon's schematics were top secret, so how was it possible this Hostile crew knew the exact location to aim first to cause maximum impairment?

Caine was never one to believe in luck or coincidence. Their attackers knew what they were doing. It was as if they had managed to get their hands on a layout of the ship. It was just one more thing that was extremely unsettling about the entire scenario.

"Primary shields are down too." Zora's fingers flew over the buttons, her eyes scanning data as it appeared. "We may only be able to pull up secondary shields at the bow." Zora's eyes widened. "They are targeting the rear reactor chambers. They are trying to kill our power. Sir," her voice rose frantically in a panic. "Sir, they-" A low whistling noise became more high-pitched.

There was a horrific explosion followed by the sound of metal screaming against metal. Caine winced. That was too close to the ship's reactors. If they lost power, they were dead. His entire ship, hundreds of crew under his command, would be lost to the Hostile Clan attacking them.

How would he get them out of this mess? Not even Flight Captain Tauran Shea's skilled maneuvering could get them out of danger at this proximity. Kuso.

Designed to lead battle, The Archon commanded as a large-scale attacker. She was bulky and slow compared to the merchant ship: far better equipped for attacking from a distance. All the Destroyers and Light Cruisers in the Fleet under his authority had their own missions throughout the system. Even his closest combat ships were at least a day's distance, busy patrolling other border planets.

A cluster of green dots on the screen moved, marking the location of his assault team. With nearly three-quarters of them left behind to help on Evid, he was fighting with one hand tied behind his back. He hoped he had enough of them to launch an effective attack. Half a dozen assault ships zipped around the Archon towards the tiny merchant craft.

As they neared, they opened fire. The lasers deflected off the merchant vessel shields. Caine wiped a hand over his face in stunned disbelief. The Hostile craft turned its focus to the assault ships surrounding it.

Caine's ships strategically swerved and dodged laser beams while firing back at the attacking spacecraft with their own. They struck one of the assault ships, and it broke apart. The oxygen from inside igniting caused a small explosion. He watched as his ships were picked off one by one.

"Commander?" Than yelled, catching his attention. Caine had to act. He was running out of time. The rest of his Fleet was too far to help. He didn't have minutes; he had seconds and needed to decide now. There was no simple way out of this mess.

The Confederation had recently supplied the Archon with a prototype weapon - an EMP.

The EMP, an electromagnetic pulse modified for spacecraft, had yet to be tested during live battle in deep space. It would shut down any and all forms of energy for five klicks, including mechanics and technology. Both ships would be temporarily disabled.

Scientists intended its use to be within an atmosphere where there were places to land safely. In space, the Archon would drift until it regained power.

If Caine could get the Archon and the assault ship's systems up and running faster than the Hostile's ship, they would be fine. Their more advanced electronics would handle the surge better, but the scientists had warned him that the EMP had the potential to cause enough damage his ship's system might not restart.

The systems reset without complications in all the trial runs, engines back running at full power under a minute. But, those trials had all been in a lab on Arctus. To utilize it for the first time in space during an altercation was an entirely different story. It was drastic and risky.

The risk was small, but if his system failed to reboot, the consequences would prove fatal. The oxygen converter wouldn't work, and he, along with his entire crew, would suffocate.

He had authorization from the Confederation to use the EMP if needed. They'd encouraged him to use it to test its functionality during battle. However, at this moment, he would be subjecting his crew to being unwilling test subjects in a trial run that could have deadly results.

One more blast from the attackers was all that was needed for Caine to make up his mind. Risk suffocation or allow his crew to fall into the hands of the Hostiles. The tortures that awaited them were far more horrific than a slow honorable death on the ship.

"Prep the EMP," he instructed. Despite the chaos, the Bridge fell silent. Everyone stopped what they were doing.

"Sir?" someone behind him asked. Still, no one moved. They were all shocked by his request: not quite believing he was planning on going through with it.

"Do it," Caine growled, not liking his crew questioning his decisions. Than's wary gaze spoke volumes. He gave Caine a nearly imperceptible shake of his head. It was a bad idea. Caine turned away to look at his screens. He couldn't meet Than's eyes anymore.

"It's ready," an officer informed him.

All eyes were on him. He took a deep breath and had one last momentary flare of doubt. This better work. If it didn't, he was about to subject his entire crew to an agonizing death. There was no time for second-guessing now. He turned to hit the black button on the wall behind him.

As soon as his fist made contact, there was a sharp, blinding flash of vivid blue light that exploded around him, and electricity crackled through the air. As the ship lost power, a concussive shockwave surged through his body, forcing all the air from his lungs.

In the darkness, blue light emanated from the EMP. His feet left the floor as tendrils of the strange light snaked around him. Curling around his legs, it crept up towards his waist. He wasn't sure if it was the light causing him to float or the sudden lack of gravity. It wrapped around his chest and twisted around his arms. There was a whooshing sound like wind blowing through a tunnel, metal screeching, and a gentle tugging sensation like he was being pulled towards something. The odor of smoke was overpowering. He could hear a woman screaming, faint at first but getting louder; closer. He couldn't tell if it was Xan, Zora, or a different member of the crew. The glow brightened until it was so blinding Caine could only see white. He threw his arm up over his face to shield his eyes. As his eyes closed, he could see another set of eyes staring back at him. Grey eyes.

There was a deafening crack followed by another surge of energy so strong it pulsated deep within him. His body convulsed. His arms and legs extended outwards, stiff and straight. He couldn't move. His muscles were no longer under his control. He was being pulled in all different directions at once. His body was simultaneously being ripped apart and crushed. He gave a sharp yell as searing pain radiated from his joints. The white light vanished, and he fell towards the floor. His head hit something hard, and he lost consciousness.

Chapter Three

Cara knew she wasn't dead. Her head hurt far too much to be dead. From what she had been taught, being dead wasn't supposed to be painful. The heaven her grandmother told her about as a child was supposed to be strictly pain-free. Not that she had ever believed her Grandma Mary's wild stories, especially the ones about seeing angels who rode on cloud ships in the sky.

She lay on a hard, flat surface that was slightly cool under her skin. She wasn't ready to open her eyes yet. The wind had been knocked out of her. She hadn't felt like this since she fell out of the back of her boyfriend Josh's truck during her senior year of high school. They had been having fun flying down the dirt roads behind his family's farm. She and a group of her friends had all climbed into the bed of the truck, screaming with laughter as they slid around with every sharp turn he took. Josh hit a bump going too fast, launching Cara out of the back. She hit the ground so hard she left an imprint of her body in the red dirt. She had been lucky to walk away with no broken bones.

This? It was even worse. She could barely even let out a groan. Cautiously opening one of her eyes, she looked around. A light above her bathed everything in a red glow. The light dimmed and brightened above her like a lighthouse, a beacon, but who was it summoning?

From what she could tell, everything should have been white. The walls were smooth with a glossy sheen, like plastic. She turned her head to the side to gauge her surroundings and found that she was lying in the middle of a hallway. It curved off ahead of her, and there were no doors or windows. It looked like a hospital, but there was no one in sight. Everything was quiet. No voices or ambient sounds that would give her clues as to where she was. Why was she on the floor? The last thing she remembered was being on the subway. How had she gotten here?

That's right, the subway. Her memory was cloudy, like a snow globe shaken up. Bits and pieces of images flashed in her mind. Something had happened there. She had been on the train.

She squeezed her eyes shut. Think Cara. She remembered the pungent smell of smoke and the sharp, metallic taste of electricity in the air. Someone had screamed. Maybe it was her. She couldn't remember. Had there been an accident?

She slowly moved. Fingers and toes first. They wiggled like they were supposed to. None of her bones felt broken, although her arms were like lead. They flopped around on the floor as she dragged them closer. The light dimmed, plunging the hall into near darkness. When the light brightened, it spurred her to move and find help.

It took immense effort, but she managed to hoist herself onto her knees. Her muscles were slow to react, and she had to push herself up with her hands. Her body screamed in protest. Each muscle was tight, every bone ached. Her head spun as if she had been put through a blender. Her legs refused to move an inch more, and she fell back to the floor. Her stomach lurched. She fought back nausea. She moved slow and heavy as if every part of her had been cut open and filled with sand. Her skin tingled, and there were goosebumps on her arms. The walls rippled, and the room spun.

Cara rocked back to sit on the floor, letting her eyes close, waiting for the gut-churning sensation to pass. Her head bowed, she sat hunched over, taking deep breaths. It took a while, but the sick feeling subsided. She looked around for her purse. It had pain killers in it, and she was in desperate need of a few or maybe a handful. It was gone.

She swore under her breath. Her purse had everything in it - her identification, credit cards, and her money. She even carried a toothbrush and toothpaste in there just in case. She slicked her tongue over her teeth. They needed a good brush.

Cara pushed to all fours again. She had to find people. She crawled a few feet before slumping against the wall in exhaustion. She had no energy left to go another inch. Her limbs were so shaky there was no way she would be able to go any further unassisted. She looked down at her hands; they were trembling so violently she balled them into fists and shoved them down into her lap.

"Hello?" Her call for help came out barely louder than a hoarse whisper. Feeling discouraged, she wanted to scream in frustration, but no one would have heard her anyway. Her only option now was to sit and wait until someone found her. She leaned her head against the wall. A searing spike of pain lanced through her head and down her neck. Reaching up, she touched the back of her head, letting out a hiss of air through her teeth when she reached the sore spot. Her fingertips came away bloody. She recalled hitting her head on the train against the doorframe.

Every second dragged on. She could barely keep her eyes open. Somewhere in the back of her mind sounded a warning not to fall asleep. If she had a concussion, it could prove fatal. She dug her fingernails into her palms, trying to keep her eyes open. Her chin slowly dropped towards her chest, and she jerked it upright again.

She slapped her cheek. "Stay awake." It didn't help. Her eyes closed.

Moments before she heard them, the heavy vibrations of footsteps made the floor tremble under her. They pounded towards her, and the low thuds were in unison, like marching. They grew louder. At least a dozen men rounded the corner and approached her slowly. The men were wearing navy blue uniforms with gold trim and were all heavily armed.

Disoriented, Cara struggled to make sense of the situation. The men had their guns aimed at her, so fear joined the conflicting, messy mix of emotions. The largest man stepped forward. Bald and round-faced, his dark eyes stood out as he squinted down at her. His face was red. The veins in his neck bulged out.

"State your name and rank," he barked at her. Name and rank? Guns in a hospital? This was the police or the military, yelling at her. Where were the doctors? The nurses? Cara was in pain and confused, not a good combination. She had no idea what the man was talking about. She pushed up on her arms and managed to get to her knees again, but her stomach flipped violently.

"I'm Cara. Cara DeLeon," she managed to croak. Why did it sound like she was underwater? Her voice sounded muffled and distant. Her tongue was swollen and too big for her mouth. She struggled to get the words out because her throat was dry and scratchy. The lights were too bright, and her head throbbed like it was being crushed in a vice.

The walls began to bend and sway. The angry faces staring at her warped into disfigured blobs. It was like she was stuck inside a carnival funhouse and remembered running through one as a girl. The mirrors had always been her least favorite part, making her body look unnatural: too big in places and squished down in others, her face contorted like a Picasso painting.

"I think there was a train crash." With that, she unceremoniously threw up right at the man's feet and passed out.

The leader of the group, who had yelled at her, stared down at the now unconscious figure before him. Her face was ashen and pale. He glanced at the officer next to him, who simply shrugged, just as confused as he was. He heaved a big sigh and reached up to his shoulder where his communication link was. He pressed the button.

"Commander? You need to take a look at this."

Chapter Four

Minutes earlier, Caine had floated in the darkness, waiting; his heart pounding. Everything was eerily silent. Seconds ticked by as he waited for the generator and engine to come back to life. A minute went by. Two.

Caine's panic mounted until the generator finally coughed and sputtered. The lights flickered on, and a whistle of fresh air surged through the vents as the oxygen converter came back online. He fell to the floor with a crash as the gravity drive booted back up. He dropped like a rock and knocked his head against something hard during the fall. Pulling himself back to his feet, he rubbed the sore spot above his ear, and his fingers came away bloody - no time to worry about that now, likely just a bad scratch.

"Shields are up!" Zora yelled across the Bridge. Caine looked over to where she was kneeling in front of her screens. Relieved, Caine noted she appeared uninjured. He could see the assault ships power up as the green dots reappeared on the screens.

"Fire at will!" Caine commanded. Within moments, the Hostile ship broke apart, and debris scattered into the blackness of space like ashes into the wind. Shea quickly took the Archon to a safe distance awaiting the return of the assault team. Caine let relief wash through him before quickly tamping it down as he assessed the damage on his screens.

The outer hull was a mess of scorch marks and riddled with small holes. Several huge craters dented the metal. Fortunately, nothing had punctured the inner hull. Many electrical circuits had overloaded or blown and would need replacing, but all the critical components were up and running. Cosmetic damages would be fixed later.

"Send anyone injured to Medical and call up the second-string shift to fill in anywhere it's needed," Caine told Xan. She relayed the orders to the crew over the comm system. Everyone would be utilized. Until the damage was repaired, they would all be working extra shifts. Fortunately, with a crew of several hundred, everything would be fixed in just a day or two.

"Caine, we have a problem." Than stared at his screen with a frown. "The system has flagged an unknown ping on the lower levels. It appeared out of nowhere. No one should be down there right now. It is registering as a person, and I'm getting a count of an extra body on board."

A renewed sense of urgency sent a rush of energy through his tired body. A Hostile? He looked at the tiny blinking dot on the screen. It wasn't moving. How was that even possible? "How the hell did someone manage to get onto my ship in the middle of space? Send a team down there now!"

Major Danko relayed the orders to his men. "I want an eight-man team down there now. Find out who is down there. Report back to the Commander directly. Move. Now."

Caine looked at Than, his lips pressed together in a hard line. "I'll be in my quarters. I need to brief the Council on the attack. Get me when this has been handled."

Caine made his way down to his personal quarters, which included his office, bedroom, and private bathroom. He went to his office and sat at his desk.

A transparent monitor rose as he approached and touched a few icons on the glass screen. Next to his desk was a small shiny black table. The top of the table pulled apart, revealing a projector lens, and a holographic image of the Council appeared. They were sitting at their horseshoe-shaped table, dressed in their traditional, long, burgundy robes.

Head Council Leader Yuri Yugato smiled at him. Yugato was the representative from Darshan, where Caine was born. He was an ally and an old friend of Caine's family. Nowadays, Yugato stayed neutral when it came to Caine, but years before, he had helped Caine get through Fleet Training and recommended the Council place him on the Archon. Caine would never have made it this far without the small helping hand of his mentor.

"Commander." Yugato bowed his head as he addressed him, his hands clasped together resting on the table.

Caine recalled first meeting him as a boy, his raven black hair tied up in a small sangtu, a topknot traditionally worn by men on Darshan. Now, his silvery hair was turning increasingly snowier as time progressed. His thumb bore the large gold ring with the Council crest etched into the broad, square surface. Caine knew on the inside of the band, Yugato had the Darshanian motto engraved. "Sumeba miyako. Home is where you live." A motto that had come about during the long journey from Old Earth to the new system, it represented the hope the ancestors of his people had when they traveled through space, awaiting the arrival to their new planet, their new home.

Now generations later, Caine was grateful for the tremendous obstacles his ancestors had overcome and all they had sacrificed for him to be born on Darshan with clean air, clear water, and abundant food.

Yugato's smile vanished. "You're bleeding." Caine looked down at his shirt and noticed the bloodstain spreading down from his neckline across his chest. He had forgotten about the wound on his head. He stared directly at Yugato, not making eye contact with the other members as he relayed the news.

"The Archon was just attacked by heavily armed Hostile forces under the guise of an abandoned merchant vessel."

"What?" Yugato looked stunned.

The other nine council members whispered amongst themselves.

Councilman Tabu Shiro's blue eyes narrowed with suspicion. "How can that be? Hostiles have never attacked like that before."

"Hostiles will attack however they please, in whatever way will kill the greatest numbers of people," an older man with short, salt and pepper hair angrily addressed Councilman Shiro. His frown only accentuated the wrinkles around his eyes, which had more to do with the fact he always had a perpetual scowl etched onto his face rather than his age.

Caine clenched his mouth shut to keep his facial expression neutral. Turcan Saar, one of the most litigious council members, was particularly unpleasant, especially towards Caine.

Caine had been vocal about his dislike for the man initially, but he learned to pick his battles over the years. They managed to be civil, most of the time, despite the tension always simmering below the surface. One wrong word could cause it to boil over.

Saar fed off confrontation. It emboldened him and made him more determined to get his way, especially if he knew it was against Caine's wishes.

Saar was a former Captain in the Confederation Fleet, and he had worked hard to get elected to the Council after Councilman Gerrok died. Council members were the supreme law in the system. Once chosen, they sat on the Council for life. They were celebrities in their own right.

Unfortunately, Caine did not think Saar was someone children should admire. Saar was violent and unmerciful and showed little emotion unless it was anger. He was unpredictable and rash, and he preferred to promote aggression in his views on Council issues, bordering on nihilistic. Saar hated the Hostiles more vehemently than any other sitting Council member, and he was extremely vocal about it.

When Saar had been a young Confederation officer, he had been assigned a wife, Jura. As most wives did back then, Jura had gone on some of the missions with Saar, but things went terribly wrong on one mission.

The story was still unclear on how it had all happened, but Jura had been killed by Hostiles in an attack. Saar slipped into a deep depression, vowing to eradicate every last Hostile in the system. He was brutal in his attacks, even petitioning to mount full-scale strikes on their planets. He was confrontational, going after them directly rather than acting defensively. Eventually, he was ordered to stand down and focus mainly on protecting the Core planets.

Caine had long believed Saar's aggressive methods had been the catalyst that escalated the ferocity of Hostile retaliation. When Saar had been nominated for the Council, Caine had voiced his opposition, but Saar was still elected.

Caine understood the need to end the Hostile attacks on innocent civilians, but he did not harbor the same violent and frenzied bloodlust as Saar. To have such a fanatical and short-sighted influence in a leadership role could only spell trouble for the Confederation. Caine deliberately ignored Saar and addressed Yugato.

"Sir, this is unlike any attack pattern we have seen. They are using new tactics - the village attacks, now this. Things are changing and quickly. Hostiles have never been one to sneak attack. They always make sure their target knows who they are and that they are coming for them. They are characteristically uncoordinated, unorganized, sloppy," Caine paused. "They had advanced military-grade weaponry," he added, trying to avoid looking at Councilman Shiro directly.

"How is this possible?" Yugato frowned. Caine kept his gaze squarely on Yugato. If Saar was an extremist,

Shiro tipped the scales drastically in opposition. Shiro had deeply sympathetic views when it came to Hostiles. He even shared similar ancestry with the Hostiles, descending from two brothers generations ago, who went separate ways. One joined the earliest bands of rebels, eventually became the Hostiles, while the other became a member of the Confederation government.

Shiro had been at the center of more than a few conspiracies and accusations. His sentiments were questionable at times, bordering on radical. Caine had his own theories, some of which included illegal black-market weapons trading. Still, he wasn't about to throw arms dealing into the pot right now, especially without any hard evidence to prove Shiro was in any way backing the Hostile clans.

"Sir, all I know is they had cold-start fusion engines and advanced laser weaponry. This technology is only on our most advanced military ships. How they got access to it, let alone manage to install it onto a merchant ship, is beyond me."

"I want a full investigation into this. Any resources needed are at your full disposal. Keep me informed," Yugato ordered. Caine nodded in agreement, and the screen went black. He sighed and slumped back into a chair. His entire body was sore. Following a beep, a voice crackled over his comm.

"Commander? You need to take a look at this."

Caine sighed and ran a hand through his hair. Usually, Danko and his officer would handle smaller security issues. If he was being called directly, it must be severe. He left the room and made his way down the hall, but one of his leading officers, Bercu Myat, stopped him. The bald man's face was even redder than usual. His eyes bulged.

"Sir, we have the Hostile in custody," he reported sharply, clicking his heels together and saluting. "She is being transported to Medical now."

She? That caught Caine off guard. The shock that rippled through him was an unwelcome feeling. He did not like being taken by surprise.

Women rarely took part in Hostile attacks or raids. As uncivilized and savage as Hostiles were, they had some perverse sense of honor when it came to allowing women to go out on attacks.

Hostiles were more concerned with keeping the numbers of breeding partners high rather than caring about the women's lives themselves, but whatever the reason, he was glad Hostile women stayed home. He had a substantial aversion to hurting women, even Hostile ones.

Caine shook his head, trying to quickly process the information that had just been relayed to him as he made his way down the levels to the ship's Medical wing.

The doors slid open as he approached. Comprising of several recovery rooms surrounding a central treatment area, Medical was a place with which he was well acquainted.

In a small room to the left, the woman in question was lying on a table near the back of the room covered in a silver thermo-blanket. There was an I.V. in her hand pumping fluids. Her eyes were closed; she looked sickly and pale. Her hair was a honeyed chestnut color and flowed down long over her shoulders: a style unusual for a Hostile. They often dyed their hair black and wore it up in elaborate up-dos and braided buns, decorating it with anything from carved wood to bones. She didn't appear to be much younger than Caine.

Caine pulled back the thermo-blanket. She was dressed in strange, plain, civilian style clothes with no markings or rank insignia. Hostiles often wore large, elaborate embellished patterns on their clothes, and they marked their skin all over with equally distinct symbols, which signified their importance to their family, called clans.

Most Hostile men he encountered had more markings and less skin, covering all the way down to their fingertips. His people called them okraska, a tattoo, but he just referred to them as they were; the markings of war.

Hostiles wove bones into their clothes, as they did in their hair. They made their clothes from whatever cloth they could weave, such as metal or chains, ripped animal hides, and sometimes even human skin.

If he hadn't known any better, he would have assumed she was a civilian, but he did know better. This woman did not appear to be Hostile on the outside, but he had seen a few who were not as heavily marked as the rest. Inside, a whole different story could emerge.

Doctor Yalain Nadir came walking out of an adjoining room. He stopped short in front of Caine and scowled at him, his olive eyes narrowing. Wisps of grey hair curled around the thin arms of his round glasses. He continued to scowl at Caine over the lenses and waved his hands at him angrily, stepping protectively between him and the woman.

"No. No, no, no. Absolutely not. She is not ready for an Interrogation yet. She doesn't have the strength. It could kill her. Whatever she went through left her extremely weak." Nadir turned to the table, checking the machines hooked up to the woman. He pushed his glasses up onto the bridge of his nose and squinted at some of the readings. "It is as if just her body is here, but all her energy is somewhere else."

Caine didn't care about the doctor's medical assessment now. "Did you find anything on her?" he asked.

"We didn't locate any personal items. We did find a marking on her neck, but it isn't one I recognize. It could be a new clan we haven't heard of yet." Nadir brought an image of the marking up on a screen on the wall.

Caine didn't recognize it either. It was small and elegant. The delicate swirl was the opposite of the sprawling and embellished signs of the clans. He tensed as he looked at the little black symbol. She had a mark. This was a significant connection to the Hostiles, even though she showed no other outward signs of being one. Nothing was adding up.

"Have it sent over to Daedra. Tell her to run it through the full database. It could be the formation of a new minor Clan."

Hostile Clans often warred amongst themselves, and it was not uncommon for the larger major Clans to break apart into smaller offshoots, often over trivial disagreements.

Caine looked back down at the woman. She looked so helpless; he could hardly believe she was part of the Hostile attack that had just happened. Nadir looked at him, concerned.

"It's fine, Nadir." Caine knew precisely why the doctor was worried. Nadir was like family. A mentor and a friend, he had been patching Caine up since he was in the Academy. When Caine was given command over the Archon, Nadir was the first person he asked to join his crew.

"Can you be impartial about this?" Nadir knew what lay in store for the woman when she woke. He also knew of Caine's reservations about dealing with women.

"I can do my job." Caine meant it to sound reassuring despite the sharp tone.

Nadir failed to keep the skepticism from his face.

"I can do my job," Caine said more forcefully, a dangerous edge to his voice.

"Alright, alright." Nadir lifted his hands, conceding. He knew which battles to pick and when to pick them, and right now was not the time. Caine needed to be in the right state of mind to do an Interrogation. If he was upset, it could affect his ability to execute it safely.

"Since she isn't ready for a full Interrogation, move her to Diagnostic and Procedure. I want her prepped for immediate questioning when she wakes," Caine ordered. "And get the trammel on her too."

The trammel used a combination of generated gravity and pressure to immobilize. It was especially useful when disoriented patients were wakening up from anesthesia. He had seen crew members destroy the room in a drug-fueled panic.

He was more concerned about his mystery woman launching an attack when she woke up. Without another glance down, he turned and left.

Chapter Five

If being dead was painless, then Cara was coming back from the dead. She was groggy, and it took a moment to open her eyes. The room around her was dark. The only light came from a dim orange light above her head, shining down directly on her. She was on a hard table. A hospital table?

A soft beeping caught her attention. Failed efforts to turn her head to see what was making the noise made her realize she couldn't move. She tried moving her arms. Nothing. Not even a finger wiggled. She couldn't move anything at all. Fear rushed through her. Was she paralyzed?

As the beeping got louder, her heartbeat grew quicker, or maybe it was the other way around. The faster her heart raced, the louder the beeping became, almost as if it was keeping up in both speed and intensity. Where were the doctors? Why couldn't she move? She made one last attempt to wiggle her toes: nothing. No amount of willing it to move was working.

Cara opened her mouth to scream when the main lights in the room unexpectedly turned on, momentarily blinding her. Soft footsteps drew near, and her eyes adjusted as a blurred figure leaned over her. The fuzzy image cleared into a strikingly handsome man with shockingly blue eyes. She couldn't remember ever seeing anyone with eyes so blue. Maybe it was colored contacts. It just didn't seem natural. He disappeared from her view, and the beeping stopped.

"Sit up," he commanded in a deep voice.

There was a slight accent to his voice that she couldn't place. It was not overly prominent, but it was noticeable enough. She tested a finger and was surprised when it wiggled. She did a quick check; feet, legs, arms. All her ability to move had returned. She was sore but, fortunately, not paralyzed.

Cara turned her head to look at him. His dark brown hair was neatly trimmed. He wore a navy-blue uniform, with unrecognizable emblems and insignias sewn on, a military outfit. He was sitting in a chair: elbows on the armrests, his clasped hands resting in his lap.

Cara pushed herself up slowly. A sharp pinching tug stopped her. An I.V. was attached to the back of her hand. At the sight of the needle, she shuddered and yanked it out. She had never liked needles and didn't want to be tethered to something while being stuck in a strange room with an unknown man. Blood trickled out, and she pressed her fingers on the small wound to stem the bleeding. She looked up again at the blue-eyed man. He hadn't moved at all, and his face remained neutral, making it hard for her to read him.

When she made eye contact with him, a surge of nausea and blinding pain speared through her head. A wave of dizziness washed over her, and she closed her eyes tightly, biting back a moan. She focused on forcing the awful feeling away. She did not want to be sick in front of this man.

Whatever was happening to her must be residual effects from the crash. She could have a concussion. When the faint feeling finally subsided, she raised her head to look at him once again. He scowled at her. His brows were pinched together, eyes narrowed.

"Who are you?" He leaned forward ever so slightly. A vein in his temple pulsed.

Cara was trapped in the icy blue stare. Despite the thousands of questions rushing through her mind, she couldn't stop herself from answering, strangely compelled to tell him anything he wanted to know.

"Um, I'm Cara, Cara DeLeon."

The headache and nausea surged to the forefront again. She took a deep breath, trying to push through it. She closed her eyes tight and pressed a hand against her forehead, trying to rub away the throbbing ache that had rooted right behind her eyes. She imagined an invisible barrier around her, keeping the onslaught of pain at bay.

"I think I was in the crash on the subway. I think I have a concussion. Is there a doctor here? Where am I?" she asked.

The man's expression fleetingly changed to one of puzzlement. His head tilted ever so slightly to the side; his eyebrows rose nearly imperceptibly before the steely cold hardness returned to his gaze.

"How did you get on this ship?" he pressed, ignoring her questions.

What was he talking about? She had been on the subway before she ended up here. "What did you just say? A ship?" She looked around the white room. She was on a boat? "I thought this was a hospital." She looked around, alarmed. "How did I get here?"

The man sat forward in the chair, leaning towards her, his eyes searching her face. The heavy, crushing sensation flared up so intense and fierce Cara swore out loud and gagged. Bile crept up her throat, but she swallowed it down, pressing a hand over her mouth. The acid burned in her throat. The man stood abruptly, towering over her.

"You are on the U.C.S. Archon. A Confederation ship that was recently attacked. You ended up here in the middle of it all. So, I think I will be doing all the question asking here." His demeanor was stern, his tone accusatory. "Are you Hostile?" he barked, looming over her.

Tears stung at the corner of Cara's eyes. She had no idea where she was or how she had gotten there, and here was this man, yelling at her like she was a criminal. What if he believed she was involved in that attack? She had to correct him before this went any further.

"Hostile? No, of course not. I have no idea what you are talking about. I don't even know how I got here," she pleaded.

For a brief moment, silence ensued between them.

"Think about it, and when you decide you want to talk, let me know." He turned sharply on his heels and left the room.

Two men came in and took her by the arms. She was forced down the hall to a small room. She tried questioning them, but she stammered, and her words came out jumbled. Before she could gather herself, they pushed her into the room and slammed the door. Cara fell to the floor and finally let the tears spill over.

Olivia would be worried sick about her. Did her parents even know she was in a crash or that she was being held as a suspect for causing it? What would David think when she didn't show up for dinner? Guilt rippled through her. It was the first time she'd thought about David. He hadn't even been her first thought or concern. He deserved better than that from her. She didn't even know what time it was. Maybe she had already missed their dinner. Was David waiting at the restaurant, sitting at their usual corner table, as he stared at the door waiting in vain for her arrival?

Would he go to her apartment to find her or check in on her? Was anyone even looking for her? She shook her head. Of course, they were looking for her. Despite her concerns about having a concussion, she was drained, all her energy sucked from her. She had to sleep.

Cara curled up on the floor and fell into a fitful, uneasy sleep. When she woke, she had a terrifying moment of confusion until she remembered where she was. How long had she been there? With no clock in the room or access to a phone, she had no way of knowing what time it was and could easily have already been there through the night.

Her stomach grumbled, and she desperately needed to use the bathroom. She wiped the hair off her face and pulled it back into a messy bun. How could that man believe she'd been involved with the crash? She had to speak to him at once. If she was being held on charges, she had the right to make a phone call. She needed to call David. No, she needed to call a lawyer. Stumbling, she brought herself to her feet and pounded on the door. No response.

"Hello?" she bellowed. Her voice cracked with the strain. She pounded on the door again. There were footsteps in the distance. She pounded on the door as hard as she could. "Hey," she yelled. "Hey! Hello!" Her voice was hoarse and scratchy, but she refused to give up until someone came back to listen to her. Her hands were sore and red, but still, there was no answer.

She stopped and listened. The footsteps had disappeared. She had to get someone's attention. She kept pounding, hoping someone would hear her. "I don't know what's going on!" she kept yelling. "What the hell do you want from me?" It was time she set the story straight with the blue-eyed man.

Chapter Six

A young officer knocked at Caine's door a short while later with an update. "The Hostile is yelling in her cell," he reported.

Caine nodded and dismissed him. He went to his computer, taping on the glass display to establish the communication link with the Council. The screen flickered. Familiar faces appeared, tinged with an electronic blue hue.

"Any news?" Yugato questioned. Caine nodded grimly.

"We have a Hostile in custody on the ship," Caine informed them. Yugato looked momentarily surprised.

"I'm not even going to ask how." Yugato raised his hands, indicating he wanted no further explanation. "I assume you want permission to interrogate him?"

Caine nodded, not bothering to correct him on his error in gender. He didn't feel it was relevant information for him to share yet. At least not until he had more information on the female's involvement. He couldn't push away the nagging idea she might not be involved, but it was the only logical explanation he had to go on.

"Yes, in due time, but not just yet," Caine reported. "Nadir has done a medical evaluation. The Hostile is in an extremely weakened state, which could compromise any information they know. If we attempt an Interrogation right now-"

"That is unacceptable," Saar interrupted. "It has always been protocol Hostiles are interrogated immediately." Hollow cheeks and a long nose made him look hawkish. Caine knew better than to underestimate him; Saar was shrewd and conniving. He could easily manipulate a situation to shift in his favor with a few calculated words.

"The Hostile is in no condition to withstand the full procedure. It could cost us valuable information we need." Caine explained Nadir's medical evaluation, hoping it would prevent Saar from demanding it regardless.

"We cannot allow the Hostile to be compromised," Shiro argued. "This could have severely negative impacts on their-"

"I know full well the implications," Saar cut Shiro off short. "We cannot decide to modify Council procedures simply for the sake of one Hostile. What kind of precedent would that set?"

Rage surged. Saar didn't care if Hostiles survived or not. In his opinion, Interrogation was an unnecessary delay in eliminating the threat. Caine's hands clenched into tight fists.

"This is an excellent opportunity to try and rehabilitate this Hostile," Shiro interjected. Several pairs of angry eyes settled on him.

"You know full well trying to rehabilitate a Hostile has never been successful." Councilwoman Indriya Viraha swept her long, deep brown braid over one shoulder. She folded her hands on the table in front of her, the gold bangles around her wrists clinked together.

"No," Saar shouted. "These are our laws. We cannot bend the rules. What will stop it from happening the next time and the time after that? We have these procedures in place for a reason. We cannot allow anything to compromise the integrity of this organization," Saar turned his gaze to meet Caine's.

Pitted up against the more aggressive Councilman, Shiro crumbled, sitting back in his chair, looking defeated. He pressed his thin lips together, his catlike blue eyes narrowing until they were mere slits. Saar was a force to be reckoned with on the Council. When he set his mind to something, he would fight to the death to get what he wanted. Shiro wasn't willing to pay a price that high to defend his ideals.

"The Commander can do it, or he can bring the Hostile here, and we will handle the interrogation," Saar finished, a challenge in his eyes, daring Caine to refuse again.

Caine knew Saar could request to have him court-martialed for disobeying direct Council orders. His more pressing concern was how interrogations were handled back on Arctus. There was little regard for Hostile life, even if it was a female. Under Saar's command, they were treated like animals - no, even worse.

For just a brief second, he considered refusing just to spite Saar. No serious repercussions would ever come of it, but the brief termination from duty would be a huge hindrance. He also couldn't stomach the thought of the woman being brutally tortured by the Council Guard during her Interrogation.

"I would like to state I side with Councilman Shiro on this matter. The Council is making a huge mistake." It came out more forcefully than he intended.

One of the other council members held up a hand. "Your disagreement has been noted, but you must abide by the rules, Commander," Councilman Rhyden Dhar cautioned. "This is a Hostile, and they must not be shown any leniency."

Yugato looked at the other Council members. They all nodded in agreement. The battle lost, Shiro remained silent. He looked frail as if he was about to shatter under the pressure. He glanced over at Caine, unspoken apologies in his eyes. Caine knew there was no more to be discussed. The matter was settled, and he had his orders to follow. The screen went blank. The Interrogation order had been given. Caine had no more than 8 hours to get back to the Council and relay his findings.

He made his way to Bridge. "Pull up the holding cell feed at my desk," he instructed Xan as he walked back into his secondary office attached to the main room.

The image appeared on the display in front of him. The woman was sitting, knees tucked up, and arms circled around them. She looked up at the door with her head tilted to one side. She was listening. Perhaps she heard a passing officer. She dropped her head again. The tight knot of frustration grew when he remembered the panic in her voice and the fear in her eyes. Despite how convincing she appeared, it was all just an act, part of the game the Hostiles played.

One look into those dark gray eyes made him feel like he was looking into the eyes of someone who could easily match wits with him. She was smart. It would be a challenge breaking her but break her he would. She would talk. In the end, they all talked. This particular ability of his was why he was appointed to this position. He was incredibly good at what he did.

Cara. Her name rolled easily off his tongue. He assumed it was fake, just like everything else about her. He remembered how light probes into her mind had been met with incredibly strong resistance. Not many people were trained in the art of Intransigence. Out of the limited numbers who were trained, it was uncommon for any of them to master the ability. Of the small handful who actually could resist Interrogation, only a rare, extraordinarily exceptional few were skilled enough to resist him.

Yet, she had. The last time he encountered an Intransigent was years ago, just after he'd left the Academy, and he had only ever known of one Intransigent Hostile. He looked at the woman again, make that two.

He should have reported her to the Council, but he didn't know why he didn't share that piece of information. It was unlike him not to fully divulge the facts of a situation. All Intransigents in the Confederation were registered with the Council. It was an extremely prestigious and select few who were hand-picked for training. Very few were civilians.

Even if a person displayed the capacity to be an Intransigent, it didn't mean they did. It took years of training to develop the ability, and most were unable to complete the rigorous instruction, either dropping out of the program or failing. How could she have possibly slipped through the system? It was nearly impossible for her to have gone unidentified unless she was a Hostile.

He would have to push harder during the Interrogation to breach the walls of defenses she had created, but it would be a significant risk to her health. If he pushed too hard, too soon, her mind could break, and the information would be lost forever. Just like in the real world, if he knocked down the walls, he could cause permanent, irreparable damage. She trembled. Her shoulders shook. He had seen enough and made his way down to the detainment area.

A plan formed as he approached her holding cell. He would need to change his usual tactics. Sheer force was not the way to go, not with her. He had the feeling forcing her would only make her fight it more. This was not a "fight fire with fire" battle. He had a feeling they would both end up badly burned that way.

If he could gain her trust, manipulate her into letting down her guard, he would have easier access when Interrogating her, and he would not have to push as hard. He reached the cell and opened the door. She had not been expecting anyone to come in, let alone him. She yelped, scrambling to her feet, pressing back into the far corner. He noticed her hands were red. Seeing him glance down at her hands, she rushed to hide them.

"Show me your hands," he demanded. He hadn't meant for his tone to be so sharp, and he immediately regretted it. He needed to keep his emotions firmly in check throughout this process.

"Why?" Her eyes narrowed instantly.

He stepped forward into the room, and she retreated further away from him. Her entire body tensed like a tightened spring, ready to explode. Her shoulders shifted slightly, getting ready to run if she needed to. He had to diffuse the situation before she did something stupid.

"I'm not going to hurt you." He held his hands up, palms out, showing he wasn't a threat. "Please, show me your hands." He let his voice drop, softer and smoother.

Cara pressed her feet firmly onto the floor, ready to jump away from him if she needed to. When he spoke, his voice tingled down her spine, and it gave her goosebumps. Slowly, without even wanting to, she held out her hands to him, keeping a close eye on his body language for any sign of aggression. The edges of her hands were red, the knuckles too, and they were aching from the abuse they had taken. They would bruise by morning. He scowled down at her hands.

"Get Medical prepped," Caine spoke out loud, despite there being no other person there to hear him.

A chill ran through Cara's body at his words. They had been watching her all along. She did a quick scan of the room, but she couldn't see a camera. With modern technology, it was probably too small to see without looking for it anyway.

Caine noticed her glance around the room, searching for the camera. Very smart. She was incredibly observant; he would have to pay careful attention to be especially guarded with his plans to prevent tipping her off. He didn't want to fight her if it wasn't necessary.

She looked back at him, suspicion still evident in her gaze. He gave a gentle tug on her hand, and she followed.

Caine led her down to Medical and guided her to sit on a solid metal chair. He quietly cleaned her hands and gently applied a clear gel to them.

She was puzzled by the show of kindness after his harsher treatment earlier. The gel stung her raw skin. She inhaled through her teeth with a long hiss, but he patiently rubbed it in, though not meeting her eyes.

As he tended to her, Cara finally got a chance to look at him. He had classic good looks: sharp jaw dusted with just the faintest hint of shadowy growth, and a straight nose worthy of a Greek statue. He was tall, with broad shoulders and large hands made rough with hard work. He was clearly a leader who chose to work instead of sitting in a chair, doling out orders. He was formidable as well as intimidating, although she could sense there was a gentleness hiding under the surface. It unexpectedly revealed itself in the smallest ways.

She couldn't pinpoint why, but strangely, she knew she was safe when he was around, despite her peculiar and alarming circumstances.

When he was done, he stood and walked to the counter along the wall. He opened a drawer and pulled out a silver foil packet. He tore the top off and handed her a brown square from inside.

"Eat," he told her.

She looked up at him, slightly skeptical, but hunger cut through her. She took the bar and bit into it. It had a nutty yet chalky flavor, like a protein bar with more chemicals in it.

"First, I want some questions answered," Cara told him, chewing.

He was quiet. His face stayed blank; his emotions well hidden.

"You get three," he finally agreed. The cool tone to his voice told her he wasn't pleased with her request or with the fact he was granting it to her. She tried to think of questions that would give her the answers she wanted.

"Who are you?" she asked first.

There was no change in his features, but something in his eyes shifted. "I am Commander Nikolas Caine," he responded. Even though it was an intentionally short answer, at least now she had a name and knew he was military.

"Okay, Commander, where am I?" She hadn't meant for it to come off sounding so sarcastic and hoped it wouldn't ruin her opportunity to get some information.

"On the U.C.S Archon."

He was being deliberately vague. She still couldn't understand how she was on a ship. New York was surrounded by water, but why would the military be involved with an accident cleanup. She was reasonably sure American ships were labeled U.S.S., but she had only taken one year of college history. Paired with his accent, it confirmed her suspicion he was foreign.

"Are you American?" she ventured.

"I am a citizen of the Confederation."

She was right. He wasn't American. How had she managed to go from a New York subway to a foreign ship?

Caine was confused by the woman's strange question. He recalled no place in the Confederation called America, but the name sounded familiar. She opened her mouth to speak, but he held up a hand.

"I agreed to three. My turn now."

There was no use in arguing, so she glared at him instead.

"Who are you?" He turned her own original question against her.

Playing word games wasn't the smartest idea since he had the upper hand. Still, she couldn't help but try and twist the situation in her favor just a little. She didn't want to make him angry, but she hoped to at least find a little ground to stand on.

"Cara." She deliberately responded with an answer as equally ambiguous as the ones he gave her. "My name is-"

He sharply cut her off. "Yes, I know. Cara DeLeon. Who are you actually?" She looked unsettled; her forehead all scrunched up.

"I told you who I am. I live in New York, and I was on my way home from work when I think I was in a subway crash."

Caine's nerves were getting frayed. "Who do you work for?" The color drained from her face, and her eyes widened.

Dread twisted her gut. The situation she'd had some hold on slipped through her fingers. The tables had turned. She was at a loss. He did believe she had something to do with the train crash. The military would have gotten involved if they thought it was an act of terrorism. Shit. He was accusing *her* of being a terrorist.

He stood and turned away, walking over to the counter. More out of shock, a bubble of incredulous laughter worked its way up her throat. She couldn't hold back the nervous giggle, and it escaped.

He whirled, eyes ablaze. "You think this is funny?"

"No, no. I swear." The hostility directed at her caught her off guard. "Look, I don't work for anyone. I'm just a telemarketer. I don't know what you are talking about. I had nothing to do with the train crash, and I don't understand why you think I'm involved."

Caine stared at her for a moment, his mouth set firmly in a straight line. He was getting nowhere. The time had come to push further.

Cara was confused when he stood and left the room. Seconds later, two uniformed officers entered. Panic flooded her as they approached her. Something was about to happen, and she had a sinking feeling it was not going to be good.

Chapter Seven

Caine stood outside the room as the two officers went in to restrain her. He could have done it himself, but the guilt stopped him. For whatever reason, regret was creeping into his mind for what he had to do next. He had to keep his mind clear; this woman was potentially the enemy. This was his job, his duty. He needed to remain impartial. At least he had fed her. It would give her some strength to go through Interrogation.

A highly creative string of swearing quickly followed ear-piercing screaming as his men strapped Cara's arms and ankles to the chair. The officers left the room with long, red scratches on their cheeks and arms. Maybe she would handle this better than he initially thought.

He waited until her belligerent shouting had ceased, fighting a smile as he listened to the offensively colorful insults she was yelling. He took a moment to compose himself. He tugged on the bottom of his jacket, straightening it, and ran his fingers through his hair. He took a long, deep breath and entered the room.

Sitting in the chair looking at the floor, she glanced up at him as soon as he walked in. Her hair was disheveled; long strands hung over her face. Behind it, her gaze was full of venom and disgust. For a moment, he doubted his own ability to follow through and had to remind himself, ready himself. It was his duty.

He wasn't just the Commander; he was an Esper. Someone born with the unique skill of being able to go into another person's mind. His ancestor's genetics had changed, developing the ability to connect with another person's thoughts and memories, seeing their mind from the inside out.

Caine pulled a chair towards her, setting it about a foot in front of her, and sat. She turned her head, looking away from him. He was sure if her legs hadn't been restrained, she would have kicked him. He liked that little spark of fire she had.

"Look at me," he instructed.

She didn't move. She was going to refuse his orders. Fighting him would only make the whole process infinitely more difficult and dangerous for them both.

He sighed, a soft, sad sound.

"Look at me," he repeated. This time his voice was different; lower in pitch, his words clipped and crisp.

The smooth sound sent a strange tingle down her spine. A shiver rushed over her, making all her muscles contract and release. Goosebumps popped up all down her arms and legs. She turned and looked at his feet. Technically, she was looking at him.

If the situation had not been so serious, Caine would have been more amused by the display of her rebellious streak and the loophole she had managed to find in his order. She was following his command, well, mostly. However, he needed to find a way to make her comply, which didn't require the use of force. He sat for a moment, thinking of another alternative.

"The sooner we get this over with, the sooner I can let you go," he lied. "Please, Cara."

His gentle entreaty and the sound of her name caught her attention. She finally looked into his eyes. The vibrant blue stare trapped her almost immediately. He used her momentary surprise to his advantage. He pushed into her mind as she gasped.

Once inside, he stared up at the enormous walls of resistance towering in front of him. They stretched out in all directions as far as he could see. She had strong mental defenses. Caine remembered his surprise when he had attempted to gain access to her mind earlier. The walls were not at all what he had expected. He had never seen defenses like this in someone who hadn't been through extensive Confederation training. It was nearly impossible for a woman like her to be capable of being Intransigent, especially not one as strong as this. Most outer defensive walls he could easily slip through, but this was solid, well developed. Only years of intensive training would allow an Intransigent to fortify their mind in this way.

When he put his hands on the wall to climb over, he was thrown backward violently, landing hard and skidding across the surface. She was fighting back, even though she didn't seem to be aware she was doing it. Caine stared up at the impassable defenses, frustrated by the situation. He wouldn't be able to get through using the usual techniques. It was going to take more force than he had been hoping to use.

He pressed his hand against the hard surface, fighting against the pressure of her push back. He took a deep breath and pushed firmly, testing it. The tremors this time were fiercer. The wall rippled as if it had been turned to liquid, but nothing happened, so he tried again, pushing harder. His hand slipped through the wall up to his wrist.

Just as he expected, he would be able to edge through this way. Cracks spread out like spider webs from where his hand had gone through the wall. He pulled, but his arm was stuck. He tugged again, but the wall refused to let go of its grip on him. He needed to find a way to get himself free.

Caine put his other hand on the wall and pushed again, using more force than needed to break a fully trained man. The surface of the wall rippled again, and this time he didn't hesitate. He threw himself into the wall, pushing through, and piercing pain spiked through him, making his muscles clench and convulse. This was hurting her. He doubled over, clutching his stomach. He could sense everything she was experiencing; her emotions and her pain. It was one of the drawbacks of this method. If she hadn't been resisting him, it would have been so much easier. Her mind was naturally blocking his entry, despite the amount of force he was using. He gritted his teeth and pushed on. He climbed through, hoping to find some answers to settle this entire situation.

Once he crossed to the other side, he turned back. The cracks had grown as he'd gone through. They widened significantly, extending out for several meters in all directions. It was not significant, but still, it was damage. It would heal in time. How much time, though, was yet to be seen.

Caine continued, but her next onslaught of mental defenses bubbled up underneath him. His feet were stuck like he was slogging through thick mud; every step took tremendous effort. He was finding it increasingly more difficult to think and breathe. An unseen force was crushing his chest. He pushed forward, trying not to get bogged down and sink in her mental quicksand. His legs were being sucked down. In moments, he had been dragged down to his knees. To break through, he bore forward, throwing his whole body into each step. Her agonizing cry of pain echoed, faint and distant. Another savage set of cramps sent his muscles clenching in violent, uncontrollable spasms. He gritted his teeth and pushed again. A muffled whooshing roar grew louder. One more push, and he finally broke through, moments before he was hurled into her next layer of defenses.

A giant wave of resistance crashed down on him like water immediately sucking him beneath the surface. He struggled to stay afloat in the endless sea, tossing and turning in the churning waves. It pulled him down, but he needed to keep his head above it.

Gasping for air, he could find no foothold, nothing to grab onto to regain control. Wave after wave of watery defenses crashed down on him. He was drowning in them.

Caine had never encountered anything like this. The idea she would have been so strong had never occurred to him.

The surface slowly drifted further away. He had to figure out a way to slip through; otherwise, he risked getting trapped. He mustered up all his remaining strength and drove his elbows out, thrusting his arms to the sides. Shockwaves of power radiated from his palms and sent her watery defenses shooting away from him in two massive tidal waves. For a brief moment, everything was still, then as if a drain plug had been pulled, he began falling.

Spiraling through the air in the whirlwind of her mind: he fell through the sky, hurtling towards a ground that never grew any closer. He fought to regain control, to plan his next move, but the rushing wind stole the air from his lungs, making it difficult to focus.

There was a change in air pressure. The ground rushed towards him in a blur. He hurtled towards it with such speed he would have no time to stop the impending crash. This was going to hurt. He threw his arms up in front of his face to protect himself, expecting to slam into the ground face first. With a wet splash, he hit the hard surface on his back.

He moved his hands away from his face. He was lying in the middle of a busy street; water dripped from his clothes, pooling under him in a growing puddle.

Thousands of people and strange-looking machines on wheels whizzed in a blur. It was like he was stuck in slow motion as the world sped by him in fast forward. Huge buildings and screens flashing with words and color climbed high into the sky. He stood, placing his hands on his knees to push himself to his feet, and was surprised when his hands touched dry clothes. He had been drenched just moments earlier and had to remind himself he wasn't in the real world. Inside a person's mind, things worked differently; reality was different; anything was possible.

Trying to control himself, Caine scanned his surroundings. He didn't recognize the place or the people in it.

He spotted Cara standing on the side of the busy street, gazing up at one of the large screens. It flashed with pictures he didn't understand.

Caine examined her memories for cracks, but there didn't appear to be any. There were no indications of manipulation or any signs of alteration. Everything appeared to be in its rightful place. Usually, he could find strange little shifts and warps in the surroundings, places where pieces of the memory didn't quite line up. These were a clear giveaway, an indication that something had been changed or replaced.

Hostiles occasionally planted sleepers as informants in the core planets. They were easily detected unless their entire identity was replaced. The easiest way to cover their tracks was to alter their identity at the source, in their mind. This always left traces, like fingerprints at a crime scene. Caine was able to detect the flaws that exposed those changes. They appeared like the rough edges of a puzzle piece that had been sloppily cut to fit into an empty hole. A piece that had been placed in the wrong spot, never aligning with the space around it.

Cara turned and walked towards him. As she crossed the road, the people and vehicles faded away slowly. Everything she passed grew transparent and vanished behind her, leaving nothing but eerily empty streets. Caine followed as she passed by, and soon he was the only person in the whole city besides her.

She went down a set of stairs leading under the roadway. There was a big sign with the word 'subway' written on it in big black letters with a green arrow pointing downwards. Caine remembered her mentioning the word 'subway' during his questioning.

At the bottom of the stairs, Cara walked through a small contraption with tiny doors that swung forward when they opened to let her through. The little doors shut behind her. Caine pushed them, but they were stuck closed. He was losing sight of her in the crowd! He placed his palms on either side and swung himself over it. He ran after her and found her walking across a narrow platform in front of a tunnel; it stretched out in both directions as far as he could see. She stopped near the edge and waited. He could hear the screeching of metal and a deep rumbling getting closer. A massive machine roared in - sleek and silver. It groaned to a stop in front of her, and several sets of doors along its side opened. Cara stepped in, and Caine followed.

The section they were in was empty. Chairs lined its walls, and a metal bar ran along the center of the ceiling. She stood in the back near a door, holding a small, triangular metal handle above her head.

Cara didn't react to his presence, as if he was invisible. The subway moved forward with a lurch, and Caine grabbed onto a nearby pole to steady himself. A folded grey paper on one of the blue chairs caught his eye. He picked it up; The New York Times. There was a date at the top, small, tucked into the corner. He hadn't noticed it at first; his attention captured by the larger words splashed across the page. A closer look made the blood run cold in his veins. The date was over nine hundred years in the past! He rubbed the edges of the paper, looking for any signs the memory was a fake, but there were none. He whirled around to look at Cara, but as he did, the section came surging back to life. All the people reappeared around him, sitting in seats or talking. The noise was overwhelming. Every seat had someone sitting in it, and more people stood in the aisle, crowded all around him. The lights flickered.

Her relaxed expression became fearful. There was a thunderous bang followed by a bright swirl of blue light and a flash of blinding white.

Without warning, he was yanked from the moment and swept through her memories. He no longer had control. With a loud pop, he was pulled into her past.

A little girl with pigtails, tied at the ends with big blue bows, was sitting in front of a pink cake with little purple candles. She was surrounded by children singing a song. When they finished their song, she blew the flames out. The scene changed to a little girl in a red dress, sitting on a bench playing beautiful music on a large, black instrument. Cara sat at a long table, conversing with a group of people around her. She was holding a large wooden stick, hitting a ball as children ran around. A small yellow creature played with a red ball, running across the grass, wagging a long tail as Cara looked on. It dropped the ball at her feet. She picked it up and threw it. The little yellow thing streaked after it, making her laugh. She called out to it, calling it Max. Time skipped ahead; she sat sobbing on the floor as she cradled a much larger yellow creature in her arms.

Pulled forward, Cara was now wearing a black gown complimented by a square, black hat with a little tassel hanging over the flat brim. People clapped as she walked up to a man wearing impressive purple and gold robes. He handed her a rolled-up paper wrapped with a black string. He blinked, and she was working at a desk, talking into some strange comm unit on her head.

With each sharp crack, he was torn from memory to memory, through the events in her life. Kisses, running in the rain, injuries, growing and learning, happy times, and sad times. The joys as a child, tears as a teenager, and the doubts of adulthood. Recent memories and old ones. He felt all of it, knew all of it.

With another sharp snap, he found himself standing in the middle of a vast stretch of blackness. Memories scrolled by like a string of small screens playing each scene over and over. Floating about at random were small transparent spheres, little bubbles of memories. He was in her central memory cortex. He raised his hands. With quick flicks of his wrist, he filtered through the memories as they streamed by. He searched for anything that might explain what he was seeing. A milky grey sphere floated by over his left shoulder, and he reached out for it, plucking it from the blackness and held it gently in his fingertips. He allowed himself to be pulled into the scene.

Cara sat at a table with a man. He held her hand, beaming at her. She stood up abruptly.

"I can't," she said. The man kept staring and talking at the empty chair as if she was still sitting in it. His hand remained curled as if he was still holding hers. She took a few steps back from the table. She turned and looked up at Caine, staring at him as if she could see him. Reaching its end, the memory stopped and restarted.

Caine retreated to her central cortex and looked around for a cardinal memory, one of great importance that would confirm her true identity. He waved his hands, and everything around him accelerated, flying by him, moving faster until he clamped his fist shut and everything froze. There, that was the one he was looking for. He could sense it. He touched the screen-like image in front of him.

He found himself standing in the middle of a small room. He looked around. There was a table with chairs and a bed in an adjoining room. Even though he had never seen this place before, there was an overwhelming sense of familiarity. He knew instinctively this was where she lived. This was her home. He inspected everything closely, touching the walls to see if they would shift or break, indicating memory changes. There were no visible signs that anything had been altered previously. It was all real, authentic.

Cara walked over to a window drinking something from a white cup. She stared out at the city for a short time before placing the cup on the counter and walked past him.

Her energy pulled at him, trying to drag him along as she walked out the door. The door closed with a loud slam. He couldn't hold on any longer and was thrust roughly from her mind.

Chapter Eight

Caine came back to reality, his ears ringing. Everything was hazy, blurry, and deathly quiet. His heart raced, his chest heaved from oxygen deprivation. His lungs burned as he sucked in breath after ragged breath. He was hunched over like he had been punched in the stomach.

He had barely managed to keep his seat when he was violently ejected from her mind, back to reality. He looked over at Cara; her head was hanging, long hair draped over her face, blocking his ability to see her expression.

Caine bent his head and steadied his breathing, drawing in air through his nose. He raked a hand through his hair. Little dark spots appear on her pants. He reached out to touch one, and it smeared red. He could feel the hot wetness of his own blood dripping down over his lips and chin. He wiped it away with his sleeve.

Nosebleeds were the most common side effect when his abilities went unchecked. He had pushed too hard trying to get through her defenses, and in doing so, had forged a link between them that rocked him like an explosion.

Caine had never had a connection as powerfully brutal as the one he had with her. It was as if she had taken over him when they merged, causing him to lose control. An Interrogation that chaotic was unheard of. Not even throughout his most extreme training had he ever experienced anything close to what had just happened.

Regaining control of his racing thoughts, Caine recalled what he had seen and who she was. All of his beliefs about the universe, everything he knew about reality shattered around him as he began to comprehend what he had just witnessed. She wasn't a Hostile. She wasn't even from this century!

How was it possible?

Even with all the advances in technology, time travel was still not possible. He had not seen any changes in her memories and nothing had been altered or erased. Everything in her mind was real, as real as he was. The clues and signs of the memory alterations Hostiles typically performed on spies or plants were nowhere to be found in her mind.

"Cara, look at me." He kept his voice soft and gentle instead of demanding it.

She was trembling and wheezing. He reached out and laid a hand on her knee. At his touch, Cara became deathly still. He reached up, gently pushing the hair away from her face. Her eyes were clenched tightly shut, blood dribbled from her nose, trickling down her lips and chin. Her head shook back and forth rapidly in small, jerky movements.

"Cara, look at me," this time he gently commanded it, letting the direction take its hold.

Her eyes flew open with pupils dilated and looking wild. Without warning, they rolled back into her head. She convulsed, her body thrashing violently against the restraints.

Caine swiftly ran to push the red emergency button by the door. He unbuckled her ankles and wrists quickly and grabbed her tightly in his arms, holding her until Nadir came in.

One look at the scene, and Nadir grabbed a syringe from a drawer. "Hold her still," Nadir instructed.

Carefully, Caine brushed away the hair away from her neck. He held her tightly as Nadir pushed the needle in an exposed vein and sedated her. Nadir's eyes blazed with indignation.

Caine could do nothing but hold Cara until she went limp in his arms, her eyes open and glazed over as her head lolled back. It took a minute for the drugs to take effect, but eventually, she slipped into a sedated sleep.

Caine picked her up and placed her on a nearby bed. He looked down at Cara, her face pale and bloody.

"Go," Nadir said lowly, brushing past Caine to take care of his patient. He turned his back to Caine and quickly set about hooking up all the monitors and machines.

Caine knew no explanation would fix this situation, and it was highly possible he damaged her mind beyond repair. He had pushed through her defenses, breaking them down, possibly shattering her mind with them. Even the most well-trained Intransigent had ways to break through doors into the mind, but she had no doors. Just layer after layer of defenses. Her mind had almost been impenetrable. It was almost as if she had let him in on her own terms. That unnerved him the most. He wanted to assess the damage, but nothing would change by allowing her to rest and give Nadir a chance to cool off.

Caine went back to his quarters. He rinsed his hands clean and splashed some water on his face. He but couldn't help feeling a bit shaken after what had just happened. He hadn't been this unsettled by an Interrogation in years. An alert blinked on the display screen, letting him know a video message was waiting from Daedra. He played the video.

"Caine, I ran the image through our system. It isn't anything I have ever seen from a Hostile clan before. The symbol is an Old Earth symbol. It is from an Old Earth religion called Buddhism, which originated in Indo-Asian culture. It could be a new Clan or a branch off an older one, but I have never seen them use Old Earth symbols before. This is something entirely different. I hope it helps. Good luck Caine." The message ended, and the screen went blank.

An Old Earth symbol; it made sense. She was from a time when people still lived on Old Earth. He knew America had sounded familiar. One of the ancient nations on Old Earth. He shook his head as he made sense of things. It was clear now. This was real. How was it even possible? The United Colonies had made great strides in science, but time travel was still not possible.

Hours later, Caine ventured back to Medical. She was lying on a table with eyes closed, monitors beeped. Nadir had washed the blood from her face and hair and changed her into a clean outfit. Caine held her cold hand in his. Not knowing what else to do, he pulled a blanket from a cabinet and awkwardly draped it over her. Footsteps approached from behind.

"It appears she had some form of seizure from the shock." Nadir approached from behind. "When she wakes up, we will see the extent of the damage. I told you she was too weak and wasn't ready." He shuffled up alongside Caine.

"Not now, Nadir," Caine begged wearily.

Nadir sighed, knowing full well Caine was beating himself up over this. "Get some rest. I will call you if anything changes."

"I'm not leaving until she wakes." Caine looked down at Cara, pale and still.

Nadir knew better than to argue. He nodded and left.

Caine pulled up a chair and sat by her side. He would be here when she woke; he owed her that much. He rubbed her hand with his thumb. White-hot electricity sizzled in the microscopic space between their skin. For a brief moment, his hand melded with hers. He was slipping into her, or she was becoming part of him. It wasn't just his hand; it was theirs - together. He yanked his hand away and stared at it.

Something had happened when he had gone into her mind. Something had connected them. As if he knew her and always had. He was now part of her life, and she was part of his. This was only going to make everything more difficult and complicated. He would have to force himself to ignore the connection that drew him to her. He had to stay impartial and do his job. It was his duty.

Chapter Nine

Cara was back in the medical ward where she had first woken after the crash, but she was lying on a hospital bed this time. She looked around; memories of what had happened were foggy and distant. Someone had been asking her questions and then... then she couldn't remember anything. Now she was here.

Out of the corner of her eye, a slight shift of shadows caught her attention. The Commander slept in a chair a few feet away. His shoulders rose and fell gently with his breathing. What was his name again? Carl? No, he definitely was not a Carl.

Cloudy memories cleared. He had been questioning her before...before whatever it was that she couldn't remember. He must have done something to her but wasn't exactly sure what it was. One moment she was staring at him, tied to a chair; the next, she was waking up in a bed wearing different clothes. Had he drugged her? What had happened in this room while she was unconscious? Her stomach lurched as all kinds of horrible worst-case scenarios filled her mind. She was going to be sick.

She sat up, and he stirred. Her stomach lurched, and she looked around desperately. Slipping off the table, she wobbled toward a sink in the corner. Monitoring clips and cords tugged as they fell away. Her knees gave way. She wasn't going to make it. The commotion fully woke Caine, and he grabbed her arms before she fell. Keeping her upright, he helped her over to the sink.

Cara's stomach emptied. She rinsed her mouth out, and as she wiped her mouth off with the back of her hand, she noticed a tray of medical tools on the counter next to her. Maybe she could use one to protect herself. She grabbed the sharpest thing and whirled towards him. She attempted to point it at him, but he was closer to her than she expected. Her elbow hit his chest. The momentum of her swing threw her arm upwards. The sharp edge of the scalpel scraped the underside of his chin, leaving a little nick like a paper cut.

Caine had seen her grab at something on the counter next to her. He caught a glimpse of metal in her hand moments before she twisted towards him. He leaned back just enough to avoid the full brunt of her attack. He managed to get a hold of her wrist and drove her back against the wall, slamming her hand against the hard surface to disarm her.

Cara nearly lost her grip on her small weapon, but she managed to keep her fingers curled around it. She let out a sharp cry as her knuckles cracked viciously against the wall.

"What the hell did you do to me?" she roared furiously, trying to pull away.

Caine was quiet for a moment. A thin line of blood welled up on the cut under his chin. "You were weak. You fainted, and you hit your head." He hoped his lie was believable enough.

Nadir rushed into the room at the sound of their struggle. "Well, I can see she has recovered just fine." A half-smile played at the corners of his lips. "I think you have this handled," he added and left.

"Nadir," Caine growled at him as he left. The door slammed shut. Caine huffed and turned back to look at Cara. Damn the woman. She should never have been able to catch him off guard like that. He pressed his thumb into her wrist, hitting a pressure point. As he pushed on the bundle of sensitive nerves, her fingers opened. The scalpel slipped from her grip as she gave a little cry of pain. He kicked it away to a safer distance and released her. He took several steps back, trying to give her some space but she remained pressed against the wall like a caged animal.

Even though she cowered from him, he could see defiance in her eyes. He touched his chin neck and looked briefly down at the dark red smear on his fingertips. She had a fighting spirit, and her success at injuring him almost impressed him.

Caine stared at the blood on his fingers, but there wasn't any anger present in his expression. Cara didn't understand his calm reaction.

She frowned at the stranger in front of her: a man who had thrown her in a cell and treated her like a common criminal.

She was fuming, but it wasn't anger sparked by fear. It was the same kind of anger she felt when David or her brother had made her upset. It was the kind of anger one feels towards someone familiar, someone she cared about. Where had that come from?

Despite everything that happened, she sensed she could trust him. It was almost as if she knew him or had known him once long ago. When he had grabbed her wrists, lightning coursed through her veins. The moment he had touched her skin, she began to lose herself in him. Looking in his eyes, for a split second, he was all that existed, like she was part of him, and he was a part of her. It was a terrifying feeling which overwhelmed her. She couldn't explain the connection she felt. She hadn't even connected like this with David after all their time dating. There was a sense of trust, a bond with this man. Even in bed, there was a cold disconnection from David, but with this man, she knew in bed he would …

Wait a second, get a grip! Where the hell did that come from? No, no, no, this was all messing with her head too much. She couldn't think clearly anymore.

Cara looked up at the little smear of blood underneath his chin. She had come so close to hurting him.

She was not someone who resorted to violence. All she had meant to do was hold the scalpel up to make him back away, to put distance between them, and instead, she'd come within inches of nearly cutting cut his throat. What if she had killed him?

Everything crashed down on her, and she pressed her hands to her mouth with a horrified gasp. The walls started to move. They undulated as if they had become liquid and slowly closed in around her. She blinked, trying to get her mind straight. She was instantly claustrophobic, like hands were around her throat, suffocating her.

The emotions played out on her face. She was working through everything she'd been through, processing it all. Her anger gave way to shock at what she had done, and she covered her mouth in dismay. She wavered slightly, and he reached out to steady her, but she drew away quickly, taking a few shaky steps away from him. He should have seen it coming, but he was so caught up in the moment he missed all the signs of what was about to happen. Cara glanced at the door and took the opportunity. She ran.

She bolted from the room, racing down the corridor as there were shouts behind her. She had to find a way out. Cara raced around the corner at the end of one hallway and turned down another. She'd only made two turns but was already lost. She had no idea how to escape. What if she was on this ship, and it was in the middle of the ocean? If she made her way to the deck and found she was nowhere near land, nowhere near help, she would still be trapped. This fueled her panic further.

At the far end of the hallway, two officers stepped around the corner into her view, standing shoulder to shoulder and blocking her exit. She whirled around and found Commander Caine striding down the hallway towards her.

"Stay back." She stepped back and held her arms up, outstretched defensively. He stopped. She shot a glance behind her to make sure the other two officers weren't trying to sneak up on her. Caine took a step forward. She glared at him.

"Back off," Cara bit out, snarling at him like a cornered animal.

"You have two choices," Caine offered. "Either you can walk with me, and I can take you to your room, or I can have those two drag you back."

Cara weighed his words. "Room? Is that what you're calling the cell you shoved me into earlier?"

Caine took a deep breath, trying to compose himself. Cara was wound so tight the slightest push might send her over the edge. He didn't want to fight with her. He needed to diffuse the situation and his own mood.

"Yes, your room." He forced his tone to remain even and calm. "I was just about to tell you before you decided to go on this little field trip, you are no longer being detained. You have been cleared, and you are now my guest on this ship until we can take you home. You will be released as soon as we can do so."

Caine warped the lie enough to be almost the truth. He knew now she had no idea of her impossible journey and needed to keep it from her until he knew how to handle the situation. He couldn't even begin to calculate the damages and repercussions if she found out where she was. Her mind was still mending from his Interrogation and would not be able to handle any more stress. He knew there were hairline fractures all through her mind, hence her lack of memory of the Interrogation. Any more trauma could cause them to fragment completely. Not to mention the extensive stretch of cracks he hammered into her outer defenses, which could easily crumble into a larger hole that would take months to heal. Her angry gaze softened, but there was suspicion in her eyes.

There was a beeping noise as his comm unit went off, signaling his presence was needed elsewhere. Of course, he would be pulled away right at this moment.

"Cara, I have to go. But I can have my officers bring you to your room. I can assure you that you will be just fine," he told her.

Cara gave a small nod but didn't speak. Caine gestured to his officers to approach. He turned and left feeling like the encounter had ultimately been a success, despite her commendable attempt at trying to decapitate him. As he rounded the corner, he paused, expecting to hear her protesting, but there was silence, so he continued on to deal with his next encounter, one with the Council he feared would be far less successful.

Arriving at the Bridge, he found Than and gestured for him to follow. They made their way to his private quarters and entered the small office he had built off his bedroom. It was the most private place on the ship.

Caine was still shaky as he continued to reflect on what he now knew about Cara. He crossed the room and sat at his desk. He leaned forward, resting his elbows on his knees with hands clasped tightly.

"You okay?" Than asked.

"She's from the past."

Than looked incredibly confused. "What?" His brows shot up, unsure if he heard Caine correctly.

"She is from nearly a thousand years in the goddamned past!" Caine thundered, slamming his fist on his desk. Objects rattled, tipping, and threatening to fall. Caine grabbed at one, keeping it upright, and ran his fingers through his hair.

Than looked at him as if he was delusional. "Caine, you know time travel isn't possible. Attempts have never been successful."

"I know it isn't possible, but there she is. I should know. I just Interrogated her," Caine barked at Than.

As the meaning of Caine's words dawned upon Than, his eyes widened. He knew as well as Caine how dangerous Interrogations could be and the potential damage that could occur to the mind. "Is she?" he ventured.

"She's perfectly fine," Caine cut him off. "She tried to take my head off with a scalpel afterward." He gestured to the cut under his chin. Than let out a sharp, barking laugh, more in shock that someone had actually gotten the drop on Caine.

Caine shot him a murderous glare. "She's an Intransigent."

"Come again?" Than looked skeptical. He brushed a lock of black hair off his forehead and scratched his chin.

"She had mental defenses. Strong ones, at that. She was able to keep me out for a short time. I don't even think she is aware of it. She doesn't realize what she is doing."

"If she's an Intransigent, she should be registered in the system. There would have to be records of her somewhere."

Caine shook his head. "I've looked. I ran her image and her DNA through the database. Nothing. Not a fingerprint, not a surveillance photo. Before yesterday she didn't exist in the Confederation."

"So, doesn't that mean she could be a Hostile?"

The Confederation liked to keep a close eye on things, keeping track of all its citizens, even those on the most distant border planets. For someone not to exist in some format in the database was virtually impossible unless they were a Hostile. Only the prominent Hostile Clan leaders were known, along with any spy who happened to get caught.

"I don't think so. I saw it all. Her whole life, all her memories were from the past. Hundreds of years ago." Caine wiped his hand over his face and leaned back in his chair.

"You know it isn't possible." Than rubbed his chin. "Hostiles have been working on perfecting their methods for years. She could have had her memory altered. Maybe memory implants?"

Caine knew Hostiles were more frequently erasing their memories to cover their tracks. It was a brutal procedure involving chemicals and good old-fashioned brain damage at the hands of an unskilled surgeon.

He remembered seeing Hostiles with entire chunks of their brain carved out to keep the Confederation from getting information if they were captured. More often now, Hostiles were turning towards advancing technology to change memories or implant artificial memories. He knew the process well.

Decades ago, scientists had worked with Espers to develop a way to help those dealing with trauma, changing bad memories to good ones, allowing people with PTSD or other mental illnesses to regain some normalcy in their lives. It was used after that by the corrections system to rehabilitate criminals. It was commonplace to change memories of rough childhoods to ones filled with love and transform memories of violence into peaceful acts.

Soon, the government seized control of the process, banning Espers from using it on civilians. The Confederation had hoped to use the process to turn captured Hostiles into decent, ordinary citizens, but it didn't work. They would behave as if they were changed for a short time, but the effects quickly wore off, and they went back to being violent and aggressive.

Hostiles had changed so much over the centuries; fundamentally, their DNA was different, the same way his own was different. As an Esper, he could not implement changes in a mind that wasn't exactly, well, entirely human. The government scrapped the entire project but not before the idea of the process ended up making its way into the hands of the Hostiles themselves. It was one of the first things Caine remembered learning about in his education.

Hostiles utilized the research to develop technology so they could alter the mind with machinery rather than with Esper abilities. They erased memories of planned attacks, names of sleeper agents embedded in the Confederation, and more. Old memories could not be recovered, but the simple fact of knowing a memory was altered often led to some form of information being revealed by a captured Hostiles.

Cara's memories had not been changed. They were real. They were hers.

"I would have noticed," Caine shook his head. "It was as real as you or me."

Than nodded, pondering on the revelation Caine had just dropped on him.

"Tell me what you saw."

Caine described the entire scene to Than.

"There was too much detail. There is no way a Hostile could recreate a memory with that level of detail in it. Especially not one from so long ago. Everything was natural."

Caine continued describing what he had seen in her mind, but as he spoke, a detail he shared caught his attention.

"The blue flash," Caine repeated, making the connection. "There was a blue light and then a white flash while she was on some sort of transportation system, just before she woke up here!"

Than looked confused. "A blue light like the EMP?" Than asked.

"Exactly like the EMP," he confirmed. He rubbed his chin. "How could it be possible? Could the EMP have caused all of this?"

"There is a theory," Than spoke slowly, "a ripple theory about space and time. Big events can ripple through time. Not just the future but the past too. Time is all connected." He paused. "Think of time and space as a string. A line, yes, but not fixed. Points in time are like points on a string, each one representing a specific time and place in space. The string can bend, move, and twist, moving these points of time with it. The theory states if two points in time are close enough when catastrophic events occur at each one, they could momentarily touch, merging for just a second. It could be any place or time. If something happened at the same moment as the EMP, it's possible she was pulled through."

Caine's head was spinning. "It isn't possible." He shook his head.

Than shrugged. "It doesn't seem possible, but as you said, there she is."

Caine opened a bottle of araq and poured a full cup. He took a long drink, letting the spicy, herbaceous spirit run down the back of his throat. Fermented from kokerr, an astringently acidic yellow fruit with dark red pulp, which was too grainy to eat, the juice was used to make the drink.

"The Council is going to lose their shit when they get wind of this," Than told him with a lopsided grin.

Caine groaned, pouring himself another cup.

Chapter Ten

Caine requested an audience with the Council as soon as possible. He spent the next several hours typing up the formal report to send them. He had just finished when the screen flashed.

Caine did his best to explain the situation, and everything was going smoothly until he mentioned the Hostile was a woman. The outburst made him cringe. Half the Council was on their feet, shouting at each other. Some of them pointed at each other; others shook their fists.

"Silence," Yugato rose to his feet, his great wooden chair scraping on the stone floor. The arguing ceased. "Sit down," Yugato demanded. Several Council members exchanged final angry glances before taking their seats. Yugato looked back at Caine. "Proceed."

"I did the Interrogation. She is alive and well, I assure you. The only problem is she is not from this time." Mentioning aloud that she happened to have traveled through time sounded awkward and strange to him.

"I don't understand." Yugato frowned. "She is actually from the twenty-first century?" he questioned. The look on Caine's face gave him the answer. Yugato sat back in his chair, rubbing his temples. "How is this possible?"

"I am not sure, but it is true. I have seen the proof myself."

"If I may explain," Than supplied. "Caine and I have discussed a possible theory that may explain how this could have occurred." Than explained the theory to the bewildered council members. "I think when we used the EMP, it caused a ripple. Cara, the woman, got stuck in the middle of two moments in time and was pulled across."

"Are you sure you didn't miss anything? What you claim is impossible," Saar interjected.

Caine bristled.

"I assure you this is not a mistake. Her memories were not altered or changed in any way. Nothing was erased; her memories were clean. I went deep enough. I would have noticed even the smallest of inconsistencies. This woman is who she says she is."

Yugato sighed and wiped his face with his hand before addressing his colleagues. "This is unprecedented. We will need to get our top scientists working on this immediately. If she was able to get here, there must be a way to send her back."

He looked back at Caine. "This needs to be contained before any word of it gets out to the public. We don't know what kind of repercussions there may be from her arrival. In the meantime, I want continued updates on the situation."

"But what about this woman? What happens with her?" Councilwoman Viraha's deep, raspy voice was as distinct as her political views. She stroked her long, dark braid.

"She cannot be allowed to remain on the Archon," Saar stated.

Viraha nodded in agreement. "Saar is right. She must be brought here to us as soon as possible."

Caine made a mental note to inform his crew they were changing course. The Council was located on Arctus, at least a three-day journey in the opposite direction.

Yugato looked around at the council members. "It appears we are all in agreement. She will be brought here at once. When she arrives, we will keep her here at the Caelum until we can find a way to send her back. Oh, and Than, I want a full report on the engineering of the EMP. Maybe we can find a way to use it to get her home."

"I will have her there as soon as possible," Caine confirmed.

Yugato folded his hands on the table. "We will be expecting you."

Caine waited for the image to disappear, but it didn't. Yugato pinned Caine with a concerned stare.

"Is melioration needed?"

Caine knew what Yugato was implying. If the woman was aware she had traveled through time, her memory had to be wiped clean.

"She has no idea where she is," Caine replied with relief. Thank the stars for that, at least. Despite having done it dozens of times in his career, for some reason having to do that to Cara didn't sit well with him.

"Good, keep it that way until she gets here. Do what you must to keep this from her." Yugato spoke his final order, and the screen went blank.

Caine agreed; the more she knew, the more dangerous the situation could become. For her own safety, it was better if she knew nothing. The only problem was figuring out how to keep a secret this big from her until then. Caine sighed; nothing on this ship was ever easy.

Chapter Eleven

Cara was taken to a room with a bed and a small three-sided stall area containing an odd gadget that loosely resembled a toilet. She still had no more answers about what had happened than before. Commander Caine was turning out to be enigmatic, and it was frustrating. He would not tell her where she was or why. In fact, he had refused to answer any of her questions truthfully. His word games were frustrating. He had politely asked she remain in her room until they could bring her home. Although he had phrased it as a request, she knew it was an order. He claimed her presence would be a distraction to his crew.

At first, she had adhered to his request more out of uncertainty. She held a book close to her chest. In all his stately splendor, the Commander had unexpectedly arrived at her room, standing uncharacteristically awkwardly at the door, trying to find the words to say to her.

"I brought this for you. So, you have something to keep you occupied until you arrive home." He had thrust the book in her hand and crisply turned and left as she stared after him, baffled by the whole encounter.

It took her two days to finish the work of military science fiction. It was a fitting novel for him to have in his collection.

When she was done, she decided it was time to get another. She went to the door, and it slid open automatically as she approached. Wherever she was, the place was technologically advanced, beyond any other building or location she had ever been. Whatever military forces were behind its creation had spared no expense on outfitting it with the most high-tech gear. Out in the hall, a young, uniformed man stood guard.

"I'd like another if you don't mind," she advised, handing him the book.

He nodded but continued to look straight ahead at the opposite wall, remaining still as the door closed again. She let a few minutes pass before approaching the door again. It opened, and the officer was gone. She didn't see anyone in the hallway, so she couldn't get in anyone's way if there was no one there, right? Cara wanted to justify her disobedience. Just a quick walk to the end of the hallway and she would go back to the room, but one hallway led to another, and her inquisitive nature soon got the better of her.

She wandered down the hallways. It looked like a ship, white and shiny but drastically different from the battleships she had seen at the Maritime Museum near Boston as a child.

Those battleships were grey and dark with small passages and low ceilings. This one was extensive, with much higher ceilings and wide long hallways. A door opened when she walked by, revealing sleeping quarters. Most of the rooms on this level led to large sleeping quarters for the crew or small equipment or mechanical rooms. She turned down the hall, and a door to her left opened, revealing what appeared to be an elevator. She stepped in. The doors closed, and it started to move automatically. She searched frantically for any recognizable buttons to press to make it stop but found none.

After a short time, the door opened again, revealing a busy hall with crew walking around. She pressed herself into the corner, trying not to be seen, and waited nervously for the doors to close. When they were halfway shut, they stopped, and an officer stepped in. He gave her a quick look over but didn't question her. She forced herself to look straight ahead and not meet his eyes. Eventually, the elevator stopped, and he got off. She tried to exit behind him to make her way back to her room before she got caught, but her escape was prevented when several more officers stepped on, boxing her in. The next time the elevator stopped, she pushed through the group and got off. There were officers to her left at the end of the hall.

Cara turned around, heading away from them. Every floor looked the same. At this point, she had no idea how far up or down she had gone. When she passed another door, it opened automatically. She stopped and curiously peered in. Its darkness intrigued her. She stepped through the doorway to see what the room held.

Her eyes adjusted slowly to the darkness. Her heart skipped a beat and leaped into her throat. The room was exceedingly large and expansive, empty - devoid of any furniture or décor. At the far end of the room, where a wall should have been, was a massive floor to ceiling glass window.

She would have expected to see oceans, maybe even the distant outline of land on the horizon, but instead, she found herself staring into the vastness of deep space.

Actual outer space.

Real outer space.

She took a few hesitant steps, coming to stand in the middle of the room. She was in utter shock, unable to form any coherent thoughts. She approached the window, raised a hand, and slowly reached out to touch the glass. It was ice cold under her fingers.

Inky blackness was dotted with glimmering spots of light. The slender curve of a pastel blue planet, half-shaded in darkness, loomed in the distance. Space; she was in space.

Despite how illogical it sounded, she was on a spaceship.

Pressing a hand against the glass, she stared out into the unending expanse of space and found herself questioning not just reality but also her sanity. This couldn't possibly be real. There had to be some sort of explanation.

She needed answers. How had she gotten here? What had happened to her?

Stunned, Cara stumbled a few steps back and away from the window. Her mind was a tangled mess of racing thoughts and rising panic. Logic warred with the reality that stretched out in front of her.

When Cara was seven, she had been fighting with her brother, Royce. She pushed him, and he fell into a table. Her mother's priceless crystal bowl crashed to the floor and shattered into a million pieces. Horrified, Cara stood there, staring at the little crystal shards as they glinted in the sunlight, little rainbows dancing in the center of each tiny piece. It was as beautiful as it was terrible.

There was a gut-twisting dread eating away at her insides as she stared out at the stars, scattered across the sky exactly like the little fragments of glass on her mother's kitchen floor.

She pulled her gaze away from the view and managed to walk back to the hallway.

Outside the door, she slumped against the wall, allowing it to hold her up, not sure her shaking legs would be able to hold out much longer. She raised her trembling hands to her face, rubbed her eyes, and ran her palms over her cheeks. Her fingertips were still cold.

Still shocked by her discovery, her initial surprise was turning quickly into feelings of resentment. It was easier for her to feel animosity than to allow herself to be frightened. She was angry at all the lies that had been fed to her. Lies fed to her by the Commander.

Caine had to be behind all of this. He was the Commander in charge, after all. Cara leaned against the wall and closed her eyes. Her heart was racing, and her lungs were tight. She couldn't take a deep enough breath. Adrenaline levels plummeting; she dropped her face into her hands, fighting back the prickle of tears threatening to escape.

No, no, no, this cannot be happening. In a moment of absolute absurdity, she pinched herself. Cara shook her head. She was being ridiculous. As if that would somehow jolt her awake, and she would magically be back on Earth in her room.

She pushed herself up off the wall and drew in a shaky breath, and went in search of Caine. The longer she looked, the more lost she became. Thoughts circled like a merry-go-round in her mind.

Cara had no idea where she was.

She needed to find Caine.

She needed to find a way home.

Terror threatened to take control. Home… how was she going to get home? Her family was probably terrified, not knowing where she was. Footsteps echoed down the hall. As if she had conjured him, Caine appeared from around a corner; his body practically filled the space.

Damn, the man was daunting. She sucked down the rising fear and bile and gritted her teeth. It was time for her to get her answers.

Chapter Twelve

Caine was watching the screen in front of him when a security officer called out to him.

"Commander, our guest has left her quarters."

"What! Didn't I have someone posted outside her room to prevent this exact thing?"

He needed to find Cara before she got herself into any trouble. As he left the Bridge, a young officer approached, holding a book. It didn't take much time for Caine to figure out what had happened. She was clever, but the deception left a bad taste in his mouth. He found himself quickly questioning whether he had been wrong about her.

"You will report to maintenance tomorrow," Caine commanded.

The officer looked down at the book with wide eyes, realizing his error. "Yes, Sir," he replied meekly, head bowed.

Caine passed by the newly demoted officer. "Where is she?" he spoke into the comm unit on his shoulder.

"Far end of level six near the water holding area, Sir," an officer informed him.

He made his way toward her location, but she was nowhere to be found when he got there. She couldn't have gotten far. He turned the corner, and she was there at the other end of the hall.

For a split second, it appeared she was going to run, but she hesitated. If she had run, he would have gone after her. He almost wished she had; he would have enjoyed the chase. He had an unexplainable urge to be close to her. The same magnetic energy that was pulling them together also equally pushed them apart. Equal forces were keeping them connected yet separate.

Her body language changed. She squared her shoulders and stepped towards him with determination. He wasn't sure why she was so upset when she was the one who had ignored his orders. He had to remember she wasn't one of his crew members; she was a civilian. She wasn't used to following orders or his regulations. Still, she had been asked to stay in her room, and she had decided not to listen. He should be angry, not her.

"Where the hell am I? Why are we in space?" She stormed towards him and jammed her finger against his chest.

His throat closed. She knew. She had been in the ship's observatory and had discovered what he had been trying so hard to hide.

"Cara, I can explain." He reached for her hand, her finger still planted firmly on his chest. When his hand closed around hers, she struggled against him.

"What the hell is going on? I want to know what happened to me." Her voice cracked as she screamed at him.

"Kuso, stop," he growled in frustration. She landed a solid blow to his ribs with her elbow as she pulled away. "Cara," he ground out between his clenched teeth, his breath rushing from him.

"Are we on a spaceship?" she asked, trying to wrench away from him.

"Stop, before you end up hurting yourself." He was about to lose his patience with her.

"Holy shit. It's true, we actually are in space," she said when he didn't deny her accusation. "How did we get into space?" She was muttering to herself now, still trying to tug her hands out of his grasp. "This can't be happening. This cannot be happening."

"I'll answer all your questions, just stop," his tone was less pleasant.

Cara hesitated but pulled away again. One of her hands slipped free, and she struck him on the arm.

"Stop fighting," he lowered his voice, compelling her to obey.

She stopped moving immediately. Caine knew it wasn't voluntary. Her breathing was rapid and shallow, and she was pale and cold to the touch. She was slipping into the initial phases of shock. This was precisely why he hadn't wanted her to know. How could someone's mind process something as drastic as this without dangerous implications?

"Look at me," he directed.

Her gaze flicked upwards to meet his; pupils dilated. Her eyes were not entirely focused on him; it was more as if she was looking right through him. Her breathing increased, and she kept muttering something he could barely make out, but it sounded a lot like 'I'm in fucking space.'

"Cara, you're okay. I need you to take a deep breath for me."

She gasped, desperately trying to fill her lungs. Her shoulders and chest rose with every shallow breath she struggled to catch. Her head tilted to the side as her brain fought against the oxygen deprivation. She was about to pass out unless he regained control of the situation.

"Cara, stop," he demanded.

She complied immediately, a little more than he had expected her to. Her eyes rolled back in her head, and she collapsed. He grabbed her as she fell against him. That had not gone at all how he had planned. Wrapping her in his arms, Caine slid down the wall to the floor, holding her gently across his lap. Her eyes fluttered, and he used the moment to probe into her mind again.

He gently pushed into her head, surprisingly meeting no resistance. It was quiet and dim, but from the looks of it, nothing was damaged. In fact, almost the opposite, the cracks were almost fully healed, and there was no other damage from her recent discovery. As shocking as it had been, internally, she was handling the weight of it quite well.

As she regained consciousness, her defenses surged back. Sharp pole-like defenses flung up in front of him, forcing him to back out.

He looked down as her eyes opened fully. She stared up at him for a long time as she gathered herself. Eventually, she pushed herself out of his arms and slid across the hall floor to lean on the opposite wall. He allowed her to put some space between them. He waited a while to speak.

"Are you ok?" he asked after a few minutes.

For a moment, she didn't say anything. She put her hands on her temples, ran her fingers through her hair, and looked up, squarely meeting his gaze.

"Tell me the truth; start from the beginning." Strength and determination blazed in her eyes, and he knew she would be okay.

Caine knew he wouldn't be able to keep lying to her any longer. If she was going to trust him and allow him and his team to help her get back home to her own time, he had to be honest with her.

"Many years ago," he explained, "the Earth you know was no longer able to handle her growing population of humans. The water was polluted beyond saving, and there wasn't enough healthy land to grow crops. There was famine, starvation, and disease. No more food would grow, and rain never came in some areas; acid rain fell in others. In some places, there was constant cold. Billions of people were suffering and could no longer survive on Earth. They had destroyed the planet beyond repair, but there was nowhere else for them to go. Humans struggled to get by, warring with each other endlessly over the minimal resources remaining. The population which had once been so big was sharply declining. People were barely surviving on what they had stored or on government-supplied rations.

"Several nations pooled their resources to find a new home. An expedition was sent into space to find new planets to live on. It took decades, but the expedition was eventually successful. Technology advanced enough through photon particle acceleration research, allowing for the development of ships fast enough to make the journey worthwhile.

Scientists decided on a distant solar system, Theta 5, which had a sun and many planets, but the planets needed some work before anyone could inhabit them. They used a process called terraforming. It makes a planet habitable for human life, giving it oxygen, water, and plant life. Scientists had hoped it could be used on Earth, but their attempts failed."

Cara listened in disbelief, waiting for him to get to the part where he explained what had happened to her.

"Earth was too far gone. The best chance for the human race was to move on and leave Earth behind," Caine continued. "Many of the planets in the new system were terraformed, but not all of the attempts were successful. Less than half of the hundred planets in the system were considered habitable."

"The ten that had transformed the best became ten core planets of what they used to call the United Colonies. Another thirty-six planets terraformed only partially and were less than ideal for habitation. They had oxygen and water, but on some, it was difficult to grow food, while others had lower gravity. They all had their unique problems. These became the border planets and the rest beyond; most are either frozen wastelands, barren deserts, or swamps. Harsh, inhospitable environments where humans would struggle to survive."

"The many governments of Earth that came together to send out the initial exploration team formed one new government called the Confederation of United Colonies, which we simply call The Confederation. The Confederation ordered people to evacuate Earth, but not everyone wanted to leave. Some people chose to stay, refusing to evacuate with the others. The rest, about half a billion people, left the planet in several waves of transports. It took hundreds of years to get to the new planets. Many generations were born and lived their lives only on the Confederation transport ships, never once seeing the final destination they were heading towards."

"It was during this time the Confederation created the Council. Each country or region that joined the Confederation was given its own planet, and one man was chosen as its sole representative and leader to make sure everything remained fair. They were chosen by the people of their planet and remain on the Council for life. A new representative is chosen when they die. They made new laws regulating food, water, chemicals, everything that had destroyed the Earth. For many years they even regulated population, to keep it under control on the ships until they reached the new system and the planets were fully settled and stable."

Caine couldn't read Cara's expression. Nonetheless, he continued. To comprehend what had happened to her, she needed to hear everything.

"When people first arrived in the new system, they spread out across the core planets. Populations flourished, but some people did not want to be a part of this new world. They did not like the Council; the Confederation. They did not want The Confederation as their new government. Some did not agree with the new laws and wanted to make their own rules. Some just didn't want to be on the busy, congested core planets. People broke away and formed their own colonies on the border planets that had not terraformed well, claiming they were not under Confederation control."

"The Council wanted these new settlements under their control. They wanted total control of all the people. It sparked a war that killed many people and only fueled those who hated the Confederation. These people wanted power; to be king of their own worlds."

"The war lasted only a year. The Confederation was far better equipped and were easily victorious. The defeated rebels were forced to push deeper into the system, taking over the outermost planets. The Confederation claimed victory over many of the colonized planets closer to the core. They stopped chasing the rebels further out. They believed the people on those planets would never survive long under the harsh circumstances to waste resources on following them out so far. There were only so many Confederation ships, and space is vast. They were stretched far too thin to fight against them. They decided it would be best for them to become the defenders rather than the aggressors. But the rebels survived, and they have grown in numbers. It has been just over a hundred years since the Border Wars ended, but we are still fighting them."

Caine paused. Cara's expression had not changed. There was still so much left to explain. He was trying to condense a thousand years of history into minutes, and his abridged version was falling woefully short of painting the full picture. For a moment, he almost stopped there, but he noticed how attentive Cara was. She looked at him when he paused and gave him a barely perceptible nod, wordlessly telling him to go on. She wanted to hear everything.

"The ten central-most planets, the Core Colonies, are heavily guarded," Caine continued. "There are two sections of border planets. The inner ring closer to the central core Colonies and the outermost band of planets.

The inner border planets often fall victim to raids and attacks from the rebels who occupy the outer planets. The fleet's primary purpose is for protection, preventing attacks on the border planets, but we also bring them supplies. Food, medicine, clean water, whatever they need.

"We try to leave the rebels alone; the Confederation simply calls them Hostiles. They used to keep their distance, but over the years, their bloodlust has increased. They staked claims on the most inhospitable planets at the far edges of the system but as populations have grown, so has their resentment for the Confederation. They are pushing closer with every passing year. I fear we have another war ahead.

"Hostiles have different groupings called Clans, each with its own leader. Clans usually do not get along, but lately, we have seen them working together to plan and carry out attacks. They raid and kill for no reason other than to hurt people. Their hatred for the Confederation runs deep. They act like savages; they live like savages. There are eight main Hostile Clans we have been trying to keep at bay for years. When you first showed up, we thought it was a possibility you were one of them." He paused, knowing the weight of his next words.

"The year is 2936." He stopped and let her sit in silence for a long time. He could sense her confusion, her anguish; it was so evident in her features. She was so expressive; it was easy to read her. He had to keep himself from sliding next to her and consoling her. He could tell her mind was racing, her brow scrunched, staring at the floor as she processed everything he'd told her.

Cara sat quietly for a long time. She hadn't gone crazy. It had to be real. Now, she had two choices. The first would land her in a straitjacket after a mental breakdown, stuck in a padded room and heavy sedatives. Her second was to accept it and make the best of her situation.

As tempting as a padded room and endless supply of drugs sounded, this was her reality, and she needed to face it.

"Are there aliens?" she asked softly, after a long silence.

Caine couldn't help but chuckle. This woman was an enigma. She had just found out she was hundreds of years in the future and her first reaction was not one of panic but of curiosity.

"You mean little green men?"

She nodded.

"No." He could see her relief. "We have barely begun to explore space. We have found life on some planets, mostly animalistic in nature. Here though, many species were brought from Old Earth to help populate the planets upon arrival. They have evolved over generations and probably don't resemble anything you're used to from home. Even some border peoples have adapted to their planet's climate over the years and look quite different than those who live on the inner core planets."

Cara was quiet again, looking down.

"This is completely insane." She closed her eyes, pressing her fingers against her temples.

"I can only imagine what this must be like for you," Caine sympathized.

"What happens now?" she asked, pinning him with her stormy gaze.

"I am taking you to the Council. We should be there in a few days, barring any unexpected delays. They are going to try to get you home."

She looked up at him, her grey eyes full of pain. "And if they can't get me home?" she asked. There were tears in her eyes. One spilled out, rolling over the edge of her eyelid and down her cheek.

Caine didn't respond; he had no answer for her. She leaned her head back on the wall behind her. Soon she closed her eyes, breathing deep and slow. Caine stood up. His starched uniform rustled, always crisp and perfect.

"Come, I want to show you something." Caine offered his hand to her.

Cara wiped away her tears. She looked from his outstretched hand to his eyes. There was something in his gaze she couldn't quite read, but it almost resembled sorrow. She slipped her hand into the warmth of his, and he grasped it firmly, helping her to her feet. When he released her, she rubbed her hand, unable to deny the effect he had on her. The eerie magnetism was tangible every time they touched.

"This way." They walked down the hall, and he ushered her into the elevator. She couldn't be sure if they were going up or down, but the doors opened onto another long hallway shortly after. Halfway down, there was a single door, and it slid open as they approached. "In here," Caine gestured for her to enter. She peered in. Even with the minimal light, she recognized a space like this; a library.

Light from the hall spilled into the space, illuminating it. It was not a large room; it was small and cozy. The shelves climbed to the ceiling and were overflowing with books. There was a fireplace, an old wooden desk, and a high-backed wing chair covered in worn brown leather. It looked like something out of a Victorian mansion and was beautiful.

It was strange to find such a place here, a stark contrast to the rest of the ship's sharp modernity. This place was special to someone. The incredible amount of detail put into the room was not something any military would pay for voluntarily. Whoever had this space created was trying to keep memories alive. Memories of what, though, she wasn't sure. She stepped in. Automatically, the fireplace in the corner roared to life, and the lights turned on, just a dim glow over the armchair. She reached up and touched the books.

"This is yours?" she asked.

He looked around the room, the hint of a wistful smile barely visible for a fleeting moment. She could tell he was proud of this place, proud of what he had created.

"Yes, and I want you to feel free to spend as much time as you would like in here."

"Are you also going to start calling me Beauty?" she joked.

"What?" Caine was puzzled by her strange statement.

"You know, you're giving me a library? Oh, just, never mind." She shook her head. He wouldn't understand the reference even if she tried to explain it.

Did it make him the Beast? No, it made it Stockholm Syndrome. She shook her head. No, it couldn't possibly be that either. She hadn't been kidnapped, and he wasn't holding her hostage. She was just simply stuck here. But for how long? She pushed the thought aside. There was no way she could allow doubts to creep in. She was going home soon, and this would all be behind her.

Cara inspected the spines of the books, reading their titles. She ran her fingers carefully over the well-worn bindings. One caught her eye.

She pulled it out and read the cover. A History of Earth 2100-2200. She flipped it open. The date on the inside was 2468. She closed it with a snap, quickly tucking it back on the shelf. It was still all so strange. A high-pitched beep broke the silence. She turned to see Caine looking down at some sort of device before slipping it back into his pocket.

"I have to go," Caine spoke up.

Cara could hear the hesitation in his voice. He didn't want to leave her here by herself.

"I'll be okay. I think I'd like to stay here for a little while." Cara didn't want to leave the comfort of this place. Maybe he didn't want her here alone. "If you don't mind," she added, hoping he would say it was okay.

"Stay as long as you'd like. Just let any of my crew know if you need anything at all." As he turned to go, he paused. "Cara." His tone was firmer. "Only a select few of my crew know about this, about you. I would advise you not to discuss where you're from with anyone. This will only create confusion and questions I don't have answers to. If they ask you anything, just tell them you can't discuss it."

It wasn't a warning exactly, but Cara understood why he was telling her this. She was to keep her mouth shut.

"I won't tell anyone," she promised.

He nodded sharply and left the room. The small space felt uncomfortably spacious and empty without his presence. In fact, the very small world she was used to had just grown by a couple of galaxies.

She pulled out one book after another. Publishing dates all hundreds of years in the future; her mind raced. Doubt crept in. Was it all true? Actually possible? Was she crazy? Was he crazy? She picked up 'A History of Earth' and read through it. It told of space travel and new planets. She read until an overwhelming feeling took over her mind, and she had to put it back down. She remembered the events of the day, wanting to make sense of what happened on the subway.

Time travel was something out of books and movies. People who talked about time travel were either top scientists with a genius IQ or simply psych ward crazies who believed lizard aliens lived on Earth disguised as human beings. She knew she didn't fall into either one of those categories, so where did it leave her? Time travel defied all logic. It hardly seemed possible even with the insurmountable mountain of evidence to the contrary.

Even this far into the future, with all the technological advancements, time travel was still just science fiction. Yet, it had happened to her. She only wished she knew how and why.

Cara sat in the wing chair reading pages of book after book, pondering and trying to make sense of her situation. Her stomach grumbled. She was getting hungry. When was the last time she had even eaten? She had been sitting there for a much longer time than she intended to stay.

It would be best for her to head back to her room; the only problem was she didn't know how to get there. Caine had told her to ask for help if she needed it, but as she looked around, she didn't see anything resembling a phone and had no idea how to get in touch with him. She walked into the hallway, hoping to see one of the officers she would ask for help but didn't see anyone. Maybe she could just make her way back to her room on her own; she didn't want to bother him while he was working anyways.

Cara wandered the endless maze of hallways, half lost in her thoughts, and hoping to find anything that looked familiar and lead her to her room. Her mind drifted back to Caine and the library. Was the crew allowed free use of it as well, or was it exclusively his? She was curious as to what drove him to create one on a spaceship. A room like that was typically built in a home, but for Caine, this was where he lived all the time.

At that moment, it all came together for her. To Caine, this was his home and was more than just a place where he worked. His entire life was here and had been for many years. She understood exactly why he had built the library.

She came to a halt, realizing she had no idea how long she had been walking. She still had not managed to find her room, and everything looked the same. Has she been wandering in circles? Her limbs were slightly numb as the shock and panic worked its way out of her system. As her endorphin levels continued to drop and hunger took over, she was dizzy and nauseous. Now, on top of all of it, she was lost. No one was in the hallways for her to talk to or ask for help.

As busy as the ship always was, now it appeared abandoned. For the first time in years, she desperately wanted to be in New York. She just wanted to go home and be with people she knew. Cara bumped into the wall turning a corner, and it knocked her off balance. Her shaky legs couldn't recover in time. She slipped and fell. Using the wall for support, she pushed herself up to a seated position and her breath caught with a cry that just wouldn't work its way to the surface. She wanted to go home, but if she couldn't go home right now, she would settle with managing to at least get back to her room. She got her feet back under her and took a few wobbly steps.

Cara walked in a dazed fog. She stared down at her feet as she walked until strong hands gripped her shoulders, stopping her in her tracks.

Turning around to face him, she stared at Caine with a blank expression.

"I can't find my room," she murmured lightly, but he could hear the frustration in her voice. He kept his grip on her arms, knowing she needed a little bit of extra support. She needed to eat and rest.

"Come on," he said softly but firmly.

She followed him without argument. He got her back into her room and gently helped her to bed. She curled up under the blankets. Her eyes closed, and her breathing slowed to a steady pace. He pulled the blanket over her shoulders.

He should have known better than to leave her alone. He was glad he had spotted her. She could have ended up wandering around aimlessly for hours. The Archon was the largest in the entire fleet. It had dozens of decks and was hundreds of feet long. Who knows where she might have ended up?

Caine brushed a strand of hair off her face and quickly pulled his hand away, clenched his fists: mentally steeling himself against her, and left.

He posted an officer outside her door just in case and made his way up to the Bridge.

"Kendar," he gestured for Zora to follow him into his office where their conversation would be private. He didn't want curious crew eavesdropping.

"Sir?" she asked. "Everything all right?"

Caine wasn't sure how to word it. "I have a slightly, well, delicate matter I need to discuss with you." He gestured for her to sit. "During the Hostile attack the other day, there was an unexpected arrival of a guest far earlier than planned. I am asking for you to check in on her, see to it she has everything she might need."

Zora didn't respond; she just looked surprised.

"Zora?" he prompted.

"Oh yes, yes, absolutely, Sir. Of course." Zora shook her head, breaking her daze, and nodded. "Sir?" She paused with her head tilted slightly in confusion. "What exactly is she doing here? I didn't think we expected anyone to be on board for a while."

It was an innocent enough question. His core crew usually knew the schedule of anyone coming or going, and they would have known well ahead of time about any arriving guests, especially a female one. Guests were not frequent on the Archon and were typically political.

"For right now, I just need you to see to it you check in on her regularly," he ordered, avoiding a direct response to her question. "Please," he added after a moment.

Zora's eyebrows shot up, but she didn't question him, nodding in agreement instead. She stood there for a moment longer, the questioning look still in her eyes, but Caine could see she wasn't paying attention to him anymore. Her mind was too busy whirling with the information he had just shared.

"Kendar?" he questioned, not sure why she was still standing there.

"Yes, Sir?"

"Dismissed," he told her.

Zora flushed. "Yes, Sir." She turned and quickly left.

Chapter Thirteen

The next morning, Cara awoke from the strangest dream about being sucked into an episode of Star Trek. She opened her eyes and looked around the room. No, not a dream. Reality. She rubbed her eyes and stretched her arms, still sore from yesterday. Nonetheless, she was thankful she hadn't been more seriously injured. What could the side effects of time travel be on a person's body?

There was a knock on her door, and Cara's heart leapt even as she reminded herself of the realities of her situation.

The door opened, and a woman was standing there, smiling at her. The initial disappointment of not seeing Caine there wore off quickly. Maybe she had found someone she could talk with. Friends were currently in short supply.

"I'm Zora. I wanted to check on you and see how you have been holding up." She smiled at Cara. Her brown eyes were warm and kind. It was a huge comfort knowing there was another person on board who cared.

"You mean Caine wanted you to check on me." Cara could see right through the formality of the greeting. It wasn't hard to figure out who had sent her.

Zora looked sheepish, her dark skin revealing her blush.

"Guilty," she shrugged. "I told him you'd know immediately."

"He isn't hard to figure out."

Zora chuckled. "I can see why he wanted me to check in with you." She winked, the corners of her mouth curled up. "I brought you some food." Zora held out the bowl.

"Thanks." Cara took the offered bowl from her and took a small bite.

It was mush, like oatmeal but had a mild sweetness to it. With her food being delivered directly to her, it was clear Caine wanted her to stay in her room instead of poking around anymore, and she could understand why he didn't want her roaming the ship. The last time she had gone wandering, she had discovered she was living out a science fiction movie in real life. Maybe it would have been better to have never discovered what year it was. Ignorance was bliss, as they said.

Cara looked up at Zora, noticing the tight, dark curls circling her face. What a mess her own hair must be.

"Actually, before you go, there is something I could use your help with." Cara wrung her hands together, slightly uncomfortable. "I would like to take a shower, and I don't know where to go."

Zora looked confused. "A what?"

Cara pointed at her face and hair. "To wash and clean up a bit more?"

"Oh!" Zora exclaimed. "It's right over here." She led Cara to the back corner of the room and pressed one of the electronic consoles. One of the wall panels slid open, revealing a small chamber.

"Just step inside, and it will start right up." Zora smiled.

"Thank you so much."

"Of course. I'll leave you to it and bring you back some clean clothes in a little while."

Cara undressed and stepped into the small area. A fine mist of white foam sprayed out all over her, which bubbled as it hit her skin. She used her hands to scrub herself and her hair. There was a quiet buzzing, and the mist stopped. The unusual suds dissipated on their own. From above, warm air blew her skin dry with a soft whirring sound, but there were some knots she needed to work out. Stepping out, she put her old clothes on, waiting for Zora to return.

When Zora returned, she brought a change of clothes and a small plastic box. Cara opened the lid. Inside was a comb, a bottle of blue liquid, and some other toiletry items.

"Just a couple of things you might need." Zora handed her the clothes. Cara changed while Zora had her back turned. It was a simple outfit: black pants and a white shirt.

"Thank you," she said in relief. She took out the comb and ran it through her tangled hair.

"We aren't used to having civilian guests on the ship. How do you know the Commander?" Zora was cleverly prying for information.

Cara remembered Caine asking her not to reveal anything to the crew. "Actually, I don't know him at all. He's just been nice enough to help me get to the Council on Arctus." Cara hit a snag in her hair.

"Here, let me." Zora took the comb, working it through the knots and tangles Cara struggled to reach.

"Thanks. It's such a mess right now."

Zora chuckled. "It isn't the same kind of clean you're used to."

Panic speared through Cara. Did Zora know? "What do you mean?" she asked, swallowing hard.

"It's not like being back on a planet. We don't get to use our water rations on cleaning up here, unfortunately."

Cara breathed a small sigh of relief. "Oh, yeah. It's a little strange."

Zora continued combing but stopped without warning.

"Zora?" Cara asked, unsure why she froze. She turned around and was met with a look of angry confusion on Zora's face.

"What is it?" Cara didn't know why there had been such a drastic change in Zora's demeanor.

"You have a mark," Zora's barbed, accusatory tone was full of suspicion.

"A mark?" Cara wasn't sure what she meant. She didn't have any birthmarks, or large scars she could think of that would cause Zora to act the way she currently was.

"The one on your neck."

"You mean my tattoo?" Confused, Cara reached up to touch the back of her neck.

"A what?" Her eyes narrowed, brows tightly knit together.

"It's called a tattoo."

"What is a tattoo? Marks are symbols of Hostiles."

Cara remembered Caine's story about Hostiles and how he had treated her when he believed she was one. That must be why Zora was reacting so fiercely. Hostiles weren't just feared; they were hated.

"I got this a long time ago, but I promise I am not a Hostile." Cara was fighting a losing battle trying to explain.

"Is this why we're taking you to the Council?" Zora crossed her arms, glaring at her.

Cara nodded. "But I can't talk about it."

Zora let out a long breath through her nose and handed the comb back to Cara. "The Commander told me to help you with anything you need. I'm not sure why, but he trusts you." Zora grabbed the empty bowl she had brought earlier. "I hope the Commander is right about you," she said icily before leaving.

"Zora, wait!"

Zora didn't turn back, which was for the best. What could she have said anyway? She couldn't tell Zora the truth. The sharp sting of loneliness crept up on her. It was very likely she'd lost her only friend.

Absentmindedly, she opened the bottle of blue liquid and gave it a sniff; it was minty. There was no toothbrush in the box, so she took a small sip of the liquid and swished it around. She squinted as it fizzed in her mouth. The sensation made her eyes water. She spat it out in the sink and looked in the mirror. How was she going to do this? She was a stranger here, not just to this world but to the people in it. She just hoped the Commander could keep his promises and get her home as soon as possible.

***

Caine was at his desk when he noticed Zora approaching him, and he didn't like the look on her face.

"Commander, a word?"

Caine gestured for her to come into his office. She shut the door behind her with enough force to indicate she was upset as if her tone wasn't already enough of a warning.

Zora crossed her arms over her chest. "She has a mark."

Caine knew Zora was talking about Cara. He wasn't sure how Zora had seen it, but she had and now had questions and unease he needed to put to rest.

"I am well aware of the mark on her neck."

"And you are still letting her wander around the ship as a civilian when she could be a dangerous Hostile?"

Kuso. This was a mess.

"The last time I checked Kendar, I am in charge of this ship. I don't appreciate you questioning the decisions I make. The safety of this crew is and has always been my highest priority. Cara is not a Hostile. I would have never let her out of a holding cell if I had the slightest notion she posed any sort of threat to this ship or any of the crew. I completed her Interrogation, and she was released from holding into my custody until we arrive at Arctus."

Zora was turning red, not meeting his eyes. Caine could only imagine how the encounter had gone and what kind of reaction Zora must have had. He hoped Zora hadn't been too rude to Cara. Seeing her behavior moments ago, he was sure she had.

"And Kendar, I highly recommend if you made any sort of harsh comments to her about her mark or made her feel unwelcome, you go and rectify it immediately."

Zora dropped her head in shame. "Yes, Sir."

"Zora." Caine took a deep breath. "She's been through a lot and is valuable to the Confederation. She is a guest here. I know you don't have the full story. You've been part of my crew for a long time and known me even longer. So speaking as your friend, you're going to have to trust me right now."

Zora's outburst was understandable. Her heart was in the right place. His crew looked out for each other, took care of each other.

"My only request is you do not mention this to any of the other crew. I don't need any more outbursts in my office."

"Yes, Sir." She dropped her head and turned to leave, but she stopped in the doorway. "Sorry, Caine."

"You're fine, Kendar," Caine reassured her, a smile ghosting across his face.

Chapter Fourteen

Cara spent the rest of the day reading, resting, and after spending over an hour of just staring at the ceiling, she finally decided she needed a break. Caine had never actually told her to stay in her room - he had only alluded to it.

Cara made her way down the hall. A small group of officers turned a corner, talking and laughing with each other. They were in plain black pants and white shirts, not their typical uniform, which she assumed meant they were most likely off duty. Maybe they could show her to a place she could spend some time. Did spaceships have gyms? She followed them into what appeared to be a cafeteria where officers were eating and milling about. They all stopped talking and fell silent when she entered. A few gave her the same suspicious glance Zora had earlier, and her face grew hot.

"Come sit over here," someone said softly just behind her.

She jumped at the unexpected voice, turning quickly to see who had spoken. The man standing behind her was in uniform, and his nose crinkled in embarrassment.

He ran a hand through his short black hair, sweeping the longer hair in the front to the side. "Sorry, I didn't mean to startle you." He sounded sheepish. "I'm Than, a friend of Caine, and occasionally I do some work around here too. He's kept me updated on everything, about you, I mean." He stopped rambling and grinned at her. There was a mischievous twinkle in his eyes. "It's Cara, right?" Than gestured for her to sit next to him. "It's nice to meet you."

Cara was surprised by his kindness. "Nice to meet you too." She looked up right as another officer walked by, narrowing his eyes at her as he passed.

"Just ignore them. They just aren't used to strangers being on board. They're more curious than anything," he reassured her.

"How much do they know about me?"

"If you're asking if they know how you arrived here, they don't know anything, though it doesn't mean they haven't come up with their own theories." He smirked, but his cheeks flushed. "So far, I've heard you're a Hostile informant, a Council spy here to report on us, but my personal favorite is that you are a very expensive personal courtesan for the Commander himself. So, which is it?"

Cara buried her head in her arms and groaned. Of course, rumors would be flying; she just wished she wasn't at the center of all of them.

"Don't worry. You don't have long until we arrive on Arctus."

"If I survive that long," Cara quipped.

Than's rich laugh rang out. "I like you," he told her.

"At least someone does. Between Caine and Zora, my list of fans is growing shorter each day."

"What happened with Zora?"

"She saw my tattoo and kind of freaked out." Cara recalled the horrible look on Zora's face.

"Oh, Caine told me you had a mark. I'm sure Zora will come around. She just wasn't expecting you to have one. Only Hostiles have marks like yours in this world."

"So I've been told," Cara grumbled.

"You must be hungry; stay here."

Than stood up, went over to a counter, grabbed two plates of food, and brought them back to the table, sliding one in front of her. The plate was filled with brown goo and stringy green noodles. It looked terrible. She looked down at it for a minute, but when her stomach growled, she took a bite. To her surprise, the food tasted far better than it looked.

"Not exactly gourmet, but it's not half bad once you eat it for a while. I'm sure it isn't what you're used to," Than grinned.

Cara spent the next hour with him talking about the 21st century. Than was fascinated by her stories. Trying to explain everything - cars, planes, even some animals - was like explaining rocket science to a first grader. Everything was so much more advanced now. What she described was ancient, and so it was difficult for him to imagine. It was a stark reminder that the world she was in now was so different from the one she knew.

"So, you grew up with Caine?" she asked finally.

"You could say that. We first met during our first year at the Academy." Than leaned back in his chair, gently resting one foot on his opposite knee. "I remember being scared to start training, but Caine wasn't. He was fearless. I was smaller than a lot of the other students. One day a couple of the older boys were giving me a hard time, and without any hesitation, Caine marched right up to them; this little five-year-old kid facing down boys three times his age and size. After that, Caine took it upon himself to make sure no one bothered me, and we were practically inseparable."

"You start training at five?" Cara was shocked.

"The world is a little different now. You don't decide what you want to do with your life when you're nearly grown. The world decides for you. All children take an aptitude and ability test when they turn five to determine their potential skill set. Based on the results of that, you're assigned a placement for a future career."

"Where did Caine get placed?" Cara asked. Than got a strange look on his face, almost as if he got lost in his own memories, but there was something else in his gaze like he was holding something back from her.

"Leadership." He quickly flashed her a half-smile. "As soon as you get placed, you begin your education or training, and apprenticing comes a few years after. It's more efficient this way. Everyone does what they are good at and are properly trained by the time they start working."

"This is so weird," Cara couldn't help but say. "Do you think the Council can get me home?"

Than twirled his fork. "I think they will. This is new for all of us. This might be your so-called future, but despite all the advancements in technology, there is still a big difference between fantasy and reality."

Cara sighed. "If it's just fantasy, how did I end up here?"

Than reached over and gave her hand a gentle squeeze. His slanted brown eyes crinkled at the corners when he smiled. "I'm sure the Council will have their best scientists and engineers working on it. I have to get to work, but I wish you the best of luck. It was an honor to meet you, Cara."

Cara didn't want him to go. He was so different, and she understood why Caine was the protector of the two. She hoped Than was right and she would be in good hands with the Council. She wanted to go home.

***

Cara woke to a knock on her door. She went to the door and found Zora there, smiling awkwardly.

"Can I come in?" Zora asked. Cara could hear the embarrassment in her voice.

"Yeah, yes, sure, come in." She rubbed her hands together, uncomfortable with her presence.

"I wanted to apologize about yesterday. It wasn't fair of me to treat you in the manner I did."

"You talked to Caine?" Cara guessed. She didn't fault Zora for questioning the Commander.

"I talked to Caine," Zora confirmed, looking embarrassed. "He told me you were in protective custody."

"Did he tell you why?" Cara asked.

"He just said you had important information the Confederation needed, and you're not a threat. I'm sorry I assumed you were one."

"It's okay. I understand how seeing my tattoo made you suspicious. I would have reacted the same thing if I were in your position."

It was as close to the truth as she could reveal. At first, Zora had been a great help. Now, Cara was forced to lie to her every time they talked.

"How are you doing?"

"It's a little strange. I still have a lot to learn. This is my first time in space," Cara admitted. It was truthful enough but still didn't reveal too much about her situation.

"I remember how hard my first year was working up here. So much was different than on the ground." Zora grinned and folded her hands in her lap. "But there's a saying, once you've been in space, your feet are never happy on the ground again."

Cara couldn't hide her smile. "I can promise you I won't have that problem. I can't wait to get on solid ground again."

"Well, don't worry too much. You won't be stuck up here for long. We've got just another couple of days before we land on Arctus. Ever been there before?" she asked.

Cara shook her head, "No, I've never been, but I've been told it's quite a place."

"It doesn't compare to any other planet. Especially, the capital. It's the best place to stock up on all the good stuff we can't get at our supply stops. I've got a whole list already."

"You all went to the Fleet Training Academy on Arctus, right?" Cara was curious as to where Zora fit into the equation. Caine and Than were clearly friends, but she wasn't sure how close they were with Zora.

"I was a few years behind them, but yes, I was at the Academy the same time they were there. Sometimes I'm amazed we all made it out of there alive. What did you place on your test?" she asked.

Cara was thankful she had talked to Than earlier because she would never have known how to answer. "Communications." She hoped it was a real answer.

Zora pondered her response for a moment. "Never would have thought you'd have placed there," she said with a puzzled frown.

Cara forced a yawn, "I'm still so tired. I'd like to lay down for a bit."

She needed to end the conversation before she dug herself into a hole she couldn't climb out of. Zora looked deflated but nodded.

"I'll check on you later."

Cara flopped back onto her pillow and groaned after Zora was gone. How much longer could she keep up the lies?

She found herself staring at the ceiling for hours, mulling over the strange events of the past few days. She kicked her legs up the wall, tilting her feet from side to side. For being a massive spaceship, it was surprisingly quiet. After so many years in the city, she was accustomed to noise; the constant drone of motors, and endless whine of sirens. It was a comforting hum that had become like white noise, continuous in the background; the soundtrack of her life - New York's lullaby.

Here, she would have thought there would be mechanical noises, banging, or the whir of machines. Instead, the silence was deafening, making it hard to relax.

Cara closed her eyes, imagining laying in her own bed, listening to the honking horns, screeching tires, doors slamming floors below, and even the occasional barking dog breaking through the commotion. Her mind could only maintain the daydream for a short time, and soon the intense quiet broke through. She groaned and rolled over, pulling the thin pillow over her head.

***

When Caine came to see her the next morning, she took the opportunity to address the issues with her secret-keeping.

"There's no way I can keep hiding this from Zora if you insist on her babysitting me," Cara grumbled.

"She isn't your babysitter. I thought you would want to have someone to talk to."

"Yes, but I can't talk to her about anything. She doesn't know where I'm from, and I know nothing about this world, so you can see the dilemma."

"It won't be an issue anymore. We arrive in Arctus late tonight. First thing in the morning, I will be escorting you to the Council, and they will be handling you from there."

Cara didn't appreciate how he used the word handling as if she was a problem, an unwanted problem. "We will take the transport pod over in the morning," Caine added.

Cara frowned. "Transport pod? We won't walk there?"

Caine shook his head, and Cara looked crestfallen. "What's the matter?" he asked.

"I won't get to see anything?" She had hoped to walk through the city and see what a planet looked like in the future.

Caine hadn't even considered it. Naturally, she would be curious about everything and want to see things so foreign to her.

"I don't think that's a good idea."

"Why not? No one knows who I am." How would she possibly make the best of her situation if she didn't even get to experience anything about what life was like in this time?

For a split second, Caine couldn't think of a good reason not to walk. It would take less than an hour, and if they left early enough, they'd arrive at the Council in enough time.

"The Council wouldn't approve." It was easy enough for him to pass off the blame to them. Cara nodded sadly. "I'll come get you tomorrow morning." He turned sharply and left her, but Cara didn't want to be alone.

She found her way to the cafeteria, but she didn't see Zora or Than there. She went up to the library to put her most recent read back before making her way to the Observation Room. The door opened to reveal the eerie darkness within; she walked in. She sat in front of the glass, letting her eyes adjust to the lack of light.

Thousands of stars glinted, a smattering of crystalline freckles scattered across the sky. The faintest glow of the swirling green and purple clouds of a nebula could be seen far in the distance.

It was spectacular beyond imagining. None of the photos she had seen taken from the space station could do the view any justice. Cara wanted to sit and gaze out at the universe for hours but didn't notice her eyelids growing heavy. They slid shut after a time. She was sprawled out in front of the window when she woke up later.

She pushed herself to her feet and, reaching out, traced a heart on the glass, leaving the faintest, barely noticeable smudge behind. She walked to the door and took one last look over her shoulder as it would be her last.

Chapter Fifteen

Without bothering to wait for a response, Caine entered her room early the next morning, after knocking twice. Cara bolted upright at the intrusion. "Get ready," he directed curtly. "Put this on." He dropped a shirt onto the end of her bed and strode away. Cara rolled her eyes and flopped back onto the bed with a huff.

Cara looked at herself in the mirror after she dressed: loose-fitting black slacks, a plain long sleeve blue top, and jacket. Caine didn't want her standing out. She ran the comb through her hair and hurried out of the room to catch up with Caine just as he was coming back to get her.

He nodded in approval as she finished slipping on the jacket. "Good, let's go." He led her down to the loading dock. The ship had made port sometime in the night. It was in a huge hanger, large enough to handle a massive ship like the Archon.

The Archon was perched high on top of eight massive docking towers supporting its weight. These towers had been designed to allow the largest ships, such as the Archon, to make port. Before they had been built, the ship was forced to remain in orbit.

"Try to blend in," Caine instructed, although he knew it would be easier said than done.

He was dressed in full Commander attire, a dead giveaway to the public that this was official Council business. The Council had instantly denied his request to wear something less conspicuous. Damn their protocols. The fact that his ship was here would draw plenty of attention in and of itself.

The Archon was not a ship that could arrive without notice, even in the middle of the night. Word it was here would spread like wildfire, and hordes of curious people would be out on the streets hoping for a glimpse of whatever was happening. Due to her massive size, the only place the Archon could dock was on the city's southern edge.

The Council was still expecting him to take a transport pod directly there, but he found himself deciding against it. He hadn't informed the Council of his decision yet. He was sending his envoy, Havita Li, ahead to manage council business before his arrival. She would be capable of smoothing things over with them.

Hopefully, the route he chose would help them make it to their destination without too much fuss. Rather than parading Cara down the city's main streets, he instead took her through the more residential areas on the outskirts.

Even though he wasn't readily willing to admit it to her, he wanted to show her the bustling marketplace he was fond of. He had spent many years in his late childhood running around the village market, causing trouble when he was not in training.

He knew exactly what the Council would have to say when they discovered he took the long way to them. Displeased, of course, but if Cara was to be sent home, he wanted to let her have a small taste of what the universe was like now.

Cara followed his brisk pace out of the ship into a large docking bay. The entire place was more expansive than she had pictured. They were high up, dozens of floors below them bustling with smaller crafts docking and leaving.

Several ships were being loaded with massive crates. Mechanics in grey jumpsuits worked, fixing broken parts. A strange hush fell over the space as they crossed it. People glanced at them out of the corner of their eyes, and even though Cara was uncomfortable, Caine didn't appear to notice the scrutiny.

A woman with dark eyes and black hair cut in a blunt, chin-length black bob strode through the crowds towards them. She wasn't wearing the typical officer's uniform Cara was used to seeing. Instead, she wore a stately, long red jacket and black pants.

"Li," Caine addressed her.

"Sir," she nodded respectfully. "I still think you should take the transport." She disapproved of the Commander's decision. It was uncharacteristic of him to break with protocol. While it wasn't required for the Commander to take the pod, it was customary for high ranking officials to travel with their security and envoy.

"My decision is final," he added, nullifying any possible rebuttal from Li.

"Transport will be ready in about 10 minutes." An officer marched up to Li and handed her a thin square device resembling a tablet. Li shot Caine a disapproving glance and looked Cara over. Whoever this woman was, she was important enough for Caine to want to bend the rules.

"Understood, Sir. I will see you there." Li reviewed the information on the screen about her departure and tucked the device into her pocket.

"We're going this way," Caine guided Cara over to a round elevator and stepped in. She followed, sparing a glance at him. He stood straight, head forward. He wore his uniform, but she could sense he was uncomfortable in it.

"Ground rules. Don't talk. Don't touch anything, and you stay right next to me the whole time," he commanded.

She nodded, surprised he had changed his mind. The elevator descended along the edge of the building. The elevator shaft blocked any view of the outside for a short time, but when it emerged, Cara found herself staring down at a world she had only encountered in movies.

Massive skyscrapers climbed into the sky: the largest of them looked like a palace in the distance. White, stone towers jutted up towards the sky, ending in sharp, pointed spears, taller than all the rest. It was New York times a thousand, except it was cleaner and greener. It was beautiful.

Cara's mouth dropped open in awe, and she pressed herself up against the glass, taking it all in. "This is incredible."

Caine found himself smiling at her, enjoying her reaction. He had grown cynical over the years, his view clouded by bitterness, but Cara was looking at the city through fresh eyes.

The doors opened to streets filled with people dressed in bright colors. Something resembling a subway glided along silently on a single thin track overhead. Spaceships filled the sky, and a small car with only three wheels zipped past, weaving through the crowds of people. Another passed by, floating just a few feet off the ground and a motorcycle without any wheels hummed by them.

"That is the Caelum, where the Confederation Council is." Caine pointed at the gleaming white, stone building that dominated the skyline in the distance.

"This way," he gestured.

He always disliked big cities. They were too crowded and had too much potential for something to go wrong. He often trusted his instinct because it usually proved to be right, and right now, his internal alarms were going off. The knot forming in his stomach made him want to get away from the busy shipping district as fast as possible.

Cara followed a half step behind him as they left the more urban area heading towards the outskirts.

The area was a stark contrast to the sleek city center. The buildings were cobbled together from wood, brick, and red clay. The streets were unpaved, and children rushed by, kicking up clouds of dust. Street vendors were selling all different varieties of exotic looking foods. They walked down the street with Cara's eyes wide in awe and Caine's scanning for danger. There was so much to see.

Cara noticed people glancing at them quickly before averting their eyes. Some people even moved out of their way as they approached. Many stared at Caine with fear or reverence. She looked at him, walking tall beside her in his blue uniform. What had he done to gain such status? It was more than just his rank as Commander. These people must have encountered officers before, but Caine agitated them in a way far beyond any normal respect for authority. It was as if they recognized him and knew exactly who he was. He wasn't telling her everything.

Caine could feel her eyes on him and turned to look at her. Her brow was furrowed as she stared at him, an inquisitive curiosity in her eyes. She was observant, and he knew she must have noticed the reaction of the people around them. As an Esper, he was recognizable enough with his bright blue eyes giving his genetics away. His uniform only made him stand out more. Civilians would know precisely who he was.

He stopped by a stand, purchasing a small koloxi - a steamed bun filled with meat. The vendor handed Caine the bun without looking him in the eyes, bowing a few times in the region's traditional show of respect. He handed it to Cara, but she gave him a hesitant glance. Cara was taken by surprise at the small gesture. She took a bite. For a second, the combination of chewy dough and spiced meat made her feel like she was back home, eating at Chan's in Chinatown and hoped by the end of the day she would finally be on her way home. Caine tipped his head, indicating they were moving on.

The shops were busy. People were carrying bags of food or other purchases as they made their way home.

"Gun kai," a voice yelled, making Caine stop in his tracks.

A few feet ahead, a man pushed off the wall where he had been leaning and took a few stumbling steps towards them. He waved his fist angrily in the air. His stringy, black hair hung long and disheveled over his shoulders. His clothes were well worn, with ragged edges, dotted with holes, and had not been washed in some time.

"Ben dan wang ba!" The man continued his rant, spitting at the ground in front of Caine's feet. As he did, he appeared to spot Cara, and he directed his vitriol towards her. "Sha bi," he snarled, pointing at her.

Cara had no idea what the man was saying, but she had no problem interpreting his tone. Whatever the man had said to her upset Caine, who stepped in front of her protectively. Cara looked around at the growing number of people who had stopped to gawk at the interaction. She didn't like being so exposed to all the curious eyes staring at them.

"Yuan li, huo bei bu." Caine spoke sharply, and the man took a step back.

"Ta ma de." The man made a hand gesture at Caine, clearly meant to be rude, then slowly stumbled off again, muttering under his breath but still throwing the occasional angry glare at the pair. Caine quickly propelled Cara forward through the curious crowd of onlookers.

"What was that all about?" Cara ventured.

"Don't worry about it," he told her.

"Why was he angry at me?"

Caine took a deep breath. "He wasn't, not really. He was more upset you were with me," he explained.

"But why?"

"He is from Anling, one of the outlying neighborhoods here in Shiyan. Many people move to Arctus to look for work, hoping for a fresh start with a job working for the Confederation, but many are never successful in finding one. Anling is one of the, well, rougher areas here. Many people who live there are not satisfied with their living conditions, expecting the Confederation to care for them since they live in the main city. They often take their agitation out on anyone who works for the Confederation, people such as myself. There is very little money here and a lot of hunger. People can become desperate when they feel like they are struggling to survive. It can be a dangerous area, even for Arctus."

"I'm assuming what he was saying wasn't very nice," she noted.

He gave her a knowing, half-smile. "Not even a bit. Come on, let's go."

Ahead, there was a massive building made of gleaming black stone and glass. It was a sharp contrast to the pure white Caelum that speared into the sky. A little boy in a plain, grey uniform ran across the road, crossing their path, and entered the building.

Caine stopped as the boy ran past them. He was lost in his thoughts, but Cara wasn't sure exactly what in his past he was thinking back on. There was so much she didn't know about him. Truthfully, she knew nothing about him, but this small window he opened up for her was incredibly revealing. He had spent time here as a child and knew the area well, but he clearly wasn't from here.

"Confederation Training Academy."

It made sense. That was why he was so familiar with the area. He had spent his entire childhood here, growing up at the Training Academy.

With no warning, there was an incredible explosion that made the ground shake. Caine grabbed onto Cara instinctively, pulling her closer as he searched for the source of the blast. Cara followed his gaze upward. A sky craft wrapped in billowing plumes of smoke hurtled towards the ground, the back half enveloped in flames. It disappeared behind the roofline. There was a horrible crash when it hit the ground. Instinct kicked in. He grabbed Cara's hand and ran towards it.

Cara could barely keep up with his long strides. Her legs burned. They rounded a corner, and the smaller streets of the outskirts opened to the wide roads in the city center. It was a beautiful metropolitan area, dotted with spacious squares filled with greenery and beautiful fountains. Everything was sleek and shiny, a stark contrast to the neutral, earth-tone buildings of the outskirts.

The pod had come to rest near the edge of one of the main avenues. Asphalt and concrete were smashed into giant chunks that were scattered for several meters in all directions. The pod was a complete wreck, all crushed metal and shattered glass.

"Stay here," he yelled at Cara, holding his hand out to keep her from following. Cara doubled over, hands on her hips and gasping for air. She wasn't going anywhere.

He raced towards the smoldering wreckage and climbed in through a gaping hole in the side of the ship. A flash of red in the smoke caught his eye. Li was still strapped into her seat, coughing in the smoke and bleeding from several lacerations.

"You okay?" he asked, trying to assess the extent of her injuries as quickly as possible.

"I'm good." She coughed from the smoke.

He unbuckled her. As he helped her stand, she yelped, and her legs buckled under her. He eased her back down onto the seat.

He quickly assessed the large gash on the outside of her left thigh. It was deep, but he could stabilize her here before he moved her. He rummaged through a storage compartment until he found the emergency medical kit. He pulled it open roughly, scattering medical supplies across the floor and grabbed the sealed package he needed, and ripped it open. Inside was a syringe filled with a thick, blue gel.

"This will sting."

"Just do it." She grimaced.

Placing the narrow tip over the wound, he squeezed the contents out across the injury until the gel covered a wide area. It stopped the bleeding immediately, adhering to the skin to form a bandage-like seal over the wound.

"Can you walk?" He unstrapped her.

"I think so." She flexed her injured leg, breathing out through clenched teeth in pain.

Caine pulled her up, swinging her arm up around his neck so she could use his body for support as they moved. A sharp crack rang out over the crackling of the fire. Something shattered the glass of a window in the pod, but it didn't take more than a second for him to know what it was. They were under fire, and Cara was out there, exposed. He ducked and half-dragged Li out of the wreckage. He tucked her near the back of the pod, where she was protected and away from the smoke.

"Stay low," he told her.

Caine looked around but couldn't find Cara right away. He spotted her crouching down behind a large chunk of the wrecked pod. When she saw him, she stood. He raced towards her.

"Stay down!" Caine threw himself at Cara, knocking her to the street just as the blue laser bolt hit the wall near them, causing brick and dust to fill the air, sending shards of stone flying.

Debris rained down onto them. People who had come to gawk at the crashed pod fled the scene in a panic, causing a dangerous stampede. More explosions followed; laser fired from the right, no, left. Caine struggled to pinpoint their location. He spotted one assailant on a roof, another down the road using the corner for cover. There was a third in the window of a building to the right. He heaved Cara up by her upper arm.

"Run," he commanded, giving her a push in the direction he wanted her to move.

There was no hesitation. Cara ran, a full out sprint down the street. He followed, using his body as a shield to protect her.

"Left!" he yelled. Cara ducked left into an alleyway just as a laser bolt hit the wall, less than a foot in front of her. Brick shattered into hundreds of sharp fragments. She threw her arms up to block her head but did not break her stride.

"Than! I need a pickup now! Far west side of Shiyan."

His comm crackled. "On my way," Than replied.

Caine caught up to Cara. "This way." He placed his hand on her shoulder, steering her through the winding streets and alleys. He was grateful he had taken this route because he knew the streets like the back of his hand.

"Turn here."

She turned but immediately skidded to a stop. A figure dressed in muted greys and black, holding a gun, appeared at the far end of the narrow road. Caine grabbed her and slammed his shoulder against a wooden door on his left. It flew open, and he pulled her inside. It was a residence. He looked in from room to room but couldn't find any other way to exit.

"Looks like up it is."

He pulled Cara up several winding flights of narrow stairs. At the top was a small landing with a rickety, wooden ladder stretching up to a small trapdoor in the ceiling he hoped would lead out to the roof. The door below was kicked open, slamming into the wall with a loud bang; they were running out of time. Cara climbed up and pushed the heavy wooden hatch open. Caine followed closely behind. With each step up, he slammed his foot down on each rung below, snapping the thin wood in two, so their pursuers would be unable to follow, at least not easily.

"Head that way." Caine kicked the trapdoor closed, and they sprinted across the rooftops, running through gardens and lines of hanging clothes drying in the sun.

Gunfire whizzed by. He turned and fired at the attacker, still climbing out of the trapdoor. He hit his target, and the man collapsed halfway out. It would buy them precious moments while his partner moved the body.

"Jump," he commanded.

Cara leapt across the gap between buildings, but her toe caught on the edge of the roof, causing her to lose her balance. She stumbled forward, landing on her hands and knees. Caine followed after her and pulled Cara to her feet.

"Get up. Come on," he pushed her on.

The flat roof ended, and the next home had a sharply angled metal roof. Cara eased out onto the narrow ridge at the peak, sliding her feet across the narrow beam. Caine crossed backward to keep them covered, his weapon at the ready, but there was no movement. He knew he had managed to lose them, but it wouldn't be for long. No sooner had the thought crossed his mind than they came under fire again. In the moment of chaos, Caine bumped into Cara, and she lost her balance.

"Caine!" she screamed, reaching out to try and grab his arm as she slipped down the steep incline. The roof pitched down several feet before it flattened at the bottom, creating a short overhang for the room below. Cara clawed desperately, trying to get a grasp on anything substantial. She tucked her toes, trying to stop her slide; shoes squealed against the metal and slowed her descent.

One foot slipped over the side, leaving her dangerously close to falling. All the air rushed from her lungs as if they seized up in terror. Her throat closed around an escaping scream, cutting it off until it was nothing more than a harsh wheeze. She yanked her dangling foot back, leaving her crouched just inches from going over the side.

Caine slid down and reached for her. Carefully, they inched along, making their way along the roof's edge until it came to an end. There was a significant drop down to another level of rooftops below. It wasn't sizeable enough that it couldn't be done, but it was ample enough distance Caine was concerned Cara would be hurt in the fall. Nevertheless, better to walk away slightly injured than shot dead. Caine swung over the edge and dropped, bending his knees and rolling to absorb the impact.

"Come on," he called to her.

She looked terrified, but she slipped over the edge, clinging to the edge of the roof.

"Let go." They didn't have time to spare. "Cara, let go! Now!" He was harsher than necessary, but they needed to move.

She loosened her grip and allowed herself to fall. Caine reached out for her, and she fell into him, the force of the impact knocking him off his feet. They tumbled backward, but he wrapped his arms around her, cupping the back of her head with his hand to protect it as they rolled.

Getting up, they raced across the rooftop to an open area. He could see Than racing towards them on a hovercycle.

"Cara, listen to me. You need to jump. Than will catch you."

Cara looked at Than approaching and then back at Caine, eyes wide. She didn't outright refuse, but he could see her reservations. She had only known him a few days, and he was asking her to jump off a roof.

He understood her reservations, but if they were going to survive, he needed her to do as he asked, and it would be best if she did it willingly. "Right now, I need you to trust me."

She was pale, and her lips pressed tight together. Standing on this flat stretch of rooftop, they were exposed. He knew they would only have seconds before the attackers caught up with them. Those seconds passed all too quickly. He turned to cover them while Than sped towards them.

"Jump! Now!"

Cara pushed off the edge of the roof, leaping out into the sky. Than reached out and grabbed her, clutching her close as they veered off almost vertically and out of firing range.

The second cycle was running automatically, pulled along by the first. It slowed and stopped next to Caine. Blue flashes of laser fire kicked up dust. Caine grabbed a small handle on the side and pulled himself up. The cycle raced off, and Caine turned, firing at the two figures: one was on the ground and the other on the rooftop. They wore plain clothes and had cloth draped across their faces, hindering his ability to identify them. One of the men fell as his return fire struck its intended target.

Once he was far enough away, he turned back, took manual control of the vehicle, and raced towards his ship. The Archon was already airborne when he arrived. He slipped into the open entrance to the hangar, and the hatch closed. Dozens of officers were waiting.

"Take us up." Caine wanted the Archon high in the exosphere, out of harm's way.

"We need to get you to Medical, Sir."

"Did someone find Li? She was still at the crash site."

"Sir, your injuries need attention."

Despite the commotion, he turned to the young officer next to him. His brown eyes were huge, face pale. He swallowed hard before silently pointing at Caine's side.

The searing burn in his shoulder and side steadily grew more painful, forcing Caine to acknowledge it. His uniform was torn where he had been hit, the edges of the tear singed black. Blood soaked through the fabric. He held a hand over the wound on his side, pressing on it to stop the blood flow.

"I'll head down there shortly," he told the officer. Right now, he had more pressing matters to attend to, like figuring out who attacked them and making sure Cara had not been severely harmed.

"Cara!"

She poked her head between the shoulders of several officers attending to her. She had blood running down her face, her eyes wide with fear. When Caine stepped toward her, he grunted in pain.

"Kuso, eto bolno." He bit his tongue to prevent more colorful words from slipping out.

"Sir. Her injuries are superficial - just some minor scratches, nothing serious. Your injuries need immediate attention. Doctor Nadir wants you down in Medical."

Caine directed his attention toward the officer next to him once again. Who was he to order Caine down to Medical? Caine grit his teeth. Nadir was a bossy old man. He couldn't fault the young man for relaying the message. He'd take the time to remind Nadir about who was in charge if he thought Nadir would bother listening to him.

Officers quickly cleaned up the small cut on Cara's forehead. Head wounds always bled a lot, and it was not as bad as it had initially looked. It appeared to be nothing more than a small scratch from flying debris. Her hands were scraped raw from her fall, but fortunately, she had escaped major injury

As soon as she was assessed and given a clean bill of health, she was left alone. She had hoped to find Than, but she was sure he was busy navigating them to safety. She made her way down to Medical to check on Caine, making several wrong turns in the process. She hoped his wounds weren't serious. She swallowed hard - there had been so much blood. If anything happened to him because of her, she wouldn't be able to forgive herself.

Chapter Sixteen

"I want an update on Cara," Caine demanded.

Nadir did not respond. He poked the wound on Caine's shoulder. "This will impair some of your arm movement for a while."

"Kuso, stop that!"

Nadir did not meet Caine's angry glare. Instead, he pushed the cleaning pad, soaked with alcohol, onto the wound with more pressure than he needed to.

"Oof." Caine groaned. "You did that on purpose."

"Yes. I did." Nadir squinted through his round glasses at the gash he was treating. "I already told you twice Cara is doing fine; a simple scratch on the head, nothing more. Head wounds always bleed. Hold this while I work on your side."

Caine held the pad against his shoulder while Nadir bent his head to examine his other injuries.

"You're very bossy today."

"And you are very lucky this one was just a graze. It didn't hit any vital organs. Missed all of your important bits."

"I'm lucky those guys were lousy shots. They were not well trained."

Caine knew if it had been him, he would have hit them both before they even knew someone was firing at them. His blood ran cold, and he thanked the stars that whoever had hired the hitmen had managed to find two who had the worst aim. Otherwise, Cara would have been killed. He didn't want to think about it.

"It's not as deep as the ones on your shoulder. It should heal up nicely. Hush up and hold still while I close this up."

"Watch it, old man." Caine bit back a smile despite the pain.

"Do you really want to call the man with the needle old? You're the idiot who somehow got shot by the two worst assassins on Arctus."

"It's fine; I've had worse."

Nadir jabbed the needle into Caine's side. Caine hissed in through his teeth at the sting. The needle injected a foamy, white substance that filled the wound and spread out over the edges of the ripped skin. It stopped the bleeding and started the healing process similar to the gel he used on Li earlier.

"Do not pull the wounds open this time." Nadir wagged a finger at him. "You need to take it easy for two days. No lifting, no running, and no more shootouts. Think you can manage that?"

"I'll do my best." Caine slipped off the table, pulling on a new shirt that had been brought for him. He winced as he raised his arm.

"I mean it," Nadir warned, lifting the sleeve higher to a better angle. "You tear these open, and I will stitch them shut the old way."

Caine never slowed down even when wounded, and more often than not, he had to go back to be patched up again.

"You need to rest," Nadir added, hoping Caine would listen. The man never took a break.

Caine shot him a look, clearly indicating he had no intention of doing so. He did up the last of his buttons and left, heading up to his office.

Nadir sighed. He looked around his room. It was in complete disarray; the table was piled with bloody gauze and bandages. Caine's ruined shirt lay on the floor. The shoulder wounds were deep, although none of them were life-threatening. Though, from the state of the room, it looked like a bloodbath. Caine did have a point; Nadir had seen him with far worse injuries than these in the past.

He walked to the cleaning station and pulled off his gloves. A sharp gasp behind him made him look up. Cara was standing in the doorway. She took one look at the blood on the table next to him and blanched, looking at Nadir in complete horror.

Nadir recognized how deeply she cared for Caine, even if she didn't realize it herself. He remembered Caine's show of concern for her, his demands to get an update on her wellbeing.

Caine, always so rigid and rough, was finally showing an emotion Nadir never thought he would see his young friend display again - affection. His heart filled with hope as he looked at Cara. He was not a man of faith, but he knew there were strange forces, powerful forces at work in the universe.

This woman was special. She was going to change the universe, beginning with Caine. Nadir, never one to turn down an opportunity to help out those strange fates, knew precisely how to manipulate the situation. Sometimes all that was needed was a gentle push in the right direction. A push he was more than happy to supply. He looked at Cara with a shrug.

"He's not here anymore." He shook his head sadly. An innocent enough statement, a truthful statement, but a lie all the same. Mix that with a little stress and imagination, and she would do the rest of the work for him.

Her eyes widened, mouth fell open. She grabbed at her chest as shock rippled through her. Caine was dead? She raced from the room, feeling sick.

Nadir turned and chuckled as he cleaned up the mess. Yes, just a tiny little push.

Cara raced up the stairs but wasn't sure where she was going. Tears burned in her eyes and blurred her vision. She hated this place, hated everything that had happened to her. She bumped into something solid, looked up, and found herself staring into the bright blue concerned gaze of Commander Caine himself.

"I was just coming to check on you." He frowned. "Are you all right?"

Cara threw her arms around him and burst into tears. Caine bit back a groan as she squeezed his injured shoulder. She stepped away and wiped the tear from her eyes.

"Nadir... he said..." She sniffled. "He said you weren't with us."

Caine paused. She was this upset because she thought he had died? He was surprised she had such a strong reaction, but he was comforted by it. Nadir had a habit of being a troublemaker and liked to stir the pot when people were getting too comfortable.

"I can assure you I am right here." He gave her upper arm a gentle squeeze.

Cara nodded fast and brushed away a tear. He huffed out a sigh. He couldn't just leave her in this state, so he called for Zora to keep an eye on her. He had to check on Li at the city medical center and then talk to the Council. It was no coincidence his transport had gone down. The shooters were there under the assumption he and Cara would be on it when it crashed. They were there to finish the job if they survived. When he rushed in to help, he unknowingly put them both in harm's way.

Zora came up and wrapped her arm around Cara's shoulders to lead her away. Caine went back to his room and took out a clean uniform jacket. He cringed as he pulled it up over his injured shoulder; the tight pinching at the wound caused him to let out a guttural groan and swear aloud. When he finally entered the Bridge, everyone hushed.

"I want the Archon locked down. No one comes on or off except me. And if anyone tries, shoot them," he commanded.

No one protested. He spun on his heel and headed to the flight deck to get his personal pod prepared so he could address the Council in person.

Still tense, he flew the pod to the Caelum. The immaculate white calcifite steps loomed in front of him. To anyone else, they would be daunting and intimidating, but Caine took them two at a time. The guards opened the massive doors as he approached and saluted. He returned their salute and strode directly to the Council Chambers.

A young officer turned pale in his presence and pulled the door open, allowing him through without breaking stride. Breaking protocol, he walked right up to the podium without being called forward first.

"Where were you? Where is the woman?" Yugato asked.

"She is back on the Archon."

"You were ordered to bring her here," Yugato countered.

Caine shrugged. "We were attacked."

There was silence.

"What?" Yugato's shocked outburst echoed off the stone.

"There was an explosion on my transport pod, which I suspect was not due to any mechanical failures. Li is lucky to be alive. We were attacked by at least three men, maybe more."

Caine thought back to their first shot. They had been aiming at Cara, not him, which was even more disconcerting.

"How did you manage to escape unharmed?"

"I didn't take the transport pod over," he confessed.

The Council angrily began talking all at once.

"A total breach of protocol!" Someone yelled over the commotion.

"Yes, it was, but it is the only reason both she and I are alive right now." Caine looked directed at Saar. "Unless you're disappointed I'm still here."

"Obviously, we are thankful you're alive." Yugato held his hands up, trying to diffuse the situation.

"You suspect foul play?" Councilman Dhar asked. "Are you sure this was a deliberate attack against you?"

"The Aegis is investigating the cause. They should have conclusive evidence within the hour as to the nature of the explosion." Whoever the attackers were, they brought his pod down expecting him to be on board, not knowing he had changed his route only hours before the pod was scheduled to transport them to the Caelum.

"In the meantime, you need to return to the Archon and bring her back here as was planned." Councilwoman Viraha's deep, husky voice sounded even more gravelly and harsh from anger.

Caine thought about bringing Cara back to them. It was the right thing to do; get her off his ship and in the hands of the Council who could get her home. Yet, something didn't feel right. Why would they be aiming at her if no one except the Council was supposed to know she even existed? He couldn't allow her to be turned over to the Council until he could be sure she would be kept safe.

"In order to maintain her safety, I returned to the ship with her, where she will remain until she is ready to go home." Caine couldn't believe he was defying the Council's orders, but it was the right thing to do. He had been listening to the Council for so long now, allowing their regulations to become the moral compass by which he guided his life, that he had stopped listening to his conscience.

Saar slapped a hand on the table. "She cannot stay on board the Archon. It is completely against regulations!"

Saar's evident lack of concern for her safety finally broke Caine's tenuous hold on his temper. "Regulations be damned! You promised you would be able to keep her safe, and you did not keep that promise. Those men were not aiming at me; they were aiming at Cara." Caine fixed Saar with a cold stare.

"It is not possible; no one here, but the Council knows about her." Yugato looked around at the Council. Everyone nodded in agreement.

"Well, information has leaked out because someone appears to know about her and has made her a target. Until I find out who, Cara is not safe: not even with the Council."

"Are you implying the leak came from our end?" Saar didn't bother to hide his icy contempt for Caine.

"I am not implying anything. I'm simply saying that until the Council takes care of this security threat, I cannot, in good conscience, turn Cara over to you."

"Absolutely unacceptable!" Saar slammed his fist on the table. "You were ordered to bring her here! You are disobeying a direct order from the Council!"

"I was tasked with keeping her under my protection until she was safely in your hands. Since it is clear I am unable to get her to you safely at this time, this is the most logical course of action," he responded.

"Civilians have not been allowed on Confederation military ships since-"

Caine looked directly at Yugato and cut him off. "She stays there."

Several council members argued amongst themselves. Yugato raised his right hand, silencing the council.

"Quiet down!" Yugato chided. "I find I have to agree with the Commander. We did order him to keep the woman safe. This is an unusual situation, but we need to get her back to her time. We will investigate this further and arrange for a more secure exchange. Until then, she is to remain on the Archon temporarily." Yugato placed both hands on the table.

"You are willing to take on the responsibility of having a civilian on board, given your personal history?" Councilman Dhar asked.

"I am."

"It's settled. In the meantime, do not leave Arctus," Yugato directed.

Caine met his eyes, hoping to convey his unspoken gratitude. Yugato came to his defense when he didn't need to. Caine deeply bowed his head in respect to the Council and left.

He took a transport pod to the city's Medical Center to check on Li. She was lying in a bed, bandaged up.

"Are you okay?"

"Never better." She forced a smile despite her injuries.

Li was one of the first selected to join the crew of the Archon as its political envoy. She had extensive combat training, but it was her diplomatic skills that had impressed Caine.

The doctor entered and bowed his head to Caine respectfully.

"Commander, your envoy is lucky she survived the crash. She has a significant concussion, several contusions, three broken ribs, and a punctured lung. She will need to stay here for at least a few days before she can be transported to the Archon. Even then, she will still need several more weeks of rest before she can return to work."

Caine turned to Li; she shrugged.

"It's not the time off I requested, but I'll take it," she joked.

Despite her attempt at humor, Caine could see in her eyes she was shaken up.

"You get better." He pointed at her, trying to sound stern.

"If the crash didn't kill me, the food here might"

"Li," he warned.

"Yes, Sir." She nodded solemnly. "I will."

"I want regular updates," Caine ordered the doctor as they exited the room together. He couldn't stay, and he still had one more stop to make before he could return to the ship.

There was a shit storm coming, and it was about to unleash its fury and rain down upon him. Caine just hoped he could keep his people out of the mess.

Before heading back, he returned to the crash site to see what had been uncovered. Aegis Officers were milling around, inspecting, and taking notes. One looked up, spotting Caine, and immediately rushed over.

"Commander, Sir," Lieutenant Anson Choi approached respectfully. He nodded sharply and saluted.

"What have you found?" Caine surveyed the wreckage.

"As we suspected, this was no accident. There was a small detonation device attached to the underside of the transport. Unfortunately, we cannot tell whether it was placed there by hand before flight or fired up there from the ground to it while it was in motion. The blast originated near the rear, which is why your envoy survived. We will be taking the device back to the lab for testing."

Crime was relatively low in the core planets. The Aegis' strong security presence deterred most crimes. Acts of terror were even rarer, associated with Hostiles, and generally limited to the border planets. Li had been the one piloting the pod. If he and Cara had been aboard, they would have been in the seating area; in the rear of the craft.

"Nik," a voice called out.

Caine knew only one person who would call him by his given name in public while he was on official business.

"Tirio," Caine turned to greet his brother.

Tirio approached, his blue eyes narrowed. He was the Captain of the Aegis, the Arctus Elite Guard and Intelligence Service, a job he took far too seriously. Tirio stuck his hand out in a formal greeting that directly contradicted the deliberately casual way he addressed Caine. Caine and Tirio were equally matched in height, but Caine was broader and darker while Tirio took after their mother's slender build and lighter complexion. The only clue they had shared genetics was their striking blue eyes.

"What can I do for you, brother? The only time you acknowledge my existence is when you want something from me." Caine didn't bother to hide the sarcasm.

"I can see you are still as immature as always."

Caine resisted the urge to roll his eyes, but he couldn't help but take advantage of the moment to antagonize Tirio.

"And I see your uniform could use a good cleaning." Caine deliberately brushed his hand over the four gold stars on Tirio's right shoulder. Tirio stiffened and smacked his hand away.

"And yet you act so surprised someone would want you dead," Tirio scoffed.

Caine shook his head; his brother's ridicule was a sobering reminder of what had happened.

"Not to disappoint you, but they weren't shooting at me."

Tirio's frown deepened. "Who was their target?"

"A political refugee I was escorting to the Caelum," he explained.

"Ah, I did hear something about this woman you were accompanying. Whoever she is, she's made an enemy or two." Tirio looked over at the twisted wreckage of the crashed pod.

"It would appear that way."

"When do I get to question your little refugee?"

Caine deliberately ignored the bait Tirio had laid out. "You don't. She is safely under the custody of my crew on the Archon until further notice. Now, if you'll excuse me, I have some things to take care of."

Caine walked away, but Tirio wasn't finished yet.

"I heard she's marked."

This was neither the time nor place for bitter sibling rivalry, but Tirio was intent on causing a scene.

Caine spun slowly, anger radiating from him and his heel grinding into the ground as he turned. "Since this has nothing to do with your investigation, I fail to see how it's any of your business."

"It is my business if my brother is cavorting with a potential Hostile!" Tirio strode forward, planting himself inches from Caine.

"Cavorting? Do you even hear yourself? And since when have you started putting so much stock into such ridiculous rumors?"

"As head of the Aegis, it is my duty to fully investigate any potential intel, especially if you're being irresponsible."

"Yes, you have made it abundantly clear you would just love to find something to pin on me, so I get dismissed from my position." Caine didn't bother hiding the scorn in his voice.

"You realize I'm just trying to do my job Nik. Do you have to make this more difficult?"

"Don't take yourself so seriously, brother; no one else does."

Tirio threw up his hands in an exasperated huff. "You really are a child." He pointed his finger at Caine and sneered. "The only reason you got chosen as Fleet Commander is because of your abilities. You have no other redeeming qualities that make you fit for the position. You're a disgrace."

"Envy doesn't look good on you, Tirio," Caine said dryly. "Give Maynelle my regards." He spun on his heel and walked away before the conversation could descend any further into argument.

Chapter Seventeen

Back on the Archon, Cara reluctantly allowed Zora to lead her away to her room, giving her an opportunity to change before bringing her elsewhere. She didn't pay attention to where they were going until Zora was telling her to sit. They were in a small lounge area with a few comfortable looking chairs and tables scattered throughout. Cara found an oversized chair to sit in while Zora busied herself. A few minutes later, she handed Cara a mug with steam rising from its contents.

"My mom used to make this for me when I was little. It's called haldi."

Cara took a sip. The hot tea was floral and comforting. "What was your home like?"

"Greener," Zora sighed, "so much greener. I grew up on Mir. It's quite a bit different than Arctus. So much green you could walk through fields for days. There are ancient forests with trees almost as tall as the Caelum and the most beautiful purple flowers that would bloom at night."

"Do you miss it?"

Zora smiled sadly. "I haven't been back in a long time. My mom got sick years ago. After she died, I never went back. My sister still lives there. I don't talk to her as much as I'd like to. She works at the Medical Center in the capital and has a family now, but I've never even met her children. That's just life up here."

The haldi tea was warming Cara up, calming her nerves.

"You all seem so at home, though." Cara sighed, the stark feeling of homesickness tugging at her.

"That's because this is home. I've been on the Archon for nearly a decade; some have been on it longer. We were all handpicked, specially selected to be here by the Commander. We could have been placed on any of the ships in the fleet, but he chose us to be here. Caine holds us all together. The people here, they are just as much my family as my own sister is."

Cara sipped the tea, thinking about the ship's crew. They were so cohesive. She missed her family. Her poor parents must be worried sick about her. Hopefully, tomorrow Caine could safely get her back to the Council, and she would be one step closer to heading home. Zora smiled at Cara, and they quietly enjoyed each other's company. A low ding resounded through the room, like a seatbelt alert on an airplane. Cara looked at Zora for an explanation.

"Commander's back." Zora put her cup down on the table. "Back to work. Will you be okay?"

"Yeah, I'll be fine. I think I can actually find my way back to my room this time." It was a weak attempt at humor, but she needed to reassure Zora she would be alright without her.

Cara sat back in her chair after Zora left, finishing her tea. She had come so close to death. The closest she had ever come was when she had nearly drowned in her Aunt Rachel's pond when she was six. Her cousins abandoned her, leaving her on the floating platform to swim back to shore on her own. She'd only taken a few strokes when she had sunk under the surface, watching the beams of sunlight filter through the murky, yellow water. Weeds had curled around her ankles, but she didn't remember feeling scared. It was more of a feeling of confusion. Today though, she had felt genuine fear, the kind of fear that drove its way deep into her bones and lingered. She had almost died, but Caine had saved her. Just thinking back on the day made her frayed nerves spark. She got up and poured herself another cup of haldi. She would need a few more before the day was done.

***

Caine returned to the Archon and checked in with his crew at the Bridge.

"I want us ready to go back into orbit around Arctus in an hour," he directed.

"What about bringing her to the Council," Than approached.

"I'm not bringing her anywhere."

There wasn't much Caine did anymore that shocked Than, but his mouth dropped open, and his eyebrows shot up. "What? You're not actually thinking about letting her stay?"

Caine wiped his hand over his face. "I don't know what I'm thinking," he admitted.

"The Council approved this?"

"I didn't give them much of choice."

Than rocked back on his heels, surprised. This was out of character for Caine. "It's not normal for you to defy Council regulations."

"Nothing about this is normal, Than." Caine shook his head.

"How long is she staying?"

"Until this gets resolved," Caine answered firmly.

"I'm assuming you saw Tirio," Than's lips twitched with a repressed smile.

"I did. He becomes more of a prick every time I see him." Caine walked over to his desk, shuffling through papers.

"You'd think after all this time, you two would learn to resolve your issues."

Caine shot a glare in Than's direction. He was not in the mood for Than to be instructing him on proper brotherly treatment. "I don't need one of your lectures right now."

"Just saying, some of us would be thankful to have a brother," Than reminded him.

"I don't need a brother who gets on my nerves when I have you to fill that position," Caine muttered. Talking about his brother always brought out the worst in him.

"Testy, are we?"

"Than, don't push your luck," Caine warned.

Than pretended to be busy at his station, not saying anything, but Caine knew he didn't have to. Zora entered the Bridge and slipped into her seat at her post. Caine walked up to her.

"She's in the lounge." Zora didn't even bother looking up.

Caine turned to leave but turned back. He opened his mouth to say something but thought better of it and left, missing the shared glance between Than and Zora.

Cara looked up as Caine entered the lounge. She was in a chair; legs pulled up close to her chest, her chin resting on her knees. In her hand was a black mug.

"Haldi?"

Cara tilted the cup to peer into it. It was nearly empty. "Zora made me some." All the tension had slipped away from her muscles, leaving her feeling light and dreamy.

Caine was well acquainted with the calming effects of haldi. He wasn't surprised Zora had made her some, but he wanted to make sure she was clear-headed for the upcoming conversation.

"Cara, we need to talk."

The dreamy feeling vanished. Cara stiffened, instantly on guard. "Okay," she answered warily.

"Not here," he told her. He wanted somewhere more private, where any random officer couldn't just walk in on them talking.

She followed Caine into his office in the Bridge. He gestured to a chair. She sat, clenching the armrests nervously, palms sweating. Caine sat, placing his elbows on the desk, folded his hands, and rested his chin on his knuckles.

"Today wasn't an accident."

Cara's stomach dropped at the weight of his words.

"It appears someone deliberately attacked the transport ship. The shooters were there waiting to see if anyone survived the crash."

Cara frowned, trying to put the pieces together. "And we were supposed to be on the transport shuttle."

Caine nodded solemnly. He pushed his chair back abruptly and took a few steps away, looking out a window at his crew.

"Cara, I don't think they were targeting Li or myself." He was finding it difficult to look her in the eyes as he told her.

"It was me," she breathed. "They wanted to kill me." She leaned back in the chair, thankful to be sitting.

Caine looked away for a while before turning to Cara. She was looking down at the floor, her hands clenched in her lap, turning her knuckles white. He hadn't wanted her to know the attackers were after her. He had wanted to protect her, but she needed to know the truth if she was in danger.

"Why were they after me?" she asked softly.

Caine ran his fingers through his hair. "I don't know. Time travel isn't supposed to be possible, so maybe someone thinks you hold the key to figuring out how. Maybe they think you know something you shouldn't. Until we know who is behind this..." He stopped. His face hardened, and his shoulders stiffened. He was fighting something inside himself. "You'll be safer here than with the Council. I'll have an officer bring you to your quarters." He finished abruptly.

"They're allowing me to stay here?" That was unexpected.

Caine looked away, not saying anything but still revealing the truth.

"You?" Cara was shocked. "You wanted me to stay?"

Caine took a deep breath and nodded tersely. Cara couldn't believe it. He was continuously surprising her.

"You have free range of the ship and its facilities until we can deliver you safely to the Council. As long as you do not interfere with the affairs of this ship, you will not have any problems. Clear?"

It was an unexpectedly abrupt dismissal. Standing, she nodded, acknowledging the expectations he had laid out for her. She headed for the door without looking at him. He turned back to face his desk.

"Caine, thank you."

He turned to look at her, holding her gaze for a long moment before nodding curtly.

Cara left, and the door closed behind her. She stood in the hallway for a moment, confusion getting the better of her. He had gone cold so quickly, telling her she would be staying as if he didn't want her on the ship, yet it had been his idea in the first place.

Caine gripped the desk tightly as if holding onto it would keep him from going after her. He sat down in his chair, hard enough to cause it to squeak in protest, and buried his face in his hands. He wasn't sure he had made the right decision. There were reasons civilians were not allowed on Confederation Fleet ships, but she was in danger. She could have died today right there in front of him. He had promised to protect her, and he always kept his promises, despite any trouble that would come from it.

Chapter Eighteen

Caine slumped back in his chair, his head cradled in his hands. There was a sharp rap at the door. He rushed to gather himself before it opened. He smoothed out his uniform jacket before Than entered with his permission. Halfway standing, he sat back down in disappointment.

"Did you think I was Cara?" Than asked, wisely keeping any sarcasm from his voice. Caine inwardly cursed how observant his friend was.

"What the hell happened down there?" Than asked.

Caine made an exasperated sound, rubbing a hand over his face. "This is a nightmare, Than." He rubbed his temples. "They were after Cara. There were three of them, maybe four, and they attacked us in the middle of the street. They were aiming at her, not me. The only reason they didn't hit her was because they had terrible aim. Otherwise, she would have been killed. They had the drop on me."

Than let out a long breath. "How could they have possibly found out?"

"I have a few theories but nothing I can confirm. Someone's leaking information. I'm worried it could be from our end." It was the first time Caine voiced his suspicions out loud. He trusted Than more than anyone else, but to tell someone he suspected a member of his crew of leaking classified information still didn't sit well with him.

Than scowled. Caine was toying with two magnets, pushing the opposing poles together. No matter how hard he tried, the ends wouldn't meet. He turned the magnets slightly, and they snapped together. Than watched him stare at the magnets, curious as to what was going on in his friend's head.

"Do you have any ideas?" he asked Caine.

Caine shook his head and abruptly tossed the magnets into a drawer, shutting it forcefully. "I have no idea. Someone shared information about our route. I only finalized it with Li this morning. The Council didn't even know we were going the back way."

"I still don't understand why. Why would someone want to kill her?"

"Maybe they think she knows something or is a threat. Maybe the person leaking information knows how or why she got sent here," Caine threw his hands up in frustration. "I don't know. It could be anything. She traveled through time, Than. Maybe someone is worried it the public will find out." Caine was pulling at strings. It didn't make sense for someone to want to hurt Cara.

Than studied Caine's facial expressions as he talked about Cara. He knew something was different with him when she was involved. He had known Caine for a long time and knew he had a tendency to push away good things. He tried hard to be an impenetrable wall, a strong leader, but it led to a rough personality that grated on many people he met. Than had a feeling Cara was not a person to put up with being mistreated.

"She's going to be here for a while," Than said bluntly.

Caine nodded. "Yeah." He blew out a deep breath.

It wasn't what he wanted. He didn't want her around him. He didn't want her on his ship. It was against protocol, and he was breaking more regulations than he could count, not to mention the fact she was getting under his skin. Like the magnets opposing each other, he wanted to avoid her, but the harder he worked to keep away from her, the more they ended up being pulled together.

"Have you thought through what you are doing here?" Than folded his hands in his lap and leaned back in his chair.

Caine wasn't sure where Than was heading with this question, but he knew he wouldn't like it.

"Of course, I have."

"Are you sure you aren't keeping her here because you think this is some kind of second chance? A do-over?"

Caine's gaze narrowed. He knew where Than was headed with this.

"My decision is entirely unrelated to that. She is in danger right now, and at the moment, this is the safest place for her to be. The Archon has better security than the Caelum." Why did it feel like he was making excuses? And poor ones at that. He was the Commander; he didn't need to justify his actions.

"You don't have to live the rest of your life trying to atone for what happened. Let the past go, Caine." Than turned to leave. "You are responsible for her now: her safety and her feelings."

Caine's eyebrows jumped skyward. Was Than insinuating that he might hurt Cara's feelings?

Than shot him a look saying precisely that.

"Be nice to her, Caine." Without another word, he left.

Caine opened up a drawer on his desk and pulled out the string he had used to explain Cara's mysterious appearance to the council. He toyed with it in his hands, wrapping it around his index finger and unraveling it again. It was the perfect metaphor for what was happening to his life.

There had not been a citizen on board a military class vessel in a long time. He had been the one to help get the regulation passed. He upheld the law, saw to it that rules were followed to the strictest of letters - until she arrived.

Now, he was going against protocol, left and right. His crew would become more suspicious as time went on, and Caine knew the minimal information he was giving them would not be enough to explain Cara's long-term stay. He already knew rumors were flying, but he needed to brief his crew; for her protection and his own.

Caine called his core crew into his office. Zora, Than, Myat, Xan, Senn, and a few others were sitting around him.

"As you are all aware, there has been a lot that has happened in the last few days, and you deserve an explanation. We have a guest on board, and her name is Cara. Some of you have already met her. She is in possession of some highly classified information that is of extreme value to the Council. This makes her a critically important asset to the Confederation. The Council tasked me with escorting her to them, but yesterday, she was the target of an assassination attempt when I was transporting her to the Caelum, forcing me to return to the ship with her. After discussing with the Council, we agreed it best that she stay on board here until all necessary precautions are taken on Arctus to ensure a safe transfer over into their custody. I expect you to keep this information only among those who need to know and do whatever it takes to protect her while she is with us. Understand?"

Everyone nodded and murmured their agreement.

"If any of you notice anything suspicious, you are to notify me immediately. I would prefer she stay in her quarters but if she is out, keep an eye on her."

Zora was stunned. She was only now learning the real reason Cara was on board. She had been so rude to Cara, and she was undeserving of it. She turned to look at her fellow crew members and noticed a mix of surprised reactions, but Than's, by far, was the most interesting. He almost looked disappointed and not surprised at all. Than clearly knew all of this before now. Why did Caine go through the trouble of making it appear as if he didn't? The story was too clean, too rehearsed. There was much more he wasn't sharing with them, and she would find out what it was.

***

Cara threw herself onto her bed. She had been through more than she could handle. A short time later, there was a knock at the door. She groaned. When did it end? She was not in the mood to see anyone and only wanted to be left alone for a while. Reluctantly, she walked over and hit the button on the wall to open the door. Than was standing there and appeared glad to see her - as pleasant as he ever was.

"You look terrible." He grinned, looking genuinely happy to see her.

Cara was startled by his blunt honesty, but a smile tugged at the corners of her mouth.

"If you were tossed a couple hundred years into the future and everyone wanted to kill you, you would look terrible too."

"I don't want to kill you."

"That's a relief."

Than's shoulders shook with laughter. "Come on, let's get you something to eat."

He stretched out his hand, and she took it. He gave her hand a gentle squeeze, and she flushed.

"He doesn't want me here," she murmured.

Than didn't reply right away. He understood Caine's struggle. Everything his friend had gone through had made him who he was. It had changed him, hardened him.

"This isn't easy for him. Caine has a lot of pressure on him right now," he explained. "It isn't you. He's like this all the time. A lot has happened to him in his life, plus he is the leader of an entire fleet and must act like one. He can be a little cold but give it time. He'll come around."

Cara wasn't sure if it would ever happen. How long would it take for Caine to warm up to her? She wasn't sure she wanted to be around long enough to see that happen. She was still holding out hope Caine would arrive any second, telling her they had found a way to send her home.

Food and conversation helped settle her nerves. Than was so warm and open; she enjoyed talking with him. It was so easy. Communicating with Caine, on the other hand, was like talking to a rock. Than was so willing to share stories. He was the only person who took the time to explain things she didn't understand. He understood how out of place she was and took the time to make her feel like she fit in. After eating, he took her on a full tour of the ship, showing her how to get around. She made a mental note of the route back to the observation deck and library.

Back in her room, she looked at her reflection in the mirror. She was dirty; her hair was slicked back and looked greasy. She looked terrible and could use a shower. Cara pressed the buttons on the control panel to open the circular wash tube Zora had shown her. She stepped in. A fine layer of white foam bubbled on her skin. She still wasn't sure how the spaceship version of a shower worked, but it didn't bring the same satisfying feeling as her one at home.

Despite the clean feeling afterward, she missed a hot shower. She wanted to feel water running through her hair, sitting under the spray for as long as she wanted.

Water was a precious commodity in space. Storage was limited, and so were locations where the ship could refill. Her tap had shut off while she was trying to wash her face earlier in the day.

Than had explained the ship's water rationing policies. Cara marveled at how different life was for the crew. Being on the Archon for the last week had been challenging enough, but for the crew who lived on board full time? She didn't think she would ever get used to a life like that.

She stopped and looked in the mirror again. For the first time, she wasn't sure she recognized the woman staring back at her. She had been through so much. She had come this far and survived time travel, attacks on her life, and now she was living on a spaceship. A chuckle bubbled up in her throat. How was any of this even believable? She was facing the impossible every day. Wiping tears from her eyes, she took one last glance at herself. No, she didn't know who this new woman was, but she liked her. She was strong, and she would get home.

Chapter Nineteen

Caine sat on the graveyard shift. It was the middle of the night, and the Bridge was empty, save for the skeleton crew. He was in his chair, staring out into deep space.

"Commander," a voice called.

"Yes," he answered.

"Cara has left her quarters. You asked me to monitor her movements. It appears she is going up to the library," the officer informed him.

"Thank you."

He finished submitting all of his daily reports and went to see her. She was curled up on one of the antique leather chairs, reading a book titled A History of Old Earth.

Caine knew the history all too well. It had been drilled into him by his instructors during his years at the training academy. He understood the importance of learning it and would do whatever he could to ensure they never again followed the same path as their ancestors. They would not make the same mistakes twice. He bit his lip to keep from smiling at the sight of her just as Cara turned to face him.

"Couldn't sleep?"

"I'm sorry, I didn't mean to..." She looked away, face red. She closed the book, but he held up a hand.

"It's okay, please," he reassured her, gesturing for her not to get up. "I told you that you could come here whenever you wanted. I'm glad to see it being used. It's empty far too often."

Cara smiled, holding the book against her chest.

"I want to thank you for saving my life. Okay, that sounds weird to say out loud. It's hard to think everyone I knew died hundreds of years ago, and here I am, stuck on a spaceship. It's just so strange. Where I'm from, this kind of stuff just doesn't happen. In books and movies, yeah, but real life? My family, my friends, they all died, and no one knows where I am or what happened to me." She let out a long breath through her nose, trying to stave off the flare-up of homesickness. "I'm sorry."

"You have nothing to be sorry for," Caine reassured her. "This must be difficult for you."

Cara finally worked up the courage to ask the question that had been eating at her. "Do you think they will find a way to get me home?"

Caine searched for the right words. Every response he came up with fell woefully short. It would have been easier to lie to her, but he couldn't bring himself to do it.

"I don't know," he finally said, truthfully.

"It felt like I was being ripped apart."

Caine was momentarily confused until he realized she was talking about her unexpected fall through time.

"There was this blue light. It just appeared out of nowhere. It came right at me. Just me. It was as if it could think and could choose where to go. It didn't touch anyone else, and it curled around my arms." Cara rubbed her forearms, touching the skin where the light had contacted it. "I was trying so hard to hold on, but it was like it was pulling me away, forcing me to let go. Everything got bright, and I couldn't see anything, just this horrible pulling like every cell in my body was coming apart. I can't even describe it. I was being squeezed down into just one little speck in space. Then I was here. Just like that. One second I was there, and the next, I am in the future."

"I promise you, I will do everything possible to make sure you get back home safely," he told her. "May I make a recommendation?" he asked. Cara followed him to the shelves as he scanned the rows. He pulled out a book and handed it to her.

"The Complete Works of Shakespeare," she read the cover. "How did you get this?" She looked up at Caine, eyes wide in astonishment.

He smiled down at her, pleased he'd managed to surprise her.

"I have quite an extensive collection of books from Old Earth. My family was smart enough to keep them over the centuries, and now I have them."

Cara traced the well-worn leather cover of the book with a finger. "When he dies, take him and cut him out in little stars."

"And he will make the face of heaven so fine that all the world will be in love with night." Caine finished the quote.

A slow smile spread across Cara's face, lighting up her features.

"Romeo and Juliet. I have read most of the books in the library. They aren't just here for show." Caine's features were hard, but his eyes held warmth. In his eyes, she could see he was holding back things from her, secrets she hoped would eventually reveal themselves.

Neither one could look away. Unable to move. Or was it unwilling? The invisible magnetic force tugged at her as if trying to pull her forward, closer to him. Her hand moved on its own volition, no longer in control of her own body. Reaching up, she touched one of the pins on his jacket, straightening it.

"Cara," Caine's voice was tight, strained.

"I'm sorry." She jerked her hand away and pressed her fingertips to her lips. What was she thinking? Did she have zero self-control?

Caine's throat tightened as Cara averted her eyes, cheeks flushed. He was feeling it too: the same lack of control. It was the unexplainable magnetism again, the connection that kept bringing them together. If it made him feel this unsettled, he could only imagine how disconcerting this must all be for her. He was barely keeping a hold on his composure. He wanted to comfort her, reassure her. A little voice in his head told him to pull her in for a hug. He wanted to feel her melt into him as he wrapped his arms around her, but that simultaneous polar opposite force holding him back kept him from acting on it. Instead, he took her chin in his hand and gently tilted it up, so their eyes met.

"Cara, I promise you everything is going to be okay."

They stood there, stuck in the fleeting space between push and pull, rendering them both motionless. Unable to close the small distance between them, yet incapable of pulling away. Caine shook free from the hypnotic trance first. He drew his hand away abruptly and cleared his throat. With a curt nod, he left her.

Cara huffed and went back to reading. Caine made no sense. He was always so rigid and stiff, but occasionally he would show a softer side that he tried hard to hide. As soon as it was revealed, it was shut back up just as quickly. It wasn't surprising to her. She was sure this life was not easy and called for someone capable of making difficult decisions and pushing aside their personal feelings and emotions. He had made it to the position of Commander of an entire military fleet, and she was sure he didn't make it this far without having walls up to protect himself.

Be that as it may, she sensed there was another reason he was pulling away from her. She felt it herself too; the unquestionable knowing that she needed to keep herself distant, even though she wanted to throw herself at him. She was going home soon. Back to her life, back to David.

Cara groaned. David, poor David. He was probably falling apart, worried sick, not knowing where she was. Cara didn't think he would be handling the stress well. He was thrown off for the whole day if his morning coffee stop was out of blonde roast. What did everything happen to her? Her boss, Lauren, all her friends, and family. Did they think she died in the train crash? Did they think she was simply missing? Did people even remember her, or had she simply disappeared from time as if she had never existed? She wasn't sure how time travel worked in real life.

Her thoughts drifted carelessly back to Caine. It was hard to see warmth from him only to have it snapped away. It was unsettling the way he could quickly shift back to his usual formal demeanor. It gave her emotional whiplash. It was more than she could handle. She had to stay focused on getting home and was sure her presence on board wasn't easy for him to handle. Troubles had plagued her, and Caine from the moment she had arrived on the ship. At least Than didn't mind the chaos.

She fell asleep in the chair and dreamed of Caine and his big blue eyes.

Chapter Twenty

There was a strange commotion amongst the crew the next day. Cara ate slowly, watching as crew members rushed through breakfast, barely finishing their meals before rushing off again. Cara caught Zora's attention, waving her over when she walked in.

"Hey," Zora pulled a chair out with her foot and set her tray down.

"What's going on?" Cara gestured at the crew hurrying by them.

"We left orbit this morning. Makes things a little more hectic than usual."

"We aren't staying near Arctus?" Cara asked Zora.

"The Archon has too much to do to sit and float around doing nothing. Besides, Caine can be very persuasive. We have a few scheduled stops. The other ships in the fleet are too far away right now to complete them. Commander got permission from the Council to leave so we can finish these last few jobs. We'll return as soon as everything is done."

"You mean return with me." Cara was surprised the Council had allowed the Archon to leave Arctus with her still on board, but maybe his rank meant Caine had a little more sway over the Council than he liked to let on.

Zora reached out and gently squeezed her shoulder, "I wouldn't worry; you'll be back on Arctus in no time at all."

Cara didn't bother correcting her. It was better for Zora to believe she was upset about leaving the ground behind.

"So, what do I do until we get back?"

"It isn't every day a civilian gets to spend time up in space like this." Zora shrugged. "Without a job to do, I mean. If it were me, I'd just try to relax and enjoy my time up here while it lasts."

Zora's idea sounded great in theory, but Cara wasn't sure how it would end up playing out in reality. Although, it was a valid point. Cara had no responsibilities, but it wasn't like the ship had a spa she could relax in until they got back. She would just be stuck in her room with no entertainment of any form to be found and nothing to do.

After she finished eating, she made her way up to the observation room. It seemed appropriate to go back there as they were leaving Arctus behind.

The observation room was dark and quiet, just as she had found it the first time. She walked across the floor and sat in front of the window. She hugged her legs into her chest and rested her chin on her knees. Actus was shrinking in the distance, a small green and blue sphere slowly fading from view.

Cara had expected to feel disappointed she wasn't back down there, feet planted firmly on the ground. Instead, there was a great sense of relief that she was still on the ship. Caine was right; she was safer up here.

She was so small sitting there in front of the massive window. She found herself in a place that was so much bigger than she ever could have imagined. There was only vast, unforgiving blackness as far as she could see.

As Cara looked out, her eyes adjusted to the dark. Although it first appeared to be an empty void, the blackness was flecked with pinprick points of cold starlight. Out there was an entire system of planets filled with people, stars, moons, and suns. It wasn't empty; it was limitless, and this new universe she found herself in was filled with infinite possibilities. New York seemed so insignificant compared to this.

Cara found herself drifting off as she sat there, her eyes grew heavy, and she couldn't keep them open any longer. When she woke, Arctus had vanished. Her feet had fallen asleep. She stretched her legs out long and flexed her feet back and forth, letting the blood flow return. She should head to the library or find Zora to share a cup of haldi. Anything would be better than just sitting around in her room doing nothing. She pushed herself to her feet.

Halfway back to her room, a familiar voice caught her attention. She turned the corner. Caine was busy talking with two officers.

"Caine!"

He looked over when she called his name.

She flashed a smile. "Hi."

Caine's face remained passive. He didn't appear pleased to see her. In fact, it was quite the opposite.

"Cara." His tone was flat, almost apathetic. "Can I help you?"

Cara took a step back as though he had struck her; the icy greeting was cold water extinguishing her enthusiasm.

"Oh, uh, no. I was just heading back to my room."

"That's a good idea."

Caine returned his attention to the officers and continued talking with them. Cara was bewildered by the callous interaction. She hesitated another moment before leaving. As she walked away, she glanced back at him, hoping to see him look at her, but he had turned his back on her in more ways than one.

The next two days and nights crawled by agonizingly slow. Cara struggled to sleep, finding herself lying awake for hours staring at the ceiling. She holed up in her room, only leaving to get something to eat.

She had only seen Caine a few times, always at a distance. He had seen her but immediately broke eye contact and walked away. He was deliberately avoiding her. He was making it crystal clear he wanted her out of his way.

At first, she had been upset and hurt, but now she was just furious with him. Here she was, stranded far from home, and he was alienating her. In the long run, she knew it was easier not to see him since every time she did; it was like all the air was sucked out of the room. He was imposing, but the way her pulse raced was not because she was intimidated. Something about his presence made it hard for her to breathe. She was acting like a silly love-struck teenager.

Daily life on a spaceship was a far cry from the exciting interstellar travel she had seen in movies. It was just a lot of flying through space, doing a lot of nothing. Even Than had told her things were unusually quiet.

Hostile encounters were a regular occurrence, but lately, they all but appeared to have vanished. She thought it would be seen as a good thing, but Than was concerned. He shared his fears that this was the calm before the storm. Cara hoped she wouldn't be around to face that storm if it came.

Zora came by when she could to check in on her. Cara knew she was busy, but it was nice having her around.

"How are you doing?" Zora asked, flopping onto the bed with a groan. She pulled the band from her curls, allowing them to explode around her face.

"I'm doing all right," Cara admitted. "Things are just so... different. It's going to take some getting used to."

"What is so different?" Zora peered at her from behind the mass of ringlets half-hiding her face.

"Where do I even start?" She rubbed the back of her neck. "I don't think I could even begin to explain. Food. Mmm, pizza, and ice cream. I miss the food my mom would cook on Thanksgiving and movies, and music. I miss music the most. I haven't heard any since I've been here." She was rambling. She rubbed her hands up and down her arms. "I just need to know it's going to be okay."

Zora took her hand, brushing the back of it gently. "It will be okay."

"Want to get something to eat?" Cara asked.

"Yes, that sounds great." Zora smiled, but it quickly vanished when her comm beeped. "Duty calls," she sighed. "I'll come by later. You need to explain to me whatever that Thanksgiving thing is."

Zora headed up to start her shift. As she crossed the Bridge to her desk, she passed by Caine standing by his own.

"She misses music," she whispered over his shoulder as she walked by.

"What?" Caine called after her, confused by her random statement.

Zora winked at him as she sat in her chair.

"Music?" he muttered to himself. He shook his head. Women.

He glanced at the time. He had spent yet another night working. His stomach was tight. He hadn't eaten since yesterday morning. He had to update the Council in an hour, giving him enough time to get some food and clean up a bit before facing them.

The collision course was inevitable, although neither one of them knew it. Cara stopped short as she left the cafeteria with her food just as Caine was entering. There was no way to avoid each other this time. She panicked, not sure what to do. A part of her wanted to turn and run, but she also wanted to pretend her feelings weren't hurt and just walk by and ignore him. Since her head and her feet couldn't agree on a plan of action, she remained in the doorway.

"Hello." Caine's voice was tight. He shifted his weight from one foot to the other, running a hand through his hair. She had come to recognize his one tell. He did it any time his emotions ran high. Other than that, he maintained his poker face.

She blinked at him. Hello? That was all he had to say after ignoring her for days? She kept her mouth shut, afraid she would embarrass herself.

"I've been busy-" It was a pathetic excuse, and the look on his face told her he knew it was too. He almost looked sheepish.

"No, I get it." She interrupted him. "You have a ship to run. I just get in your way." It came out more sarcastic than she had intended, and she inwardly cringed at her tone.

"Cara-" The softness in his voice was infuriating. They wouldn't even be in this pickle if he'd agreed to leave her with the Council like they wanted, instead of insisting on keeping her here on the ship for her protection.

"Look, Commander, you don't need to worry about me. I know you don't want me around. I'm so sorry I have been such an inconvenience to you," she snipped. She was being immature, but she was on a roll now. "Maybe we all would have been better off if you had just let them shoot me." She stormed off.

"Cara!" Caine took a step towards her. He wanted to reach out to grab her so he could set her straight, but he balled his hands into fists and released a frustrated huff. How could she think he regretted saving her? Did she believe she was causing him that much trouble? Yes, there was trouble because she was here, but in his life, trouble found him one way or another.

It wasn't worth trying to reason with her now. She was being overly dramatic. He didn't have time to deal with her tantrum. His appetite suddenly gone, he returned to the Bridge, poured a cup of amka, and downed it. He slammed the mug on the desk at his Commander's Station in frustration, the metal clang reverberating through the room.

"Oh, you must have run into Cara." Than appeared next to him.

"Shut up," Caine growled.

He brought up the glass monitor and scanned the information on the display. There was a supply ship meeting them in the morning. He needed to make sure everything was ready to go so that it would be a quick drop. He stomped back over to Than, still scowling. They stood in silence for a moment.

"Don't say anything," he snapped at Than.

Than feigned shock. "What? Me? Would never dream of it." The fake look of shock on his face was broken by the hint of a smirk curling up the corners of his lips.

By the third night, Cara discovered she was talking to herself and needed to get out of her room. Sitting around her room, doing nothing for days, was finally pushing her to her breaking point. She needed a break in her self-imposed reclusiveness, so she headed towards the one place she knew she had full access to: the library. As she approached, the door opened. She came to a sharp halt.

Sleeping in a chair was Caine; a book lay open on his lap. A blanket had fallen to the floor.

Cara froze. She had not expected to find him here. What a ridiculous thought to have. Why shouldn't he be in it? It was his library.

She stood in the doorway, deciding whether to stay or go. He didn't stir. Even though the room was warm, she shivered involuntarily. She turned to leave but thought twice about it and turned back. All she wanted was a new book. She wasn't going to wake him, just quietly grab a book and leave. She'd be in and out in a few seconds. He would never know she had even been there.

Cara crept over quietly and picked out a book. She stared at Caine sleeping - so peaceful and still. As if against her wishes, her body moved towards him. She picked up the blanket from the floor, draped it across his lap, and tucked the corners up around his shoulders.

His hand shot up and grabbed her throat as his eyes flew open. His pupils were huge, making his eyes look black. The small sliver of blue that ringed his eyes was a violent blue, almost glowing.

"Caine," she managed to croak out, gasping for air under his tight grip.

The room faded around her, and her vision went black.

Chapter Twenty-One

Cara sat straight up in her bed, gasping for air. She was back in her apartment. Alone. Where had Caine gone? The clock on the nightstand read 3:47 in the morning, and her heart was still pounding. She wiped her hands over her face. Strands of hair stuck to her forehead and cheeks. Her shirt, damp with sweat, clung to her chest.

Had she been dreaming? She'd had vivid dreams in the past, but this took it to a whole new level. Every detail was still crisp and clear in her mind as if she had lived it. She reached over and flipped the switch on the lamp. Nothing. Dammit, she needed to replace that lightbulb. She would have to remember to run to the hardware store tomorrow after work. She untangled herself from the sheets, twisted and wrapped around her legs, and carefully walked to the bathroom. She wasn't risking another collision with her nightstand again.

She turned on the tap and splashed cold water on her flushed cheeks. Eyes closed, she fumbled for the hand towel hanging on the wall. As she wiped her face dry, she looked at herself in the mirror. Her eyes had dark circles under them as if she hadn't had a good night's sleep in days.

Unfortunately, she was wide awake. Work in the morning would be rough if she couldn't get another hour or so of sleep.

Cara walked into the kitchen. A cup of tea would soothe her nerves enough that she'd fall back asleep. She looked around as she picked up the teapot from off the stove. Everything was exactly as she had left it in the morning. Or had morning not even come yet? She skimmed the edge of the counter with her fingertips. Was this real?

She looked out the window. Even in the middle of the night, the city was busy. A man walked along the sidewalk, his shadow dancing every time he passed under a streetlight. Taxis cruised down the road, safely bringing their passengers home. The streets were wet, and a taxi drove through a puddle sending a spray of water flying into the air. The man on the sidewalk leapt away, narrowly missing getting soaked. He raised his middle finger, flipping off the taxi - good old New York.

Everything she remembered from her dream faded away and became a distant memory. She was home. That was all it had been - just a dream. It was a very realistic one, but a dream, nonetheless.

She shivered. Her apartment was freezing. She hoped her heat hadn't been turned off, but it wouldn't be the first time she had missed a payment. One more late arrival at work again, she would have more to worry about than one late bill. She couldn't miss the subway in the morning.

Wait.

The crash.

She wasn't home.

Only moments earlier, she had been with Caine, in his library. In space. Then, inexplicably, she had ended up here. She put the teapot down, looking around the kitchen, confused. Had she somehow time-traveled again?

There was wet warmth on her nose, and she touched it. Deep red blood discolored her fingertips. She rubbed her fingers together, smearing the blood: it was hers.

This was wrong, all wrong. She walked to the window in the kitchen and looked out at Central Park. The lights were glimmering through the trees, the moon shining overhead, the lights and sounds of the city at night, they looked distant as if she wasn't even there.

She reached up and touched the glass. With a sharp snap, it cracked under her fingers. She took a step back as the crack grew and spider-webbed out.

The window exploded inwards, shards of glass slicing into her skin. She fell to her knees on the tile floor, and her body bent backward, contorted in agony. Every muscle jerked and twitched.

"Caine," she screamed, her eyes shut tight. When she opened them again, she was back in the library with him, and his hand still circling her throat. His eyes widened, and he let go, yanking his hand off her neck. She collapsed to the floor, gasping for air.

Caine rushed to her, "Cara, are you okay? I'm so sorry." Blood oozed from his nose in an uneven streak of crimson.

"It's okay. I'm okay." Cara wasn't sure if she was telling him the truth, mostly because she wasn't even sure exactly what had just happened.

He crouched down and reached out for her, but she recoiled away, putting her hand up to maintain the distance between them. He rocked back on his heels to stand and withdrew a few steps, bowing his head in shame.

"I have to go." Cara pushed to her feet and rushed from the room. She was fleeing, but she didn't understand why. Something inside her was telling her to get away, but she didn't even know what for. What had just happened?

***

Caine watched her make a quick exit. He turned and slammed his fist into the wall, letting out an angry roar. He could have killed her. Still in the fog of being half asleep, he had lost complete control of his abilities. He would have a lot of explaining to do in the morning. It was like every time he took a step forward, he ended up taking two more back.

Despite being off duty, he made his way to the Bridge. He wiped his nose off on his shirtsleeve and pulled his jacket down to hide the stain. Than didn't look too surprised to see him in the middle of the night.

"Can't sleep."

It wasn't a question, and Caine didn't feel the need to respond.

"She's getting under your skin."

"Like an infection," Caine retorted, knowing Than was right.

Than's lips twitched, but he didn't say anything. Caine let the subject drop. The more he protested, the worse it would be. It was better just to keep his mouth shut. Cara was getting to him. He had to keep her away and keep her distant because she could get hurt so easily. He couldn't control himself around her: tonight, in the library, proved that.

Besides, he didn't want to explain what had just happened with Cara. He didn't need another lecture from Than. He had been doing so well, keeping his distance from her, until today. He wanted to protect her. The best way he could keep her safe would be to stay away from her until she was ready to go home. The more she was around him, the more trouble followed. An unwelcome twinge of hurt shot through him at the thought of her leaving. Forcing all thoughts of Cara aside, he dove into his work.

Cara raced back to her room. She looked in the mirror at the blood she had smeared over her cheek and lips. If she had been part of a haunted house, she would have looked scary enough to terrify small children, but this wasn't fake blood. Whatever Caine had done to her caused it.

Wiping at it with a cloth only succeeded in spreading it even more. She dug through the box Zora had given her until she found the small bottle of cleanser. The liquid bubbled on her skin. When she wiped it away, the blood was finally gone.

She threw the towel on the floor and curled up on the bed, pulling the covers over her head. Home, she had been home. It had been so real. Her desire to return home came back with fierce intensity. She wanted out of this place, away from Caine, and back to her own time. She wanted to go back to her simple, ordinary, and boring life.

She blinked away tears, but they spilled over. She roughly brushed them away, closed her eyes, and pictured herself back in her apartment until she fell asleep.

Chapter Twenty-Two

The next morning, Cara found Than in a hall. "What the hell is Caine?" she demanded, sliding on the bench across from him.

Than coughed, nearly choking on his food.

"Does he have magic powers?"

"What?"

Cara stopped, and her eyes widened. "Is he an alien?" she gasped out, shocked by this sudden possibility she had discovered. "He told me there weren't any aliens."

"Whoa, slow down." Than held up his hands defensively. "What happened?"

Cara told him how Caine had somehow transported her back to her apartment, but Than showed little reaction. When she was finally finished, he stared at his food for a long time before he spoke.

"Cara, I have been friends with Caine for a while. This isn't easy for him. This is something Caine needs to tell you himself," he said softly.

"What? No!"

Than shook his head in a way that told her he was trying to control his tongue. "This is not my story to tell. You deserve to hear it from him, and he deserves to have the chance to tell you himself."

Cara knew when to accept defeat. "Fine," she pushed away from the table. If she wanted an explanation, the only way she would get one would be by talking directly to Caine. She admired the loyalty he had earned from his friends.

She stood up and whispered into Than's ear. "I knew it. He is an alien."

Than's wild laughter followed her out of the room.

She was halfway up to the Bridge, steeling her nerves to confront him when sirens blared. All the lights in sight turned red and flashed. Crew ran down the hallways, and she pressed herself against the wall, trying to stay out of their way. Than was at the end of the hall. She shouted his name, but the deafening frenzy drowned out her voice.

"Than!" She pushed through the swarm of people.

He turned, trying to determine who had called his name.

"Than! Over here!"

He deftly wove through the rush of officers.

"Follow me." He led the way to the Bridge, yelling at crew to get out of his way. "Go sit." He pointed at a chair bolted to the wall. He vanished into the crowd.

Cara stumbled as the ship shook beneath her. She reached out for the chair to steady herself but instead, she found herself grabbing hold of a strong arm thrust in front of her.

Caine's gaze was like ice: not looking at her but through her. He had a firm grip on her upper arm, pulling her towards the chair. The floor tilted beneath them, and they slid across it. Caine managed to hook his fingers on the edge of the chair. He heaved her towards it and pushed her roughly down to sit. His grip hurt as his fingers bit into her skin. He grabbed the harness, yanking the harness across her chest to buckle her in.

"I got it," Cara cried out. He didn't listen. "I got it," she snapped sharply, slapping at his hand. "Caine, stop." She didn't like raising her voice that way, but it broke through his robotic trance. His hand stayed, gripping the harness, but he looked at her. The fear in his eyes caught her by surprise. She wasn't expecting such a reaction from him. Seeing it made her acutely aware of the danger she was currently in. Reading science fiction in the comfort of her own home was one thing but living it, she wasn't prepared for that.

She placed her hand gently on top of his. "I can do it. Go."

He gave her a sharp, curt nod and turned back to his crew. She was thankful he'd listened to her. He had a job to do, leading his crew through whatever dangers they were facing. He didn't need to be distracted with simple tasks like buckling her into a seat. She didn't want to be the cause of him losing focus.

She jammed the harness buckle closed, breathing a sigh of relief when it clicked into place.

Another blast rocked the ship. She was glad she was strapped in; otherwise, she would have gone flying across the floor. She finally had time to listen to what people were shouting. Hostiles were attacking the ship. Something about cloaking, she couldn't be sure. The blood drained from her face as she remembered Caine telling her how vicious the Hostile clans were. She closed her eyes, hoping he would be able to get them out of the situation safely.

Caine turned to shoot one last glance over at Cara, who was as safe as she could be, given the situation. He couldn't worry about her right now. He had an entire ship to protect. He would talk with Than later about what he was thinking, bringing her onto the Bridge while they were under attack. He should have just sent her straight back to her room, but Caine understood it would have taken too much time. He gripped the desk in front of him as the ship trembled from another explosion.

"Get me out of this," he shouted to Tauran.

Tauran had the controls in his grip so tight his knuckles were white. "I have one trick still left up my sleeve," Tauran said through clenched teeth. "Zora, get the rear guns ready to fire. We need to get below them and attack from underneath."

Caine knew this maneuver when this close to the Hostiles was risky. Tauran would cut the engines, allowing the ship to drop below the other ship, then launch forward.

If one thing went wrong, the ships could crash into each other.

The Archon was massive and not built for moves like this, but right now, a move like this could save them from massive damages and loss of life.

"Strap in," Caine commanded. Everyone moved quickly to secure themselves to their desks or chairs.

Cara tensed when Caine grabbed hold of the two silver bars on the wall near the door and pressed his body against the wall.

The ship lurched forward, slanting downwards at a sharp angle. Her whole body slammed back into the seat: causing her head to crack against the wall. She understood exactly why everyone had strapped in. She floated towards the ceiling held in by the harness. As the ship leveled off, she slammed back down into the chair. The sirens turned off; the sudden sharpness of the silence was eerie. She could hear everyone breathing heavily, relief palpable.

Her hands shook, fingers struggling to unhook the harness.

"Are you okay?" Caine appeared, his face still stony. He gently reached down, moved her hands, and lifted her from the seat. She wobbled. The adrenaline in her system caught up with her, and her stomach rolled just like the ship had.

Caine was speaking to her, but the sharp buzzing in her ears drowned out his voice. She rubbed them. Everything was muffled like she was wearing earplugs. The back of her head throbbed viciously. A black container appeared in front of her face, and she threw up into it, unable to hold out longer. A hand gently rubbed her back, where the slope of her neck met her shoulders.

"You okay?" he asked again.

She was too woozy to look at him, so she nodded over the container.

Caine, assured she was okay for the moment, stood and turned to address his crew.

"Where the hell did they come from?"

"I don't know, Sir. We never even registered a heat signature on the radar," Tauran told him.

"This is the second ship that has had a cloaking system. We need to figure out how they are getting their hands on military weapons and stop it. I want an investigation started to find the source," Caine instructed.

"What about the Council, Sir?" an officer queried. "Have they sanctioned one?"

Everyone quieted. Caine looked around the room at the crew. These were his people; the ones he handpicked for these positions. He trusted them with his life.

"I'm not sure there isn't a leak in the Council. They can't be trusted until we get more answers." Caine shook his head and ran a hand through his hair. "For the time being, nothing leaves the Bridge. That's an order." He pointed at Cara. "Than, get her out of here."

Cara hurried after Than, ready to get back to some calm and quiet.

"Is this normal?" she rubbed the sore spot on her head as Than escorted her away.

"Unfortunately, yes," he nodded. "Lately, they are getting bolder, venturing further into the Core Planets. The Clans are uniting for coordinated attacks. It is a new tactic. Not to mention they are getting their hands on weaponry they should never have access to."

"Where are they getting it?"

"No one knows. Not even Caine can say for certain, but he has his suspicions."

Cara stopped dead in her tracks. "Wait. Are we safe on here? Am I safe?" Her voice wavered.

Than exhaled heavily. He reached out and gently grasped her upper arms in a comforting grip.

"Cara, the Archon is a warship. She's designed to withstand a lot more than whatever those Hostile ships can throw at her. Caine is one of the best Commanders the Confederation has ever seen. You have nothing to be worried about. Now, let's get you to Nadir so he can look at your head."

Cara forced herself to nod, but the feeling of unease in her gut took root even deeper despite Than's best efforts to put her mind at rest.

"What have we this time?" Nadir walked up and gently gripped her chin in his fingers, tilting her head.

"I hit my head on the wall."

He pointed her into one of the smaller recovery rooms. "My dear, you are becoming a frequent visitor here." He shone a light from one eye to the other. "I hope this doesn't become a habit."

"It seems impossible to avoid trouble around here."

"You need to be more careful, my dear." He took her head and gently pressed on different spots, checking for soreness. There was an underlying hint of a warning in his words that made her think he wasn't just talking about injuries.

"I have no idea what I'm doing." Cara winced as Nadir found the lump on the back of her head.

"As is to be expected. You are not of this world. You will face many challenges navigating it. All sunshine makes a desert."

"I have no idea what that means."

"It means, my dear, you are going to be fine," Nadir patted her on the arm.

"My head or me?"

"Yes," Nadir chuckled as he walked off.

Cara couldn't help but smile at Nadir's quirky response. Nadir brought her a pill and a cup of water.

"This should help with some of the ache. Get a little food in your stomach and get some rest too. Come back and see me tomorrow."

Cara swallowed the pill and slid off the table, following Nadir into the main treatment area.

"You'll be right as rain, my dear." Nadir winked and wandered off into an adjoining room.

Than was waiting for her near the door. "What's the diagnosis?"

"Just a bump and some strange advice about a desert."

"Ah, yes. Nadir is known for dispensing wisdom as much as he does medication."

"I'd like to process all his wisdom with some food."

"Coming right up." Than draped an arm around her shoulder. "Let's go."

Chapter Twenty-Three

Once the day's initial uproar of the earlier incident died down, Cara decided it was an excellent opportunity to question Caine about what had happened.

"Have you seen Caine?" Cara asked Zora.

"He went to his quarters." Zora looked at her with curiosity. "Why? Do you need to talk to him?"

Cara frowned. "No, it can wait." She tried not to sound overly disappointed. She had only been to his room the one time, and the ship was so large she didn't think she would be able to find her way to it without getting lost.

"He said he didn't want to be disturbed," Zora winked at Cara. "He'd be angry if I told you his room was two floors down, first door on the right." Zora put her index finger over her lips. "Shhh."

The door to Caine's room opened for Cara as she approached, and she found him sitting at his desk in his office, writing in his logbook. His eyes narrowed when she entered.

"You think you can just barge on in here?" he grumbled, clearly annoyed with her. "Who even told you where I was? Never mind."

She scowled at him. She had a feeling he wouldn't want to talk, being in such a foul mood, but since she was already living dangerously, the risk was worth it.

"The first time we met, you did something to me. It hurt like you were breaking my skull open. I thought it was because of the crash, a concussion, or something, but it wasn't. It was you. You did it again when you were questioning me. And the other night when I woke you, you sent me home. I was there. In my apartment. Touching things. I woke up there even though I was still here. How did you that? What did you do to me?"

Caine didn't look up. His fists clenched on the desk, and the muscles in his jaw twitched. "Cara, you need to leave."

She was done being ignored. She was done allowing herself to be pushed aside. "Caine, you-" He threw her a lethal stare that made her think twice about pushing the issue.

"I am not discussing this with you." The frigid edge in his voice was enough of a warning on its own, but Cara refused to back down.

"We have to talk about this."

"I am busy. I do not have the time nor the patience to have this talk. Let me remind you, I have an entire Fleet to manage. My work does not stop on a whim every single time you feel the desire to have a conversation with me."

She crossed her arms and sat in the chair across the desk from him. She was willing to force him to acknowledge her or admit she had a point.

"You have tried to get rid of me since the first day I was here. Getting any answers has been like pulling teeth. You owe me an explanation. After everything I have been through and now being stuck on this ship. I deserve it."

"Get out now," he barked.

Cara wasn't budging. She'd had enough and wasn't going to allow him to treat her like she was a bystander anymore. She was as much part of this as he was. She had an even more significant stake in it since she was the one stuck in the future.

"No," she bit back.

She was playing with fire, but she was beyond trying to reason with him. Caine stood abruptly, his chair scraping backward. Cara nearly jumped out of her skin. His eyes flashed bright blue, nearly glowing the same way they had in the library the other night. He was angry, angrier than she had seen him before. For a moment, she worried she had gone too far, pushed him past his breaking point.

He stalked around his desk towards her. "Stand up."

There was something different about how he sounded. His voice was stranger, deeper. She wanted to refuse to listen to him barking commands at her, but she stood, feeling pulled up like she was being hoisted on strings. Her body just did it on its own. Instinctively, she took a step back.

"Turn around." His voice was soft and smooth but had a faint, hollow ring to it. Her entire body tingled as he spoke.

Her muscles clenched, unable to control their movement. She spun in a circle.

"Now, the other way."

Again, the strange tugging sensation returned, like ripples pulling at her skin, her muscles spasming like she had been electrocuted. This unseen prickle like pins and needles surging through her forced her to do what he told her. She spun around again, her body moving unintentionally. She took another step back, eyes wide, fearful. How was he doing this? It was like he was in her head, in her body, controlling her like a puppet on strings. She couldn't stop it even if she wanted to.

"Back up," he ordered. Her feet propelled her backward until she hit the wall.

Caine was beyond reasoning with her at this point. "Come here."

She took three steps toward him, closing the distance. They were standing nose to nose, both of them breathing hard, one from fear, the other from anger.

walked her through "Kiss me," he whispered. She did. But deep in the back of her mind, she registered his voice had sounded different that time. She had wanted to kiss him. He wasn't making her do it; he wasn't forcing her. She was doing this out of her own free will. His hands fisted in her hair, tugging at it. It was explosive, and she was shattering into tiny pieces. It was as if, in an instant, the whole world vanished. They were alone in the universe, melting into each other. Finally, he pushed her away, and she was pulled back to reality. She was gasping from the intensity of it all when he turned away from her.

"Get out," he barked.

She didn't hesitate. She ran.

Caine stared at the door, trying to slow his breathing. He walked around his desk, kicking his chair back with his toe, slumped into it, pushed his work aside, and rubbed a hand over his mouth. He had done his best to diffuse the situation, but she kept pushing. His ship did not revolve around her. He knew he would have handled the situation differently if he hadn't already been on edge from the earlier attack.

What he had just done was not just stupid, but unprofessional. All she had wanted to know was what had happened to her in the library. She was right to demand an explanation. He didn't know how to tell her. He had thought the only big bombshell he would have to diffuse was the fact she was in the future. He hadn't expected her to be around long enough to be questioning who he was.

Than burst in minutes later.

"Does anyone knock around here?" Caine muttered. He was going to start keeping his door locked if everyone thought they could just come into his private quarters whenever they felt like it.

"What the hell were you thinking, Caine?"

Caine didn't need Than to explain what he meant. Than was angry, and rightfully so.

"I know." It was all Caine could say. Anything more would sound like he was justifying his actions.

"You swore an oath never to use your ability to harm a civilian."

"I didn't hurt her. She needed to learn a lesson Than. This isn't her world. I'm trying to keep her safe." It was a weak attempt to defend himself.

"Safe? Safe isn't me finding her running through the hallways like she's being chased by Hostiles. Then she starts rambling on about how you've used your freaky alien powers on her. You say you're keeping her safe? Safe from who?" Than yelled at him.

Pretending not to care, Caine poured himself a glass of araq.

Than shook his head, disgusted with Caine's nonchalant reaction. "Kuso. Get yourself under control." He stormed out.

Caine huffed. Yes, he was definitely reinstating the lock settings on his door immediately.

"Alien powers," Caine muttered incredulously and took a long drink.

Chapter Twenty-Four

Caine sat for a long time in his chair: one leg crossed over the other, tapping his metal stylus on his knee. He thought about events that had taken place over the last week. This woman had brought him nothing but trouble yet, even though everything she did ended up backfiring, he found her to be endearing and charming. He owed her an explanation.

A couple of quick taps on the glass screen in front of him displayed her location.

She was in the library.

He was surprised after everything that had happened there. This was becoming their meeting place, whether by choice or accident.

When he walked through the door, Cara gasped and jumped up. She scurried behind the chair, her eyes darting around as she frantically searched for a way to escape.

"Can we talk?" Guilt surged through Caine.

"Stay away from me!" If he wasn't willing to make the time for her when she wanted to talk, she wasn't going to make the time for him.

"Please, let me explain. I'm so sorry," he pleaded. It didn't help. It just made her angry.

Her eyes blazed in narrow slits. He was almost afraid of her reaction.

"You're sorry? Sorry!" she hissed. She stepped out from behind the chair and marched towards him, waving the book she was holding. "I'm almost a thousand years in the future, stuck on this stupid spaceship, people are trying to kill me, you're using your crazy alien powers on me, and no one will tell me what the hell is going on, and you're sorry?" she exploded. She smacked him on the chest with the book, tears brimming in her eyes. "All I want to do is go home." The tears spilled over.

He reached out for her, but she swatted his hand away. He grabbed her and pulled her in to hug her anyway.

"No, stop it. Don't touch me. No, go away," she mumbled into his shirt, protesting, although she was returning his embrace. The book tumbled to the floor with a thud. A moment later, she stepped away. She sniffled and wiped away the tears, refusing to look at him.

"Cara, you have to understand-"

"No. I don't have to understand anything. You have no idea what it's like to be in my shoes. You haven't even tried to see things from my point of view. Do you know how it feels? I know nothing about anything. You've been hiding things from me from day one. Why don't you try telling me the truth for once?"

Caine sat in one of the big leather wing chairs. Cara hesitated but reluctantly sat down across from him. He was hunched forward, silent, thinking of the best way to explain everything to her. This was the second conversation he'd have with her about this world he lived in, and there would be so many more to come. She didn't know anything, understand anything.

"I'm an Esper," Caine said, feeling the sound of the words on his tongue as he spoke slowly. It had been a long time since he'd had to explain what he was to anyone.

Cara's expression remained blank.

"I come from a long line of people who developed the ability to see into another person's mind."

Cara looked confused. "What?" she paused, her head tilted slightly to the side. "You can read my mind?" She sounded skeptical.

"No, I can't read your thoughts. It's not telepathy. That doesn't exist. I have the ability to go into someone's mind. I can place my consciousness inside of yours and see your memories, desires, ideas, and thoughts you've had."

"Oh, and somehow that's supposed to be more believable than being telepathic?"

In this world, everyone knew; children were taught in classes or told about it by their parents. Explaining it was never something he had ever been expected to do.

"The best we can tell, something in our DNA changed many generations ago. We aren't sure how or why. My ancestors discovered they could not hear people's thoughts but could go inside a person's mind: see what they think, see what they have done, and everything they know. An Esper's ability can sometimes go beyond just entering a person's mind. Espers can change memories, alter memories, and even erase them completely. We use it in a process called Interrogation. It is how we get information from Hostiles and prisoners; by taking it directly from their mind,"

"How are you able to enter their mind?" If it weren't for her circumstances, she never would have believed his story.

"I can enter a person's mind through their eyes. I have to be looking into your eyes to gain access. It links me to you."

"They always said the eyes were the window to the soul," Cara said sarcastically. "But what about how you get me to do things I don't want to. You weren't looking into my eyes that time."

"It's another part of our ability. Cognitive manipulation. It's a form of compulsion. Civilians call it Silverspeak. I can put thoughts into your head and make you do things and control you. We do not use it often, and we are forbidden to use it against civilians. I do not have to be looking at you to use it. We use it during questioning before an interrogation, to make suspected Hostiles and other prisoners give us answers we want."

"You mean it's forced coercion?"

Caine gave an awkward smile and nodded. She had a point. "Silverspeak is not as strong of an ability for many Espers. If there is enough resistance, it doesn't always work. Sometimes we can't get the answers we want, so we have to go to the source, in their mind."

Cara shivered, remembering the pins and needles sensation whenever he compelled her to do something; the unrelenting pull to obey.

"It feels funny." She unconsciously rubbed her arms.

Caine nodded. "It's a force, pulling you. Sometimes it does feel like something tugging at you. Once it takes hold, it is nearly impossible to break free, but you are different. When I first tried to gain access to your mind, you were able to resist me, which is not common. You put up walls, mental blocks in your mind, and fought me, which is difficult for even trained military personnel to do. It's called Intransigence. It usually takes many years of difficult training to learn how to resist Interrogation and hone those particular skills and abilities. Many are born with the capabilities to become an Intransigent, but they never successfully learn how to use them."

"You were still able to make me do things. You could still see into my mind even though I'm an Intra-" She looked to Caine to finish for her.

"Intransigent." He chuckled. "And yes, I was."

Cara pulled her legs up and wrapped her arms around them, listening intently. "Can everyone do what you can do?"

"No. Espers are not common. We all descended from a few people hundreds of years ago. We are all part of the military, so we can use our abilities to protect the Confederation. We are trained from a young age to control and strengthen our abilities. I was five when I moved to the Academy."

"What about your parents? They were okay with that?" Cara couldn't begin to imagine what it must have been like for his parents, forced to send their five-year-old son away for military training.

Caine didn't look sad, but he had a distant expression as he reminisced on days long gone.

"My parents were both Espers too. They were in the military, as we all are, from the moment we are born. They knew the day I was born; this was what I was intended to do."

"It's like they own you."

He gave a twisted half-smile, "In a way, they do."

He remembered what it was like going through the training. So much pressure for someone so young. He had excelled, exceeding everyone's expectations for him, and they had pushed him harder, challenged him to his breaking point.

He was only seven when he began Resistance Training; something trainees typically started at thirteen. They had one of the more powerful Espers teach him, train him, and try to break him. The pain he'd endured had been excruciating, but it had made him strong. The mental defenses he developed were nearly impenetrable.

"There are different classes of Espers, depending on how powerful they are. One is the lowest level, not able to fully breach someone's mind. Ten is the most powerful. Powerful Espers are highly valued and often given high-ranking positions because of their capabilities. But Espers have many rules we must follow. We cannot use our abilities on civilians unless under direct order from the Council. Our abilities are used only for military operations. Since this ability is genetic, we pass it on to our children. Espers are only allowed to have children when dictated by the government, and the selection process for a suitable mate is long and hard. Everything we do is regulated, down to the number of children we can have. That way, there aren't hundreds of Espers. Not everyone can handle having this sort of power; this kind of responsibility. We pledge our whole life to protecting the Confederation and the people."

"It doesn't seem fair. You were created for this. You didn't have a choice. You get no say in anything? What about love?" Cara blushed as the last question slipped out before she thought better of asking.

Caine smiled, but it didn't quite reach his eyes. There was a fleeting glimpse of sadness she caught before it was gone.

"Our duty comes first. Keeping the people safe from Hostiles is more important."

"It just doesn't seem fair," she said again almost to herself.

Caine went quiet, thinking about all the events in his life that had led him to here. He never thought he would be in this situation. If it weren't so serious, he would have thought it was humorous, albeit ironic.

"It's why people knew who you were when you were taking me to the Council. They knew you were an Esper."

Caine nodded, confirming her theory. "One of the genetic traits is our eye color. It's just something we're born with, kind of like an external genetic marker, signifying what we are on the outside. It makes us stand out in a crowd. People also know I am the Commander of the entire Confederation Fleet. Put the two distinguishing factors together, and yes, people know who and what I am."

Cara looked at his unusually vivid blue eyes. "So, all Espers have blue eyes like yours?"

"Yes, some civilians do have blue eyes, although they are not as common. Espers have quite a significant color difference."

He was quiet for a moment, rubbing his chin. He clasped his hands together. "I know I have not been as forthcoming as I could have been with you, and for that, I apologize."

He walked to the screen on the desk. "I hope maybe this will make up for my error in judgment yesterday." He pressed a few buttons.

A soft, strange melody began to play.

Cara's eyes widened as her heart fluttered in her chest at the first soft notes: music! It wasn't anything like the music she was used to hearing, but it was beautiful.

Caine's comm beeped. "I have to go. Stay as long as you want."

"Caine?"

He turned partially around but didn't quite meet her eyes.

"What level are you?" she asked softly, even though in her gut, she already knew the answer.

He looked up at her and held her gaze for a brief moment before looking away. He didn't say anything. Silently, he left the room.

The ten little gold stars on the patch on his shoulder appeared to wink at her as he retreated.

Chapter Twenty-Five

Cara rolled a pen back and forth across the surface of the desk mindlessly as the music continued to play in the background. She was lost in thought. Caine, being an Esper: all of it was more fiction than science, and if she hadn't experienced it for herself, she would have been more hesitant to believe him. It explained so much. All her questions had been answered, and yet she still knew nothing. She wanted to know so much more, wanted to see these worlds he spoke of, and learn what life was like now. However, with her impending departure to the Caelum and her subsequent journey home, it didn't appear it would ever be possible.

Later that night, Caine joined Than, Zora, and Cara for dinner. Everyone in the dining area threw curious glances at them the whole time. Cara surmised the Commander did not regularly take his meals with the crew.

"Has there been an updated status on the border run departure time?" Zora asked near the end, between mouthfuls.

Caine shot her a murderous look because he knew Cara's curiosity would cause a problem.

"What is a border run?" Cara piped up as expected.

"We are going to one of the border planets to drop supplies and pick some up," Than offered when Caine didn't explain.

"Can I go?"

"No, it isn't safe," Caine instructed firmly.

Zora rolled her eyes. "Please, Turah is one of the safest border planets."

Caine glared at her.

"Gotta get to work!" Zora chirped and quickly made her exit.

"She's right. It is one of the safest planets we go to." Than attempted to make the argument in favor of Cara going, but Caine fixed him with the same dark look he had given Zora.

"She is not going, end of conversation." Caine swiped his tray off the table and left in a huff.

Than looked at Cara and shrugged. "I tried."

"It's okay. I can just read in the library." Even though Cara was disappointed, she was grateful Than and Zora were on her side. Unfortunately, even working together, they were no match against Caine's final decisions.

"There is no reason you shouldn't be able to go." Than sipped his drink. "He's just being stubborn."

"Seems like he's always that way," Cara noted.

"Pretty much. Doctors think it's incurable," That deadpanned.

Cara burst out laughing, welcoming the humor to break the tension. Cara wiped a tear from her eyes as her last chuckles faded.

"I talked to him last night. He told me what he is."

Than did not look surprised. He needed no explanation as to what she was referring. He nodded, acknowledging her statement but didn't respond.

"Do you have any abilities?" She pushed for more information. He didn't have the blue eyes of an Esper, but at this point, Cara wasn't sure what other kinds of powers people in this time had.

"Oh, no, not me. Completely normal. Caine is the only Esper on the ship."

"He's powerful." She had put enough of the pieces together to feel like she had a pretty good picture of the situation. Caine wouldn't have been selected to be the

Commander of an entire fleet if he wasn't incredibly talented.

"Caine is the first level ten Esper in over a hundred years."

Cara knew how hard it must have been for Caine with all the pressure and expectations. It must weigh so heavily on him, and it explained some of his strange mannerisms. Than wasn't an Esper, but he was incredibly astute.

"Caine can fly a ship and control a legion of men without any problems, but when it comes to having a simple conversation with a friend, he's lost. He doesn't always handle the emotional stuff well. If it isn't in the rule book, he doesn't know what to do. He can be too critical. He may be hard on others, but he's even harder on himself. Go easy on him. He means well, even though it doesn't always come across that way."

Than looked at Cara sitting across from him like a sponge soaking up everything he was saying. She had been on the ship long enough; she had earned the right to learn more about who Caine was.

Cara understood. She just wished he would relax a little instead of always trying to be so damn perfect. "This is all he knows, isn't it?"

"Caine has never experienced a normal life. He was raised in a special branch of the Training Academy for Esper children. He was sent directly into military service afterward. Everything he is and does is regulated. He has a hard time removing himself from all of it. There is no difference between the Commander and Caine. Everything he is and everything he knows was trained into him. He can't separate his personal life from his job because his life is his job. They are one and the same. He's never had a chance to have his own life. When he finds himself in moments where there aren't rules or protocols to guide his behavior, he gets a little lost."

Cara understood. It also explained his behavior the other day. The kiss they shared had been on her mind non-stop. She couldn't stop thinking about it; about him. She kept herself focused on going home. She reminded herself she wouldn't be around much longer, but she wanted to go on the border run while she was there.

Cara looked for Caine in his office on the Bridge, but he wasn't there. She meandered down to his room. The door didn't open as usual when she approached. She knocked on it. Nothing. She noticed the panel next to the door, and she placed her palm on it. With a flash of green, it scanned her palm.

"Entry unauthorized," a computerized woman's voice reproved. Seriously?

She knocked again. It took a few moments, but there was a beep, and it slid open. She entered, but Caine didn't turn to greet her. He was tapping away on some sort of glass tablet.

"Caine, look, I know this whole thing hasn't been easy for you. But, since I am here, I think it would be a good idea for me to go with you on this-"

"No." He cut her off, not looking up from the tablet in his hand.

She stepped closer to plead her case but tripped on the edge of the rug. Caine turned as she steadied herself. He pinched the bridge of his nose, letting out an exasperated sigh.

"Please? I just want to see it."

"Weren't you the one the other day who reminded me there are people out there who want to kill you?" He turned her own words against her.

"Than said it would be perfectly safe."

"Than's an idiot," he retorted, shooting her a quick cautionary glance warning her to drop it

Clearly, she'd caught him in a great mood. Exasperated, she put her hands on her hips. "You won't even know I am there."

"That is impossible," Caine said sarcastically.

"Look, I know you don't like me too much, but I'm doing my best to make the best out of this whole situation." Cara put her hands on her hips. "I'm only here for a short time before they are sending me home. I already know everything. I can't just stay stuck in my room the whole time. You don't even know how long it will be."

Caine closed his eyes, glad he wasn't facing her. She had no idea how much he didn't not like her, but he knew it was better this way. She was so excited, though. He remembered her face when he walked her through Shiyan on Arctus for the first time.

"This isn't a holiday. This is work. We are meeting the locals to bring them supplies they desperately need. We will be busy transporting the supplies to the village. We leave the following morning as soon as we finish."

Cara had to find a way to go with them. This was potentially her only opportunity before they returned to Arctus. "In the morning? I can help. It can't be that hard to stack some boxes."

Caine knew she wasn't going to back down. He looked into her storm grey eyes filled with dreams, ambitions, and… hope; something he hadn't felt in a long time. His resolve slowly crumbled. They would be on the planet for less than eighteen hours. If she was any trouble, he could easily stick her on a pod back to the ship.

"Fine," he snapped.

Cara bit her tongue as hard as she could to keep from smiling.

Caine pinned her with a stern look. "You stick by my side the entire time, and you don't say anything."

"I told you already; you won't even know I'm there."

"I've got work to do." He was more frustrated he had given in to her than with her specifically.

"Got it," she gave a little click with her tongue and pointed her finger at him with an awkward wink. Her cheeks reddened, and she quickly retreated before he could change his mind.

Caine shook his head, exasperated with Cara, and disappointed in himself. Why couldn't he say no to her? He had no problem saying it to everyone else. He knew better than to bend the rules, but what were the rules about this? She was in his custody, and he was supposed to keep her safe. Didn't that mean he needed to keep a close eye on her? How could he do that if she was on the ship while he was on the ground? It was a weak defense at best; one the Council would quickly shoot down, but one of the benefits of being the Commander was he had complete autonomy to run his ship as he saw fit. It meant he had complete authority to handle situations involving Cara as he wanted while she was on board.

He considered calling her back and telling her he changed his mind, but he thought better of it. An extra set of hands wouldn't hurt. The faster they got all the supplies unloaded, the sooner they could return to the ship, and he would be able to put this entire thing behind him.

***

When Cara showed up on the loading dock to join them, Than looked over at Caine, surprised. She was fighting a smirk and losing horribly. Walking in front of Caine and past Than, she boarded the smaller pod. When she was safe on the pod, she winked at Than. Than looked back at Caine.

"Don't say anything," Caine growled at him, brushing past him too.

Than laughed and walked away, shaking his head.

Chapter Twenty-Six

After landing on Turah, Cara walked out of the pod behind Caine. It was like stepping into a third world village. People lived in tiny, thatched-roof huts made from local plant material. There was no running water or electricity and only some rudimentary weapons to protect themselves. Farming was almost impossible, forcing them to rely on food and supplies from the Confederation to stay alive.

The village Jalan was the largest on Turah. Huts were clustered around a large, central gathering space. Beyond the village was a dense forest, where the locals hunted and foraged for whatever was edible.

A flock of grey and brown camu birds flew overhead and vanished beyond the treetops. It looked so similar to Earth, but distinct differences reminded her she wasn't home anymore.

Most people wore simple, loose clothing that covered all their bodies to protect them from the sun.

Cara waved at one of the children, who quickly hid behind her mother. They were afraid of the soldiers dressed in their uniforms. The men of the village thanked the officers and began to move the stacks of supplies.

"There are only a few hours of workable light here. Find somewhere to sit and stay there. Don't get in the way of my crew, or I will have you sent back on the next pod." Caine's stern tone made it clear he wasn't joking.

Caine assisted his crew in unloading the supplies off of the transport pods. Cara made her way off to the side. She sat on a large crate, observing. She spotted a little boy peering at her curiously from a distance. His facial features were slightly different than those of a typical human. He had larger eyes and a smaller than average nose. She smiled and waved. He slowly walked up to her, looking around nervously. He stood on his tiptoes and leaned in to speak into her ear.

"I'm it," he whispered in a heavily accented voice. He poked her in the arm and ran away.

She heard the giggles of children all around her from their various hiding places.

"You little sneak!" she exclaimed. "I'm going to get you!" Caine's orders forgotten, she ran after the boy, and he shrieked with mock terror.

Caine saw Cara get up and rush after the little boy. He almost went after her to tell her to sit back down but seeing how her face lit up as she ran off made him stop. She looked just as innocent as the children did. As he unloaded and stacked supply crates, he watched her play with the children of the village. She knew these old-world games like tag and soccer that was played with a tattered and dirty ball of rolled-up string.

Cara scooped up the little boy, who shrieked with laughter. She looked happy: cheeks rosy and eyes sparkling. He didn't think he had ever seen her look genuinely happy since he had met her. She brought light to his dull life and shook up his routine.

At first, he had hated her for it, turning his world upside down, but she had unlocked something. The doors he had long kept shut now opened to reveal parts of himself he hadn't believed he still had. There she was running around, kicking up clouds of dust, practically glowing. She looked like she belonged. He couldn't risk those kinds of thoughts. Cara was going back to her own time, where she belonged. It was inevitable, he just didn't know how long he had, and a small part of him wanted to enjoy whatever time they had left.

Cara was thoroughly enjoying herself playing with the children. Out of breath, she took a seat on a large crate as the children finish their game. A small girl came up to her, her long hair braided and twisted into little knots across the back of her head. She pointed at Cara and smiled shyly.

"Hello," Cara gave the girl a little wave.

The girl pointed at Cara again.

"I'm Cara."

The little girl beamed. "Toril."

"Nice to meet you, Toril."

The little girl handed her a small white flower, the stem broken where she held it in her hand.

"Thank you." Cara took the flower gently.

The group of children called to Toril, and she went bounding off to play. Cara turned and caught Caine staring at her. She spun the flower between her fingertips. Caine nodded at her curtly and continued with his work.

As the brief daylight faded, a group of women took Cara and braided her hair, weaving in small flowers and vines as decoration. They took some of the earth and mixed it with water, and painted rust-colored stripes and dots on her face. They dressed her in loose garments made of woven grasses and soft furs. The women led her to the gathering, talking and laughing amongst themselves. Some of the children ran alongside them while others ran ahead, excited for the celebration.

The men had covered their faces and arms with a grey clay mixture. As it dried, it turned a ghostly white. As a gesture of acceptance and respect from the people, Caine had the same white clay streaked across his forehead, cheeks, and chin. It was eerily beautiful. It suited him.

The villagers handed bowls of stewed meat and vegetables and bowls to everyone. They sat around a great big fire with the locals, some of them singing and dancing. A few men wore more ornate clothing with fringe on the arms and legs that flapped as they danced.

One of the men danced by Cara and grabbed at her. Caine got tense, but Cara willingly allowed herself to be pulled up and into the dancing crowd. It was a simple circle dance. Cara followed along as best she could, learning the steps. Their dance around the large bonfire was in celebration of the supplies the Archon had brought to them. Their voices filled the air. A group of men sat off to the side, beating their palms onto large drums as they sang. The tempo changed, and the dancing became faster. Cara could feel the joy.

"Come on, Than!" Cara held her hands out as she danced by him and pulled him up into the whirling frenzy too.

A pang of jealousy flared inside Caine.

The festivities ended when the fire had died down to smoldering coals.

A woman came up to Cara and pulled on her sleeve, but Cara didn't understand what she was saying. Unsure, she turned to look for Caine.

"It's all right. Go with her. There has been a place prepared for you to sleep." Caine translated for the woman. Cara was led away. He wished he could keep an eye on her; wished he could be the one taking her to bed. His throat tightened, and he swallowed hard as his thoughts took a scandalous turn. He sensed Than walk up next to him.

"Jealous?" Than asked, following his gaze.

"I have no idea what you mean."

"You know it's okay to be worried about her."

Caine gave Than a sideways glance. "She's an asset; of course, I'm worried about her safety."

"You know that isn't what I meant," Than said, unsurprised by Caine's attempt to deny his feelings. "Have a good night all alone in your bed." Than moseyed off into the night. Alone, Caine watched the smoke dance up into the black sky and vanish.

Cara was taken to a small hut. The woman gestured toward the door, indicating this was hers for the night. Cara nodded her head.

"Terima aitah." Cara thanked the woman in her native tongue.

The woman beamed. Cara pushed open the wooden door. There was a simple, hand-carved, wooden bed, and a wooden chair. She crawled into the creaking bed and fell asleep to the gentle sounds of the night creatures calling.

***

Cara bit back a shriek of surprise as she opened her eyes and found herself face to face with Toril, smiling above her. The little girl giggled at her reaction, and her large brown eyes sparkled mischievously.

"Hetai bornan," she whispered. "Hyvaa beyani habarii."

Cara had no idea what she was saying. The girl laughed again and ran out of the little hut, leaving the door swinging. Beams of light streamed through the one small window of the hut, illuminating the dust Toril had kicked up. Cara stood and washed her face in the small bowl of water on a table in the corner.

Outside she found the villagers already busy with their day. They were tending to gardens, fixing huts, weaving clothes in a circle, and it looked like there was a group of children huddled under a tree being taught. Men helped the Archon's officers move the last of the large wooden crates around while others were opening and unpacking them.

Supplies were distributed to villagers while others were transported to storehouses on the outskirts of the village. A large majority of what was unpacked was food supplies. The planet had thin soil. Paired with minimal precipitation, growing food was a challenge for the villagers, and they relied heavily on regular deliveries. The villagers worked in the quiet heat of the rising sun. It was too quiet. Where were the rest of the children?

Toril raced up, tugging on her hand. She looked scared.

"What is it?" Cara asked.

Toril spoke frantically, but Cara couldn't understand her words. She did, though, understand the urgency. She allowed the little girl to pull her away towards the edge of the village. Through the trees, she could see water ahead, a small river.

The children were pointing to the water, all talking at the same time. Not far from the bank, a young village boy clung to a rock in the rushing water. Cara raced to the edge, searching for anything she could use to throw to him. Fueled by terror, the boy let go of the rock, trying to reach out for her. He was quickly swept away with the current. Without hesitating, Cara jumped in. Several strong strokes closed the distance between them. She grabbed the boy by the back of his shirt, pulling his head out from under the water. He spluttered and coughed.

"I got you. You're okay." She gripped the boy tightly. She started swimming back to shore, but with only one free arm, she made no headway. She was getting pulled further and further downstream by the strong current. She noticed there was a rock right in their path, and they were traveling rapidly towards it. There wouldn't be enough time to get out of the way. With the collision inevitable, Cara wrapped her arms protectively around the boy and did her best to turn her body so he was facing away. They slammed into it. Cara's side took the brunt of the impact. She yelled out in pain, the air rushing from her lungs.

Ahead, another massive rock jutted up from the water. She kicked towards it, using all her remaining energy to reach it. She grabbed hold, and her fingers dug into the stone.

The group of children had disappeared from her view. She hoped they had gone for help. The water crashed into the rock, sending up spray, and Cara coughed as she swallowed water. She clung tighter to the boy. Her fingers ached. She wasn't sure how much longer she would be able to keep a grip on both the boy and the rock at the same time.

Chapter Twenty-Seven

A large group of children rushed into the village, yelling and calling out. The commotion caught Caine's attention. They were so scared their words were not clear as they all shouted over each other. He could only understand a few words, but he managed to translate enough to understand there was something dangerous at the river. Some of the men motioned for him to follow when they ran off to figure out exactly what was going on.

The children ran with them. When they reached the river, they all screamed at once, pointing towards the water. Downstream, Cara clung to the rock with one arm and clutched a boy to her chest with the other.

Caine didn't think twice. He ran down the bank towards them, pulling his jacket off. Throwing it to the ground, he jumped into the river without hesitation and swam out to them.

"Are you okay?" he asked when he reached her.

"Yes." Her voice was weak.

"Stay here," he told her. She rolled her eyes at him, giving him some relief that she was okay.

Cara shifted her grip on the boy to get him in position to grab onto Caine. The boy reached out and clung to Caine's neck. As the boy moved, her tenuous hold on the rock failed, and she was ripped away. Caine grabbed the rock and reached out for Cara. He managed to get a grip on her shirt sleeve and yanked her towards him.

The fabric ripped, and the rushing waters sucked her downstream.

"Cara!" he screamed her name, though he knew it would do no good at this point. "Kuso." He needed to get the boy to safety before he could go after Cara. He hoped she was a decent swimmer.

He adjusted the child on his back and, with a few powerful strokes, reached shallow water. One of the village men pulled the boy off Caine's back. The child burst into tears as the man scooped him up, safe at last.

Caine's attention turned to Cara. He raced along the edge of the river, trying to spot her in the water. Not far ahead of him, her head broke through the surface. His soaked clothes were weighing him down. His legs burned under the strain, but he pushed himself faster. He had to get ahead of her if he had any hope of getting to her. He would never be able to swim fast enough to catch up to her. The rapids became more dangerous up ahead. With a few long strides, he leapt off the side of the embankment into the water.

He sank under the churning whitecaps, fighting against the current that took hold of him. He broke through the surface, scanning it, trying to find her. He spotted her not far behind him, and moments later, Cara slammed into him.

"Hold on to me," he yelled over the roar of the water. She wrapped her arms around him. The water picked up speed, and the thunderous roar of the rapids increased. The river took a steep drop sending them careening out of control over the edge, plunging several meters before hitting the surface with a smack. Cara shrieked and spluttered as water filled her mouth.

"I need you to help me kick back to shore. I can't do this alone." Caine had to get them back to safety before they went over another drop up ahead. "Ready?"

Worn out, Cara could only nod. He pushed off a rock with his feet, and they shot through the water, Cara kicking with him in unison as hard as she could. They closed the distance to the edge, where villagers were waiting to pull them out of the water.

"Are you okay?" Caine knelt in front of her and pushed wet hair out of her face.

She coughed hard, clearing her lungs. "I'm okay," she croaked.

The villagers surrounded her, shouting joyously, some of them tapping her shoulders, others patting her head.

"They're calling you a hero." Caine took a blanket from a woman handing it to him, and wrapped a shivering Cara in it. "You saved the boy's life."

Cara blushed, but her blue lips trembled. Caine lifted her to her feet, but she swayed. He bent down and tucked an arm under her knees and scooped her up. He held her close as her eyes drooped closed.

***

Underneath Cara's closed eyelids, her vision was turned red from the sunlight. She was warm and comfortable. She opened her eyes to a silhouette blocking the sun. Her eyes adjusted and revealed Caine looking down at her. She was lying in his lap, her head resting gently against his chest. She pushed herself up to sitting. The sun was setting just over the trees.

"How are you feeling?"

"Like I got hit by a bus."

Caine frowned. "I'm assuming that's a saying from your time?"

"Something like that." Cara's sharp gasp cut her laugh short. She hissed through her teeth and winced.

"What's wrong?" He looked her over, concerned he had missed seeing an injury.

Cara sat up, rubbing her left side. "I hit a rock in the river. Just sore."

"You need to let Nadir take a look at you. Make sure nothing is broken."

He helped her to her feet and escorted her over to Nadir's medical tent. Nadir was tending to a young pregnant woman. He spoke to her in her native tongue, gave her a small container of pills, and sent her on her way with a smile.

"You had quite an adventure today." He waved a hand, motioning for Cara to approach.

"She hit a rock in the river." Caine didn't allow her to respond. Cara shot him a glare, displeased with him dominating the situation.

"It's just sore; I'm sure it's fine," she didn't want to trouble Nadir when he was supposed to be caring for the villagers.

"Come on, let's take a look," Nadir patted the exam table next to him. Cara groaned as she slid up onto the surface.

"May I?" Nadir gestured to her shirt.

Cara nodded. He lifted her shirt, and Caine forced his eyes away. Cara noticed and bit back a smile.

Nadir adjusted his glasses on his nose. "You have quite a bruise, my dear."

Cara looked down; Nadir was right. A blotchy, purple mark covered a large part of her side, from her ribs down to her hip. Caine stole a glance and was surprised by the size of the injury.

"I wouldn't say it's fine, Cara, would you?" Caine couldn't keep the hint of snark from his tone.

She didn't argue. The look she gave him told him she agreed, although reluctantly.

"You could have been killed out there," he said sharply.

Cara couldn't stop the small sigh from escaping.

Just like that, the comforting, understanding Caine from moments ago was gone, and now he was cold, almost angry at her. "Going in after him was incredibly stupid."

"What was I supposed to do? Let him drown?"

"No, you should have come to get one of my officers or me."

"By the time I would have reached you, it would have been too late." Cara wasn't sure why she needed to defend her decision. It had been the right thing to do.

"What if it had been too late by the time I reached you?" Caine countered.

There it was; the real reason he was angry. Some of her annoyance ebbed.

"Caine, get me the container of cream over there on the middle shelf." Nadir pointed, cutting the tense moment short.

Caine turned to get the cream, and Cara watched as the great Commander took orders from the short, older man in front of her. Nadir had such a fatherly quality to him she wasn't surprised Caine did as he asked. It was evident Caine had deep-rooted respect for the doctor.

"This will help the blood reabsorb and relieve some of the pain. You should be just fine by tomorrow." Nadir pulled the lid off. As he did, a woman entered the hut, carrying a wailing baby. Nadir handed the cream to Caine. "You can finish up," Nadir directed at a very dismayed looking Caine before walking away.

Caine approached Cara slowly. "I need to..." Caine ran a hand through his hair. "I guess I just, uh, should..." He trailed off awkwardly.

Cara pulled the up hem of her shirt, revealing the bruise. Caine carefully spread the cream across her skin. She sucked in a breath as the combination of cold cream and warm fingers startled her.

"Sorry, did that hurt?" Caine apologized, pulling his hand away.

"No, no, you're fine." Cara didn't want to admit he was affecting her as much as he was. He searched her face for any sign of discomfort as he worked. He lowered her shirt when he finished.

"Um, thank you," Cara told him. Caine helped her off the table.

"Cara?" Nadir called her name as she was leaving. "No more adventures," he chided lightly. As much as she wanted to promise him, she had the uneasy feeling that her adventures were only just beginning.

Chapter Twenty-Eight

The Iyas, the village leader, requested the crew stay another night so they could celebrate Cara's rescue of the boy that morning. He had also requested she sit next to him that evening at dinner. His dark hair had been pulled back and woven with green vines. White clay paint dotted his forehead, and there were two stripes down each cheek. Around his neck lay a circle of black feathers tied around long, woven grasses.

When he stood, the whole village quieted down. She could hear the crackling of the bonfire, twigs snapping, and damp wood hissing. The night creatures hummed and chirped in the distance.

The Iyas gestured to Cara as he spoke. She didn't understand his words, but she grasped the meaning and the depth of his gratitude for her saving the child's life. He presented her with a black stone pendant on a cord and placed it over her head. It had been carved into the shape of a seven-pointed star, except the ends were rounded off, making it looked more like a flower. It had been polished until it glinted like glass in the firelight. The simplicity of the design made it even more stunning. Cara rubbed it, enjoying the feeling of the smooth surface under her fingers.

"Terima aitah," she hoped he would grasp the depth of her appreciation for such a meaningful gift.

The chief smiled broadly, magnifying his deep wrinkles. After dinner, everyone remained seated around the fire until it was just a dim flickering flame. The villagers and crew talked in hushed tones while children lay sleeping in their mother's laps.

Cara rose to make her way back to her small hut. When she stood, so did Caine.

"I'll walk you back."

"You don't have to do that," she protested, but he was already by her side.

"I want to apologize for what I said earlier. What you did today was incredibly brave."

"I couldn't sit there and let him drown. Anyone would have done it. It was the right thing to do." She looked up at the sky. "Back home, we have stories for different shapes made by stars."

"Constellations?" he asked, surprised they both knew the concept.

"There aren't any I recognize, but I doubt I would here."

Caine glanced up, searching the sky. "There," he pointed up. "See the small triangle of stars right there?"

Cara followed his finger, and there were three stars in a small triangular cluster, shining just slightly brighter than all the others around them.

"They're called the Three Sisters. There is an old legend. When the journey was made from Old Earth, three sisters were born on one of the ships. They all looked exactly alike, identical in every way. Even their own mother couldn't tell them apart at times. One night a passenger attacked one of the sisters, doing horrible things to her before she managed to escape. The sisters informed the authorities, but before the man could be held accountable for his crimes, he was found murdered in his bed. Everyone blamed the sister who had been attacked for getting her revenge, but when they came to arrest her, they were unable to tell the three girls apart. They tried to get the girls to admit to who was who, but they wouldn't confess. They refused to turn against each other. Even their mother refused to admit which daughter was which.

In that time, if you were charged with a crime, the punishment was far more severe. Keeping criminals alive was seen as a burden, wasting the limited resources the ship had for its citizens. Eventually, the one sister was found guilty of murder, but still, they refused to give their sister up. In the end, all three were sentenced to death.

Their mother begged for their lives to be spared, but the ruling was final. So, she was given a choice; pick two daughters to save. The hope was she would pick the two innocent daughters, revealing the guilty one, but the girls told their mother not to choose. When the time came to cast the sister off, the three held hands together. As she watched her daughters taken away to die in space, the mother kept her silence and prayed to the stars for the sisters to be protected, saved somehow. The sisters were cast into space, still holding each other's hands. As they floated away, they began to glow, brighter and brighter until they turned into stars themselves. Their mother's prayers had been heard. Their love had saved them, and they remained together in the sky for all eternity."

Cara stared up at the stars, thinking about the three sisters who sacrificed themselves before they would betray each other. "They loved each other so much they died for each other."

"Sometimes, when you love someone that much, dying is the least you would do to protect them." His voice was hushed as he gazed skyward.

The way he said it made Cara suspect he knew what that was like from personal experience.

They stopped in front of her hut. He stared at her so intensely, for a moment, Cara thought he would kiss her, but he cleared his throat, said goodnight, and walked away. Cara went inside and threw herself onto the bed, yanking the covers over her head as if to ward off the dreams of Caine she knew would be inevitable.

Caine woke up in the middle of the night. Something wasn't right; it was far too quiet. The night creatures should have been humming away, but there were none of the usual calls and songs he expected to hear.

He sat still in the darkness, listening. At first, there was only silence, but he waited. There. The faint crack of twigs in the distance. He reached over and slipped his laser pistol out from under his jacket and quietly swung his legs over the side of the bed. Caine's bare feet hit the dusty dirt floor without a sound. Carefully, he pushed the wooden door of the hut open and stepped out into the night. The village was bathed in ghostly starlight. He searched the shadows for any movement, but even the breeze was holding its breath. The dead of night exploded into chaos. Laser fire chattered, and instantaneously, the whole village was lit up like Christmas. Huts were on fire. People were running. Women were screaming. Caine rushed towards the panicked villagers, yelling orders at his officers.

"Zora, find Cara!"

Zora ran off towards the huts on the far side of the village. Caine grabbed a woman stumbling out of a hut engulfed in flames, bleeding from a wound on her side. He wrapped his arm around her and pulled her away to safety. Hysterically, she screamed something at him. He roughly translated her panicked cries. It sounded like 'little child,' but he couldn't be sure. He raced back into the burning hut. A baby shrieked in a basket on the floor, tucked in a corner by the bed. He grabbed the wiggling bundle and raced out, coughing. Handing the baby back to the sobbing woman, she clutched the infant close to her chest. He couldn't stay to comfort her; he was needed elsewhere. Caine ran towards the chaos.

Cara woke with a jolt to the sounds of screaming. She rolled off the bed, hitting the hard floor with a thud, and squeezed under it for cover. When the door burst open, Cara froze in terror.

"Cara!" Zora screamed her name frantically; fear stained her voice when she spotted the empty bed.

Cara rolled out from under the bed.

"Stars, Cara." Zora yanked her off the floor abruptly. "We need to move." The urgency in her voice was echoed in the frenetic nature of her actions.

"What's going on?"

"Hostiles!"

Cara's heart skipped. Zora pulled her out the door.

"Where's Caine?"

"Fighting," Zora guided her along the edge of the hut, but they came under fire.

She pushed Cara down, and they crouched on the ground, occasionally peering around the corner of the hut to return fire.

"We aren't going to make it back to the ship," Zora said, mostly noting it for herself. "Okay. New plan. You get to the woods." Zora pointed at the trees about a hundred yards away. "Find cover and stay there until I come for you." She pushed Cara away. "Run," she shouted and turned to fire on the attackers trying to draw their fire as Cara escaped.

Cara fled towards the woods as fast as she could. She was halfway across when the Hostiles spotted her. Laser fire hit the ground around her. She only hoped to find a hiding spot from them in the thick forest. She had just reached the edge when an agonizing burning sensation ripped through her arm. She stumbled but pushed on, her drive to escape outweighing everything else.

Cara was running blind, her hands out in front of her pushing away branches. Laser fire ripped through the leaves all around her. She ran faster, unable to see where she was going and hoping to find somewhere to hide before they caught up.

She tripped and fell to the ground, hitting her head on something hard. She clutched her injured head, biting her tongue to hold back a scream that would reveal her location to her pursuers.

Hands reached out from the darkness and grabbed at her. They had found her. One last deep moan of agony escaped her before she blacked out.

Chapter Twenty-Nine

Cara tried opening her eyes, but they would only open into thin slits, crusted shut by something. She was being dragged across the dirt by her wrists, tied together over her head. Every stone gouged into her sides, each jerk making her joints feel like they were being pulled apart.

There was ear-splitting shouting and shrieking, like wild animals fighting. She squinted, trying to make out her surroundings. There were people around her, cheering as she was dragged through the crowd.

They were dressed as if they had been ripped from the pages of a medieval Viking book. Furs and bones adorned their bodies mixed with more modern-looking pieces of leather-like material covered in metal spikes. Their faces were painted - no - tattooed. Many had black hair hanging in long matted dreadlocks around their faces. Some of the women had their hair crudely cut in spiky, matted messes. Many had facial piercings.

They were howling at her, shaking their fists at the sky victoriously. One of them threw a rock at her. It smashed into her shoulder as she turned her head away, trying to protect her exposed face. A woman approached and called out a command to whoever was dragging her. They stopped. The woman stood over her for a moment. She spat out harsh, angry-sounding words Cara did not understand. The woman balled up her fist and slammed it into Cara's head. Blackness descended once again.

When she came around again, every fiber of her being was in excruciating pain. She could barely lift her head to look around at her surroundings. Her left eye was swollen most of the way shut. She could see she was chained to a chair in a small room. The metal panels bolted to the walls were rusted, and chains hung in one corner. On the door were scratch marks as if someone had been trying to claw their way out. Her heart sank at the realization she was being held prisoner by Hostiles.

She wasn't sure how long she had been sitting there. It could have been two hours or ten, but time seemed irrelevant. The rusty metal door in front of her creaked open. A man with short, curly black hair and black eyes entered. He was wearing all black. His arms and hands were so heavily covered in tattoos there was very little skin showing. There was also one long tattoo on either side of his face. It was a web of intricate curved lines interspersed with strange symbols that curled their way along his skin, from his forehead down the sides of his face and continuing down his neck. He walked over and crouched down in front of her. Cara couldn't stop a gasp from escaping when she found herself staring into ink-black eyes. Even where the whites of his eyes should have been, they too had been colored black. He reached out and gently touched her cheek. She jerked her head away from him.

"It truly is amazing to finally meet you, Cara." He spoke in a quiet, lilting tone. "I have been waiting a long time for this. Time travel certainly suits you."

Panic flared. He knew who she was. He knew about her not being from this time. He smiled warmly at her, but his horrific black eyes remained cold; it wasn't genuine. She could see the truth in his stare. He was nothing short of crazy.

"Do you know who I am, sweet Cara? My name is Re'em Samas, the leader of the Samandran Clan. I am their tu'le, a title earned through blood and fire. As unfortunate as it is that we have finally met under such regrettable circumstances, I am sure you and I will be able to become good friends."

Cara kept her mouth shut and looked away. She was not going to give in to him.

Samas reached up and grabbed her chin. She tried to pull away, but he held it firmly in his grip, forcing her to look at him.

"All you have to do is give me what I want, and you can go - free as a bird." He fluttered his fingers towards the door and dug his nails deep into her skin.

Cara couldn't help it; her eyes automatically flicked towards the exit.

"Ah, I can see I finally have your attention." He leered at her with a sardonic grin. Cara squeezed her eyes shut when he leaned forward. He gently ran his fingertips down her cheek. "You are so special, Cara. Did you know that? I am sure you do. The Commander must tell you every day. All you have to do is help me get what I want, and I will let you go. I give you my word as my solemn vow." His voice was almost sing-song.

"I won't help you!" Cara yanked her chin away.

He grabbed her face again, pressing his fingers into her cheeks, and squeezed so hard her lips pursed. "Oh, sweet Cara, don't you want to know what I want first before you turn me down? This offer will not come again."

He laid his hands on the dirty floor and rubbed them around. He pulled them up, looking at the wet, muddy grime now covering them. He stood and grabbed her arms, his dirty hands covering her wound. He squeezed.

Cara screamed. Samas grasped the sides of her face, smearing the muck on her cheeks. She gagged as he hovered over her.

"You are going to deliver our dear Commander's head to me in a box," he cheerfully whispered in her ear. An icy wave of fear rolled through her.

"No!" She pushed against her bonds. If only she could leap up and tear his throat out. "I would never do that!" Tears rolled down her cheeks.

"Oh, Cara, but don't you realize you already are?" The harsh, maniacal laugh that emerged from him made her skin crawl. "Caine, your precious Commander, he will come for you and-"

"Caine will never negotiate with you," she snapped at him. Deep down, she hoped her words were true. She knew he would risk his life to save hers, but the Council would never allow it. Negotiations with Hostiles were strictly forbidden.

"The dear Commander has always liked to pretend he plays by the rules. He's just a little boy in some very big shoes. Besides, if he doesn't want to come, I have lots of other ways to convince him." Samas giggled like a child.

"You're a monster." She bared her teeth at him.

"Oh, sweet Cara, we all have a monster inside us. Maybe if you let yours out of its cage, you'd see just how much fun it can be. Maybe you could even join us!" He gasped as if it was the best idea he'd ever had.

"You're insane!"

"So uptight, sweet girl. Are you afraid the Commander won't love you anymore if he sees the darkness hiding inside you?" Samas mocked with an exaggerated pout.

"You don't know what love is. You're disgusting." Bile rose in her throat. She spat at his feet.

Samas brought his hand up and backhanded her. Her head snapped back. She tasted blood on her tongue. "You think you have all the answers. You think you know what we are. Condemned by a bunch of self-righteous bastards, sitting up there in their white tower believing they are entitled to the universe and everything in it, acting like they are the greater good. They want to destroy us, but don't you see? They need us. They need us to make themselves look good for the people. They have made us the enemy, but they have done terrible, terrible things. We all have." Rage glinted in his black eyes.

"I've done nothing."

Samas stared at her, a delirious look of raving lunacy twisting his features. "You've done more than you can imagine."

A sickening squeeze worked its way down her neck, and a slimy feeling curled like an oil slick over her limbs. There was a piercing pain like someone was drilling a hole into her forehead. She recognized it immediately. He was trying to access her mind like Caine had.

"You're an Esper," she whispered. How was it even possible? She looked into the void of his black eyes. He had managed to disguise the shade of vibrant blue she was sure they should be.

He laughed, his tone gleeful, yet cruel. "Oh, so smart, my sweet little Cara. Our dear Commander certainly shared some of his little secrets with you, but he has so many more."

Cara frowned, not understanding his meaning.

He bent forward and whispered menacingly into her ear. "Monsters, my dear." He turned to go.

"How are you an Esper?"

Samas turned. "Isn't it wonderful?" He clasped his hands together, grinning as if he was taking great pleasure in this. He chuckled and slammed the door shut behind him.

Cara sat in the cold cell, tied to the chair for hours. Her limbs were numb. They ached every time she moved. She could barely flex her fingers and toes and couldn't stay awake. She fell into a restless sleep, which did little to dull the punishing throbbing in her arm. She kept drifting in and out of lucidity, losing track of time, of reality. No one came to see her. Samas had just left her there alone. She hoped Caine would rescue her from this place, but she knew he would never be allowed to negotiate with Samas. The Council would just call her a loss and move on. In the end, it was almost better if Caine just left her here. It would be easier for him to go back to living his life without her, as he had been before she showed up and turned his whole world upside down.

As her thoughts descended into darkness, she dozed off again and dreamed; bright blue eyes haunting her.

Chapter Thirty

The door flew open, slamming into the wall. The crash echoed off the metal. Cara jerked awake with a choked gasp. A different man entered, his long black hair braided and held up with bones. He had bones strung around his neck, and a tattoo circling his eyes made it look like he was wearing a mask.

He untied her from the chair and heaved her up to her feet. Her weak legs couldn't hold her weight, and she struggled to stand. Disoriented, Cara didn't know where the man was taking her. He pulled her down a long corridor as she stumbled alongside him, struggling to keep her feet under her. He shoved her through a door, and she fell to the ground. Bright daylight blinded her momentarily.

A crowd had gathered in a circle. Everyone was cheering and screaming like wild animals. The man grabbed her by her shirt, dragging her several feet on her knees before he roughly shoved her into the center of the ring of people, causing her to fall to her knees. Cara scrambled back to her feet, trying to keep an eye on the crowd surrounding her.

Above her, Samas stepped to the edge of the roof and extended his arms towards the crowd.

"We have long wanted to see the Confederation suffer for their crimes. We may not get the justice we seek today, but at least we can revel in the suffering of one who has caused us pain beyond measure!"

The Hostiles jeered at Cara. Some reached out to grab at her; others pushed at her, trying to make her fall down again. At the opposite end of the circle, the people stepped aside, parting to make way for a woman to enter the ring. She was tall and muscular, carrying a long wooden staff. The woman pinned her black eyes on Cara. She bared her teeth; they had been filed into sharp points. The woman stuck out her tongue, running it over the points, and growled. She laughed cruelly, spinning the staff in a circle in front of her. People around her patted her on the back, cheering at her.

Someone threw a broken staff at Cara's feet. Cara was struck with the terrifying realization she was expected to fight this woman. The woman made a mock lunge at Cara, and she jumped away, but the surrounding crowd pushed her back into the middle. As Cara bent to pick up her meager weapon, the other woman charged at her, aiming a kick at her legs. Cara found herself momentarily airborne and landed flat on her back with the air rushing from her lungs.

Before Cara could move, the woman was on top of her, her arm across her throat. Unable to breathe, Cara clawed at her arm as she kicked her feet frantically, trying to find purchase. She couldn't get away. Just when she was about to lose consciousness, Samas called out, and the woman roughly released her. Cara rolled to her side, coughing and gasping. Hands grabbed her and dragged her inside, back to her cell, throwing her in and slamming the door shut, but they didn't rechain her to the chair. Cara pushed herself into the far corner and found a small chunk of rock. She scratched a small tally mark onto the wall.

Cara wasn't sure how much time passed, but all too soon, she was dragged back outside. Samas stood above her again, but the look in his eye was different. Cara knew this time he wouldn't call the woman off. He wouldn't stop her.

She needed to think fast if she was going to survive the next few minutes. She had taken a few self-defense classes in college, but nothing even close to what she was about to face. She was weak, injured, and hadn't eaten or drank in far too long. She didn't stand a chance if she directly defended herself.

The large Hostile woman stepped towards her. Cara clenched her small weapon defensively, knowing Samas hadn't given it to her to make it a fair fight. He was toying with her. He wanted to watch her try and fail; to give her false hope, make her think she had a chance. He was like a predator playing with its meal before the kill. She wasn't going to allow it to happen, not today.

The woman swung at her, and Cara ducked out of the way. She rushed to the other side of the circle, trying to put distance between them. Avoiding attack was her only option. Again, the woman came at her. Cara jumped away, dodging the blow. The crowd roared angrily. Above her, Cara could hear Samas laughing wildly. The woman turned, looking even angrier than before. Cara couldn't avoid the full force attack this time. The woman leapt at her, knocking the staff out of Cara's hands. Cara saw the fist flying towards her face only a split second before it knocked her into quiet darkness.

When Cara regained consciousness, she was back in her cell. She had been dumped facedown on the dirty floor. Her head throbbed. She struggled to roll over onto her back, amazed she was still alive. Her body shook uncontrollably.

A cup of dirty water was by the door. She drank it, not even caring about any health risks. Hours later, a bowl of tasteless broth was slid in for her. She considered not eating it. What was the point? Samas was only trying to give her the energy to fight again, for his amusement. She would rather he kill her outright instead of torturing her for hours. Either way, the result was the same.

A sharp jolt of pain broke her out of her stupor. No, she wasn't going to die here. Even if Caine didn't manage to save her, she refused to give Samas the satisfaction of her giving up so easily.

She picked up the crudely forged metal bowl. Her hands were shaking so hard she could barely hold it steady.

Most of it spilled on the floor. Cara lifted it to her lips, drinking down the remaining lukewarm liquid. Her stomach churned. She lay back against the wall, trying to keep it down. She needed it and needed to be ready.

The door opened not long after. Cara's heart sank; she wasn't ready for another round. When Samas walked in, she pushed back into the corner as far as she could go.

He sat on the chair she had been tied to, slinging one of his legs casually over a metal arm. "Are you enjoying the entertainment?"

Cara refused to answer, pinning him with a frigid glare.

Samas tutted. "I'll take that as a no. Too bad. I was hoping you were enjoying your stay here with us." He carefully pulled something from the front pocket of his jacket. He hid it in his clenched fist for a moment before he released his grip. The stone pendant gifted to her on Turah dangled from his fingers.

"That doesn't belong to you."

"The Turian symbol of protection. Ironic, isn't it? Maybe they shouldn't have given it away. It didn't do you any good, did it? They certainly could have used it." He was mocking the villagers, making fun of the fact he had slaughtered them.

"They were good people. You killed them for no reason."

"No reason? Oh, sweet Cara. We are sparing them. What would you have us do? Leave them with no food, no supplies so they can die a slow and painful death? Let the children suffer? No. We make it quick. Killing them is mercy."

"You actually believe that," Cara breathed. "You're insane."

Questioning the validity of his motivation sent Samas into a rage. He rushed at Cara, grabbing her by the throat, pinning her to the ground.

"Death is better than any life under the choking rule of the Confederation. They think they are the only ones who get to choose who deserves life? What makes us any different?"

"You're Hostiles," Cara wheezed.

Samas released her. He rocked back to crouch on his heels in front of her, his fingers over his chin and lips.

"Quite the name they've given to us. More like exiles. You know nothing about us. You don't know our history except what they wrote in the books. The victors always get to write whatever they want. We ended up here because we didn't bow down to their authority. They cast us out and now look at us. Look at what we have become. We are survivors!"

"What does killing Caine prove?"

"An eye for an eye, my dear. The Confederation will only respect force; therefore, we must show it." He stood in front of her with his arms outstretched, as if he was a god in his own reality. "They think they are the saviors of this system, that they saved humanity. They did not. They chose the worthiest ones to live in their perfect planets and left leave the rest to rot away in the wastelands. They call us their enemy simply because we questioned their authority. We saved ourselves. We do what it takes. The question is, will you?"

When the door slammed behind him, Cara broke down. Samas killed out of a perversely twisted sense of sympathy, making him even more terrifying. He truly believed his actions were justified. Yet, his hatred of the Confederation was not all ideological; it was also personal. He had an intense, deep-rooted vendetta against Caine. What kind of history did they have? Caine hadn't been forthcoming with the truth twice already, until she had confronted him. Samas said Caine had more secrets. Cara believed him.

She dragged herself across the room, trying to make it to the chair. Feeling faint from exhaustion and dehydration, she collapsed to the floor, unable to make it any further.

This time when the door opened, she was ready. She didn't know why she was being used as a human gladiator, but with her hopes of a rescue slipping away with every passing day, she knew one of these fights would be her last.

She wouldn't be able to keep this up for much longer, not in her current condition. If she used sheer force, she would lose against a much stronger opponent. Any kind of stealth strategy wasn't a feasible option given how weak she was. At least she had managed to come up with a few feasible options for how to deal with whatever Samas planned on throwing at her this time.

She was still trying to formulate an alternate plan as she was shoved into the ring.

Every single plan she'd thought up turned to smoke when the crowd parted. A young boy walked into the ring with her. He had black paint smeared across his face. He bared his teeth at her in a snarl as he raised a long sword in front of him. Someone in the crowd tossed Cara a slim staff for defense. It rolled up to her feet, stopping when it hit the toe of her boot. Cara looked up at Samas in panicked confusion. They expected her to fight a child?

He smiled down at her with deranged glee, eyes wide with exhilaration, and made a waving motion with a hand.

The young boy launched himself at Cara with a battle cry, slicing through the air with his sword. She dodged the first strike, but he kept coming at her, forcing her to participate. She lifted the staff to block the blows he rained down on her. The boy moved quickly. With one easy swing, he slashed the side of her calf. She fell to the ground, clutching her leg with one hand, and raised the staff with the other as the boy brought his sword down. The sharp blade stuck into the wood, and he ripped it out of her grasp. She was defenseless. The boy advanced, holding the sword out.

"Stop," she pleaded, tears rolling down her cheeks. "Please stop!"

She pushed herself across the ground, trying to keep her distance. With another shrieking cry, the boy raised the sword and rushed at her. It happened in a split second. Something slid across the dirt and hit her leg.

A gun.

Instinct drove her to grab it and raise it, aiming at her attacker. Cara pulled the trigger. The boy collapsed at her feet, mere inches away, with the sword still clutched in his grasp. Cara swallowed hard as time seemed to slow and grind to a halt. A pool of blood slowly spread out from the boy's chest, oozing over the ground until it touched Cara's shoe.

"No!" She threw the gun to the side and pressed a shaking hand to her mouth, biting her knuckles to keep from screaming. She killed a child. She killed him without even thinking about it: her body had just reacted.

The Hostile woman she had fought walked towards her but did not attack; instead, she stopped a few feet away. Hands grabbed Cara from behind. Two strong men forced her to her knees, holding her arms out to the side. The woman knelt in front of her and dipped her hand into the pool of blood, and dragged her hand down over Cara's cheek, smearing her face with the hot blood of the boy she'd just killed. Cara gagged, but her stomach was empty. Nothing came up as she retched.

The woman pulled a small dagger from the waistband of her pants. She tugged the collar of Cara's shirt aside and dug the knife into her skin. Cara screamed in agony, trying to rip herself free. As the dagger sliced through her skin, she wished she would pass out, but the blissful black never came. When the men let go, she slumped over. The woman shoved her. Cara fell backward to the ground. The woman climbed on top of her, straddling her stomach to finish this attack. When she finished, she climbed off and vanished. Samas strolled up to admire her handiwork.

"Oh, sweet Cara. I told you, we do what it takes to survive. It's them or us. You let the monster out. And now," he pulled at her shirt to look at the wound on her chest, "you will always be one of us."

Samas kicked her, there was a sharp snapping noise, and pain so bright and fierce Cara couldn't scream, let alone breathe. Adrenaline coursed through her and mixed with shock, numbing all sensation until cold tremors washed over her.

Cara let her head roll to the side. Dark spots dotted her vision. The crowd dissipated, leaving while she lay bleeding on the ground, unable to move.

Cara laid there long into the night, not moving. The stars peeked out as the sky darkened, and she found the Three Sisters constellation. They never gave in; they never gave up. But they weren't alone; they had each other. She was alone. She didn't cry. Her final shred of willpower faded away to nothingness.

At some point in the night, men came and dragged her back to the cell. She crawled to the corner, empty and numb. She wished sleep would take over her, but the escape she was desperate for never came.

Chapter Thirty-One

Caine scrambled in the darkness, trying to make sense of the attack that had just taken place. Backup support from the Archon had just arrived, but they were too late. The attack had ended as abruptly as it had begun. The Hostiles had invaded the village, killed dozens of people, and left. Their ship had arrived out of nowhere, cloaking mechanisms keeping it hidden from the Archon's radar.

Caine picked his way through the destruction. The transport pods were evacuating the remaining villagers to the ship to be treated for injuries and held until they could be returned to the village to rebuild.

Than walked out of a nearby hut. "Caine, we have to go. The last pod is leaving."

"We have to find Cara; Zora was with her." He turned to look for the pair.

Than stopped him, placing a hand on his arm. "Caine, they already did a life-scan. No one is in the woods around the village. Zora probably already got them both back on the ship. We have to go," he urged as the last transport pod's engines roared to life.

Caine looked down at the destruction as they lifted off. Than was right. Zora would have headed for the safety of the ship, where Cara was better protected. Still, he couldn't shake the sensation that something wasn't right. He wasn't going to ignore his instincts this time.

"Do another life scan," he instructed the pilot. The pilot nodded and circled the village, scanning the ground for signs of life. There were none. Caine clenched his fists. Cara had better be on the ship; otherwise, he was about to rain hell down on the universe.

As soon as they landed on the ship, he searched for her. He went immediately to Medical, where Nadir was struggling with the overwhelming number of patients. Villagers were on tables; wounded crew were sitting on the floor. Zora leaned against a wall, holding gauze to a wound on her leg.

"Where is Cara?"

Zora paled even more. "You don't have her?" she asked, nervously wringing her hands.

Caine's blood ran cold.

"Where is she?" he thundered.

"We came under fire. I told her to get to the woods and hide until I came for her. I drew their fire so she could find cover and hide. I went to find her but couldn't. I assumed she had made her way back here, or you had found her."

Caine punched the wall next to Zora, causing her to flinch. "You better hope she's back on this ship," he growled at her.

Zora's eyes filled with tears, and she looked down.

Caine went back up to the holding area where the surviving villagers were being triaged, but Cara wasn't there. She wasn't in her room, either.

Caine stared at Cara's empty bed for a minute before making his way to the Bridge. "Than," he spoke into his comm.

"Yes?"

"Check all vitals on the ship. I want her found."

"Working on it now."

Caine stood next to his commander's station at the back of the room. Than came up a short time later and looked at him with a worried look creasing his brow.

"Sir," Than spoke, his official tone instantly put Caine on guard. "I cannot register any heat signature belonging to Cara. It doesn't appear she is on the ship." He sounded almost apologetic.

"Run it again," Caine demanded.

Everyone on the Bridge was silent and still.

"We'll find her."

"I want everyone sent back down there to look for her. We are not leaving until we find her."

Than gestured to the other officers following his orders, and everyone went scrambling to do their job.

Caine stepped into his office. He needed to get himself under control. He swiped at an empty mug on his desk, and it flew across the room, hitting the wall with a clang.

Than came in, lips pressed together. "We will find her."

"This would never have happened in the first place if she had stayed on the ship like she was supposed to."

"I know. This is my fault." Than apologized, but Caine held a hand up.

"No, the blame is entirely mine. I made the final call. Whatever happens now, it's on me." Caine straightened his jacket and took a deep breath. "I just hope we aren't too late."

***

Caine and his crew scoured every inch of the village and woods. Dozens of bodies were found, none of them was hers.

"Sir, we found blood in the woods, on a fallen log."

"Take me there."

The officer led him into the thick grove of trees. Caine imagined Cara running through these woods, pushing at the branches, and looking for somewhere safe to wait. The officer stopped, pointing a light down in front of them. The light glinted off something shiny. There was a thin film of dried blood on the log. Caine picked off a chunk of the wood and handed it to his officer.

"Get this to Nadir."

The officer took it and ran off. Caine sat on the log in the dark, rethinking the attack and sending Cara off with Zora. He'd made so many mistakes.

A deep, gnawing sensation settled in the pit of his stomach. He knew in his gut the blood was hers. She was the only one unaccounted for, and they hadn't found her body. She had gone to the woods to hide and had been injured, or, worse, taken by the Hostiles. How had they even known where they would be? Only the Council and his crew knew when and where they would be stopping. It wasn't public information. Someone had told the Hostiles where they would be and when. It could not have been purely coincidental they attacked while they were there.

He did a mental rundown of his crew. He couldn't afford to be overly suspicious right now, but the circumstances just were too coincidental to be purely an accident. He feared he had a leak on his ship, and Cara had been caught in the crossfire. She was just another innocent victim of his poor judgement.

A beam of light swept across his face, breaking his train of thought. Than pushed through the underbrush and spotted Caine sitting on the log.

"You've been out here for over an hour."

Had he been out there that long? He had been lost in his own self-pity when he was supposed to be the one leading rescue and recovery efforts. His brother was right; he was a disgrace to his position.

"We need to get you back up to the ship. Nadir wants to see you."

Caine got back to the ship as quickly as he could and hurried to Medical.

"Is it Cara's?" he asked as he entered the room.

Nadir nodded.

Caine upended his chair. It crashed against the wall with a sharp crack.

She was gone. He had failed to protect her. He should never have let her go with them.

Xan came running into the room at breakneck speed, breathing hard enough he knew she had run the entire way from the Bridge. Whatever she had to say wasn't just urgent; it was critical. "Commander, we are receiving a link for communication. Source unknown, it's highly encrypted."

Caine raced to the Bridge with her. "Patch it through," he ordered as he crossed the room to his desk. Xan slid into her chair, working quickly.

The screen crackled. It was blurry for a second before a face appeared. A familiar face Caine never wanted to see again. Re'em Samas, leader of the Samandran Hostile Clan, smiled coolly at him.

"Hello, Commander. I think I have something that belongs to you."

"If you hurt her-" It was a weak and empty threat at this point. He had no idea where Samas had taken her.

"Please, please," Samas held his hands up, an equally empty gesture of peace, "I assure you, she will remain alive as long as you comply."

"What do you want?" Caine snapped.

"Let's try and keep this civil Commander," Samas mocked. "I want you, Commander, if I may be frank. You will deliver yourself over to me, alone, and I promise Cara will go free, unharmed. You have twenty-four hours to give me your answer; otherwise, Cara dies."

"I am coming. I will get Cara, and I will kill you," he said sharply. Samas grinned and laughed gleefully as Caine cut the link abruptly. He turned to his crew.

"Set a new course to…"

"Caine, I don't think this is a good idea," Than interrupted.

"It's a good thing I wasn't looking for your input." Caine turned and tapped away on the display screen, bringing up maps and charts of the system.

"Nik," Than said firmly. Several crew members nearby went deathly quiet and hurried away. Caine turned to face him. Than hadn't used his given name in a long time, but it was the only way to get through to him.

"You need to think about this. The Confederation-"

"Damn the Confederation. I will not let someone else get killed because of my mistakes!"

Caine stormed out of the room. His greatest nightmare had come to pass. Than followed him into his quarters.

"Caine, please," Than pleaded. "You know as well as I do, he will not let Cara go if you turn yourself over to him. He will kill her either way. There has to be another way to get her back."

"There is no other way!"

There was no reasoning with him right now. Than would have to wait until he calmed down and speak to him then.

**

Than found Caine the next morning.

"We are going after him," Caine greeted him.

Than hurried behind him to the Bridge. Caine contacted Samas using the encrypted link.

"We will not be negotiating for her release. I am coming to get Cara, and I will kill you." Caine cut the link abruptly without giving him a chance to respond.

He turned to his crew. "Locate his ship and prepare for an attack."

Chapter Thirty-Two

Caine called the Council, dreading the conversation he was about to have. The screen flickered with the blue-tinged image of the Council.

"Samas has Cara."

No one spoke, not even Saar. Caine specifically looked at Shiro for any sign of reaction. There was none. He remained stone-faced.

"I believe someone on my ship has been leaking information to the Hostiles. I am requesting permission from the Council to get Cara back."

"Absolutely not," Viraha responded with a shake of her head, and the long, delicate gold chains she wore on her ears jingled.

"How exactly was Samas able to take her?" Saar asked.

Caine had known the question would be asked eventually.

"We were attacked during our supply drop."

"It still doesn't explain how she ended up in his hands." Viraha tilted her head questioningly.

"She was in the village when they attacked and was taken."

"Let me make sure I understand this. You took her on the supply drop with you, allowing her to be taken hostage by a Hostile clan? All completely unauthorized, of course," Saar appeared almost pleased at the gold mine Caine was hand-delivering him.

Caine ignored him. He would not be baited into an argument.

"And now, you're requesting permission to rescue her. I find your lack of good judgement in this situation extremely disturbing, Commander," Saar finished.

"You may hold me accountable for my decisions, but do not punish Cara for my errors."

"Oh, mark my words, you will be held accountable." Saar now turned to the Council. "Under no circumstances should we allow a rescue mission."

"It's far too risky," Viraha added. "We cannot send out the best in our fleet for one civilian. Think of the precedence this would be setting."

"May I remind the Council, Cara is currently a valuable asset to the Confederation, more than just a normal citizen. If Samas somehow unlocks the key to her ability to travel through time..." Caine warned.

"That is assuming she has some sort of ability to be able to do that. We have done no testing, no research, as you have yet to turn her over to us," another Councilman Dhar interrupted.

Caine was losing ground by the second.

"I make my next statement with the utmost respect for the authority of the Council. If I am not permitted to rescue her as the Commander with the full backing of the Council, I will have no other choice but to step down from my current position as Commander and do it on my own as a civilian." Caine held his breath, waiting to see if they called his bluff.

Seconds ticked by.

Saar got to his feet, but Yugato raised his hand and stopped him from speaking.

Saar sat back down, glowering.

"Of course, such a drastic measure does not need to occur," Yugato spoke. He turned to the rest of the Council. "The Commander has a point. She is no ordinary civilian. If we are to learn about how she arrived here, she must be returned to us. Any information she has cannot fall into the wrong hands. She has been on the Archon for some time now, and if she reveals anything of use to the Hostiles, we could have a much larger problem on our hands. I move to approve his request," Yugato waited for the others to speak.

"I move to approve the Commander's request, on one condition," Saar began. Caine knew Saar would try to work something into this that would ultimately benefit his agenda.

"As members of the Council, the leaders of the people, we cannot allow this to continue any longer. The Hostiles have been more violent than ever. We have been too lenient for far too long. How much longer do we let this continue before we put a stop to it once and for all?" Saar's features warped in his fury; his nostrils flared as he spoke.

"And what exactly do you propose we do, Saar?" Councilwoman Oria asked skeptically. She folded her arms slowly onto the table.

"We attack."

The Council erupted.

"We cannot just go and senselessly kill out of revenge," Shiro argued. "What do we do, try and destroy an entire planet of people?"

"That is exactly what we do!" Saar shouted.

"You're talking about human beings here!" Shiro looked horrified that Saar was considering such violence.

"They're barely human," Saar justified. "Our top scientists have confirmed their DNA isn't even the same as ours."

"Which is also the case for the people on the border planets, but you consider them human." Shiro looked close to leaping over the chairs and strangling Saar.

"This is madness," Viraha shouted.

"No," Saar turned to her with such force his robes fluttered and wrapped around his legs. "Madness is letting the Hostiles grow like a virus, multiplying, and spreading through the system." He slammed his fist on the table.

"You're calling for a war!" Shiro accused.

"If that is what it takes! What happens if we let them continue to go unchecked and grow bolder in their attacks. When do we start defending our Confederation? When they attack one of the core planets? When they come here and attack the Council itself? We have the power to stop the Hostiles, and we choose to look the other way. It is time we stop this nonsense and do what we were chosen to do: protect the people of the Confederation and end the threat of the Hostiles once and for all." Saar was so incensed he was out of breath by the end of his tirade, his mouth turned down in a disdainful grimace.

The other council members murmured, some of them nodding their heads in agreement.

"Councilman Saar has a point," Councilman Rouben spoke up. "Our predecessors fought the Border Wars against the Hostiles, but the threat has only grown since then. I agree; it is time that we bring this to an end. There would finally be peace in the system."

"And what about Samas?" Caine asked.

"What about him?" Oria queried.

"Samas has a connection somewhere in the Confederation. He has been given military weaponry along with highly classified intel. We need to find out who his contact is. If we kill him before I can Interrogate him, we will never know who is behind it."

"If there is an opportunity to kill Samas, we must take it. There is no guarantee we will get any useful information that would lead us to the source of the leak," Saar argued.

"We have to try. Why would we eliminate our best source of information? I only need a short time with him," Caine defended his idea.

"The Commander is right," Dhar agreed. "This could be our only chance of finding out who is responsible. Samas should not be killed."

"This is a big mistake," Saar warned.

"I think it is a risk we need to take. The benefits could far outweigh the consequences," Yugato chimed in.

"There has to be another way," Shiro sounded frustrated. "If we concentrate our Fleet around the far perimeters of the border planets, we can prevent further attacks."

"The Fleet is already spread thin as it is. There are not enough ships to- "

"We will build more ships," Shiro countered.

Viraha and Oria exchanged a glance, unimpressed with Shiro's suggestions.

"It will take far too long. We must act now," Rouben locked eyes with Shiro.

"After the Border Wars, the members of this Council," Shiro tapped the table with his index finger, "voted not to take any more direct military action against the Hostiles."

"The Border Wars were a hundred years ago. Times have changed. The Council voted to let the Hostiles govern themselves outside of Confederation rule, but their intention was never to sit back and allow them to kill citizens. I move to sanction a direct military assault on the Yedrus," Saar said.

"This is senseless retaliation. I implore you to see reason," Shiro pleaded.

Caine harbored such a bitter loathing for Samas he found himself agreeing with Saar.

"I move to vote on the matter," Councilman Shida said.

"No, this is far too presumptuous. This must be discussed further," Shiro argued.

"The time has come for us to vote, and it has run out for the Hostiles," Saar said. "I second Shida's motion. The Council needs to vote now."

Caine's fists clenched. Their vote could seal Cara's fate.

"By a show of hands, who agrees with the motion to strike Yedrus," Yugato asked. Eight hands rose high. Shiro and Yugato were outnumbered.

"The Council has decided." Yugato's tone was somber. "Commander, you have been authorized to use full military force to strike Yedrus and capture Samas for Interrogation." Yugato rapped the table three times with his knuckles indicating the vote was final. "May the stars forgive us for this."

Caine's screen went blank. The plan was in place, but he had no time to relish the small victory. He had to find Cara. They were days away from Yedrus, and there wasn't a second to lose. Caine pushed the Archon nearly to its breaking point to make its way to the outer planet as fast as possible. Even at maximum speed, it would still take too long. Each hour that passed, Caine's stoic demeanor slipped. By the end of the second day, Than was concerned enough about the crew's welfare and safety he needed to address it.

"Caine," Than found him in his office, pouring over satellite images of Yedrus. "I'm not sure how much longer we can keep this up before we have a catastrophic system failure. We've been pushing the engines to the brink. They're critically close to overheating. Mechanics has been working without a break, trying to keep them running."

Caine couldn't think logically: his only focus was moving as quickly as possible to get to her.

"I know you want to get to Cara; believe me, I do too, but we are dangerously close to an engine malfunction. If we break down, we lose any chance we have at saving her. Is it worth the risk?" Than reasoned with him.

Caine mulled over Than's concerns. "Divert air coolant into the engines to bring the temperature down. Give Mechanics a break, two at a time. Pull from

Engineering to fill in if you must, but we are not slowing down," he finished firmly, emphasizing the finality of his decision.

The crew would survive the ship being a few degrees warmer than usual, but if they stopped, Cara would not.

Chapter Thirty-Three

Cara was freezing. Shivers violently racked her body, and her teeth chattered. She was shaking so hard the chair she was tied to rattled against the stone floor. Her memories were murky. She couldn't put together any coherent thoughts. All she could focus on was the all-consuming cold penetrating all the way to her bones. Her head sagged, and the wound on her arm caught her attention. It was inflamed; red and puffy. Blood and pus oozed out from the dirt-encrusted edges. It was getting infected.

Samas stormed into the room and tipped her head back to look at her. The cruel hammering resumed behind her eyes, radiating across her skull. She heaved and spat up bile. He was trying to get into her mind.

He cut her ties and yanked her from the chair. He dragged her from the room, down the corridor to a smaller cell, and threw her in. As she lay on the floor, he reappeared with a cup. He poured cold, dirty water on her head. He bent down and squeezed her wound.

"This is not looking good. But this," he tugged on the neck of her shirt to reveal whatever the woman had carved into her skin, "this I like."

She couldn't see it, but it burned like she'd had hot coals pressed against her skin. She almost passed out as he pulled the fabric away from the hardened blood. She sat in the corner, too deep in shock to cry, and was sure she was not getting out of here alive.

They dragged her outside again later to fight. As soon as they let go of her, she collapsed to the ground. She could see the dark spot on the dirt where the boy's blood had soaked into the ground and dried.

She had no energy left to stand; no will to try and protect herself. She lay there; lifeless, as the Hostiles screamed at her. The woman kicked her in the ribs a few times, unhappy she no longer had a punching bag to play with. Cara couldn't even cry or beg. She had nothing left.

Realizing they weren't going to get a show, the disappointed crowd dispersed. She laid there sprawled out in the dirt until she was dragged back inside to her cell.

Samas came back to see her. He sat cross-legged on the floor in front of her. Again, the familiar pinch at the front of her forehead indicated he was trying to gain access to her mind, but she squeezed her eyes shut, trying to fight away the feeling and keep him out. Samas scowled, angry she was able to resist his attempts to breach her defenses.

He grabbed a chunk of her hair, yanking her head off the floor. "I will get what I want," he snarled. "You can't keep me out forever." He slammed her head down onto the floor, causing her to blackout.

Samas came in frequently after that. Sometimes he would try to enter her mind. Sometimes he took her blood and even a chunk of her hair.

"You will show me how you got here and how you can move through time," he demanded.

All she wanted was to scream at him that she didn't know how. She didn't even have enough energy left to whisper.

"Why do you protect them?" He backhanded her across the face, and blood filled her mouth. Too weak to swallow, the blood trickled out of the corners of her lips, dripping from her chin onto her clothes.

He continued to rant and rave about going back in time with her. He wanted Cara to take him back with her, and he would rule the Old Earth.

"Sweet Cara, you and I, we can stop the Confederation. We can save Old Earth and change this future." His eyes glittered in front of her like black holes, sucking the life from her.

Other times he would come in and just wander around the room talking as if he was having a conversation with someone only he could see.

One night when Samas came back, she was too weak to fight him off physically, but mentally she fought off all his attempts to access her mind.

The next time he came, everything had shifted unexpectedly. Samas was no longer concerned with getting whatever information he thought she possessed. He was only focused on destroying Caine and her along with him. Angrily, he squeezed her wound, wrenching a guttural scream from her.

"Yes, Breeta, can you feel her pain?" He was speaking to someone who wasn't there. "The same pain I have felt every day since you were stolen from me." He grabbed Cara's wrist and twisted it. The crisp snap of the bone was followed by unbearable pain, and Cara blacked out.

She dreamed of her family, her life in New York, and how things used to be. From this perspective, it didn't all seem as bad as she had thought it was. As she drifted in and out of consciousness, Samas continued to come. He would talk to Breeta and rage about Caine. Most of what he said made no sense. He would wander around her and laugh, speaking half-sentences and making up words.

The next time he came to her, he yanked her up and out into the hall. He pulled her down the narrow corridor, turned, and looked down at her with scorn.

He took her on a small spacecraft, and they zipped away. She lay on the floor, cold metal under her cheek. She closed her eyes and drifted off, finding some relief from the horror she was living.

She had no idea how long she had slept, but she woke to Samas heaving her to her knees.

"Oh, my sweet Cara, I had hoped we would have more time together, but alas, it appears the time has come where we must part ways," Samas frowned.

"Just kill me and get it over with," Cara managed to whisper.

Samas crowed with laughter. "Oh, Cara, I'm not going to kill you. Where would the fun be in that? You and I still have some unfinished business. I am sure we will see each other again very soon." He pulled a mask over his face and dragged her down the gangway to the ground.

"Goodbye, Cara. Parting is such sweet sorrow." He stroked the side of her face and left.

She had no idea where she was but unable to move; all she could do was lay there. The pain was excruciating. Hours crawled by before she finally managed to roll onto her side.

Breathing in to mask the pain, she managed to get to her knees, cradling her broken arm to her chest. She looked around. She was in a desert, an empty wasteland. There was nothing as far as she could see except for rolling mountains of sand. It was hot and dry. Cara knew she had to find shelter and water; otherwise, she wouldn't survive for long. With the very last bit of sheer willpower she had left, she pushed to her feet. She was exhausted and weak, but the desire to survive spurred her forwards.

Her legs ached with each move. With every step, she sank into the sand. It pooled around her ankles. One step became ten; ten became a hundred. Eventually, she lost count, pushing on inch by inch. She made her way to the top of a small hill of sand. In the distance, a rocky formation cast shadows on the sand. She had to get there and use it as shelter.

It felt like hours, but she finally collapsed under a small sliver of overhanging rock, giving her just a little protection from the harsh sun. She lay back and fell asleep, with no energy left to stay awake any longer. Cara drifted in and out. She had a hard time breathing, and it hurt like she was breathing in acid. The sand abraded her sensitive, sunburned skin like sandpaper.

When Cara regained consciousness later, the sun had sunk below the horizon. The sky was a deep midnight blue, speckled with stars winking against their backdrop. Several of the stars were markedly brighter than the rest. Planets. Cara gazed up at them, trying to pinpoint which one was Arctus.

She wished she had been more forceful with Caine about going back to the Council and not staying on the ship. She had been so excited he had wanted her to stay. It had seemed like a once in a lifetime opportunity to be in space, but looking back, she had been so naive. This wasn't a movie; she wasn't an actress. This wasn't some fun adventure; she was on the razor edge of death. All she wanted was to be home, safe in her boring apartment, living her boring life. A tear slipped from the corner of her eye.

Cara was surprised she even had anything left in her to spare. She sucked in a rough, ragged breath, wincing as her lungs filled. She was barely getting any oxygen; the levels in the atmosphere must be low. She shifted her weight to try and get the blood flowing in her legs. Lightheaded, she gasped for air. Samas may not have killed her with his own hands, but he would be responsible for her death, leaving her here to die on this barren planet.

Cold sweat washed over her as she regained consciousness. The wind was whistling like high pitch screaming as if the whole planet could sense her pain. The sky was dark with clouds. No, not clouds - sand and dust. A dust storm.

The whipping wind turned the sand into stinging bullets, hitting Cara's already damaged skin so hard it broke through, causing small pinprick droplets of blood to well up. She pressed a hand over her mouth, breathing through her fingers to keep the thick clouds of dust out of her mouth. She couldn't get a full breath.

Finally, she succumbed to the lack of oxygen and fell unconscious.

Chapter Thirty-Four

The distance to Yedrus shrank by the morning.

"Sir, a ship appears to have left Yedrus and is on track directly towards Caltha," Xan informed Caine, displaying the image.

Instinct and experience told Caine that Cara was on the ship. He was getting too close, and Samas, feeling the pressure, was fleeing with her while he still had time.

"The Archon will stay on course; there is still a mission to complete. I will be going after that ship," Caine instructed.

Caine prepped a scout ship and took a few crew members with him, leaving Than in charge to oversee the strike on Yedrus. He boarded the small craft and readied for departure. He looked out at the Archon and silently hoped everything would run smoothly in his absence. Caine was nearly a day's length behind the ship they were tracking. If Cara was on that ship, he needed to close the distance and fast.

The ship landed briefly on Caltha before exiting its atmosphere. As it did, a transmission was forced through an encrypted frequency.

"Hello again, Commander." Samas smiled gleefully. "I've left a little present for you. Hopefully, by the time you get there, it's still something you'll want to play with."

Caine didn't sleep that night as they raced towards Caltha, knowing Cara was somewhere down on the planet, hurt, dying, or worse.

"Scan the surface," he instructed when they reached orbit the next day. A faint heat signal appeared. "It's her. Bring us down!"

Caine ran to the airlock as they descended, ready to move as soon as they were close enough to the ground. Before the ramp had fully extended, he jumped down, holding a small oxygen mask to his face. The wind was whipping, swirling thick clouds of dust and sand around him.

Dust storms were common on Caltha, but they whipped up a toxic plume of dust. Caltha's atmosphere was barely breathable, with lower oxygen levels and higher carbon dioxide levels. Each speck stung any small spot of exposed skin.

Caine raced across the ground to the dark spot on the ground in front of him. His stomach lurched as he reached Cara. She was lying there, skin red and blistering from the heat and sun. Her eyes were closed, and she was gasping like a fish out of water. Every attempt to breathe contorted her body, causing her to convulse with shoulders arching up and head jerking back. She was caked in dust.

Caine slid his one arm under her shoulders and the other under her knees, lifting her. Her broken wrist swung wildly. He grabbed the spare air mask from his belt and pressed it to her face, allowing the oxygen to fill her lungs. He raced back to the pod. It zoomed off with him sitting on the floor, clutching her close to him, pinning the mask to her face. Her breathing turned into a gurgle as if she was choking.

"We need to stabilize her until we get back to the Archon." He gently laid Cara flat on the floor.

The ship's emergency medical ward was limited. Caine kept the oxygen mask on her as he inserted an I.V. into her arm. Her breathing was dangerously shallow, her chest barely rising. She wouldn't be out of critical danger until they made it back to the Archon, and even then, he wasn't sure she'd make a full recovery.

He sat by her side the whole time, talking to her in gentle, reassuring tones, telling her it would all be okay;

she was safe now. He was overwhelmed with emotions: hatred and rage, fear, and something else that had long laid dormant within him. She had worked her way under his skin and into his heart.

***

Nadir was waiting with a rolling stretcher as the scout ship landed in the docking bay. Cara was carefully transferred onto the stretcher, and Caine followed Nadir to Medical.

"We have to bring her back slowly, or she will go into shock," Nadir said. "Starting with her skin first. Water will work best to remove the contaminants. If we try to wipe it away or remove her clothes now, her skin could peel away." He pointed to the medical shower used to wash off chemicals. "In there."

Caine turned it on and ran his fingers under the spray.

"Not too hot," Nadir warned.

Caine adjusted the temperature and carefully slid his arms under Cara, cradling her to his chest. He carried her over and stepped under the water with her, still in his uniform.

***

Cara was warm. She couldn't see anything, but she didn't care. She was light, as if she was floating on clouds: complete bliss. Sharp, agonizing pain broke through the hazy bubble of euphoria, and she screamed, begging for it to stop. She wanted the pain to end. Every fiber in her body had been set on fire.

She broke down into frantic cries as the fine mist of the chemical wash hit her burning skin, rinsing away layers of sand and dust. Caine looked at Nadir, distraught by the shrill sound. The gut-wrenching sound shredded away the remaining thin veil of stoicism he was trying to portray.

"Do something!" Caine yelled at him.

"Let her scream. It is a good sign. It will help clear out her lungs."

Caine held her delicately; afraid one wrong move would break her even more. "Kuso, Nadir," he growled as Cara's head drooped to the side. He wasn't sure how much more of her pain he would be able to handle.

"Enough." Nadir turned the wash off when some of the intense redness faded.

Caine stepped out and laid her on the table. Nadir quickly intubated her and hooked her IV up to a large machine.

Nadir could see Caine was worried. "This will cleanse her blood and get out the infection." With the press of a button, the machine sucked the blood from her arms. It slid through the tubes into the machine. "The next few hours will be the most critical. Let me do my work. I will come and find you after."

Caine didn't move.

"Caine, I cannot take care of you and her at the same time. You look like you're about to collapse. If you want her to make a quick recovery, you need to let me focus on her. I can't do my job if you pass out in front of me right now."

Nadir brushed by him and took some large towels from a closet, laying them over her so she could dry slowly.

Nadir could see the hesitation in Caine's eyes. "You have known me a long time. You know she is in safe hands. I need you to trust me and let me do my job."

Using Cara's well-being was the right manipulator. Caine left without protest. He was exhausted. He went to his room and fell into a deep, dreamless sleep. He slept long into the next morning, but not even Than said a word when he showed up late for duty.

He could barely concentrate on his work the next day, waiting anxiously for an update.

Nadir called him down to Medical later in the evening. "She's finally stable, but she won't be ready to wake for a few days. I need to let her arm heal first and stop the infection. She has two broken ribs and an oblique fracture at her wrist, along with several smaller hairline fractures. I can try to help speed it up a bit, so she won't need to be bedridden for long."

Nadir sighed deeply. "This, though, will be a little more challenging." Nadir pulled the sheet back, revealing the mark cut into the skin near her collarbone. Disgusted rage flooded through him. He recognized the symbol of the Samandran Clan immediately.

Samas had branded her.

What had she been through? He couldn't imagine the horror she had faced.

"Can you remove it?"

"I will do my best, but it is not the outward scars I am worried about."

Caine pulled a chair up next to Cara, rubbing the one small spot on the back of her hand that had the least amount of skin damage. The redness had faded; the blisters had either popped or reabsorbed, but the skin was peeling around where they had been. Her skin was mottled and blotchy, darker areas healing contrasting with pale skin.

Nadir handed him a small bottle. "Here. Put this on her skin."

Caine carefully rubbed the cream onto the cracked, burned skin, avoiding any open cuts. "You're going to be okay." The reassurance was only meant to convince himself of that fact.

Now that he was sure Cara was out of the critical stage, Caine knew he was on the clock to follow through on his orders from the Council. He took one last look at Cara before leaving the room.

As he walked to the Bridge, he allowed his mind to push her to the background: compartmentalizing. If he wasn't focused, he could put his crew and the entire mission in jeopardy. He couldn't afford to have any distractions.

Cara was safe with Nadir, but there were millions more at risk if he failed.

Chapter Thirty-Five

This was the moment he had been dreading for days. He entered the room, and a few of his crew nodded their heads at him, acknowledging his presence but most continued to work unfazed.

"Are you okay?" Than approached. Caine hesitated to answer. This was Than his friend talking, not Than his crewmember.

"I just want to get this done." He didn't want to reveal his doubts. He worried voicing them could manifest them into reality.

Caine geared up and made his way to the hangar. Rows of small, stealthy scout ships were prepped, each with a pilot waiting for instructions and several armed officers standing by.

"Today will be the first direct strike on a Hostile planet since the Border Wars. We do not know what to expect, but we need to set the right example for the Confederation. We need to do this the right way. No mess, no mistakes. We will drop in with small teams of four. Our target is Re'em Samas. He is to be taken alive. If you should come across him or capture him, you contact me directly. He will likely be in the capital's main citadel, but he will not go willingly or quietly. We should have the element of surprise here but be prepared for traps. We know Hostile women and children are just as dangerous as their men. Do not underestimate them. You are not just a team today; you are a family. Take care of each other out there. Have each other's back. Be aware, be alert, and be ready so we can all come home safely."

His men murmured their agreement and loaded onto the ships. Caine looked down at the screen on his handheld tablet. Light cruisers formed a wide perimeter, and combat ships were on standby, awaiting their orders. Caine boarded the last Scout and took one last look at the Archon's hanger as the ramp shut behind him. He took his seat and strapped in, leaned his head back against the wall, and closed his eyes. It would be a few hours before they landed. A little extra rest wouldn't hurt.

He woke to the rough jostling of atmosphere entry. The descent on these smaller ships was far more turbulent than on a ship as massive as the Archon. Yedrus was small but had several dozen small camps and outposts of Hostiles scattered across the surface. Caine and his team were dropping into the area near Daiyu, the largest encampment on Yedrus. If Samas was on the planet, this is where he would be.

The Scout landed several hundred yards away from the village. He unbuckled and geared up along with his men. Comms, night vison visors, protective equipment; he had everything he would need for any full military assault. They were going in as a team of five. Caine had picked four of his best soldiers to go in with him. He could count on these men to have his back. They would fight until they took their last breath if it came down to that.

They climbed from the ship silently, spreading out in a v-formation, with Caine leading them. He waved two fingers, and they made their way through the dense growth towards their target.

Caine ignored the increasing sense of apprehension as they approached the outskirts. This hadn't been done in a hundred years. There was so much that could go wrong, so much risk being taken. He would hold the Council, namely Saar, fully accountable should this take a turn for the worse.

Attacks on this scale were typically planned out weeks, if not months, ahead of time, but this had been thrown together in mere days. The plan was a rough outline at best, and most of it would be improvised as they went along. He only hoped his men were ready to adapt to whatever was thrown their way in the next few hours.

A large structure loomed; its black shape prominent even against the dark backdrop of the night sky. This was the main building in this village - the citadel. From surveillance imagery, it appeared to be heavily fortified. It was the hub of activity, a place for people to gather but also work and sleep. There was the potential for dozens of people to be inside.

Caine led his formation through the scrub as it became sparser. He pointed silently in either direction. His men silently spread out to both sides. They stopped at the edge, each one using a scraggly bush for cover. They held their position, scanning the village area for movement.

He flicked his hand forward twice to signal their advance. His men rose and quickly crossed the open space towards the citadel. Caine kept a close eye out for movement. They made it to the wall and pressed up against it.

Caine tapped on his mouthpiece, and the men turned on their comms.

"Check," he whispered. The men signaled the channel was working. "We keep comms on from this point forward. Stay together. We do not want to get separated in there."

They eased along the edge until they reached an entry point. Daiv Arpad slid by Caine and took a knee. Arpad deftly dismantled the locking mechanism on the door, and grabbed the handle.

"On my count." Caine held up three fingers and lowered them one by one. When his last finger dropped, Arpad swung the door open. Caine leaned around the corner, aiming his weapon in, checking for signs of Hostiles. They were at the end of a long hallway lined with several large doors on either side.

"Clear." Caine waved his men inside.

Caine turned his mind off as he entered. Detaching made things easier to process in the moment. In a fight, emotions could get you killed. With his weapon raised and ready to fire, he scanned the hall for movement. He walked backward, pressed up against the back of a fellow officer, covering them from attack from the rear.

They continued down the hall, nearly silent except for the muffled padding of rubber soles on concrete. Just at the edge of the outside door, Caine thought there was a slight shiver of blackness. He scanned the opening, waiting for a person to appear, but none did. Maybe it was just his imagination, or maybe it was something moving in the breeze. No. He wasn't going to make that mistake again. He had to trust his gut.

"Halt," he whispered into his comm, holding up his fist. The team froze mid-stride. Caine waited a breath. Two. Nothing. The shadow moved again, and Caine fired. The figure of a large man, dressed all in black, slumped into the doorway, followed by a mass of Hostiles racing inside towards them.

Caine instantly dropped to a knee and fired, allowing his men behind him to fire at the Hostiles over his head. Bodies piled up until they all lay dead, but now their cover was blown. It was only a matter of time before they would be up against a much large number of Hostiles, ones who would have had time to better arm themselves.

"Be ready," he whispered to his men.

The storm was about to unleash itself.

The next moments were a hurried blur, moving in mass down the hall, kicking in doors only to find empty rooms. Their advantage of surprise had been lost. Stealth was no longer needed.

Caine kicked in a metal door. It crashed against a stone wall and stopped. A single chair was in the middle of the room. A chair he knew. His mind raced, trying to place it. The chains on the arms triggered the violent flash of memory.

Cara had been held prisoner here, in this room. He had seen her memories of this place. The knowledge of it made his blood boil. It had been one thing for him to see the room only as a memory in her mind, but to be physically standing in the same spot was entirely different. Knowing what had been done to her here made his stomach churn. His wrath grew. He kicked the chair over. It crashed to the ground, the metal clang echoing off the stone walls. Streaks of lighter color on the wall stood out against the backdrop of dark stone. He squatted down to see jagged tally marks scratched into the wall. Cara had been marking days.

A firm hand on his shoulder pulled him away from his thoughts. Arpad was looking down at him, lips pressed together. His eyes flicked from the tally marks back to Caine. Arpad jerked his head toward the door, his silent message clear; there was still a mission to complete.

"Move out," he directed to his men. Now, more than ever, Caine's desire to get his hands on Samas grew. They moved on down the corridor until it ended at a large central chamber. The circular room had several other hallways running off it. Caine held up a fist, stopping his small group. He looked down the hallways, searching for movement, trying to decipher which way to go. They had no blueprint for the building. Going down these halls blindly could get them lost or lead them into a trap.

There was a faint hissing sound, a quick pop. To his left, Colvin Verus collapsed to the ground. They were under fire. He and the remaining three men looked up just in time to see a man far up the side of the wall, taking aim at them again. Caine fired, and the sniper fell from his precarious perch to the ground.

"We have company," a voice crackled over his comm. Caine turned to see a massive wave of Hostiles racing down a hallway. No, two hallways. All of them. His breath hitched for a split second. They were surrounded, grossly outmanned, and very likely outgunned.

Caine fired into the crowd swarming towards them. The Hostiles had taken the best tactic they could, overwhelming them with their sheer numbers. For every two Hostiles Caine shot, three more were rushing up behind them.

This was a suicide mission. It was a diversion to keep them occupied.

Samas was here. This had his writing all over it. He was sending his people in to die for him so he could escape while Caine and his team were distracted. These were the sacrificial lambs being led to the slaughter. The most terrifying part was they were more than willing to do it without question.

There was no other option for Caine at this point. He pressed a small button on his comm. High above, still hovering in the atmosphere, were his combat ships, and he had just signaled for them to bomb the facility they were currently standing in. He had to get his men to safety.

"We need to leave. Now," he commanded. They went back the way they came, Caine flanking the rear, firing at the oncoming onslaught of Hostiles. A massive explosion ripped through the compound. Caine was blown off his feet. As he hit the ground, tumbling end over end, consciousness faded away.

Caine awoke in blackness with his head pounding and ears ringing, but alive. The concussive force from the blast had shattered the visor on his helmet, leaving him in the dark. He pushed himself up but couldn't hear any movement. He banged on the side of his helmet a few times, and it finally flickered on. There were cracks all down the screen, but at least it was mostly functional.

He could see the fallen figures of his men. He raced over and pressed his fingers to each of their necks. All three had a strong pulse. Thank the stars. His breath rushed out in relief.

There was a snapping sound, and he looked up to see a young man approach. He was holding a gun; he must have stolen off one of Caine's fallen teammates. He was barely out of boyhood, not yet a man, and yet he was already a trained killer. "Balamo matala auvi ikio naga tonay!"

Caine knew enough of the Samandran language to understand the directions screamed at him. He slowly raised his hands. The boy stepped forward, over the fallen body of one of his team.

Without warning, Arpad reached out, grabbing the boy's ankles and yanked him off balance. He fell to the floor, and Arpad swiftly grabbed his head and twisted, breaking his neck with a clean snap. The sharp sound made Caine visibly wince. It was such a senseless waste of life. Kuso. War was hell. Caine stood, and they lifted Jorund to his feet.

"We need to rendezvous with J Team," Caine directed. The team crept along the hallway until they reached the door leading outside. They stuck to the wall and glided stealthily around the edge. J Team was on the far end of the city.

A cry broke through the quiet. Small and weak, but enough to get Caine's attention. He lifted a fist, and his men came to a halt.

Caine crept around the side of the building. A woman lay sprawled out dead on the ground, an infant at her side. Still unable to walk, it squirmed around, gripping a fistful of his mother's hair. Caine stared at the crying baby. There was a soft rustling sound, and a young girl emerged from the rubble. Jorund stepped up next to him and trained his weapon on the girl. Caine reached out and pushed the end down, giving Jorund a sharp shake of his head. Jorund gave him a strange look.

The girl rushed over and picked up the baby, and scurried off into the dark.

"Move on," Caine ordered.

If the girl and the baby managed to make it far enough outside the village, they had a chance of surviving, but Caine knew the destruction that awaited the immediate area. Even if they did survive the upcoming final attacks, the baby would ultimately die without its mother, and the girl would not survive long on her own.

"Commander," Alri Orhil's voice sounded through Caine's comm. "Three Samandran ships have managed to leave the atmosphere. Do we engage?"

"No, do not engage. Track all three." It was one of the most challenging calls he had to make. Samas was on one of those ships, but he needed Samas alive. Without knowing which of the three ships Samas was on, Caine risked killing him if they attacked. Caine needed to be able to interrogate him.

"Back to the ship," Caine commanded his teams. It was time to end the ground operation. With Samas gone, it was time to move on to phase two of the assault.

They made their way back to the ship. Once they had lifted off, they could see the plumes of smoke in the distance from other strikes called in by his team.

The final blow to the Samandran Clan would come shortly, in the form of large explosives dropped on several of the massive compounds in the cities. He hoped it would be worth it in the end, and there would be some break in the mounting violence in the system.

Caine climbed onto the pod last and surveyed the citadel one last time. The craft silently ascended into the sky, the brush bending and blowing around in the downdraft. Caine took his seat and strapped into the harness just as the first bumps of turbulence rocked the pod.

Relief flooded him. His men were all safe, and now they were returning home.

Chapter Thirty-Six

Three days later, the anger had subsided, and Caine found himself questioning his decisions. Losing Samas aside, the attack had ultimately been successful. Once he and his men had exited the atmosphere, combat ships dropped into the atmosphere on the Yedrus and decimated it.

The Samandran Clan would no longer be able to pose a threat to the system. He could only hope the other Clans would end their violence in the wake of the assault, taking it as a warning. The Confederation was no longer going to play a defensive role in the conflict.

He sat at his desk, twirling a pen, thinking of all the destruction in the past weeks. So many lives lost, and despite the numerous Hostile casualties, he didn't feel as if it had been worth it, had been necessary. Had his desire for vengeance clouded his judgment? Was he no better than the Hostiles, killing senselessly, indiscriminately?

"I'm going to wake her," Nadir called to tell him.

Caine hurried down, wanting to be there for her. He stood over her, holding her hand. Slowly her eyes opened.

"Hey," he said. Her mouth curved into a small smile. She opened her lips to speak, but no sound came out. "It's ok, it's ok," Caine hushed her. "Rest. You are safe."

Her eyes drooped closed involuntary. He started to pull his hand away. She weakly squeezed it in protest. "I'm not going anywhere. I promise." Reluctantly, she let his hand go.

Caine pulled a chair up and kept vigil over her all night. Nadir shooed him away to sleep, but Caine refused to leave. He made a promise to her he intended to keep and would be here when she woke up again.

The next day Caine was able to help her sit up, and she spoke a few words. Her wrist was healing rapidly, and so were her ribs thanks to the cocktail of chemicals she was on. By day four, she was able to sit upright with no assistance. She was sitting up when Caine walked in. She was already trying to speak as he approached her.

"Samas," she rasped, her voice still hoarse from the breathing tube that had been down her throat for so long. "He's an Esper."

He shook his head. "That's not possible."

"Dammit, Caine." She glared at him. Her throat was still raw, and talking sent her into a fit of coughing. "I'm not lying."

"I never said you were." He grabbed a glass of water for her. She was still scowling at him as she took a sip.

"There are a lot of things that are impossible. Including me, yet here I am. So how can you say something is impossible when you have proof right in front of you. He's an Esper." Her voice cracked, near hysteria.

"I believe you; I do. I just don't know how it would have happened."

"It doesn't matter how. It happened, and it is a big problem."

"I'll look into it," he promised. "Now, get some rest."

Caine went up to research Samas, not like he didn't know everything already. Than had the same reaction Caine had but nodded grimly when Caine said Cara was positive in her assessment. An Esper had illegally fathered a child, and worse, it was with a Hostile. An unregulated child was enough for imprisonment, but to have one with a Hostile? This had never been heard of before. Caine thought of the Espers old enough to have possibly fathered Samas. There were several.

Cara was sleeping when Nadir entered. The sound of the door opening startled her awake. She gasped as she bolted upright in bed, and her healing ribs sent a shockwave of pain up her side, causing her to wince.

She had been dreaming. No, it was a nightmare. Samas' face and his twisted laughter were haunting her.

Nadir looked at her. "You feel like you are still there."

"I can still feel him all around me." She rubbed her arms. "It's like he's watching me."

"It will take time, but you will heal." He wanted to give her some hope. People in dire situations could not survive if they didn't have hope.

Cara sighed. She wanted the memories gone. She wanted to forget, not spend every moment reliving it over and over.

"This will help." He handed her a small, white pill. She took it with a sip of the warm tea. Within minutes, her body relaxed. She rolled over onto her good side and fell asleep.

When she slept, she didn't dream, but when she woke, the thoughts of Samas were still there. She rolled onto her side, wincing at the lingering aches from her injuries. The door to the main treatment room slid open. Cara sat up in bed, expecting Caine or Nadir to walk in, but no one entered.

"Hello?" she called cautiously. But there was silence. Cara stood on weak legs, using the bed to support her weight. Slowly she walked to the doorway of her room and took a few steps into the treatment area.

"Hello?" she called out again. Still no response. Her heart beat faster. Irrational fear took over. What if Samas was here? What if he had come back for her? Soft laughter echoed, and she whipped her head around, looking for the source. There was no one in the room. Something shuffled behind her and whirled around again.

A figure filled the doorway that had been empty just seconds earlier, but it wasn't Samas. It was the boy she had killed. He was standing in a pool of blood as it poured from the gunshot wound in his chest. The boy's eyes turned from jet black to blood red, and he laughed, but it wasn't the laugh of a child. It was Samas' cruel cackle that echoed around her. The boy raised a pale arm and pointed at Cara, baring his sharp, pointed teeth in a snarl.

Whirling around and trying to escape, she twisted her ankle. She cried out in pain as she fell to the floor. Her arms windmilled, knocking over a tray of medical tools. They clattered to the floor and scattered around her. Absolute terror blurred her vision. She could only think one thing- escape. Hide. She needed to get away. She scrambled across the floor.

"Cara." Samas' voice called her name.

She had nowhere to go. She was trapped. There was a muffled buzzing in her ears like she had cotton stuffed in them. Her name was called again, but this time the voice was muted and distant. Somehow it broke through the thick haze, piercing through her fear, trying to pull her back to reality.

***

Caine wasn't prepared for the chaos that met him when he walked through the doorway into Medical to see Cara. She was out of bed; her back turned to him. When she turned to face him, the look on her face made him stop. She was so pale her skin appeared translucent. There were dark circles under her eyes, and she looked drawn and frail. Her gaze was one of sheer terror. She raced backward away from him but stumbled and crashed into a metal instrument table, both collapsing to the floor in a heap.

He spoke her name softly, but it only fueled her fear. She pushed away from him, through the mass of medical tools strewn about the floor. She wasn't seeing him; she was so lost in her panic that she'd lost her grip on reality. He didn't know what she was living through in her mind, but he knew it wasn't good. He held his hands up, palms out, to show he wasn't a threat and crouched near her.

"Cara." He gently touched her knee with his fingertips. Her eyes finally focused on him, her brow furrowed as if she was confused.

She burst into tears. Gently, he picked her up and carried her back to the bed. He set her down and checked her twisted ankle.

"What happened?" He hit a sensitive spot causing her to hiss through her teeth. "I think it's ok. It will be tender for a few days." He rubbed her skin gently and looked back up at her. "Cara, what just happened?" he prodded.

"I heard him. He's coming back for me."

Caine made a sad sound and took her hands, giving them a squeeze. "He can't get to you. You're safe now."

Cara wanted to assure him she believed him, but she couldn't bring herself to lie.

"Do you want to talk to me about it?" he asked. He hoped she would open up with a little encouragement.

She shook her head. "Not yet."

Caine knew he could go into her mind to see what happened to her, but he had promised her he wouldn't without her permission. She would talk when she was ready, and he would wait for her, as long as it took.

Caine walked to the large cabinet where Nadir kept the medications and took out a mild pain killer. He handed it to Cara with a glass of water. Nadir came back as she swallowed. He glanced at the two of them and shuffled up.

"You've got work to do, Commander, and I have a patient to check up on." He shooed Caine away with a wave of his hand. "Come back later."

Caine took a few steps back, raising his eyebrows at Cara, sharing a look with her that spoke volumes, as Nadir placed himself between them. Cara's eyes warmed, and a smile crossed her face. Caine gestured to the door with his thumb and left.

Nadir busied himself getting the items he needed, gathering things from drawers and out of cabinets.

Cara slipped off the bed and went to the mirror on the wall. She pulled down the collar of the hospital robe so she could see the mark carved into her skin. She stared at it. It was mostly healed and faded, but she could still see where the puckered pink skin swirled around in a gruesome brand.

"It will heal," Nadir's voice came from behind her. "In time, you will barely even be able to see it at all."

She glanced at his reflection in the mirror and back at the mark. "I'll still remember it." She wasn't sure whether she was talking about the scar or what she had happened to her.

"Yes, you will," Nadir said in a way that made her realize he wasn't talking about the scar either. He milled about the room checking on machines and equipment.

"Nadir," Cara turned to him. "Thank you."

Nadir smiled, approaching her. He placed a warm hand on her cheek and gave a small nod of approval before returning to his work.

Turning to face the mirror again, Cara found herself staring at a stranger. A murderer. What if Caine found out what she had done? If he knew she had killed a child, he would hate her. Who would blame him? Even she hated herself for it.

Nadir patted the bed. "Come on, let's get you all checked out."

After a thorough exam, he smiled. "You are healing up nicely, my dear. I think you will finally be able to go back to your own room tomorrow."

Cara forced a smile, not wanting to tell him she was scared to be by herself. At least in Medical with Nadir, she had someone to talk to about what was happening to her. Back in her room, she would be alone with her nightmares.

Visions of the boy and hearing Samas; it was as if everywhere she looked, they were there. Walking down the halls, sitting in her room: it didn't matter. Like ghosts only she could see, they were haunting her.

She couldn't explain the feeling, but she knew he was following her, lurking in the shadows and biding his time until he could come back for her.

The nightmares were constant. The face of the young boy she killed haunted her dreams. Cara dreaded falling asleep. She couldn't bear to relive it over and over every time her eyes closed. She avoided sleeping for as long as possible until she had no other choice but to collapse. She barely ate. She was hollow; everything inside of her had been ripped away. Cara barely recognized herself. It wasn't that she only looked different; she was a different person than she had been. She thought about telling Nadir or Caine, but she chalked it up to being leftover nerves and didn't want them to worry.

The next day, Nadir escorted her back to her room, leaving her with a warm embrace and a kiss on the cheek.

"You come see me if you need anything," he instructed. The door slid shut behind him. In Cara's eyes, it was a jail door closing on her, trapping her.

She stood in her room, not sure what to do. It was too suffocating in there. She dropped her belongings on the bed and left.

She went to the cafeteria and grabbed a tray. Than and some crew walked in just moments later. He spotted her and hurried to wrap her up in a big hug.

"I'm so glad to see you up and about." He grabbed a tray of food. "Come on and sit over here with us."

She sat across from Than, picking at her food, unable to take more than a few bites. The food sank to the pit of her stomach like she was eating rocks. She listened to the crew chatting idly, only half paying attention to what they were discussing. It just felt nice to be around people.

"You have to eat something." Than noticed her tray.

Cara shrugged. "It's the medicine," she lied. She pushed the food around on her plate with her fork.

Than made a skeptical noise but didn't argue further.

Looking up from her meal, she spotted him sitting at a table across the room.

Samas.

His cold, black stare pinned her in place. She made a strangled sound as a scream crept up her throat, trying to escape. Than followed her gaze to an empty table.

"Cara? You okay?"

She didn't seem to hear him. Her eyes were wide, and she was breathing rapidly. He placed his hand on top of hers.

The touch jolted her attention back to him. She quickly looked at Than and to where she had seen Samas. The table was empty. She glanced around the room and looked back at Than. He was looking at her through narrowed eyes, head slightly tilted to the side.

"Cara?"

"Yeah, I'm okay," she said hurriedly, hoping Than wouldn't press the matter.

She looked down at her food covered in blood. Or, at least it appeared that way. Cara gagged, pressing a hand to her mouth. She looked up at Than, who was still staring at her intently, and knew he was analyzing her every move. She looked down at her plate again, but the food was back to normal, no blood - another hallucination. She was going crazy.

Cara forced the food into her mouth little by little, so she wouldn't continue to raise Than's already growing suspicions about her mental state. It tasted like ashes in her mouth. She chewed and methodically swallowed, trying to follow the conversation, but her mind kept retreating to a quiet, thoughtless place. She managed to choke down the last bite, relieved it was over. When they got up to leave the table, she raced from the room before he could stop her.

She barely made it back to her room in time before everything she had just eaten came back up. She pushed herself up to rinse her mouth, pressing the button on the side of the sink to access her drinking water rations. She let it pool in her cupped hands. When she raised them to her lips to take a sip, a sharp metallic tang filled her mouth. Instead of water, she spat out blood instead. The liquid she held in her hands had also turned to blood. With a scream, she recoiled, red splashing onto the floor.

She wiped her hands on her pants, but the blood refused to come off. She looked up into the mirror. Standing behind her, half concealed in the shadows, was the vision of the boy she had killed. Turning around swiftly, she was met with empty air. There was nothing there. She slumped against the wall and slid down to the floor, shaking and trembling.

She closed her eyes tightly and opened them again slowly. The blood was gone. She bent her legs and tucked her knees to her chest, using her toes to rock herself back and forth. She closed her hands into fists and pressed them up against her mouth, biting her knuckles to keep from screaming. What was wrong with her? She was falling apart, and she couldn't stop it.

Chapter Thirty-Seven

"I'm worried about Cara."

Caine's gaze snapped up to meet Than's. "What? Why?" He pushed his work aside, giving Than his full attention.

"I think she is suffering from some form of PTSD." Than looked concerned.

"What do you mean?" Caine frowned. He had run into Cara yesterday in the halls, and she had told him she was fine.

"Are you totally blind?" Than asked, surprised Caine hadn't noticed. "She's barely eating and sleeping. One of the officers informed me he went to check on her, and she was sleeping under her bed like she was hiding. She jumps at the sight of her own shadow, and she acts like she sees things that aren't there. Almost as if she is having flashbacks. She just goes somewhere else sometimes. Yesterday, she was eating and just froze, looking off to an empty table like she saw something there. I called her name three times before I got through to her. She looked terrified."

Caine wiped his hands down his face. "She keeps telling me she's fine."

"Of course, she will say anything to keep you from finding out. If we have learned anything about her, it's that she's not stupid. She knows how much you have on your plate already. Do you think she wants to worry you?"

"She needs to go see Nadir."

"I agree, she should, but I don't think it's what she needs right now to help her through this." He frowned. "It's possible she may not even realize what is happening to her; how severe it is."

Caine knew how PTSD could affect a person. He had seen it many times in his career, even with his own officers. Trauma could bring even the strongest soldier to their knees. Civilians like Cara didn't have the same training and knowledge on how to handle it.

"Thank you," he told Than. "I think I know who I need to have a conversation with."

Caine paid a visit to Nadir. "How is Cara improving?"

"Her body has healed almost completely."

"There is a 'but' coming," Caine said warily.

"But, her spirit is broken."

"That's what I am afraid of." Caine filled Nadir in on Than's concerns.

"She is dealing with an incredible trauma. She may not be able to handle it on her own," Nadir agreed. "Have her come down and see me. I have something I think could help her."

Caine agreed. The only issue now would be convincing her to get the help she needed. Caine went to her room, but when the door opened, it was empty. As he turned to leave, something Than had mentioned earlier stopped him. He crossed to the bed. Crouching down, he peered under it. Cara was sleeping underneath, curled up on her side.

"Oh, Cara," he breathed softly. Guilt tore at him. Than was right. How had he missed how bad things had gotten? He reached out and gently touched her arm. She opened her eyes. He helped her as she crawled out and stood up. She was pale, dark circles under her eyes.

"What were you doing down there?"

"Sometimes I-" she hesitated, "I don't know how to explain it. I feel safer there." She hated admitting it, like saying it out loud was exposing her weakness. "Caine? Samas said something to me when he was leaving." She frowned, a puzzled look furrowing her brow. "Parting is such sweet sorrow," she said quietly.

"What?"

"He quoted Shakespeare. How could he possibly know Shakespeare?"

"I'm not sure. I'll look into it. In the meantime, Nadir wants you to go down and see him."

"Why?" She stepped away from him. She was tense, watching him warily.

"He just wants to check on you and make sure everything is healing as it should be."

"I'm not stupid, Caine; you think I'm losing my mind."

Caine shook his head, "I don't think that at all."

"Don't lie to me, Caine. I'm fine. I'm completely fine."

Caine gently took her shoulders. "I believe you. Just humor an old man who's concerned about his patient."

"Fine." It was reluctant, but she had agreed.

"I'll bring you down there." He walked out into the hall with her.

She forced a weak smile, her eyes darting all around as if she were on the lookout. She shifted anxiously from one foot to the other. He reached for her, but she shrank away.

"Come on," he coaxed, holding out his hand.

She reluctantly took it, and he led her away. As they rounded a corner, she let out a strangled cry and slammed to a stop, her hand slipping from his grasp. He turned to see her staring straight ahead, eyes wide and face white. Following her gaze, he saw his officer Reytu Parks talking to another crew member down the hall. Reytu had curly, black hair. By the time he realized who Cara thought she was seeing, she had already gone running in the opposite direction.

"Cara!" He lunged for her. She was light on her feet, weaving between officers. He caught up and grabbed her. She fought him.

"Cara, calm down."

"He's here. He's coming for me. I need to hide!" She kept trying to pull away, eyes wild with terror. "Let me go!"

"Cara, Samas isn't here. It wasn't him. It wasn't him."

Cara wasn't having any of it. "Please, let me go!" Tears filled her eyes. "Please," she begged.

The sound tore at him. He pulled her into his strong embrace, and she collapsed against him, sagging into his arms and sinking to her knees. Members of his crew stepped towards them. He shook his head, indicating he needed no assistance.

"I'm not fine," she sobbed. "I'm not fine."

He gently curled his arms under her legs and shoulders, cradling her close to him, and carried her down to Medical.

***

Nadir gently convinced her to take a pill to help calm her down. She quieted, sitting in the chair and staring off into space.

"Dammit Nadir, she's half-drugged," Caine complained.

"You tell me what else to do since you are the doctor," he retorted.

Caine scowled at him.

"She went through tremendous trauma. She will have to process this in her own way. You of all people should know the mind is a complicated place," Nadir chided.

Caine went over to Cara. He gently took her chin in his hand, and she looked at him for a second. She frowned and turned away, but not before he caught a glimpse of something dark slither behind her gaze.

"I'm sorry. I didn't sleep well," she murmured lightly, in a faint, dazed voice. She pressed her hands to the sides of her head, shaking it.

"Cara, look at me," he gently commanded.

When she met his eyes, he pushed into her mind. A tendril of black fear coiled around her mind. As he reached out for it, the vine-like curl recoiled from his touch. It was deep-rooted, weaving around her thoughts and memories like a vine. He grasped a part of it and pulled, trying to detach it, but it fought back, writhing and slipping from his grasp. He pulled harder, trying to rip it out, but Cara jerked and thrashed until he backed out. He couldn't do it without causing her immense pain.

She slumped forward in her chair, elbows on her knees, resting her face in the palms of her hands. "I can't make it go away."

His heart broke for her. Fear was an incredibly powerful emotion. It could affect her mind for a long time if she didn't figure out how to manage it. He knew it wasn't just fear. There was something else lurking in the background, something she was trying to suppress. Grief, guilt, and shame: a combination of feelings he knew well. Somehow, she blamed herself for this.

"Cara, please talk to me?"

"I don't know what to tell you." She sounded weary and hopeless.

"Why don't you start with why you're sleeping under your bed? Why don't you feel safe here?"

"I told you; he's watching me. When he left me, he said he wasn't done with me. He told me he would see me again. I still have to help him finish something. He knows where I am. I can feel him; he's following me."

"I won't let that happen. You're safe here. He can't get to you here." Caine stood abruptly, running a hand through his hair in frustration. He was powerless and unable to help her. "I'm sorry."

"Yeah, you should be," Cara said sharply.

Caine was taken aback by the venom in her voice, the sudden shift in her demeanor.

"You blame me for this?" he asked.

Cara's eyes flashed. "Yes, I do. You never even came for me. You sent Zora to find me. I should never have been sent running off into the woods in the middle of the night on a strange planet. None of this would have happened if you had come for me yourself,"

"Of course, I sent Zora. We were under attack. I did the best I could in the situation. I made a difficult call. I am the Commander. There were hundreds of other villagers there who needed protection, not just you. I had my job to do."

Cara huffed and rolled her eyes, displeased with what he was telling her.

"My crew was out there fighting back. A crew I promised to protect at all costs. My duty will always come first, always. Above everything, friends, family, even you. If you were expecting anything otherwise, you will find yourself sorely disappointed."

Cara was angry with his explanation even though she knew it was right. "Then why did you come for me? Why bother saving me?" She scowled bitterly.

"How could you ask that?" He was stunned.

"I didn't deserve it. You should have left me there to die."

The fragile hold he had on his anger gave way.

"You have no idea what I had to go through to save you, what I had to do. None of this would have even happened in the first place if you hadn't insisted on going with us. You should never have been down there to begin with. You shouldn't even be here."

Cara's eyes narrowed. She went deathly still and quiet. As if a switch was flipped, she released some of the pent-up rage. It was like she had shut down, wasn't thinking, just releasing her anger. She let out a cry of frustration and threw a metal tray across the room. She tipped a chair and knocked over a container of metal tools.

"Enough," he commanded harshly.

Cara froze under the influence of his words, chest heaving.

"Enough." He released the command.

"Don't. Ever. Use. Silverspeak. On. Me. Again." She ground out each word sharply, spitting them at him like knives, one by one. She turned and stormed off, leaving Caine in stunned silence. He turned to Nadir, who didn't look the least bit surprised by the exchange he had witnessed.

"We have a long way to go." Nadir sighed.

Chapter Thirty-Eight

The Hostile woman lunged at her. Cara dodged to the left, and the woman's fist just missed her cheek. Instead, the woman grabbed a handful of Cara's hair, yanking backward hard enough she was ripped off her feet and slammed into the ground.

The woman wrestled with Cara in the dirt. She fought back, striking out and trying to get herself free. She managed to land a blow on the woman's cheek, snapping her head to the side, blood spraying from her mouth. This was her chance to get free.

Cara pressed her feet firmly on the ground for leverage and pushed upwards, using the momentum to thrust the woman off her.

She rolled to her stomach, clawing at the ground to stand, when a pair of feet stepped in front of her. She looked up to see the young Hostile boy staring down at her with blood covered his face.

"Why?" he asked hauntingly. "Murderer," he yelled at her.

The Hostile woman grabbed Cara by the back of her shirt and flipped her over. Cara pulled her along as they rolled. She grappled with the woman, but she managed to get a hold of Cara's arms. Cara was trapped and struggled to get free.

Cara's head cracked on the floor when she fell out of bed. The last echoes of her scream died in the darkness.

She lay on the floor, heaving. Her sheets were twisted around her arms and legs in a tangled mess. It was the third night in a row she had woken with the front of her shirt soaked with sweat and her hair clinging to her forehead and cheeks. Her ribs ached as she breathed as if they were still broken.

She went over to the comm unit on the wall. She wanted to call to Caine, but he had been so distant she found herself calling for Than instead. He hadn't asked any questions. He just showed up and wrapped her in a warm hug.

"You didn't tell Caine I called you?" She worried about him finding out.

"If you had wanted Caine to know, you would have told him. Talk to me."

She did. She told him about the nightmares and feeling the pain. She talked to him about hearing Samas when she was alone and seeing him when he wasn't there but didn't tell him about the boy. She still wasn't ready to share that story yet. Than listened intently, nodding as she spoke. With every word she spoke, some of the pain inside diminished. When she finished, he didn't speak right away.

"I know this is hard for you, but I think you need to tell Caine."

Cara shook her head frantically, pleading with him not to get Caine involved. "I don't want to bother him with this, Than. He has too much to worry about as it is. I don't want to add to that. Besides, he already thinks I'm crazy."

"I know sometimes dealing with Caine can be a bit like getting whiplash." He gave her a knowing smile. "He cares about you. He doesn't think you are crazy. You're processing everything that has happened to you. I haven't seen Caine dealing with his feelings for a very long time, but you make him feel things, whether he cares to admit it or not. You bring out a side of him I haven't seen in years. He would want you to tell him." Than rubbed Cara's shoulders.

"He hasn't come to see me for days. We had an argument." She wished she didn't sound as desperate as she was feeling.

Than looked away for a moment. "He's angry," he admitted. Cara's face must have portrayed a look of shock because Than quickly clarified. "Not at you. At himself. He blames himself for this; for allowing you to be hurt. Every time he sees you, it reminds him of what happened to you. He believes it is his fault. For Caine, it has always been easier for him to avoid his issues than to confront them."

"It's not like I'm going anywhere. He can't just ignore me," she pointed out.

"I think it is why this is so hard for him. He doesn't want to, but he feels like he has to. Instead of confronting his feelings, he's thrown himself into work. It keeps his mind occupied and keeps him from thinking about you," Than trailed off.

Cara slumped back into the pillows.

"Talk to him. Give him a chance," Than gently encouraged.

"I'll do my best," Cara said, and she meant it.

She would try to explain what was happening to Caine. How he reacted was out of her control. When Than got up to leave, Cara desperately grabbed at his hand.

"Please, don't go. Stay, just until I fall asleep?"

Than sat back down, and she curled up next to him. In the darkness, he began to hum. It was a soft, comforting tune - a lullaby. He hummed the tune his mother once sang to him as Cara drifted off.

The poor girl had been through hell and made it back. He had seen officers go through less and come out worse than her. She was stronger than she realized. When her breathing softened and evened out, he left her. He wasn't on duty, but he made his way up to the Bridge anyway. Caine was there, overseeing the night shift. He shot Than a quick surprised look but went back to his quiet observation.

"Why do I have the feeling you are here to lecture me."

"No lecture." Than stood beside him, staring out over the quiet Bridge. He didn't give any further explanation. Caine put the puzzle pieces together.

"Cara called you?" He shouldn't be jealous, but he was. He understood why Cara had called Than instead of him. He had closed that door on her. Than nodded, confirming his suspicion.

"This isn't easy for her either."

"I said some horrible things to her," Caine admitted.

"So make it up to her. Do something nice."

"Like what?" Caine wasn't sure how anything could fix this.

"You could start by telling her how you actually feel," Than offered.

"How? There can't be anything between us."

"You've been breaking the rules since the moment she showed up. What makes this any different?" Than laughed dryly.

Caine turned to defend his actions, but he was already walking away. Than was right. Since her arrival, he had been breaking rules left and right, and it was unlike him. He had to re-center himself; he just didn't know how.

Chapter Thirty-Nine

Than found Cara eating. "Finish up and come with me."

Cara cleaned up her tray quickly and followed Than from the cafeteria. "I remember the first battle I was in like it was yesterday: the first time I felt like my life was in real danger. I realized how incapable I was at protecting myself. I felt hopeless and terrified. I doubled my combat training. It was the only thing that helped me regain my confidence."

They entered a large space with mats on the floor. "Fighting?" She looked questioningly at Than. What was he up to?

"Just don't tell Caine," Than winked. "I don't think he would approve." He crossed the room. "I won't presume to know what you are going through, but I remember being so angry for not being able to defend myself. The anger and fear kept growing until I faced it down."

"I don't think this is a good idea."

"Trust me. Here, put these on." He handed her some gloves and wrapped cloth around his knuckles. "Let's start with the basics. Come on. Try and hit me."

Cara shook her head, mortified.

"Believe me. You won't be able to hurt me… yet." He smiled. "This will be good practice for me too. Fire away." He readied his stance; arms raised defensively.

Cara threw a punch, clipping his hand.

He nodded approvingly. "Good, but next time don't move your feet before you hit. It gives you away."

Cara swung again. Reality blurred, and she no longer was on the Archon fighting Than. In her mind, she had been transported back to Yedrus and was fighting for her life. All the pent-up emotions she had been holding back finally broke through the carefully built mental wall she had constructed. She lost control, blindly lashing out.

"Woah, woah, Cara." He tried to dodge a blow, but her knuckles split his lip open. "Cara, sweetheart." He wrapped his arms around her, pinning her arms to her sides. Pupils dilated, chest heaving; she looked feral. She was trapped somewhere else.

"Cara."

She blinked and looked around.

"You good?" he asked after a moment, watching her with concern.

"Fine," she snapped, pulling away. "We're done for today." She left.

He didn't try to stop her. That didn't go how he had planned.

Than wiped the blood away from his lip with the back of his hand.

"Shit."

"What the hell happened to your face?" Caine asked later, referencing Than's swollen and bruised lip.

"Dropped a tool fixing some wiring," Than lied, brushing the subject aside. "How are things looking out there?"

Caine gave him a suspicious sideways glance but let the conversation carry on. "It's been quiet."

Than glanced around the room at everyone working silently. Caine had been on a rampage for the last few days, making sure everything was in order. He had the whole crew running scared every time he walked into a room.

"You know, when I mentioned you had been breaking rules lately, I meant it as a good thing. I didn't intend for you to go completely off the deep end."

"You were right. I can't let her change how things are done."

"Maybe you should," Than muttered.

"Excuse me?"

"You heard me just fine. Maybe you should. You've been so uptight for years, never taking a second to breathe. Then she shows up, and you finally let loose for just a moment, but it's like you refuse to give yourself a break. You won't let yourself be happy even for a second. You know what? It's fine. You want to be miserable? Fine. Be miserable but don't take the rest of us down with you." Than stormed off.

Zora stood at her post nearby, staring dead ahead, trying not to show any sign of having overheard their exchange.

"Is Than right?" he asked her.

She turned to him with big eyes. "Sir?"

"Am I uptight?"

She looked away; lips pressed together as if she was weighing her options. She met his gaze squarely. "Sir, if you have to ask me, I think you already know the answer."

Caine took a few steps before turning back. He pointed at her. "Not a word of this to anyone."

"Wouldn't dare, Sir."

***

The next day Caine tracked Cara down in the library. She looked momentarily startled when he entered. The expression on her face changed, and she glared at him. It was as if a switch was flipped just as before. He could see it in her eyes. The hair on his neck stood up. This wasn't right.

"Hi."

She scoffed. "Hi," she parroted in a sarcastic tone.

"How have you been?"

"Fantastic. Never better," she snapped.

She turned, mumbling under her breath as she placed the book back on the shelf. Her head twitched, and she squeezed her eyes shut momentarily before turning to Caine with a cold smile.

"Goodbye," she said in an eerie singsong manner, her head slightly tilted to the side. She turned to go.

"Stop," Caine commanded before he could stop himself.

She froze in her tracks. She whirled to face him, murder in her eyes. "I told you, never-"

Caine cut her tirade short. He was done talking.

He grasped the sides of her head, forcing her to meet his eyes, and pushed in. He slipped through all her defenses he knew so well. Inside was darker than he had ever seen it. Worse than before. Everything coated with the thick black residue of trauma. Her mind was like a wasteland. In the great stretch of darkness before him, there was movement. He walked towards it. It was a memory, bigger than any other, consuming her mind. It stretched out in front of him, growing larger as he got closer until it was almost like he walked directly into the scene itself.

A Hostile boy appeared from a wisp of black smoke. He couldn't have been more than ten. He took slow, deliberate steps towards her; a sword clutched in his hands. He paused momentarily. With a harsh yell, he rushed at Cara; sword raised high overhead.

Caine turned to look at Cara just as a gun appeared in her hand. She fired, striking the boy. He collapsed dead at her feet; blood pooled around him. Cara pressed her hands on his wound to stop the bleeding as the boy's body faded and vanished. She rocked back and forth, teeth digging into her knuckles as she bit back a scream.

From another curl of black smoke, a Hostile woman stormed towards her. The Hostile knocked Cara down and cut into the skin on Cara's chest with a knife. Alarmed, Caine attempted to grab the attacking woman, but she vanished into a cloud of black smoke as his arms went right through her.

Of course, he couldn't grab her because she wasn't real. This was just a memory. This had happened to Cara.

As he stared at her lying on the ground, the woman reappeared from black smoke and continued her attack on Cara.

The scene flickered and started anew. She was reliving this memory over and over in her mind. The horror of it washed over him.

She hadn't revealed many details of her time with Samas. He hadn't pried, hoping she would open up to him over time. All she had been doing was bottling it up and letting it eat away at her. He'd known what she'd been through was terrible. This was beyond his worst fears.

"Cara." He crouched in front of her. She didn't move. She lay there on the ground staring into space, eyes unfocused and blank. He spoke her name again, still nothing. It was like she was somewhere else. He gently took her shoulders and shook her, trying to get her attention back.

Her pupils grew larger, black spilling out over her grey iris until they were entirely black. She held her hands up in front of her face looking at them. Her hands were covered in blood. Slowly, the blood on her fingertips darkened and turned black. The black spread across the pale skin of her hands, up her arms and neck, taking over like a vine strangling its host.

Cara smiled up at him, menacing and cold. "Goodbye." She thrust her hands up at him, pushing at him. The force of her defensive move broke their connection. Caine couldn't keep a foothold inside her mind anymore and was forced to withdraw. Cara was standing there in front of him, a pained look of embarrassment and frustration on her face.

"And now you know," she said bitterly as if he had discovered some dark secret she had been hiding.

He wanted to comfort her, but he couldn't quite find the words. He wanted to tell her it would be all right, but that would be a lie. Caine had seen the torture she'd endured and how deeply it was affecting her. He recalled her hands and arms turning black, the effects of the fear and trauma spreading through her. She would have to fight this in her own way, in her own time.

Cara stared at him a moment longer as if waiting for him to say something. The frustration in her eyes turned to disappointment, and she shoved past him. Caine's hands balled into tight fists as he resisted reaching out to her.

Cara just wanted to go back to her room, curl up, and hope to disappear. Caine now knew what she had done. She was afraid he would think less of her, be angry with her and pity her. Or worse, hate her. She'd walked away, and he hadn't stopped her. She wanted to be angry at him for breaking his promise and wanted to feel like her privacy had been violated, but instead, there was a strange sense of relief that he finally knew.

What did he think about her? How did he feel now that he knew what she had done? His reaction had spoken volumes. He had let her go. He didn't make any attempt to comfort her. It was clear he wanted nothing to do with her. Maybe, it was better that way.

She looked up and stopped short as she met Zora's eyes. It was the first time Cara had seen her since the night of the attack. Cara wasn't sure if Zora was avoiding her or if she was avoiding Zora. Maybe it was a bit of both. She knew they would have to face each other at some point, but Cara didn't think she was ready. Seeing Zora brought her right back to that night, making her remember.

"Cara." Zora approached her, wringing her hands awkwardly. Cara knew where the conversation would head. It was only natural Zora would want to talk about it.

"Not right now, Zora."

"Cara, please," Zora pleaded.

Anger exploded inside Cara. She was irritated Zora wanted to bury the hatchet right here and now. "I told you I don't want to talk about it. I don't want to talk to you," Cara's voice rose.

"I know you're angry with me." Zora grabbed Cara's hand. "I'm sorry. I never meant for you to get hurt."

"You should be sorry." Cara yanked her hand away.

"I tried to keep you safe," Zora choked up, barely able to finish.

"Why does everyone want to keep talking about this? It won't change what happened. I can't help but be angry with you, but I'm also angry at Caine. He sent you to find me. You did what you thought was best, but it still happened, and no amount of apologizing will undo it." Cara turned away, trying to breathe and not lose control of her anger.

Zora never intended for her to get hurt. It was a chaotic moment, and Zora did what she believed was the safest thing for her. How could Cara fault her? But there was so much anger built up inside she couldn't control it. She didn't want to be mad at Zora; she didn't want to blame her, but she did.

Cara turned back to see Zora crying. "I'm sorry. I am so sorry," Zora sobbed.

Walking up to her, Cara let out a deep sigh and embraced her. It was strange, comforting Zora even though she hadn't been the one taken. She hadn't intended to make Zora so upset, but she couldn't help how she reacted to the events that had occurred.

"So sorry, so sorry, my sweet Cara," Samas' voice whispered mockingly in her ear, mimicking Zora's crying. "Did you miss me?"

Cara ripped herself away. Samas was standing where Zora had been standing just seconds before. Terror closed up her throat; she couldn't even scream.

No! How could he be here? He couldn't be. This couldn't be real. Cara squeezed her eyes shut and grabbed the sides of her head, trying to make the image disappear.

"It's not real," Cara said to herself.

"Cara?" It was Zora's voice. Cara opened her eyes. Samas' laughing face flickered and faded into a blur as Zora's face reappeared. "Cara?" she asked again. She looked concerned and reached out for her. Cara wrapped her arms around herself, a cry of sheer and absolute frustration tried to break loose from her throat, but no sound would come out.

"Oh, Cara, what happened to you?" Zora held her close as Cara shook, unable to find the words to explain that her soul was being torn to shreds.

Chapter Forty

Work swamped Caine for the next day and a half. He'd meant to find a moment to check in on Cara, but between Nadir, Than, and Zora, he knew he would have been notified if there had been any more issues. From what he had been told, Cara hadn't left her room once. When he finally found a break in his schedule, he visited her there. He found her sitting on her bed. Her legs were tucked up in front of her, hugged to her chest. She wasn't doing anything, just sitting, staring blankly off into space.

"Come on," he instructed.

She glanced at him, her eyes sad and tired. Robotically, she got off the bed and followed him down to the gym area Than had taken her to.

"What are we doing here?" she questioned.

"Training." He didn't elaborate just yet. If she knew what he was about to do, she would leave before he had a chance to work with her.

"I don't need any more training," she grumbled.

"What?"

Cara shook her head quickly. "Nothing." What Caine didn't know wouldn't hurt him and would keep Than out of trouble.

The look on his face told her he had questions, but he didn't push.

"Turn around."

She could feel the compelling pull of his command. Her body had no choice but to respond. She was glaring at him furiously when she came back to face him.

"Listen. You need to learn how to resist Silverspeak," Caine said. "It isn't easy, but it is possible. You're Intransigent. You already naturally fight against it.

Now you just need to figure out how to push a little harder. So, the next time I tell you to do something, I want you to give it everything you've got and try as hard as you can not to comply."

Cara wasn't sure how this would help her.

"Close your hands in a fist," he commanded.

Instantly, her fingers curled. She looked helplessly at him.

"You can do this. You need to get your hands open. Fight it."

She stared down at her hands, trying to get them to open with all her might, but nothing happened. A strand of hair fell over her eyes. She couldn't move her hands, so she blew it off her face.

"Dammit, Caine." She wanted to take her fist and use it to punch him in the face.

"Ok, enough. Take a breath. Let's try again." Caine released his command on her. "I'm going to tell you the same thing, don't let your fingers close."

Cara flexed her hands and readied her stance.

"Close your hands into fists."

His command tingled, like static electricity across her skin. The muscles tightened, and her hands trembled from the force of her resistance. She gave an angry cry as they curled up anyway against her will.

"I hate you," she growled at him. This was his opening.

"Yes, use your anger. Get mad and fight me. Fight back."

She threw everything she had at it, letting all her rage and anger bubble to the surface. Her fists trembled slightly, but not a single finger moved. Tears burned in her eyes.

"Come on now, don't give up."

He would have to push her harder. He didn't want to, but anger was working for her. She needed to find the power and strength he knew she had locked away.

"You need to do this, Cara. You can't be weak. You need to get angry. Angry at everything that has happened to you."

She bit her lip. Her brows pinched together, eyes darting around as she puzzled over his words.

"Now, take that feeling and focus it."

She was still staring at him, frustrated.

"Kuso, Cara. Fight!" he yelled at her.

She let out a wordless shout of sheer exasperation.

"Don't be weak. If you're weak, Samas will hurt you again."

He couldn't pull punches anymore. It was time to bring out the big guns.

"Everyone thinks you're weak. You're a complete disgrace. You're pathetic," he taunted her.

He hated saying such things to her, but she needed fuel for the fire that had died inside her.

Finally, he used the one last thing he knew would spark a violent emotional reaction inside her.

"Come on, Cara," he taunted with a mocking sneer. "This should be easy for you. If you're capable of killing a child, you should be able to do this." He ignored the bile creeping up the back of his throat.

Cara let out a desperate roar. It was a sound of pure anguish that nearly broke Caine's resolve. He almost ran to her, so he could hold her and comfort her, but he forced his feet to remain firmly planted until she broke through. She was so close, nearly there.

Cara couldn't believe Caine was saying these things. She was so angry with him, blaming him for this. How could he try to turn this around on her? And now, he brought it up.

The one memory that ripped her to shreds.

There was an audible crack, like a plane breaking the sound barrier. As the bond broke, her fingers flew open with such force she wobbled.

She looked up at Caine, astonished. She couldn't believe she had freed herself. A rush of confidence flooded her, making her head spin. For a split second, the sheer surprise made her forget the awful things Caine said.

Caine couldn't help it; he rushed to her, wrapped his arms around her, and kissed her before he could stop himself. The spark exploded through him when his lips met hers made every cell in his body sizzle. He felt proud and something else he refused to name. Breathing hard, he pulled her close, and she clung to him.

"You did it," he whispered, resting his chin lightly on the top of her head.

Cara was shaking as the adrenaline drained from her system. Caine's praise was like a drug, and she could become addicted. She slumped against him, using his body to hold up her weight.

"I knew you could do it." He pressed a kiss on the top of her head. "You can free yourself from Samas too."

Cara pushed his arms away and stepped back. She had done it, but he had pushed her by saying things he knew would hurt. All the hurt rushed back, and his words ran through her like poison. If she could kill a child...

She couldn't stop the tears, the same as she couldn't stop the sun from setting. They overwhelmed her, and she wept, feeling bitter and angry.

"Don't cry." Caine cradled her close. "I'm so sorry. I didn't mean any of that."

"But you're right; I killed a child. What kind of a monster does that?"

"You're not a monster, Cara. If anyone here is, it's me, not you. You didn't do it on purpose. I would know. I've done far too many terrible things in my life."

The darkness swallowed her up, sucking all the life and joy from the moment. She was cold and hollow - dead inside.

Dead like the little boy whose life she had stolen.

"We all have monsters inside us." Cara turned to go.

The sharp change in her demeanor was instantly recognizable in her eyes. They went dull and lifeless; all the spark had fizzled out. Whatever dark place she had just gone to, it had consumed her.

He reached out and grabbed her wrist as she walked away from him.

"Cara, you have to forgive yourself."

"He knew I would." Sadness furrowed her brow.

"Who?"

"Samas. He gave me no choice. He knew I would shoot the boy. He wanted me to. He said he wanted to see the monster inside me, and I showed it to him."

"You are not a monster," Caine countered firmly.

"But I am. I killed a child, Caine. Who does that? Who kills a child?"

"Someone with no other choice."

"There's always a choice, Caine."

"Then, you would be dead." He yanked his hand away. The disappointment in his eyes stung.

Caine wished he could explain to Cara that he understood exactly what she was going through, that he had been in her place before, but some things were better left unspoken.

Chapter Forty-One

Cara sat with Zora and Than at dinner, venturing out of her room for the first time in days. The company was refreshing.

"Do you want me to grab you some more?" Than asked her.

She was surprised when she looked down, and her plate was empty. Than smiled at the sight. She knew he was worried about her, and maybe he was right to be.

She couldn't remember the last time she had eaten more than a few bites. The hunger had finally caught up with her.

"No. Thanks, though." She was content sitting there with them, a welcome moment of peace. It was an oasis of calm in the middle of the chaos brewing inside.

The conversation was light; idle chit chat about work until Zora said something that caught her attention.

"At least the attack went well," Zora muttered absentmindedly, lifting her cup to take a drink.

"What attack?" Cara was confused. She looked to Than for an explanation, but he averted his eyes and shot a nasty look at Zora, which clearly showed she had said something she shouldn't have.

"I thought you knew." Zora looked mortified. She turned to Than. "I thought she knew."

"Knew what? What happened?" Cara demanded.

Than was quiet for a moment. Cara could tell he was carefully choosing his next words. "The Council authorized a strike against the Hostiles on Yedrus."

"You attacked them?" She was still trying to put the pieces together, but the image was getting clear.

"They're Hostiles, Cara. They hurt you," Zora said defensively. With her statement, the final piece clicked into place, and Cara understood Zora's meaning clearly. The Archon had used full military force against the Samandran Clan, the people on Yedrus. Cara pushed her plate away.

"No. No." She shook her head rapidly. "I can't believe this." Her chair scraped against the floor as she stood abruptly. "And Caine was okay with this?"

Their silence was enough confirmation for her. She wiped her hands over her face. "This is unbelievable." The darkness lurking inside her surged to the forefront again. She had been trying so hard to cage it, but it broke down all the barriers she had constructed and swiftly dragged her mind back down to the mental hell she was trying to escape.

"This can't be happening. I can't believe this." She walked away, rubbing her hands on her cheeks, clutching the sides of her head.

"Cara, wait!"

She quickened her pace, wanting to be anywhere but there. Than caught up to her, reaching out and grabbing her arm.

"Don't touch me!"

"Cara, please listen," Than attempted to reason with her.

"I'm done listening," she growled. She wanted to talk to Caine and no one else. She knew Than was following her, but her mind was set, so she ignored him.

"Caine," she yelled his name, storming onto the Bridge.

Caine looked up, taken by surprise. Cara was marching toward him with Than right on her heels, looking deeply apologetic.

"I tried to stop her," Than mouthed at him behind her, giving him a helpless shrug.

Cara wrung her hands. "Please tell me it's not true."

Caine glanced behind her at Than, not exactly sure what she meant.

"You attacked their planet?"

Kuso.

"Cara, I don't know what you heard-"

"How could you? Why?"

Caine hated the accusatory tone in her voice.

"The Council…"

"Screw the Council! You could have told them no, but you didn't want to. You wanted to kill them. All you wanted was revenge. This is bullshit!"

"Cara, listen."

"No. He was right. You think you can justify it because you all think you're better than everyone else, but you're no better than they are."

Caine needed to diffuse the situation and fast. She was making a scene in front of his crew. He grabbed her, pinning her arms to her sides. He dragged her into his office.

"Let go of me." She kicked and squirmed in his arms. He kicked the door shut and released her.

"I get it, you're angry…"

"Angry?" She let out an enraged laugh. "I'm disgusted. And you want to know the worst part?" She shook her head. Her expression changed to one of profound sadness. "You used me to justify it. More people died because of me." Her voice faded off quietly as she finished, her demeanor far more passive than it had been on the Bridge just moments earlier.

"You're right." His admission caught her attention. "I wanted to kill them for what they did to you. The Council wanted to retaliate, and I didn't try to stop them. I didn't want to."

He let out a long sigh. How could he make her understand? She had every right to be angry with him, but if she could only see it from his perspective.

"You haven't lived in this world. We've spent too long fighting this war. Too long. There have been too many casualties on both sides. Maybe it was a mistake, but I made my choice, and I have to live with it. This is a black and white world, Cara. We all need to pick our sides. I don't have to justify anything to you, but know this, if I had to do it all over again, I wouldn't change a thing. It's the only reason you're back," he finished.

"What does that mean?"

"I agreed to the attack to get your rescue authorized by the Council. I did what I had to do to."

She hated how his words sounded so similar to Samas.

"Well, that was a mistake," she said sarcastically, her tone dry and icy.

It didn't matter in the end if she had killed all those people directly or not. They were dead because of her. Yes, she had killed only one person with her own hands, but she had ultimately been responsible for the thousands of other lives lost. She caused their deaths.

Caine hit the table with his fist, making her jump. "Kuso. I am sick and tired of hearing you say that," he thundered. "I put my entire crew at risk to make sure you were safe, to make sure you came back alive. You, of all people, should know that. Believe it or not, I understand what you are going through. You haven't even given me a chance to help you. You won't let anyone help you. I have waited patiently, hoping you would open up to me. I have been in your shoes, and I know how much this must hurt. You killed a child, and you hate yourself for it. But you did what you had to do to survive."

"You weren't there," she whispered, remembering the horrors she had live through.

"No. No, I wasn't, but I have been in your shoes before. I've had to make that impossible choice. Kill or be killed. It's them or us, Cara. At the end of the day, I will always choose to return home to my crew. Sometimes you make the hard call, and you have to live with it, but at least you're alive."

Cara chilled as Caine's words continued to eerily echo Samas. Them or us.

"I wanted to," she whispered. "I wanted to kill him." There was a sense of relief as she finally said it out loud; finally admitted it. She looked up, searching Caine's face for any sign of disgust or hatred, but she didn't see any. She didn't see pity or sympathy either. There was only understanding.

"You wanted to live. Truthfully, I'm glad you did."

Cara's father had grown up on a farm. As a little girl, he had made sure she knew the truth about where her food came from. Necessary evils, he had called them. Survival had always been centered on one life triumphing over another since the dawn of time.

Cara understood she was only back on the Archon because Caine had agreed to the Council's orders, but she was alive because she had made the difficult choice. Them or us, Samas had told her. Survivors. Yes, they had taken her hostage, tortured her, but there was still blood on her hands, and she wasn't sure she would ever be able to wash it off.

Chapter Forty-Two

Cara made her way to the sink after she was torn from another vicious nightmare. She splashed a few handfuls of water from her drinking bottle on her face and stared at herself in the mirror, noting how terrible she looked. The dark circles under her eyes were even more prominent.

She noticed a small dark spot on her cheek that hadn't been there before. She spilled a little water on her finger and rubbed it. As she did, it grew. The more she scrubbed, the bigger it got. It was dark red.

Blood. Dried blood.

It spread across her cheek in the same familiar pattern as the boy's blood that the Hostile woman had smeared on her face. She kept trying to wipe it away, rubbing her skin raw, but the blood dripped down her cheek. A drop hung suspended on the edge of her chin for a moment. It fell into the sink with a sickening plop.

As she stared at herself, the image of Samas appeared in the mirror next to hers. She let out an angry cry and smashed her fist into the mirror, cracking it. The broken image just laughed. The laughter echoed behind her. She turned to see Samas materialize behind her, standing next to her bed.

"Well, hello." His voice made her skin crawl. He reached out and grabbed her throat, shoving her back against the wall and choking her. How was he here?

The air rushed from her lungs. Caine's voice filled her mind, telling her to fight. If she could break free from Silverspeak, she could break free from this too.

Cara planted her feet and drove herself into him. The momentum sent them both tumbling. As they fell, she could feel his grip loosen. When they hit the floor, his hold released, and she rolled away from him. She jumped to her feet with her fists up, ready to defend herself, but he vanished into a swirling puff of black smoke.

Her breath caught when the smoke cleared, and she was standing inside her apartment. This was still a dream; this wasn't real. Rage boiled inside of her. She was angry at Samas, Caine, and especially herself. How much longer would she have to keep suffering? She hadn't asked for any of this, yet she was the one having to bear the brunt of the consequences. She was fed up; enough was enough.

Samas appeared in front of her again, called to her, and vanished. He would appear around her in different spots, laughing and calling to her. She braced herself, and when he appeared right in front of her, his face morphed into Caine's but the voice calling her was all Samas.

Tricks.

She launched at him, striking him with her fists. His image swirled into clouds of black smoke again, and from it, the Hostile woman who attacked her stormed out towards her. She knocked Cara down with a solid kick to the chest.

Cara knew the pain that was coming. Her collarbone burned where the faded scar was. The woman's face morphed into David's face, then her own. Her own face looked down at herself, laughing, but the laugh sounded like Samas. The vision of herself growled and slapped her hard across the face.

The face changed again, into Caine's. "You're weak," he yelled at her angrily. "Pathetic." His fingers closed around her throat, choking her.

Cara fought back, trying to escape. She managed to pry herself away and rolled out from under him. She ran to the window, but Caine's laugh made her freeze. Out of thin air, a gun materialized on the countertop, and she spun back in time to see a swirl of black smoke take form. The boy hobbled towards her; his hand pressed over his stomach and blood oozing between his fingers. He raised a hand and pointed at her. "Killer," he murmured.

Something shifted inexplicably. She looked down to see the gun had moved and was now in her hand. "Killer," the boy hissed again. She wanted to drop the gun, but she couldn't open her hand. She wouldn't shoot the boy again. She held the gun up to her head. The boy vanished, and her duplicate appeared and walked towards her.

"Killer," her copy sneered, circling her.

"No, stop!" Cara refused to lose control this time.

"You can make it stop. You can make all of this go away. It's easy."

"How?"

"You know how."

Cara looked down at the gun in her hand. Was this her only way out? Would it wake her up from the nightmare? She pressed the barrel to her temple.

"Do it, you monster." Caine's vision was back. His face flickered, and she caught a fleeting glimpse of Samas before it melded back into the image of Caine. Cara pointed the gun at Caine.

"Cara." Caine's voice was soft. "Hey, you're just dreaming. You're okay. You need to wake up." He brushed his hand down the side of her face and kissed her forehead. "Come on, wake up."

"I can't."

"Yes, you can. You know what to do."

She shook her head.

"You already know what you have to do." He reached for her, gently took her wrist, and turned her hand, so the gun was pressed against her head. "You've got this."

She wanted to wake up, but maybe this was the way. "Okay," she said weakly. She looked up at and found herself looking at herself, laughing.

"Pathetic," her copy sneered. The same word Caine had used. She was weak; she was pathetic. "Killers deserve to die." Her double laughed.

Cara cried, tears streaming down her face. She wanted to pull the trigger, but her finger wouldn't move. Why? She deserved this. She was a monster. She was a killer. She killed a child. A child who would have killed her had she not acted. She was alive because she had defended herself.

Cara could physically feel the change in her mindset. As if she had physically moved to another level to the next phase in recovery. There was an immense feeling of acceptance, and a newfound strength coursed through her.

She was everything Samas had said she was, but it wasn't a bad thing. She was a survivor and would do whatever she had to do to make it home. She pointed the gun at the image of herself standing there in front of her, and it shimmered into the vision of the boy.

"Killer." He raised the sword.

"No. Survivor." Cara fired.

The boy's image shifted back into one of Samas, and his face contorted with rage. He cracked and shattered, letting out a shriek of anger as he exploded around her, knocking her down and blowing her across the kitchen floor until she slammed into the wall. The sound of his final screams echoed. He was gone.

Slowly, her apartment walls faded, and her room on the ship came into view. She was leaning against the wall near the door. Her head pounded where she had cracked it against the wall. Real life and nightmare merged into one. Had she been sleepwalking? Or possibly, in some strange way, she had actually been fighting Samas off. Quiet settled around her. The weight on her chest had lifted, and she could finally breathe. She looked into the mirror: no blood on her face, no visions of Samas, and no voices in her head.

Maybe, just maybe, she was finally heading in the right direction.

She had to report to Medical the following day, and when she got there, she smiled at Nadir.

"Now, there is a face I have not seen in some time," he sounded relieved. "What changed?" He walked over to her, embraced her, and pulled a chair over for her to sit.

Cara relayed her experiences in her dream and how she was finally able to move forward. She was getting stronger.

Nadir held her hands gently in his. "My dear, you are more powerful than you can even imagine. You are special. I have not met someone with a mind like yours in a long time. Do not doubt your strength. Use it, and you will accomplish amazing things." He winked at her and checked her healed wounds. He pressed his fingers along the sides of her ribcage. "Still having aches around here?"

"Not anymore."

"And what about here?" He tapped her chest over her heart.

Cara blushed, looking down in embarrassment.

"I may be an old man, but it doesn't mean I'm blind. Have you told him how you feel?"

"What's the point?" Telling Caine would be counterproductive. She was still going to be sent home at some point. If she acknowledged her feelings for him, it would just make it harder to leave when the time came.

"What do you mean?" Nadir looked at her inquisitively.

"He doesn't feel that way."

"And how would you know for certain if you haven't asked him? But what do I know? I'm just an old doctor."

Nadir's words sent a flutter of hope coursing through her. She was antsy to talk to Caine privately. When Nadir finished his examination, she hurried to Caine's private quarters.

Cara knocked softly on his door, but there was no response. Curious, she pressed her hand against the scanner next to the door.

"Entry authorized," the computerized voice chirped. She was pleasantly surprised and couldn't stop a smile.

She walked a few steps in, trying to see if he was working in his private office. Caine wasn't at his desk.

"Caine?" Maybe he wasn't in his room. She would try the Bridge next and turned to leave.

He walked out of the adjacent washroom, startling her. He was bare-chested, wearing only his blue uniform pants and boots. A towel was draped around his neck, and he used one end to dry his wet hair.

Cara quickly averted her eyes. Embarrassed she had barged in on him like this, she turned to escape from the room but turned the wrong way and ran into the wall, missing the doorway. She would have hit the floor, but Caine was instantly by her side, holding her steady. She opened her eyes and found herself staring at his chest, her hands planted firmly against it. Woah, damn. She couldn't breathe. She swallowed hard but couldn't talk.

"What are you doing?" Caine asked, helping her to a chair. "Are you okay?" he asked, softer.

She nodded rapidly. She didn't speak, unable to find the right words.

He stepped away, pulled on a shirt, and buttoned it. "Are you sure?" he asked over his shoulder as if he didn't quite believe her.

"I'm fine." She didn't know how to start the conversation about Samas or ask him who Breeta was. Caine's bare chest was more than a little distracting.

He finally turned back to face her. He searched her eyes, and she knew what he was trying to find. He was looking to see if the cancerous poison Samas left behind was continuing to spread.

"Yes, I'm okay. You can look."

Caine frowned, puzzled. He didn't understand her meaning.

"You can look." She pointed to her head.

"Are you sure?"

"Absolutely." She looked him directly in his eyes, allowing him full access.

There was a comforting pressure, like a warm hug, as he entered her mind.

Caine slipped in easily; all of her defenses had vanished. Her mind once again looked normal. Memories scrolled by, and thoughts floated around like bubbles. Everything looked the way it was supposed to. He could still sense her worry, the underlying belief Samas was watching her, but most of the outright dread and tension had receded. Not entirely gone but held back and controlled. He had a renewed sense of confidence in her.

His mouth unexpectedly twitched into a little smile. "I was saving this surprise for a little later, but I guess now works too. I want to show you something," he took her hand and led her back into the washroom. He led her to a circular glass chamber, one of the ship's cleaning chambers, and pressed a button on the panel outside.

A familiar sound filled her ears.

Water. Real water.

She peered inside. Steam clouded the glass. Her jaw dropped. "Is this…" She looked at Caine wide eyed.

"I decided you deserved this after everything you've been through. I allotted some of my personal water rations."

She stuck her hand under the water. She had been dreaming about this for weeks. A real shower. One of the luxuries she missed about being home. "Thank you." She smiled, still in disbelief.

He squeezed her hand and walked out. The door quietly slid shut.

Cara stared at the water for another moment before undressing quickly and getting under the spray. She almost cried as the water hit her skin. The hot water cascaded down her face and body.

As if sensing her thoughts, the water became hotter, and it turned her skin pink. She stuck her face under the spray, just letting it rush over her. For that small moment in time, everything felt normal. She felt normal. It was as if she was home in her own shower.

She stayed in there until her fingertips wrinkled, enjoying every single second of it while it lasted. Her muscles relaxed. Her body and mind were refreshed. She stepped out and wrapped herself up in a towel before heading back into the bedroom.

Caine was sitting on the end of the bed, elbows on his knees and hands clasped with his chin resting on them. When she stepped through the doorway, he stood. Cara stilled. There was an unmistakable look in his eyes.

They stood there, neither one moving, staring at each other for a while. All the signs were there. Cara waited for Caine to say something, do something, but he just stood there staring at her.

She would have to be the one to make the first move. Caine wouldn't act unless he got the signal that it was okay. It was just part of his nature. There were no protocols for this.

Her heart drummed rapidly in her chest, and she swallowed hard. Cara held eye contact and took one small step forward. Caine inhaled sharply, and with two long strides, he closed the distance to her. He reached for her, pulled her towards him, and leaned forward to ensnare her in a kiss.

She let her grip on the towel release, and the world faded away around them.

Chapter Forty-Three

Cara woke the next morning and rolled over. As she moved, one blue eye opened, peeking at her. A lazy smile curled up his lips. Her heart melted as long-lost feelings of normalcy returned to her. There had been no dreams of Samas.

Caine slid closer to her and pulled her on top of him. She winced as she placed too much weight on her wrist.

Immediately, Caine rolled her to the side. Both eyes were open now and filled with concern. "Hurts?" he asked.

She shook her head; it was sore but not because of the injury. "No, I just slept on it funny."

"Better let Nadir take a look at it just once more to be sure." He dressed and brought her a set of folded clothes. "I had these washed for you. I have to report to the Bridge, but I will check in on you after you go see Nadir about your wrist." He finished getting ready, kissed her on the forehead, and left. She sat on the bed and caught her breath, smoothing out the sheets next to her.

Last night had been unexpected and wonderful, but as she lay there, the stinging pang of loss sent aches through her. The plan hadn't changed. She was going to be going home at some point.

Strangely, something had shifted inside her, and getting home no longer seemed like it was a priority. In fact, she was leaning more towards trying to fight to be allowed to stay. What would it mean if she stayed? What would her life be like living in this foreign world of the future? She didn't feel like she'd fit in, but Caine was a part of her life now, and she didn't want to lose him so soon.

If she didn't go down and see Nadir, Caine would have a fit, so she dressed and went down to see him.

"Back so soon?"

"I slept on my wrist, and it was a little sore when I woke up. It's fine, but Caine wanted you to look at it. You know how he gets."

"It's always better to be safe than sorry. Let's take a look."

Cara extended her arm and let him examine her wrist.

He flexed it back and forth and massaged the joint. "It appears to be completely fine to me, my dear."

"That's what I told him when I woke up, but he didn't want to listen."

"So, it seems you took my advice."

Cara couldn't stop the hot blush from climbing up her neck to her cheeks. Nadir was far too astute to have missed the clue in her words.

"Good, you deserve to be happy. You both do." He patted her hand. "You're good to go, my dear. Don't let him boss you around too much."

She was just about to slide off the exam table when Caine entered the room, passing by Nadir as he left.

"So, how is the wrist?" he asked.

"It's fine. Told you, I just slept on it funny."

"I just wanted to be sure." He took her hand and rubbed her wrist gently, moving it around as if testing it.

Cara decided it would be a good time to broach some of the more difficult topics she wanted to discuss. "I wanted to talk to you."

"About?" Caine asked absentmindedly.

"Samas."

Caine looked up at her, hopeful she was finally opening up about what had happened while he had held her hostage.

"He would come in and talk to someone who wasn't really there. He called her Breeta."

Caine tensed visibly. For someone who was usually quite adept at hiding emotional reactions, he wasn't doing a good job of it this time. His eyes caught hers, and the look in it was chilling. All of the pain Caine had spent so long trying to suppress came flooding through him. Along with the pain, came the anger and rage so intense that he had a hard time finding an appropriate response.

"Cara, you need to let this be." He tried to keep his voice steady. It wasn't her fault that she didn't know.

Cara opened her mouth to protest, but he stopped her with a raised hand. "I am not having this discussion with you. You're back here now. It's time to move on. I'll have an officer help you back to your room," he finished sharply.

Cara stood, upset by his adamant refusal to discuss it. "I can make it by myself." She crossed the room, trying to stand as tall and steady as she could until the door shut behind her, and she slumped against the wall. Why didn't he want to talk to her? He obviously knew something about Breeta and knew what Samas had been rambling about; otherwise, he wouldn't have reacted the way he did. She made her way back to her room and stayed there. What was so bad that he didn't want to talk about it? She knew someone who might be able to give her answers.

Cara decided to confront Than about it. He would have the answers she wanted.

She hurried to the Bridge, knowing her chances of running into him were higher there. As fate would have it, he was leaving the Bridge as she approached.

"Looking for Caine?" he asked.

"Actually, I was looking for you."

He cocked his head to the side, eyebrows raised. "Oh, is that so. Well, what can I do for you?"

"I know about Breeta." She knew it was sneaky, but Than's loyalty to Caine was strong. It would be the only way he would open up.

Than looked stunned. He glanced around and took her by the arm. He quickly steered her into a small alcove.

"He actually said her name?" he asked quietly, caught off guard.

"Yes," Cara lied.

Than hadn't specified that it was Caine who had mentioned her.

"Caine never talks about her." Than wiped a hand over his face. "I haven't heard him talk about her once or even mention her name a single time since he buried her body. What did he tell you about her?"

Her blood ran cold. "He killed her?" She covered her mouth with a hand. She had known something was being hidden from her, but this secret was far more explosive than she had ever imagined.

Than narrowed his gaze, realizing he had been tricked. "Caine didn't tell you anything, did he?"

"Samas was talking about her," she confessed.

"Cara, promise me, you need to leave this alone. Do not talk to him about this. Don't bring it up at all. Please, promise me you will drop this." He tightened his grip on her arm. His expression was grim.

"All right."

He dropped his hand away from her arm. "Just go back to your room, and I'll come to get you for dinner later."

His warning gave her chills. Something was very wrong. Both Caine and Than were so adamant about refusing to answer. Than stood and left. Obviously, there was something they did not want her to find out.

She remembered there was a computer up in the library. Its primary purpose was to help locate books from the expansive selection on the shelves, but she hoped it would also be a database for information. Cara hurried to the library and went over to the computer. She typed in the name. A picture of a woman appeared. She was a Hostile covered in marks with black hair twisted into thick rope-like braids that hung long around her shoulders.

Breeta Samas. Deceased half-sister of Re'em Samas. In an unsanctioned raid on a Hostile planet, the sister of the Samandran Clan leader was captured. She was interrogated by the newest officer assigned to the ship, a young Nikolas Caine, fresh out of Fleet Training. During her Interrogation, she died, and after her death, it was discovered she was pregnant. On the orders of the acting Captain, her death was not reported, and she was buried in an unmarked grave on an unnamed Border Planet. A short time later, Officer Caine went against the orders of his Captain and reported her death to the Council. There were severe consequences. The Captain was removed from his position, and the crew involved in the cover up were disciplined. Nikolas Caine had been assigned a wife, Phoebe, only the year before. As part of the Council's disciplinary action against him for aiding in the coverup and for causing the death of Breeta, Phoebe was reassigned from Caine to another Esper. One year later, Phoebe and her husband were found murdered in their home, but the assailant was never caught.

The room spun around her. Caine had killed Samas' sister and her unborn child. Caine once had a wife, and now she was dead. There was a buzzing in her ears like a million bees swarming. Cara stepped away from the computer in shock. A soft shuffle of fabric behind her made her turn. Caine was standing in the doorway.

He was looking directly at the display; Breeta's picture was clearly visible. His face went dark. Without a word, he turned and left.

Cara raced back to her room and was sick in the toilet. This was why Caine could be so cold. These were the demons he was fighting. It was why it had been so controversial when he kept her on his ship for protection, because of Phoebe.

***

Blinded by his fury, Caine stomped back to his room, downed an entire bottle of araq, and cracked open a second one. Cara was infuriating. He had risked his life to save her, sacrificed his chance to catch Samas, and she had to go snooping around after everything he had done for her. She couldn't leave well enough alone. He hated her for digging up his past, bringing up such horrible memories. He had done everything in his power to forget what had happened; what he had done. He had been so young and hadn't known any better. He thought he was fighting for the cause and fighting the enemy. Until they had broken the rules and gone after a woman...

Caine rubbed his temples, recalling the backlash he had faced from the crew after he went to the Council, but he knew he had done the right thing.

All of this was reminding him of Phoebe. The feelings he had for her. It had been a complicated relationship, but they were fond of each other, and Phoebe had wanted to be a mother so badly. After his mistake, though - no, it wasn't a mistake. He had lost control. He killed a pregnant woman, hid it, and had lost Phoebe because of it.

Phoebe had been so quiet and calm and even. Cara was a whirlwind, stubborn, and determined. She was fire, and Phoebe was ice. Cara was strong, where Phoebe was weak. Still, Caine found himself missing Phoebe's mild mannerisms.

They had met at the Training Academy. She was two years ahead of him. Tall and blonde. She had been so far out of his league, but of course, he fell for her. She was smart beyond belief and incredibly talented. When her abilities had scored at a Level 8, Caine knew they would be matched. Phoebe was unwaveringly devoted to the Confederation, and even more so to being an Esper. She had an unshakable sense of duty, but she was never able to fulfill hers, and it was his fault.

He remembered hearing she had been killed and immediately knew Samas had done it in retaliation. He had tried to protect her. Secretly, he had fought with the Council to get her assigned to someone else, far away from him, so that she would be safe. He had done everything in his power to protect her. Phoebe would never have a child, never be a mother, just like Breeta would never be a mother. Cosmic justice. He should have known better. She was never safe after what he had done.

Then Cara had arrived, bringing up feelings long repressed, and it had seemed like the powers of the universe were conspiring against him. The alcohol dulled the hurt inside. Halfway through his second bottle of araq, he found himself stumbling down the hallways of the ship with no recollection of how he got there. The ship was quiet. No officers were wandering the halls. If there had been, he wouldn't have made it this far. He found himself standing in front of a familiar door. He didn't bother to knock.

Cara looked up as the door opened. Caine stumbled in. She rushed over, and he fell forward against her. She was immediately overwhelmed by the smell of alcohol.

"Woah there. You're drunk," she accused as he went limp in her arms.

"You're pretty." His words slurred and were barely understandable.

Cara couldn't hold up his weight. She gently leaned him against the wall and hit the comm button. "Than Theoi," she called.

It beeped as it connected. Than's groggy, sleep-filled voice crackled through the speaker, "Hello?" he asked gruffly.

"Than, I need your help."

"On my way." Than didn't question. It was one of the things she liked about him.

A few minutes later, Than arrived. He looked down at Caine, who had slid down the wall. Caine smiled up at him. "Hey there, buddy," Caine slurred.

"Ok. Come on, big guy." Than heaved Caine up.

With Than under one arm and Cara under the other, they half-dragged him back to his room.

"You know," Caine looked over at Cara. The pitch of his voice was higher than usual, and each word sloppily slid into the next. "This is all your fault. If you hadn't shown up, then you never would have been taken by Samas in the first place."

Cara knew it was the alcohol talking, but there was truth in his words.

"You are so damn stubborn, not like Phoebe at all. Not like her at all." He rambled under his breath; words ran together, and Cara could not understand him. Caine groaned as they lay him on the bed. "So pretty, Phoebe." His hand brushed Cara's cheek.

"My name is Cara," she said brusquely and turned away.

Than looked worried as he gazed at Caine, who had passed out. "I'll stay with him to make sure he doesn't wander off again."

Cara shook her head. "No, go get some sleep. You have an early shift tomorrow. I'll stay here and keep an eye on him. I don't think he'll be going anywhere again."

"You sure?"

"Yeah, I got it. You go." She kept watch over Caine until her eyes couldn't stay open any longer, and she fell asleep in a chair next to the bed.

Caine woke sometime in the night, still woozy from the alcohol. Seeing Cara asleep in the chair by the bed, he gently picked her up and tucked her in the bed next to him before falling back to sleep. He woke the next morning with a splitting headache. When he discovered Cara sleeping soundly next to him, surprise quickly faded into memories of the previous night. He groaned and rubbed his face. He slipped out of bed, dressed, and quietly left so as not to wake her.

Later, Cara woke to find she wasn't in her own bed. The events from the previous night came flooding back. She sat up and remembered falling asleep in the chair. How had she gotten into Caine's bed?

The door opened, and Than walked in. He spotted Cara in Caine's bed. "Oh, um, I'm sorry." He quickly exited the room, a bewildered look on his face.

"Than, wait!" Cara cried out after him but to no avail. He was gone.

Than knew exactly where Caine would be. He stalked across the Bridge towards him, trying to keep some sense of composure but couldn't control his emotions. He gave Caine a shove. "Why the hell is Cara in your bed?" He jerked his thumb towards the Bridge door.

Caine regained his footing; his eyebrows raised by the unexpected onslaught. He looked around, checking to see if anyone noticed the exchange but fortunately, it appeared everyone had their back turned to the pair.

"I put her there," Caine responded to the accusatory question.

"What the hell were you thinking, taking advantage of her like that?" Than asked angrily.

"Taking advantage?" Caine scoffed. "I woke up, and she was sleeping in the chair. I figured she would be more comfortable in the bed."

A flush crept up Than's face. "Nothing happened?"

"No, you overprotective idiot, nothing happened," Caine said, not bothering to tell him about the other day. He didn't need Than going off on one of his holier-than-thou speeches. "You push me again on the Bridge, and I will lay you flat. If you want to get something off your chest, you do it behind closed doors. I don't care how long we have been friends. I am still the Commander here, and if you undermine me again in front of the crew, you will be scrubbing every toilet on this ship for a year. Understand?" Caine knew it was an empty and meaningless threat. He was angrier at the fact Than thought so little of him and thought he would take advantage of Cara when he was drunk.

"Really Than, really?" Caine asked him, shaking his head.

Than at least had the decency to look ashamed, dropping his head and lowering his gaze.

"I'm sending her to Alina."

"What? Why?" Than asked. "Is it because of Phoebe?"

"No. I should have done it a long time ago. This is getting too dangerous. I can't risk her life keeping her here any longer. Alina's home is safe. She will be able to stay there until she can be sent home safely. Follow me."

Once they were out of earshot, he stopped. "The situation is worse than I first suspected. I think there is a leak here on the ship, not just in the Council. He attacked Turah with the specific purpose of kidnapping Cara. He could easily have come after me, but he didn't. He only wanted to get to her. Samas knows she traveled through time. He is getting information somehow. If he truly is an Esper like Cara claims, we can't let anyone know where she is going, or the information could potentially be leaked to him."

"It makes sense." Than nodded in agreement. "Do you think it is connected to the problems with the Council?"

"Yes. I'm afraid it could be. This is much bigger than I expected. Keep an eye out."

"When are you going to tell Cara about Alina?"

Caine sighed. "Right now."

Chapter Forty-Four

Caine found Cara still in his bed. He knew how easily he could get used to seeing her there, but he couldn't allow himself those desires. He sat on the edge of the bed. "I need to speak with you."

Cara tensed, immediately suspicious.

"I am sending you to stay somewhere safe until I can get you back to the Council."

"What?" Cara cried out. "No!"

"You will be safe there, I assure you. It is a location that is well hidden and highly protected. It is my own home."

Cara opened her mouth to protest, but he held up a hand.

"This is not up for discussion. You have been targeted before. Samas knows you are on this ship. What is stopping him from attacking us?"

She didn't argue with him. This was the right choice. Still, she wished she could stay. It was hard not to believe she was being sent away as punishment.

"I will be taking you personally in an unmarked ship so the location cannot be traced. The sooner I get you there, the better chance we have at going unnoticed and keeping you safe."

Cara sighed and slumped back on the bed. Caine frowned at her.

"Cara, this is the best option right now. We can use this opportunity to flush out the leak, especially if we spread false information."

Cara couldn't find the words to respond, so she nodded. She wanted to tell him she understood and that it was okay, but something was breaking inside her.

"Go get cleaned up if you'd like. I've set aside some water again. Pack your things, and we will leave. I need to go brief the crew. I'll be back in a bit."

Cara went into the washroom and stepped into the shower. The hot water washed away her tears. She wasn't sure how long she stood there but sometime later, the water shut off automatically. "Water ration limit reached," a computerized voice spoke. Cara dried, dressed, and packed her things into a small bag.

Caine came for her shortly after. "We leave in five minutes." He turned halfway around but looked back at her again. "I'm just trying to keep you safe."

She picked up the copy of A History of Earth, the book Caine had given her, tucked it into the bag, and went to find him.

He was in the hangar area, finalizing the last checks on the pod. He waved her over to him. Her bag grew heavier with each step she took closer.

"Are you all set?"

Cara nodded. If she had tried to speak, it would have given away how close she was to tears.

"Let's go." He pressed a button on the outside of the small ship, and a narrow set of ladder-like stairs dropped down. Caine took her bag and tossed it up into the ship. She grabbed the handrail and climbed up. Caine placed his hand on her hip to keep her steady. The contact sent tingles up her spine. She twisted her body slightly and stepped up so he couldn't hold onto her any longer.

Caine knew she was upset, but she made it even more apparent when she pulled away from his touch. He didn't blame her, but she needed to understand he was doing this to protect her.

"Do I get to know where you're taking me?" she ventured as she settled into a seat next to him.

"One of the inner-most border planets is called Jalan. It is mostly uninhabited."

"Because it didn't terraform well?" She remembered Caine's brief history lesson.

"No, actually, it is quite lush and beautiful. There are a few small cities on one half."

"And the other?"

"It belongs to me."

Cara's mouth dropped open. "You own a planet?"

"Just half of one." Caine smiled at her reaction. "I haven't been there in a long time. Unfortunately, my job does not allow for a lot of downtime."

"When will we get there?"

"Tomorrow. In the meantime, get some rest."

Cara considered sleeping. She still found she was often tired, an unwanted side effect of her recovery, but Nadir said it was to be expected as her body healed.

Instead, she settled into her seat, getting comfortable, and stared out the window as the infinite stretch of space whisked past. "I just want to watch for a bit."

Far off, she could see the hint of a blue and green planet; their destination. Stars glinted. It was simple: no massive pink and purple nebula clouds or swirling green and blue galaxies she had often seen in pictures. It was breathtaking.

Caine kept a close eye on the controls through the night, piloting the pod towards the small planet. In the morning, when they descended through the atmosphere, Cara was jolted awake by turbulence. The pod shook and rattled as it dropped in altitude. Once they were through the planet's exosphere, it evened out. He flew the pod over beautiful rolling hills, vast forests, and sparkling lakes until she spotted their destination.

A palatial home sat on top of a hill with a sprawling green lawn fanning out toward expansive gardens and a forest beyond. To the left of the house was a hedge maze with a large fountain in front of the entrance.

The pod landed, and the hatch opened. Caine stepped out onto the grass and offered Cara a hand as she jumped down from the step.

A beautiful woman with long brown hair raced off the porch and across the yard towards them. The woman threw herself into Caine's open arms. He picked her up and twirled her around, and she kissed his cheeks. Cara tried to squash the twinge of jealousy before it took root.

"Alina, this is Cara," Caine said when he set the woman back on the ground. "Cara, this is Alina, my sister."

His sister? Cara's mouth dropped open.

"I can see my little brother decided not to tell you about me." Alina laughed at the stunned look on Cara's face. "Are you ashamed of me, little brother?" She nudged him in the side with her elbow, her tone playful and mocking,

"Don't forget," Caine pulled her close, "your little brother is much bigger than you." He ruffled her hair.

Cara liked seeing this side of Caine, the playful and affectionate side. For a moment, she forgot he was the hardened Commander of a space fleet. He was simply Caine, the pesky younger brother. Alina slipped her way out of the headlock and swatted at him.

"Ignore his manners, Cara. He can be a big brute sometimes." Alina smoothed her hair and reached out to take Cara by the arm. "Come."

Alina led Cara towards the large mansion. "Caine never speaks of this place. He prefers this to be his secret."

There were more gardens and ponds beyond the house. In the distance, it was all surrounded by snowcapped mountains, their jagged peaks piercing the sky. "Caine keeps me locked away here under the guise of protecting me." She winked. "I think it's because he's worried about what could happen if he let me loose on the rest of the universe." She said it loud enough for Caine to hear, and she laughed.

"Don't let the innocent look fool you, Cara," Caine called out after them. "She's a hell-raiser."

Alina pushed open the doors to the mansion. "I am so happy you are coming to stay with me here. It has been too long since I've had a friend." She pulled Cara along. "I have a room all ready for you." She turned down a long hall, telling Cara about the house and the different rooms along the way.

Cara stopped listening. The whole thing was overwhelming. Caine had a sister, hidden away for her protection, who lived in a huge mansion where Cara would be staying. Caine, sensing her distress, came up behind her and squeezed her shoulder reassuringly. Cara looked up at him.

"I want to stay with you."

"I know, but you will be safe here until I can find out who is responsible for all of this." He cupped her cheek and kissed her.

"This is your room." Alina opened a large wooden door, revealing a sprawling bedroom with a balcony overlooking the gardens. "There are clothes in the closet for you, and there is a washroom just behind that door. I hope you like it."

"It's beautiful," Cara breathed, feeling overwhelmed. The room was lavish, beyond anything she had ever stayed in before, and the one thing she wished for right now was to be back in her small room back on the Archon.

He cleared his throat. "I have to go."

"Already?" She didn't want him to leave so soon. Alina seemed nice, but she didn't know anything about her. It didn't matter that it was his sister; he was leaving her with a stranger.

"I've spent too much time here already. I don't want there to be any chance of someone locating you here." He brushed a strand of hair away from her face. "You will be fine here. I promise."

He leaned over and kissed her, tasting her bitter tears on his lips. He barely registered Alina quietly slipping out the door, closing it behind her. He wrapped his arms around her, burying his fingers in her hair. Cara dug her fingers into his back as if it would keep him there.

Caine pulled away, holding her face in his hands. "Cara-" Words failed him. He dropped his hands and left. He didn't say goodbye.

Each step was more difficult than the last as he walked away from Cara. He was doing the right thing. This would be the best place for her to be. He should have brought her here right after the initial attack on Arctus.

The stairs dropped down for him. He gripped the handhold and pulled himself up into the pod, taking his place in the pilot's seat. He took the controls and tilted the lever to lift off.

The pod lifted off in a cloud of dust. "No!" She didn't want him to leave. She raced down the steps towards the pod. "Wait," she called out. She ran across the grass after the pod as it slipped through the sky. Tears welled up in her eyes, blurring her vision. She kept running across the field after him, wishing he would turn around, but the pod kept moving. Her lungs burned, her legs ached, but she pushed forward as if she would be able to chase him down, go with him. The pod rose higher and higher into the sky.

Caine could see her running out of the corner of his eye. It took every ounce of his willpower not to turn around. His grip tightened around the control, and he pushed the lever forward, increasing his speed until she dropped back, unable to keep up. He swallowed against the lump in his throat.

Cara was forced to come to a halt as the terrain took a sharp dip down into a valley. She collapsed to her knees, breathing hard as the craft shrank and vanished into the clouds.

Chapter Forty-Five

"How do you like Jalan so far?" Alina brought Cara a steaming cup of floral tea.

"It is beautiful…" Cara trailed off, unable to finish.

"But, it isn't with my brother," Alina finished. "He means well," she continued. "You have to see it."

Nearly a week had passed. Cara was homesick, but not for New York. She had developed a close connection to the Archon and its crew in the last few weeks.

"How much has Caine told you about me?" Cara finally found the courage to broach the subject.

Alina smiled over her teacup. "My brother has many skills; communicating is not one of them."

Cara snorted. Despite the distance between them, Alina understood her brother perfectly.

"I have not heard from him in over a year. He thinks it keeps me safe. Ever since-" She paused.

Cara sipped her tea, "I know about Phoebe," she admitted. "I found out about her."

Alina smiled sadly. "I worry about him. He tries so hard to hide his past. Sometimes the walls he builds crack, and little things slip through. After Phoebe was killed, he moved me here. He told no one where I was. Not the Council, and for a long time, he didn't even tell Than. He had fought so hard to protect Phoebe, but even after she was reassigned, it didn't stop Samas from killing her."

"It must have been hard on him when the Council reassigned her."

"It was Nik who requested Phoebe be assigned to a different Esper."

Cara choked on the tea. Alina frowned at her. "He didn't tell me that part."

"When Breeta died, Nikolai knew Samas would never stop looking for him. Samas would never stop trying to hurt him in any way he could. He also knew the Council needed to punish him publicly because of what he did, so he negotiated with the Council to have Phoebe assigned to a new Esper as her match and publicly announce it as a part of his punishment. He hoped by having Phoebe taken away from him that Samas would leave her alone, but he didn't. Samas killed Phoebe anyway. After that, we knew. Samas would not stop with her. Caine feared I was next, so I was brought here, and I've been here ever since. Caine had this all built for me. He doesn't visit often, but after he finally told Than my location, at least he would come to see me as often as he could."

Cara smiled. "So, you and Than?" she asked.

Alina blushed. "We have known each other for a long time. He's a good man."

Cara had to agree. "Yes, he is." She looked at Alina and noted the remarkable resemblance between her and Caine, but her eyes were brown, not blue. "You're not an Esper like Caine," Cara noted.

"No, I'm the normal one in the family," she laughed.

"But Caine said both your parents were Espers."

Alina nodded. "The Esper genes are recessive. Not every child born to an Esper is born one themselves. Our older brother Tirio is also an Esper, but it skipped me."

Cara's face gave her away again.

"I'm not surprised he didn't mention him. Their relationship is not exactly close. Tirio has always been, well, jealous of Nikolai's abilities. He feels like our parents favored him."

Cara was confused.

"Tirio is not nearly as strong as Nikolai. He always felt like he was second best. He was in direct competition with him rather than becoming allies during training. It was a view encouraged by our father, who wanted nothing more than to see both of his sons climb to the very top of the ladder of success." Alina sighed. "Unfortunately, emotions are not always rational. The rift between them only grew as Nik climbed the ranks and became Commander, a job Tirio had hoped to hold himself. Tirio thought it was his birthright as the first-born son and that he had been overlooked. Most Esper parents are only sanctioned to have one child, but in the years after Tirio was born, there was a sharp drop in Esper births. My parents were permitted to have one more child, me. But I was born normal, and so they were allowed to try again. Nikolai was a miracle. One of the most powerful Espers in over a century. My mother used to say she could hear him talking to her when he was still in her womb. I didn't believe it at the time but seeing what he is capable of, I believe her now. We knew when he was just a boy that his future was already planned out for him. His path was set. Someday he will be on the Council and help rule over the Confederation."

Cara wasn't sure what kind of warning Alina was giving her. A warning that this was the life Caine was leading, and she would have to get used to it, or was it a warning that she was not a part of the plan.

Espers were expected to have children to produce more Espers. Cara understood the genetics part well enough. Since the Esper gene was recessive, there was no chance that Cara would bear one with Caine. There would never be a possibility for the two of them to be together. She wanted to be angry, but Alina was making sure she understood the reality of life here, of Caine's life.

"Tirio has never been able to move on. He looks at Nik and sees him living the life he stole from him."

Cara pitied Tirio. She could understand why he was so angry, but none of it was Caine's fault. He couldn't help who he was.

"Come on," Alina broke the tension. "It is too beautiful of a day to waste it inside. Let's go for a walk."

Cara followed her outside, and they crossed the great lawn. As they walked the winding path through the property, Cara was reminded of Central Park. It sent a stabbing spike of loss through her, making her breath catch. She wanted to stay, but the Council still had the end goal of sending her home. What would she be going home to? A life she was ultimately unhappy with? Yes, she had friends and family there, but they knew a different person, a person she no longer was. She wanted so desperately to stay. Would it be possible?

Cara was so lost and alone. She didn't have a home anymore and didn't even feel like she had a planet. She didn't belong in New York in the past and didn't belong in this world in the future. She didn't fit in either one. Where did she belong? As if sensing her uncertainty, Alina tucked her arm around Cara's.

"I remember when I first got moved here. I can't remember a time where I had ever been angrier. I had been taken away from my home, my friends, and even my job. My whole world had been pulled out from under me. I had to start over here, but I was forced to do it almost completely alone. I don't think I spoke to Caine for months, but eventually, I adapted. It's what we do. We have to. Looking back now, I'm not the same person I was when I first step foot onto this planet. I don't know what you have been through, but I do see a lot of myself in you. I see the same look in your eyes I saw in my own reflection for months. Sometimes all we can do is take it moment to moment, breath to breath, and eventually, the breaths turn into days and the days to months, and you wake up one morning, and you can't even remember exactly how long it's been." Alina stopped and sighed. She gave Cara's arm a little squeeze. "Sorry, I was rambling."

"No, it's nice to have someone who understands." For the first time in weeks, she finally was at ease.

***

Caine was standing behind his Commander's chair, gripping the top with both hands to support his weight.

"When was the last time you got any sleep?" Than asked. Caine refused to acknowledge him, continuing to stare off across the room. "You're going to fall over. You need sleep," he continued.

"I need to figure this out," Caine muttered.

"It's been five days, Caine. What do you think you'll solve running on no sleep? You're barely functional. You can't do your job like this."

Caine turned, anger blazing in his eyes. "Do not question my ability to do my job." He spoke harshly. Some of the nearby crew threw him sideways glances from the corners of their eyes and scurried away.

This was a mess. Although, as usual, Than appeared unfazed. Nothing ever bothered him. He took everything in stride, always trying to look for the solution to any problem. It was one of the main reasons Caine got along so well with him. Than was no-nonsense, but his sense of humor kept Caine balanced when he needed it most.

"I'll be in my quarters," Caine conceded with a less than professional huff.

The walk back to his room felt longer than ever. He had been avoiding it. He stood in his doorway, looking from the bed to the washroom door, half hoping Cara would come walking through. He wished he didn't feel so guilty about sending her away, despite knowing it had been the right thing to do. He had done it in her best interest.

He missed her. The thought made his stomach clench painfully. He wasn't used to allowing himself the luxury of that emotion, and its strength surprised him. He had been working hard to suppress it, but sheer exhaustion had weakened the typically rigid grip he had on his emotions.

Than was right; he did need sleep. He climbed into bed and, within seconds, had drifted off.

***

Cara wandered through the gardens, soaking up the bright rays of sunshine she had not seen in over a week. It had rained for days without stopping, the gloomy weather matching her mood. When she woke to the sun that morning, it was the small lift her spirits needed.

At the far end was the hedge maze, its walls blooming with white flowers. She walked up to it, smiling and smelling the fragrant blooms. She wandered in.

Getting lost in the maze was the perfect metaphor for her life. The longer she spent there, the more relaxed and comfortable she became, and she hated it. She didn't want to be satisfied with staying here forever. She understood how Alina must have felt when she first was brought here. Cara didn't want to be hidden away and rarely visited, if at all. She needed something to do; she needed a job. The thought caught her off guard. She had hated her job back in New York so much, but now the mundane, repetitive phone calls were something she craved. There was the strange split that kept her heart and mind divided. The desire to stay and yet the pull of home still lingered.

"Cara!" Alina's voice called out, echoing over the hedges. Cara turned, trying to find her way out but found herself at a dead end. "This way!" Alina appeared behind her, laughing, and led her out. "Just remember, a lot of left turns," she told Cara with a laugh. "I've gotten lost in here more times than I can count."

"Don't you ever get bored?" Cara ventured.

"Of course, I do at times. But there is a lot to do around here if you know where to look. I try to keep myself busy, and I spend a lot of time outside enjoying the beauty of this place. It can be lonely if you let it, but it is precisely why you must make your own entertainment. You should learn a new skill while you're here. There is always plenty of work to do in the gardens."

"I've barely been able to keep a cactus alive."

"A cack-tess?" Alina's head tilted slightly to the side as she tried to decipher what Cara meant.

"I just don't do well with plants."

"Oh hush, come along. I'll have you mastering the garden in no time." Alina steered her to the gardens. They spent the afternoon pruning and planting until Cara's hands were black with the rich soil. It helped the time pass, and she could see why Alina enjoyed it so much. They collected some of the vegetables Alina had grown. Cara helped her cook up a delicious soup for dinner.

They ended the meal with some of Jalan's native rapa fruit for dessert. It was a strange fruit that grew on long vines, with a soft, bumpy, red rind that easily peeled away to reveal green flesh dotted with tiny black seeds. They ate out on the large porch as the sky darkened. Cara sat back, unable to eat any more, as Alina finished off her last bite of the bright green rapa.

Despite working in the gardens all afternoon, when night came, Cara was restless. She tossed and turned and finally slipped from the bed to get a drink of water. She padded down the hall. There was a soft thud. "Alina?" she called out. No answer. The door to her room was cracked open. Cara pushed it open to check on her.

As she entered, she came to a halt at the sight of Alina kneeling on the ground. Standing over her was a face she had hoped never to see again: Samas. He had a vicious grin on his face. Alina was bleeding from a wound on her head.

Samas looked up. If his evil grin could get any bigger, it did.

"Oh, there you are." His black eyes glittered with glee. His words made all the hair on Cara's arms stand on end.

Her stomach flipped.

Cara knew if she stayed there, they would both end up dead. She needed to give Alina a fighting chance to escape. The only way to do that would be to draw Samas away.

"You bastard," Cara screamed at him. His grip on Alina loosened.

His eyes narrowed as he took the bait. At least Alina would be safe for the moment. Cara turned and ran, feet padding on the cold stone stairs. She threw open the front door and raced across the grass. She needed cover, a place to hide. If she stayed out in the open, she would be an easy target. The maze... she had to get him into the maze. It was her best option at this point. She ran to the entrance. She needed to get as far into the center as possible. If she could draw him in, she could get out, and it could give her enough time to figure out a way to fight him off.

Turn after turn; she raced through the maze. She knew Samas wasn't far behind. She hit a dead end, and her heart dropped. She turned to try and find another way out, peeking around the corner of the hedges. The coast looked clear.

As she stepped out, Samas turned the corner at the far end of the path.

"Stop," he yelled, the hollow pitch of his voice echoed around them.

She recognized the pull, the tug of the Silverspeak. She needed to listen. She fought it but knew the more she resisted, the stronger it would become. She let the command take hold; she stopped. Samas stalked slowly towards her, taking his time, like a lion approaching its prey before it pounces.

"Silly Cara," Samas chuckled. He took a few steps closer, pulling a laser gun from his belt. He pointed it at her. "Why did you run from me? I thought we were friends," he pouted, faking a frown.

"How did you find me?" Cara gasped out.

Samas laughed again. Using the end of the gun, he traced the curve of Cara's cheek, dragging the cold metal across her skin. He pushed the barrel under her chin, forcing her head to tip skywards. "I may have slipped a little something under your skin. I needed to keep an eye on you. Friends always have each other's back, don't they?" He smiled.

Cara wanted to scream. He had been tracking her all along. He had known exactly where she was. It explained why she couldn't shake the feeling that she was being followed. It was as if she had known.

"I love this game we have. You run. I chase you. I catch you, and now," he stepped closer, "I kill you." He twirled in a circle. As he came back to face her, he shrugged at her. "You lose," he said in his childish, sing-song tone.

"You didn't kill me before. Why now?" She needed to stall, to buy time for Alina to get free and hopefully call for help.

"I wasn't done with you yet." He circled around her, stroking his chin. "You were supposed to help me, show me how to make the jump, but you failed me. You let me down. So now, you die."

He laughed at her as if the whole situation was comical. Her life that was at stake, there was nothing funny about it.

Anger and hatred burned. She could use it to power herself; to fight. She was strong, just like Nadir told her. She would not lose. She would not let him control her. Cara thought back to the day Caine taught her to resist the pull of Silverspeak. She allowed the anger to build and burn through her. Cara made her move; she used as much force as she could and pushed back against it. With a scream, she broke free of it.

If she hadn't known any better, she would have thought she jumped into a wall. There was the slam of an impact, breaking the air around her that had kept her frozen in place. She reached for the gun. Samas, caught off guard by her ability to escape his clutches, was unprepared for her attack. They grappled with the gun, and her hands clutched around it.

Twisting her body around as hard as she could, her finger found the trigger, and she pulled. The laser blast hit him in the chest. He stumbled backward from the impact. Cara expected him to collapse, but Samas kept his footing. With a roar, he lunged at her, but she swung and her fist connected with his jaw. He shoved her to the ground. The gun fell from her hand. She reached for it, but it had landed mere inches from her fingertips. He fell on top of her, blood dripping from his mouth, and grabbed her throat. He pushed into her mind, ripping and tearing it apart, but she pushed back, fighting it, trying to push him out. She screamed as he tore at her memories. She reached for the gun, her fingers barely grazing it. Samas wrapped himself around her mind and squeezed harder. Cara struggled to breathe. Her mind shattered like glass; shards of her memory blown everywhere. Her fingers grasped the gun just as her world began to fade. Samas looked down at her with a wicked gleam in his eye. Gathering every ounce of strength he had left, as the life drained from him, he kept her trapped in his gaze.

"Kill Caine," he commanded.

The words twisted around her spine, curling up her back and into her mind, wrapping themselves around every tiny, fragile shard of her memory. Cara raised the gun and fired.

When she became aware of her surroundings again, she was on the ground. There was pressure on her, weighing her down and making it hard to breathe.

Kill Caine.

Breathe.

Kill Caine.

Breathe.

Blink.

Swallow.

Kill Caine.

Everything she was had been turned into one singular thought. She had no name, no past, and no future. She was simply a job that needed to be completed. Every memory, every thought, was coated with the mission she had to finish. It blacked out everything else.

Kill Caine.

She pushed the weight away. It was a body. It was covered in blood. She was covered in blood. She scrambled away from the body. It wasn't Caine.

Kill Caine.

She looked around. She knew nothing.

Kill Caine.

She only had one thought. It repeated itself over and over and over and over.

Kill Caine.

She closed her eyes.

Kill Caine.

She stood.

She wandered the maze. She was lost.

Kill Caine.

How could she get out? Shuffling footsteps. Movement. She looked up, and there was a woman. She was bleeding. Not Caine. The woman was speaking to her, but she didn't listen. She couldn't listen. She curled up by a bush and allowed the words consuming her to become the sound of her heartbeat. They became the rhythm of her breathing.

Kill Caine.

Kill Caine.

***

Caine's system got an emergency alert from Alina. He raced from his office. "Than, now." He didn't explain, but the urgency in his voice made it clear to Than that it was urgent.

Caine called Nadir and told him to meet them in the hangar. "We need to go now."

They rushed into a scouting vessel and departed the Archon. He had taken the Archon far enough out into space so it wouldn't draw attention to the small, isolated planet where his sister lived. He didn't want to hover. He still had missions to complete, but he did his best to remain close enough that he could reach them if he needed to. He only hoped they would make it in time.

When Caine and Than landed a pod the following evening, Alina was already running across the great lawn towards them, the silken fabric of her long blue dress whipping around her legs. Than grabbed her by the side of her face, tipping her head towards him to inspect her wound.

"What happened?" Than demanded, angrily looking at the large black and blue bruise encircling the gash across her forehead.

"I'm fine," Alina brushed his hand away, "but Cara isn't." She glanced at Caine. "She's alive, but she is still in the hedge maze. She isn't herself. Samas did something to her. She won't come out. I tried already." Alina looked up at Than, her face pale, "Than, it has to be you. You have to be the one to go in there and get her out."

"Like hell." Caine turned. He was going in there to get Cara himself. He learned his lesson and wasn't sending anyone else to get her. This was his job to do, and would face whatever was waiting for him in the maze; he at least owed her that much.

"Nik, you do not want to go in there," Alina cautioned, grabbing his arm.

Caine pulled away from her. He had to help Cara.

"Nikolas, no!" Alina screamed at him. Than grabbed her around the waist, holding her back.

Caine raced into the hedge maze. He made his way through the twisting turns and dead ends. He had helped design the maze, but years of being away were making it difficult for him to remember the exact path to take. He turned a corner.

There.

***

Cara looked up. There was a man. She knew him. She had to kill him. She did not know why. She did not want to, but she had to. She looked down. There was a gun in her hands. She wasn't sure where it had come from, but there it was. It was heavy and cold. She looked up at the man. He was walking towards her. He stopped. She raised the gun. The reassuring feeling of knowing exactly what she had to do washed over her.

"Cara," the man spoke. He knew her. She knew him. She had to kill him.

"Kill Caine," she whispered. She fired, and the man collapsed to the ground. Having fulfilled her purpose, the pull of the command release. She had completed her job - her task. Now she was nothing. She was an empty shell, hollow and cold.

***

Caine turned the corner. Cara was sitting on the ground, drenched in dried blood. She was holding a gun. As he crossed to her, she raised it and pointed it at him. "Cara," he breathed her name in shock as she whispered something he couldn't discern and fired. He dove to the side to avoid a direct hit, and the shot grazed his arm. He looked at the wound. It would leave a burn, but it was far from a severe injury.

He turned his attention back to Cara. She was tucked into a ball, holding her legs to her chest. She rocked back and forth. The gun had slid to the ground. She started scratching at her arm, clawing at it.

"Get it out," she begged, sounding more like she was speaking to herself than acknowledging his presence. "Get it out." She rocked back and forth, digging her nails into her skin, ripping at it. He knelt and tried to grab her hands, but she shrieked like a wild animal and went back to tearing a hole in her forearm. Blood spilled down her arm and onto her hand, coating her fingers.

He grabbed her hands, preventing her from causing any more damage. She struggled for a moment before going still. He picked her up gently. She wasn't okay. She stared at the sky with a vacant and expressionless gaze as if there was nothing in her mind anymore except empty space. He pushed into her mind. There was no resistance. He found himself floating in a dark void, surrounded by millions of little shards of glass, no, not glass, her memories, all of them covered with a thin black sticky film. He pulled out. Her mind looked like it had gone through a shredder and was set on fire. He carried her out of the maze.

Alina sobbed at the sight of Cara. "It's all my fault!" Her knees sagged. Than grabbed her to keep her standing.

"You stay with Alina until I get back." Caine's jaw was clenched so tightly he ground the words out between his teeth.

Than nodded, hugging Alina close to him as she wept into his chest.

Caine raced with Cara back to the pod, and it zipped up to the scout ship.

Even though Nadir was waiting, ready for them, he was not prepared for how horrific Cara appeared. He paled at her blood-covered body. "Biaism alnujum," he whispered.

"The stars had nothing to do with it," Caine placed her on the transport bed. Nadir quickly sedated her.

"The blood isn't all hers. She killed Samas." Caine spun on his heel. Cara was in good hands, and he had a body to retrieve.

Than was sitting on the stairs to the house, Alina seated next to him. His arm was wrapped around her shoulders, and she leaned against him, her head resting on his chest.

Caine hated knowing he had to separate them, but he needed Than. Once everything was figured out, he would grant Than a well-deserved leave from duty.

Than looked up as Caine approached. He didn't look upset, more resigned to the fact he would have to leave Alina. They had known each other long enough; they were able to understand each other without always needing to speak.

Alina raised her head. Her eyes were still red and puffy, but she had stopped crying.

"Is she okay?" Alina wrung her hands together.

"She will be. Are you all right?" He was touched by Alina's concern for Cara, but sometimes his sister needed a gentle reminder that her own well-being was important too.

"I'm fine," she pointed to the wound on her head, "Than took care of it. Nothing serious." She looked from Than to Caine and back again. "I guess this means it's time to go."

"You know I wouldn't make him leave unless I needed him."

Alina put on a brave face. Her little brother was the Commander of the entire Fleet. After all these years, he still wanted to explain his reasoning to her.

"You don't need to explain yourself." She touched his arm. "Take care of her."

Caine looked towards the hedge maze. "We need to take Samas with us."

Alina turned to Than and cupped his cheek. "I'd like to say goodbye before you touch the body."

Caine took the hint. He didn't want to stick around as his friend and sister said farewell. He retreated towards the pod to get the equipment to transport Samas' body.

Together, Than and Caine loaded Samas onto the pod and took flight back to the Scout ship.

Caine looked over at Than seated next to him. He was looking at the display screens, but Caine could tell his mind was elsewhere. He didn't want Than to hold any hard feelings towards him for asking him to leave Alina so soon after a traumatic experience. "I will make sure you get to see her soon." It was a promise he intended to keep.

Than shrugged. "Duty first," he said evenly, without taking his gaze away from the display screens.

"You're starting to sound like me," Caine admonished lightly. "I'm supposed to be the cynical one here."

Than looked at Caine through the corner of his eyes. "Maybe I've been hanging around you for too long. You're starting to rub off on me."

"I don't think I've rubbed off on you nearly enough," Caine quipped.

Than finally cracked a grin. At least his sense of humor was still intact.

"You don't have to worry about me," Than told him. "You wouldn't have asked if there was any other way. We need to get to the bottom of this."

"We will," Caine vowed.

Once the body was stored in a cryo-tank on the scout ship, Caine went down to check on Cara.

"How is she?" he asked Nadir.

"Stable, for now. Vitals are strong, but there could be a very different story to be told inside."

Caine knew Nadir was concerned about her mind. He was too. Knowing Samas had Esper abilities, paired with Cara's unexplainable behavior, Caine could only imagine what horrific things Samas had done to her.

Nadir walked up with a jar. Inside was something Caine didn't recognize; It was small and covered in blood. "I don't know how I missed it, but there was a tracking device in her arm. It appears he had put it into the wound on her arm when he captured her." Nadir shook his head, looking at the tiny device he had removed.

Caine could tell Nadir was distraught. "The systems missed it, not you."

Nadir looked down at his patient. "He had been following her the whole time, and she knew it. I should have listened to her."

"You can't blame yourself. You know Samas. He wasn't going to give up and walk away. We knew he would try something again. Right now, I need you to wake her up so I can get in there and repair whatever damage he caused."

"Waking her up could cause even more damage."

"I don't need her fully conscious. Just light enough for her to open her eyes so I can get in."

Nadir turned to the machines and gently reversed the sedation. When her eyes fluttered open, Caine pushed into her mind. He slipped into the blackness. There was no surface where he could land. He floated through the emptiness. Shards of memories hung in the air around him like snowflakes. He delicately plucked one out of the air, then another. With excruciating care, he put the broken bits together piece by piece, like a puzzle. Hours later, he had to pull out, exhausted. Nadir quickly sedated her again.

"This will take days." He hit his knee with his fist. "I haven't seen damage like this in a long time. He didn't just break her mind apart; he practically blew it up."

"There has to be another way."

"No. I have to go in and fix it. This won't repair itself on its own." He ran a hand through his hair. "I have a meeting with the Council in two days, and I have nothing to show them."

Nadir looked contemplative.

"You're thinking of something."

"There may be something. It's never been done before. In fact, it technically isn't even possible."

Caine snorted at the irony of it all. "I've been hearing that a lot lately."

Nadir smiled conspiratorially. "You are going to Interrogate a dead man."

Nadir's plan was straightforward but illogical. He wanted to shoot electricity into Samas' brain. In theory, it would revive the dead cells for a short time, sending the neurons firing. During that time, Caine could enter his mind and see the last few hours of his life. Caine was skeptical.

"I don't think it will work," Caine stared down at Samas' body.

Technically, his brain was no longer functional; therefore, he could not gain access to anything.

"It's always worth a try," Nadir said. "For Cara."

It was a low blow, but it was all the convincing Caine needed. Nadir turned on the machine. Electricity sizzled and crackled in the air. "Ready?" he asked.

"Let's get this done."

Nadir placed the electric prod against Samas' skull. Electricity sparked. As soon as Nadir removed the prod, Caine opened one eyelid and was swept inside his mind. It was dark and sickening. He fought back a wave of nausea. In the darkness was a single string hanging down. He pulled at the strand of memory. It unraveled, tangling him up inside the last chaotic moments of his life. It was Samas attacking Cara. The whole scene played out in front of him. Samas was being fed inside information relayed from Caine's ship leading him right to Alina and Cara. There were orders to finish the job and kill her. Cara raised the gun and fired, and Caine was blasted out.

Caine found himself lying on the floor, struggling to take a breath. He gasped as if he had been punched in the gut. Nadir helped him up.

"He did it," he wheezed. "There is a traitor on the ship. We need to find out who."

Hours crawled by as they made their way back to the Archon. Once they had her stabilized in Medical, Caine knew he could finally get to work repairing the damage Samas had caused.

He spent nearly two days inside Cara's mind, meticulously piecing it all back together. He picked each little, shattered sliver and shard of her mind, connecting it with the rest, one by one.

When he had put the final piece back in its rightful place, he looked at the wall of images in front of him like an endless display of moving pictures on screens. He could see the cracks and fractures still. He could do his best to help glue everything back, make the repairs more permanent. Caine closed his eyes, drawing from what little energy he had left. His fingers closed around the energized air as if he was holding a ball. He clapped his hands together, sending shockwaves out in all directions across her mind. The memories playing on their screens rippled like flags waving in the wind. He stepped closer for inspection and found the cracks had fused together. It would still take some time to finish healing, but this was a step in the right direction.

"I think she's ready," Caine informed Nadir.

"She's been under a long time. It may take a while for her to come around. I can get the trammel on her."

"No need. I'm not leaving."

"Don't be alarmed if she is disoriented at first. She may not remember what happened. It's likely she won't recognize you at first. If she starts to panic, get me immediately."

"I will."

Caine sat patiently as she opened her eyes, still groggy. He waited anxiously for the confused hysteria he had seen so often as officers emerged from the fog of drugs. She looked around the room. When she saw Caine sitting next to her, she frowned, head tilted slightly to the side. Memories would come back to her little by little. Seconds ticked by. Minutes passed. She slid her hand across the bedsheet toward him, a tear running down her face.

"Hey." He wiped the tear away. "You're okay. You're going to be okay."

Overwhelmed, Caine leaned forward and kissed her on the forehead.

"Ah, she awakens," Nadir chirped. "Is this man bothering you? Because, if he is, I can have him thrown into the brig." He looked at Caine. "Do we even have a brig?"

Cara's lips curved upward. Caine's heart somersaulted. That was the magic of Nadir. Not all of his healing was done with medicine.

Cara shook her head and reached for Caine's hand. He took it, and she gently squeezed. Even though she didn't speak, her eyes were clear and bright.

"I guess he can be allowed to remain then." Nadir checked all her vitals. "You know, I've seen grown men tear this room apart as they come around. You did remarkably well. Although, that should be no surprise.

You're a remarkable woman. Best keep that to ourselves, though. Don't want any feelings getting hurt." He hummed merrily as he poked and prodded.

"Tired," Cara rattled.

"Of course, my dear. You rest. Ignore the ministrations of a worried old man."

Cara closed her eyes.

Nadir motioned to Caine, and they stepped out of the room.

"She seems to be in exceptional health, considering the amount of trauma she has endured. I can only see what is on the outside. You will have to make sure her mind heals with the rest of her. I wouldn't worry too much, though. Our girl is a fighter."

Our girl. The words washed over Caine. Ours. His. He looked at her, sleeping peacefully in the bed.

Nadir patted Caine on the arm. "You know where to find me." He tottered away, a mischievous glint in his eyes.

Cara, as strong and determined as she was stubborn, quickly proved Nadir correct. After a day of rest, she started to sound like her old self, demanding to be allowed to walk around.

Nadir decided her condition had improved enough to sleep in her own room. Caine and Than helped to walk her there, but her legs gave out on her halfway back. She didn't protest when Caine scooped her up in his arms and carried her to her bed, where she promptly fell asleep.

Hours later, when she woke, there was a bowl of broth waiting for her. It was still warm. She drank it down; the liquid soothed her throat and filled her belly. Cara swung her legs over the side of the bed. She rubbed her thigh muscles, massaging a few tight spots. She was glad to be back on her own two feet.

She picked up the empty soup bowl and walked to the door to bring it back to the cafeteria. The door slid open, and she tripped over something. Something grunted as she collapsed onto it. The bowl went flying. It clattered against the wall and fell to the floor, spinning.

"Caine?" She pushed on his chest to look down at him. "What are you doing?"

"I wanted to be close by in case you needed anything." He untangled himself and helped her stand.

"You're sitting outside my door on the floor?"

"I guess it does sound ridiculous." He rubbed the back of his neck, looking at the floor.

"Do you want to come in?"

Caine looked embarrassed. "Yes." He picked up the bowl and followed her inside.

"How are you feeling?" He sat on the side of the bed.

"I'm okay, but I could use a break from being kidnapped and tortured."

Caine was glad to hear the humor, but guilt ate at him. "Samas is dead. You have nothing to fear anymore. You're safe now."

"Where have I heard that before?" she quipped.

Caine looked away. Heat crept up his neck. A muscle in his clenched jaw twitched. He promised her he would keep her safe, and he had failed again.

Cara grabbed his hand. "Hey, I was just trying to make a joke - a bad one. I'm sorry. It isn't your fault." She sat next to him.

"You're right. I told you that you would be safe."

Cara shrugged. "How could you possibly have predicted Samas would have tracked me the way he did. There is no one to blame except Samas. Like you said, he's dead now. I have nothing to worry about anymore."

Caine didn't respond. Cara placed a hand on his cheek, gently turning his head to face her. She slid her hand behind his head and pulled him closer to her. He didn't fight it. He leaned in and kissed her.

Cara wove her fingers through his thick hair and held him tight, worried he would pull away from her. Instead, he did the opposite. His hands traveled lower and grabbed the hem of her shirt. Breaking the kiss momentarily, he pulled it over her head and let it fall to the floor.

Caine wrapped his arms around her and lowered himself on top of her. In the back of his mind, his worry for her flared up.

"You sure?" he murmured against her lips. She had been through so much. He didn't want to be the one to hurt her again.

"Mmhmm."

It was all the assurance he needed to hear.

Chapter Forty-Six

Two days passed awkwardly. Caine had grown distant again. He was polite when he ran into her, but his easygoing nature had vanished. Did he have regrets? There was a flutter in her belly as she remembered. There was something so electric about being with him. They just fit together so perfectly, until afterward, when he would withdraw physically and emotionally. She credited his behavior to his ongoing challenges reconciling his past with his present. She could tell the guilt was eating away at him.

She spent most of her time reading, stargazing in the observatory, or talking with Than and Zora in the cafeteria.

When she returned to her room one afternoon, she found a note stuck to her door. Library, someone had written in bold strokes and signed with a single initial, 'C.' She couldn't help but smile despite feeling puzzled by the request. Why hadn't he come to talk to her directly? She raced up to the library, taking the stairs two at a time. She was being foolish, being this excited over a silly request. She had no idea what it was about. She avoided eye contact with the crew she passed on the way, feeling her cheeks grow hotter the closer she got. The library door opened slowly, but it was dark. She entered.

"Hello?" she called out. "Caine?"

There was no answer, but someone was breathing heavily. A sharp blow crashed down on the back of her skull. This wasn't Caine. She was in trouble.

Cara fought back, pushing and punching her attacker. There was a satisfying crunch as her fist connected with something hard, followed by a pained shout. She ran for the door. She skidded out into the hallway, slamming into the opposing wall. She pushed off it, running as fast as she could to the elevator. She hit the button, but the doors didn't open.

She didn't have time to wait. Whoever had attacked her would be right behind her. There were service stairs down another hall. It was her only other option to escape. She raced towards them, listening to the pounding footsteps behind her.

***

Cara made it down two levels before the man caught up. He grabbed her arm. She yanked away, but her momentum caused her feet to tangle. She tripped and fell down several steps and landed with a thud on the floor. She moaned, her vision blurring, but she could see the figure of a man coming down the stairs. As her eyes adjusted, she recognized him, one of the officers on the ship. Cara scrambled across the floor, using her hands and feet to push backward. He came down the stairs, pointing his gun at her.

She closed her eyes. This was it. This was how she would die.

There was a loud bang from behind her. She opened her eyes. The officer had fallen to the floor and was bleeding from his chest. Cara looked back to see Than rushing toward her.

"Caine," he spoke into his comm. "Get down here now, Level 8." Than pulled Cara away from the man. "Are you okay?"

"Yeah, I think so," Cara did a quick check of her body. She was sore, but nothing felt broken.

"How did you know?" she asked.

"I didn't," Than said grimly. "I was heading to the engine room to check on an electrical short when I heard you fall."

Cara went cold as she realized just how lucky she was that Than had gone by at that exact moment. If he hadn't, she'd be dead.

Caine turned the corner and surveyed the scene. He ran past Cara and grabbed the young officer who clutched at his chest, coughing up blood.

Caine pushed into his mind. Death and coldness surrounded him. This man was moments away from death, but he searched for clues. He grabbed at memories - encrypted messages to Samas, money transfers, and an order to kill Cara from an unknown source.

Seething, Caine shredded the man's mind, ripping it to pieces as Samas had done to Cara's. He withdrew, breathing hard. The man's breath was shallow and ragged until he stopped breathing. He was dead.

Caine clenched his fists, trying to keep his composure. He forced his attention back towards Cara.

He marched to her and squatted down where she was leaning up against the wall. He grabbed her shoulders.

"Did he hurt you?" Caine asked harshly.

The look in his eyes was unlike any she had ever seen. It was murderous. She knew his wrath was not directed towards her. "Did he hurt you," he barked again. His hands clamped down, fingers biting into her skin.

"No. No, I'm not hurt."

She looked at his hands and winced. He got the message and let go.

"Get her back to her room." He pointed at Than. "Do not leave her side, or I will kill you myself." He spun on his heels and stormed off down the hallway.

He went straight to Bridge. "Pull up all files on Officer Frederick Vance," he demanded. The order was not directed at any one crew member in particular. Everyone scattered.

They knew that tone and look. It was one the crew rarely saw, but it was one that did not go ignored. Screens around him blinked and filled with images of documents and personnel files. "I want all of his financial transactions." Traitors rarely worked for free. He swiped through the images coming up on the screen in front of him until he found the file he needed. Inside were lists of deposits from an unnamed account. "Pull up all data on this account. I want to know where every cent is coming from."

Everyone furiously searched. It was late in the evening before the crew hit a dead end in their investigation. Multiple accounts funneled enormous amounts of money one to another with no name attached to any of them. The money jumped from account to account before being deposited into Vance's account at United Confederation Bank. All the transactions were ten days apart. Each one was deposited at the same time through an automated system.

It appeared Vance had set up the account only months prior and had closed out all his other accounts in other banks. The unknown financier had been paying Vance to leak information off the Archon to Samas.

"Vance? Why does that name sound so familiar?" Than asked from behind.

Caine turned to look at him with murder in his eyes.

"You're supposed to be with Cara."

"She's safe. Zora is with her. She needed to be with another woman."

Caine glowered at him but agreed with Than's decision. "What do we have on his personal background?"

"This is everything we have, Sir." Xan sent everything to Caine's screen. Vance's record was immaculate. High marks at the Academy. Not a single disciplinary issue to be found. He had started working as a Petty Officer on the Concordat until it was proposed he be moved to the Archon.

"Kuso. Vance is Shiro's nephew. His sister's son. Shiro signed off on his transfer recommendation last year."

Than folded his arms across his chest. "I guess there is no need for me to point out the coincidence in all of this?"

"Pull up all surveillance video from the Confederation Banks on Arctus. I want to know which branch Shiro used." Caine walked past all the display screens, looking for anything he might have missed that would lead him to the source of the money.

The computers beeped.

"The video files have been designated as a Level 10 Clearance," someone read aloud. Only Council members had a security clearance that high. Whoever had classified these files was on the Council.

"Pull them up. I want to know who classified these files," he roared, although he already had a good idea of who was likely behind it.

"Commander, my systems are not allowing me..." Xan began.

"Can you breach their firewall?"

"Yes, but-"

"Then do it."

No response. The Bridge fell silent.

"Did you not hear me? Hack in." His tone was deathly serious.

"Commander, if you hack into encrypted files, the Council will be alerted. You will be suspended from duty." Than had walked up behind him.

Caine looked back at his questioning crew. He was well aware of the consequences of his actions. "Do it."

It took the officer over an hour to crack into the system. The name of who classified the files didn't surprise him at all.

Shiro.

He had classified all of Vance's files the day the Confederation Bank account was opened. Surveillance video captured him frequenting a small branch in Shiyan. It was highly unusual for a Council Member to go so far outside the city center to do some banking.

Caine regretted not bringing his suspicions to the attention of the Council sooner. He would have maybe prevented much of the chaos that had plagued the system lately. He could have prevented so many deaths. He understood why Shiro would want to help the Hostiles with money or weaponry. He had always been a strong supporter of leaving them be. What didn't make sense was why he would want Samas to know about Cara. Why would he want Cara dead? It was possible Shiro may have had a hand in Cara's arrival in the first place.

"Send everything directly to Yugato. Get us to Arctus as fast as you can."

Chapter Forty-Seven

They docked at Arctus around midday two days later. Caine marched to the Council, Cara in tow. He refused to leave her in the care of anyone except himself or Than.

The three of them took a pod to the Caelum. Once they landed, Than took a plain, unmarked folder Caine handed him. They exchanged a look Cara couldn't decipher. Instead of joining them, Than turned and walked in the opposite direction.

"Come on." Caine turned. Cara had to take the massive white steps two at a time to keep up with his long-legged stride.

"Where is Than going?" Cara was breathing hard, practically chasing after him. "What was in the folder?"

"That doesn't matter right now. Stay close to me. I'll handle this." He burst into the Council Chambers. The enormous wooden doors slammed against the walls with a crash.

"Caine." Yugato raised his hands peacefully to diffuse the situation. "I am sorry for the loss of your officer. We are looking into this horrible betrayal."

Caine's fists balled up. "That's not good enough!"

Every Council member stared at Caine, shocked by his outburst.

"Excuse me?" Councilwoman Viraha choked out.

Shiro reached out and placed his hand on her arm. "It would appear the Commander has simply had a momentary lapse in Council policy."

Caine glowered at him. "And it would appear to me you have forgotten the oath you took to protect every citizen of the Confederation when you became a Council member!"

Shiro leaned forward, eyes narrowed. "How dare you-" It was as far as he got. Everyone was shouting over each other.

Half of them were standing, pointing at each other or Caine. The situation was escalating rapidly.

"QUIET," Yugato thundered. Everyone hushed. "Caine." He looked at something over Caine's shoulder.

Caine turned to see Shiro in front of Cara. Without him even noticing, Shiro had left his seat and was standing dangerously close to the woman he had targeted.

"How does it feel knowing you are responsible for all of this?" Shiro asked her quietly. "So many dead, because of you. You come through time and bring nothing but death with you."

Cara looked stunned. She looked over at Caine, wide-eyed and unsure of what to do.

"How can we be standing here defending this woman and protecting her?" Shiro turned to address the Council.

"Because it is our duty!" Caine took several protective steps towards Cara, hoping to get between her and Shiro.

"You say it is our duty? Who is our duty to? It is our duty to protect citizens of the Confederation, and she," Shiro pointed at Cara, "is not a citizen. She is an interloper. A trespasser. She comes here and causes all of this unnecessary upset, and we continue to allow it to go on." He turned to Cara. "Because of you, the Confederation ordered a direct attack on the Hostile planet where you were held. You are responsible for the deaths of thousands of people. They may be Hostiles, but they were still human beings."

Cara looked mortified.

"Hardly," Saar stood up, pounding his fist on the table. "They are not human at all. They're monsters. Their DNA isn't even the same as ours."

Shiro grabbed Cara by the shoulders viciously. She shrieked. Caine jumped in, placing himself between Cara and Shiro. He punched Shiro, who stumbled away, holding his nose. Blood seeped through his fingers and dripped to the stone floor.

Council Guards leapt in, grabbing them both and forcing them away from each other.

"Shiro tried to have Cara killed on my ship. He paid his own nephew to do it to help cover up the fact he has been illegally outfitting Hostiles with Confederation technology and weaponry for the last year," Caine yelled.

Shiro's face paled. "Friedrick? He would never! Where is he?"

"He was killed in his attempt to murder Cara."

Shiro's actions were revolting. He had sent his own family in to do his dirty work. He was no better than Samas, using the lives of others as sacrificial pawns in their games.

"You bastard!" Shiro scuffled with the guards trying to get to Caine. A swift kick from one caused Shiro's legs to buckle, and they wrestled him to his knees.

"Remove him," Yugato ordered.

"This is your fault!" Shiro pointed at Saar as he was dragged away. He turned to look at Caine and Cara. "You are all responsible!"

The doors closed behind them with a resounding thud. It echoed through the chamber.

"Caine!" Yugato shouted. "I know this has been a trying time for all involved, but you are making some heavy accusations against a Council member."

"I have evidence of Shiro's involvement. It was all sent to you personally," Caine said.

Yugato took a moment to look through some of the files. "We will have this discussion in private. You will stay in Council Quarters and await further instructions there."

Caine didn't argue with the orders as they were escorted out of the Council Chambers towards separate rooms in the Caelum.

"You'll be okay. Stay in your room until we get this settled." Caine gave Cara's hand a squeeze as she was led away from him. She nodded despite her fear of being separated from him.

She was brought to a small but well-furnished room. She walked to the window, looking out over the city, hoping it wouldn't be long before she was allowed to be with Caine again.

The city streets below were bustling with activity. The skies were just as busy. Cara rested her head against the glass.

She jumped when the door opened. A tall, grey-haired man strode in. She recognized him as one of the Council members who had spoken out against Shiro. Caine had mentioned him once. She remembered deducing from his tone that he wasn't particularly fond of the man.

His long, burgundy robes swirled around his legs as he approached her. He smiled at her.

Cara noted his bright blue eyes. He was an Esper, like Caine.

"My name is Saar. I have come because I would very much like to speak with you. Please, come walk with me."

Cara followed him into the hall.

"You must be exhausted after all of this."

"I don't understand why that man was so angry with me. What did I do?"

"I am so sorry for the way Councilman Shiro treated you. That was unacceptable. It does not matter if you are one of our citizens or not. While you are in our presence, you are under our protection," he told her.

At least Saar didn't blame her for all the mess that had happened.

"I am sure the Commander has told you of our... tense relationship." He clasped his hands together in front of him.

"He doesn't tell me much," she answered truthfully.

"Caine and I have not always seen eye to eye. I only want what is best for the Confederation. I must admit that sometimes my ways might appear to be a little extreme, but protecting the integrity of the Confederation and its people is my top priority, as it is the Commander's. I wish we agreed more on the issues. Councilman Shiro and I also disagree on many things. He sees the best in the world while I see the reality of it. No matter our differences in opinion on policy, he never should have attempted to harm you. I wanted to check on you personally."

"I'm okay." Cara was intrigued by the man. He was practical, but she could tell he had real passion for his job. In many ways, he reminded her of Caine. Maybe that was why they didn't get along; they were too similar. Caine didn't like him, though, and it made her slightly wary of his concern.

Saar looked down at her as they continued. "Neither Shiro nor Caine have ever been ones to think outside the box. They live their lives according to doctrine. The rules and regulations dictate their every move. Caine, Shiro, they see the world in black and white but, my dear, there is so much grey that cannot be ignored. We live in a world where there is a threat to our peace and democracy always looming in the distance."

They reached a small sitting room. "Please, sit." He motioned to a chair. He went to a counter and poured her a drink. He handed her the delicate glass cup. She took a sip; it tasted like haldi.

"I don't understand."

"I do not want to see the end of this system. The measures we take are always in the best interest of the people. We have been given the sacred duty of protecting the planets and citizens. It is a duty I do not take lightly. Shiro blames you for the deaths of the Hostiles on Yedrus, but do not feel like you are responsible."

"I don't," Cara said awkwardly.

These were problems that existed long before she had arrived. She had merely been caught in the crossfire as the situation escalated.

"The assault was inevitable. It was only a matter of time before we were forced to take a firmer hand. You were merely the catalyst that sped up the timeline. You gave the Council a reason to fight back instead of allowing the Hostiles to continue to be emboldened by our inaction and complacency."

There was a knock on the door, and Yugato entered.

"I hope I am not interrupting." He smiled.

Cara tried not to let her relief show on her face. Rescue had arrived just in time.

"Not at all." Saar bowed his head in respect.

"May I please speak with Cara alone?" Yugato asked.

Saar looked between them. He bristled at the abrupt dismissal. "Of course," he said reluctantly.

"Thank you," Cara said with a half-smile once Saar was gone. She

"Saar means well, but he can be a little intense at times."

"I can tell."

Yugato stood. "Would you like some more tea?"

"Yes, please."

Yugato crossed the room to the counter. "I suppose it is what makes him so effective as a Council member. He will go to whatever lengths are necessary to protect this system and his people. As will I."

He handed Cara her refilled cup and took a seat across from her.

"When I first heard about your incredible arrival, I could scarcely believe my ears. I didn't know how it was possible. It was only when I finally met you that I understood the implications."

"What do you mean?"

"Caine is quite enamored with you, my dear. Have you not noticed?"

Cara blushed.

"I do believe that you have developed feelings for him as well."

"I have."

"Caine is a remarkable man. I have known him since he was a small boy. I took him under my wing when he entered the Academy. He has been groomed since birth for greatness. I am sure you want the best for him."

"Of course I do."

"As do I. Which is why I hope you will understand why I have to do this."

"Do what?"

Cara rubbed her hand over her eyes.

"Are you all right, my dear?" he asked.

"Yes, I think I'm just tired." She looked up at him. Her vision doubled and became blurry. She looked down at the cup and back up at Yugato, whose face had turned somber.

A chill ran through her. Something was wrong. She looked back down at her cup as she grew increasingly unwell. "What did you do to me?"

Yugato opened his hand to reveal a small glass vial half-filled with a clear liquid. "Aconite." He gave the bottle a little shake before tucking it into a pocket in the folds of his robe. "A handy little poison. Undetectable. Your heart will stop beating soon."

Cara pushed herself up and stumbled to the door, jerking it open. Shiro wasn't the one who wanted her dead. It wasn't even Saar.

It was Yugato.

Cara grabbed the doorframe, using it to support her weight. She needed to escape. She pushed off and tried to run down the hall but didn't make it far before she collapsed to her knees, unable to go any further.

Yugato came up behind her and grabbed her by her shirt collar. He pulled her across the floor and leaned her against the wall.

Cara tried to grab at his hands, but her arms were heavy and wouldn't work. She tried to yell, but her shouts were merely raspy whispers. She squeezed her eyes shut, thinking of Caine and hoping she could somehow get him to hear her mental cries for help.

"Why?" Cara managed to ask.

"Why, Cara?" Yugato sighed as if this conversation was boring him. "I need Caine. I cannot lose him. Not now. I have worked too hard preparing him for his future. I cannot allow you to distract him. Not when we have come so far."

"You were his friend." Cara's voice cracked, barely coming out much louder than a whisper. Why would he turn on Caine like this? He had been his mentor, like a father to him.

"Hostiles have become a plague in our system, but for years the Council has been unable to come to an agreement on how to handle them. The threat they pose grows exponentially. It needs to be eliminated. The only way to unite the Council was to give them a reason to agree on a way forward. But it couldn't be me. It had to be Saar. He has been pushing for us to use more aggressive measures for years. Then you arrived. You were the key to unifying the Council to take action. The sins of the father always fall upon the shoulders of the child..." he paused at the unintentional slip.

"Samas." Cara retched, but nothing came up.

Yugato let go of her. Cara slowly slid further to the side, unable to keep herself upright as the poison worked its way through her system.

Yugato crouched down in front of her, balancing lightly on the balls of his feet.

"He said you were clever. He wasn't lying, I see. I can see why both of them became so infatuated with you." He stood, turning partially away from her as he spoke. "His mother was one of my first Interrogations. When she was captured, it was my job to get information from her. I was young and couldn't control myself. When I found out she was pregnant, I had no other choice. I had to get rid of her. I took her off the ship on the next supply drop and brought her into the woods. Saar's wife discovered us. Using my surprise to her advantage, she managed to escape. Unfortunately, I couldn't let Jura go after what she had seen. If she reported me to the Council, I would have been arrested. When Saar found Jura's body in the woods and later realized that the Hostile prisoner was gone; even I couldn't have planned it any better. He was so quick to blame the bitch."

Yugato sighed again. "Samas could have been my greatest achievement, but you can't choose what your children become."

With great speed and agility, he turned and squatted, grabbing a fistful of her hair, pulling her upright. Cara bit her lip to keep from crying out.

"He grew up smart, too smart. When he came to power, he demanded supplies in exchange for his silence. It was hard to get him what he wanted, especially as his demands grew -weapons, money, information. Samas should have been the one killed instead of his monstrosity of a sister. But we can't go back, can we?" His eyes flashed. "And then you came along. Saar had been on the edge since Jura died. His hatred for the Hostiles growing with every passing year. He just needed that extra push so the Council would approve a direct strike on Yedrus. Even then, Samas somehow managed to escape. I should be thanking you, my dear, for taking care of that little problem for me. I never would have thought it would be you to take my son down."

"You're crazy," Cara spat. Yugato's blue eyes were no longer sad. They were cold and hollow.

"The ends will always justify the means. I have to do whatever it takes to protect this system, even if it means doing the wrong thing for the right reason. I never wanted it to come to this, but I have worked too hard to allow it all fall apart. Caine is in line to take the next open seat in the Council. Your death will be the spark he needs to continue the assault against the Hostiles until we erase them from existence. It won't be too much longer now. Don't worry. It won't hurt. I will make sure that there is justice for your death. Councilman Saar will be arrested for your murder by the end of the night."

He dragged her down the hallway. Where did he plan on taking her? It wasn't as if he would be able to keep pulling her body around behind him much longer without being seen.

Guilt and regret spiked through her. It was her fault they were in this predicament. The moment Yugato had discovered she was a time-traveler, it had put a target on her back. Samas wanted to use her, hoping she would hold the secrets and the key to jumping through time while his father was simply trying to keep his secret from getting out. She had put Caine and everyone else in danger just by being there. Guilt and regret spiked through her.

A sharp crack echoed around them. Blood sprayed across Cara's face. Yugato let her go, and she collapsed onto the cold floor. His body fell next to her.

Caine was rushing towards them, tucking his gun back in his holster. He knelt beside Cara as she tried to tell him Yugato had poisoned her, but her voice wouldn't work.

"What is it?" he asked her.

She couldn't move a muscle, not even her lips.

"What did you give her?" Caine demanded, grabbing Yugato by the front of his robes. "What have you done?"

Yugato coughed up blood. "I did what I had to. I did this for you." He spoke through blood-stained teeth, gritted in pain.

"Whatever you thought you would accomplish, you failed." Caine shoved him roughly away.

"You of all people should know." Yugato let out a strangled gurgle as blood bubbled up, trickling from the corner of his mouth. "There is always a contingency plan." Blood dripped from his chin onto the white floor. He stopped breathing.

Angrily, Caine shook Yugato's lifeless body. He looked over at Cara, who was pale and barely breathing. He rifled through Yugato's cloak and found the vial of clear liquid. He opened it and gave it a sniff. "Aconite." Caine recognized the sweet aroma.

Hearing the commotion, it seemed as if officers appeared out of thin air. Two men grabbed Caine.

"Commander Caine, you are being arrested for the murder of a council member," one man informed him.

Saar emerged through the crowd, looking down at Yugato's body, Cara lying motionless next to him.

"Cara has been poisoned. Aconite. She needs an antidote immediately. She's barely breathing." Caine looked down at Cara as her eyes fluttered closed. She was fading fast. He turned back to Saar, not trying to hide the terror he was feeling. "You'll take care of her?"

"I will." Saar nodded, the start of an uneasy truce between them. A medical team arrived. They quickly worked on stabilizing Cara as Caine was hauled away.

Chapter Forty-Eight

Caine was escorted out of the Caelum. He would be taken to the Aegis to go through the full Questioning and Interrogation process. Protocol called for another Esper to go into his mind, checking his memories for the facts.

Caine knew he would be cleared as soon as the truth was revealed. His biggest concern was Cara and whatever contingency plan Yugato had mentioned before he died.

Yugato was thorough. If he had planned on setting Saar up as the scapegoat and start a war with the Hostiles, he wouldn't stop with his attempt to kill Cara. He needed to warn Than that there could still be hidden danger.

At the bottom of the white steps was a prisoner transport pod. He turned to Officer Vesa on his left. "I need you to get a message to Than."

A massive fireball shot skyward, followed by an earth-shaking boom.

An explosion near the south end of the city.

"The Archon!" Caine pulled away, rushing towards the sound of the blast. Vesa was right behind him, already shouting into his comm calling for help.

As he rounded a corner, Caine could see the docking hangar and his ship both engulfed in flames.

"No. No," he repeated in horror.

Than would have been heading back to the ship. Caine ran towards it as fast as he could, his mind reeling.

The scene was chaos when he arrived. There was a massive hole in the side of the ship with flames shooting out and smoke plumes billowing high into the sky. Crew members emerged from the docking tower elevators, stumbling through scattered chunks of metal wreckage that had fallen to the street. Some of them collapsed to the ground, coughing, their uniforms singed. It was utter devastation. It looked like the scene of a Hostile attack, but the reality was, Yugato had done this.

The area was soon swarming with medics and Aegis Officers. Even the Council Guards, who had been escorting him to await his sentencing, had stepped in to help.

Caine grabbed people stumbling out from the smoke, checking to see how serious their wounds were and directing them to safety. A few yards away, Zora emerged from the smoke coughing hard.

He called her name, and she rushed to him, sobbing uncontrollably. His heart leapt to his throat.

"Are you hurt? Where is Than?" he asked.

Zora attempted to draw in a choppy, shaky breath. "I'm okay," Zora cried. "But," she burst into hysterics again.

"Zora, what is it?" He held her steady as she collapsed against him.

"Nadir." She couldn't even finish, but she didn't have to.

It couldn't be true.

Not Nadir.

He stared up at the ship. The upper back portion was where the blast had originated, where the Medical ward was.

Nadir had been with him since the beginning. He had healed every one of Caine's wounds, even the invisible ones. After Phoebe had died, Nadir was the one who suggested Alina go into hiding. Nadir was the heart of the ship. He was everyone's shoulder to cry on; he was the one who lifted their spirits during dark times. Caine owed him everything.

Caine wanted to collapse to his knees and scream, cry and mourn, but this was not the time. He had to remain their Commander, no matter how dire the situation was. He could grieve later. He mentally closed off that part of his mind, compartmentalizing and detaching.

"Where is Than?" he asked.

"I don't know. I don't think he was back yet."

"Go get yourself checked out." He directed her to the medics. He had to find Than.

"Than!" he yelled over the crowd. From across the crowd of people, a dark-haired man turned around. Relief flooded through him. Than was dragging an injured officer to safety. Caine ran to him and helped him gently lay the injured man down, and signaled for medics.

"I was almost into the elevator when the whole ship exploded." Than's face was smudged with ash and soot.

Caine swallowed hard. Just a few minutes later, and Than would have been up inside the ship when the blast had gone off.

"We lost Nadir." The words sounded strange, almost robotic, as he said them. Caine compartmentalized so he could survive the next few hours.

Than gave a strangled moan and sank to the ground, burying his face in his hands.

"Hey," Caine squatted in front of him. "We have to keep it together right now. We need to get through this. You're going to get up, we are going to get everyone evacuated, and we will deal with everything else later." He knew the pain his friend was going through. He was feeling it himself. He ran his hand through his hair. "I need you right now."

Than swallowed hard, wiped his palms on his pants, and pushed himself to stand. "Okay. What now?"

***

Cara woke in a hospital. Every breath hurt. Memories flooded back. Yugato was dead. Caine shot him.

She couldn't believe she was still alive despite being poisoned. The door opened. She hoped it was Caine,

Than, or Zora, but instead, a tall man in an official-looking grey uniform stepped in. He had sandy blond hair combed back neatly, a sharp jaw, clean-shaven and blue eyes. He looked a lot like, well, he looked like Caine.

"You're Tirio." Her voice was deep and thick. She cleared her throat as he approached and stood at the foot of the bed.

"I'm surprised my brother mentioned me at all."

"He didn't," she admitted. "Alina did."

Tirio looked genuinely surprised by her admission. "So that's where he shipped you off to for safekeeping. How is my little sister?"

"She's wonderful," Cara said, slightly disconcerted by the small talk.

"I suppose you want to know why I am here."

"That would be helpful."

"I'm the Captain of the Aegis. I was sent here to find out a little more about what happened between you and Councilman Saar." He brought her a glass of water and sat on the bed next to her. "You are familiar with Interrogation?"

"You want to read my mind."

Tirio gave a winsome smile, "In layman's terms, I guess that is somewhat accurate, yes." He reached out for her.

She flinched, leaning away from him.

Tirio looked surprised, but understanding flashed in his gaze. "Not all Espers are powerful enough to go into someone's mind without having any physical contact. We aren't all as talented as Caine is. I need to be touching you."

Cara hesitated but agreed. He gently placed two fingers on her temple. She could feel him enter her mind. It was a strange sensation. Different from Samas and Caine. Almost as if every Esper's sensation was unique, like a fingerprint. She could almost feel him moving through her memories. She found her mind wandering, and she thought about Caine as he lay on top of her, taking off her shirt.

Tirio had guided her to this memory. She drove Tirio out roughly, angry he had invaded her privacy. Inside her mind, giant defensive walls shot up in front of Tirio as he was surveying the memory in front of him, blocking him and knocking him off balance. He was pushed out with such force he grabbed the edge of the bed to hold himself steady.

"You are quite remarkable," he murmured, impressed with her strength. "I can see why he is so taken with you."

"He doesn't push his limits," Cara snapped.

Tirio narrowed his eyes slightly, looking her over as if analyzing her. Cara squirmed under the intense scrutiny. As if pleased with his assessment, he nodded, stood, and walked toward the door.

"Why do you hate him so much?" The question tumbled out before she could stop herself. Alina had already explained everything, but she wanted to hear it from Tirio himself. Tirio stopped, his hand on the door frame. His shoulders rose and fell with a great sigh. It almost sounded sad. He turned and ran a hand through his hair. It was a mannerism she knew well. Even though they may not have wanted to admit it, the brothers were more similar than they let on.

"I don't hate him." He looked sad, almost guilty. "Yes, I admit when I was younger, I was envious of his talents and abilities. He got all the attention. He was favored. But I saw what he was capable of achieving. So much potential. By then, our relationship was at its breaking point." He rubbed his jaw. "Not long after, our father got sick. He made me promise to help Caine and take care of him. When he died, Caine took it hard. He wanted to drop out of the academy to take care of our mother and Alina, but I couldn't let him do that. He was meant for greatness. I did what I had to do to drive him away, to make sure he stayed at the Academy and lived up to his potential the way our father wanted him to. Eventually, we just fell into those roles. We saw each other so little; each time was like seeing a stranger. If Nikolai thinking that I hate him pushes him to strive to be the best, it is the part I am willing to play."

"Why don't you tell him this? That's all so far in the past now. Don't you think it is time to move on?"

Tirio's smile was warm and genuine. "You make me feel like a schoolboy being lectured by his teacher. No one has been able to put me in my place in a long time. Maybe you have a point. I doubt it is one my brother will be willing to entertain."

"Maybe you don't know him as well as you think you do."

Tirio laughed. "Touché, Ms. DeLeon. I hope our paths will cross again someday." Cara had a sinking feeling this would be the first and last time she would see him.

Chapter Forty-Nine

The doctors cleared Cara for release the next day after multiple rounds of tests confirmed the poison was out of her system. She was escorted back to the Council building.

"Sit here," the Council Guard instructed her, pointing at a bench. The Caelum was busier than usual. She could tell in the hustle no one knew what to do in a situation like this.

The revelation that Yugato was a traitor with an unregulated son was sending shockwaves through the entire Council. She leaned against the cool wall and shivered, partly from the cold but mostly because she had a horrible feeling things were not going to end well.

Amid the crowd, she caught sight of a familiar face. Saar noticed her, and he quickly ended his conversation with the officer next to him. He approached her and handed her his cloak. Grateful, she took it and wrapped it around herself. Despite the warm cloth, she was chilled to the bone and could not get warm.

"Where is Caine?" she asked.

Saar's face was somber. "There was an explosion aboard the Archon last night. We allowed Caine a temporary reprieve to assist in the rescue and recovery efforts."

So many awful things had happened. This was the icing on top of it all.

"Do you know who didn't make it?" she asked plainly. She knew crew members would have died. She hoped none of them were names she recognized.

"I am not sure. I have not been given the full report yet, but when I find out, I will make sure you are informed as well."

"What will happen now, with Caine?" she asked him.

Saar sighed. His face was grim. He looked exhausted, sad. Dark circles under his eyes gave away his age.

"Unfortunately, we have laws for a reason. Laws that apply to him as well. Not even I can protect him now. He will be stripped of all rank, pending investigation, and put in a military jail. We will try to speed things along and get him into house arrest, but it will still take some time. The evidence will clear him in the end, but he will have to go through the entire criminal trial. When it is all over, his record will be clean, and he will most likely be restored to his current position as Commander."

"Most likely?" Cara squeaked.

Saar's face softened. "He will be just fine, Cara. I'm meeting with the rest of the Council today to try to move the process forward as quickly as possible. We have never had to deal with anything like this before. Yugato's betrayal was-" He wiped a hand over his face.

Cara sighed. "When can I see him?" She wanted to make sure he was okay.

"Not tonight. He will be at the Archon until tomorrow. I will have an officer take you to your sleeping quarters but I will bring you to see him in the morning. For now, get some rest."

Saar's suggestion was nearly impossible to follow. Cara paced her small room for hours until her body finally betrayed her, and she fell asleep. She tossed and turned restlessly.

By morning, Cara still hadn't received any updates from Caine. Not knowing what was happening was more challenging than she had expected.

Saar came to see her as he had told her. "Before I take you to see Caine, I have to speak with you." He sat at the end of her bed.

Cara knew something was wrong. Had something happened to Caine? No, that that wasn't possible because he had just told her he would take her to see him. Maybe something had happened to Than or Zora. She braced herself for bad news.

"I had the meeting with the Council and the trial judge last night. He has agreed to begin the trial immediately on one condition."

Cara's heart was beating wildly. "What condition?"

"We have to send you home before it begins."

"No!" That was not the news she had been expecting.

"As we speak, our scientists are doing the final tests on a machine they built to get you back where you belong."

"When?"

They had done it; they had figured out a way to get her home. For some reason, she had almost stopped expecting it would ever happen and had gotten used to the idea she would be staying.

Saar paused as if debating revealing the next piece of information. "Tonight."

Cara's heart sank. She hadn't thought it would be so soon. "I don't want to go back," she pleaded.

"Cara, do you love him?" Saar asked pointedly.

"Of course I do." There was no point in hiding her feelings for Caine. She had tried denying them long enough. Saar was smart enough to know the truth.

"Cara, your presence here is hindering my ability to help him. It has sparked all of this."

"So, this is all my fault?"

"No, no, that is not what I am saying. What I am saying is your presence here will not help him. If you love him and want to protect him, then you need to go home. This is not your time. It is not where you belong."

"I do belong here with Caine," she protested.

"You will never be able to be with him. With the truth about Samas's paternity revealed, this will be enforced now more than ever. The Council would never allow it. There are laws for men like him. Laws even I cannot change. A union between you and him; you would never be together since you are not an Esper. An Esper must be genetically matched with another in order to bear an Esper as a child."

"I understand genetics just fine." She didn't need a science lesson explaining to her why she couldn't be with Caine. It was clear enough to her already. One eyebrow raised slightly at the hint of attitude in Cara's voice, but Saar continued.

"Caine is one of the most powerful Espers we have seen in over a hundred years. His child has the potential to be just as powerful. He has his mission to protect and serve the Confederation. He will be moving up in the military or even potentially have a place on the Council someday. He has a great future. None of it can exist or will exist with you."

"I want to see Caine."

"You cannot discuss this with him," Saar warned. "He will fight for you; he will give up everything and his entire future for you if you asked him to. Do not ask him to. Do not make him sacrifice all the good he could do for you."

Cara stared at him, bewildered.

"Caine will be assigned to marry another in a year or so. He will not want any of it if he believes he could be with you instead. If he refuses his match, there would be significant consequences for him, and you still wouldn't be allowed to be together. He would be forced to watch you live alone on a foreign planet struggling to survive. How would you work here? How would you live here? Go home to where you belong. Your family will want you back."

Tears fell freely.

Saar touched her arm gently. "You know this is all for the best. Get ready, and I'll take you to see him."

Cara dressed quickly. Saar led her to a transport pod, and they made their way to the smoldering wreckage of the Archon.

When the ramp lowered, she scanned the crowd for Caine. He was talking to several Aegis Officers. He looked over at that moment and hurried towards her, weaving in between people. He grabbed her and hugged her close.

"Cara," he whispered and kissed the top of her head. "My brother told me he went to check on you and make sure you were okay. I'm sorry I didn't come."

Cara gently pushed back so she could look him in the eyes. "Don't be sorry. You had to take care of this. Zora? Than?" she asked, hoping to hear they were safe.

"They're fine, but…" He stopped.

"Tell me."

"Nadir," he stopped again, his voice heavy with grief.

She let out an anguished cry and pressed her face against Caine's chest. "No," she protested. Nadir was the only reason she was still alive today. She owed him everything, her life being the least of it. After a moment, she turned to look at the ship she had wanted to call home.

"Are you okay?" Caine asked.

Was she okay? She had just been told Nadir was dead, and she still had to break the news to Caine that she was being sent home. She absolutely was not okay.

She looked away, not wanting to tell him she was leaving, as if not speaking the words aloud made it less real. Caine noticed her sudden anxiety.

"What? What is it?"

Cara looked at him. She looked in his eyes, those brilliant, unnaturally blue eyes. They were a stark reminder of who he was. He was different and special. He did have a future.

Saar's warning echoed in her mind. There was a look in his eyes when he stared at her. He cared for her. He would give up everything for her. She could never ask that of him.

"Cara." He tilted her head to make her look at him. "Tell me." He sensed her fear and anxiety. He felt her indecision.

"They want to send me home."

"How? They have no way." He stopped and took a deep breath. "They found a way."

"They will push your trial forward as long as I leave today." Her voice wavered as she spoke.

"No, I won't let them send you back. The trial doesn't matter."

Cara looked up at him, tears spilling down her cheeks.

"What aren't you telling me?" he asked. He could see she was holding something back, something she was avoiding telling him.

"I don't have a choice; you don't have a choice. He said you can't stop it."

"Who said that?" Caine demanded.

"Saar." She wouldn't meet his eyes, her voice barely above a whisper.

"Kuso." Caine ran his hands through his hair. He knew Saar had the final say in this. With Yugato gone, even he would be unable to fight the Council on this. They would never change the laws just for him. He wanted to fight, but he knew it was time for her to go home. She had a family, friends, and a life waiting for her there.

"I thought we'd have more time." Caine held her close, one hand cradling the back of her head.

Cara couldn't speak, tears flowing readily. She had wanted to go home for so long, and now she wanted nothing else but to be allowed to stay.

Saar approached, cutting their time together short. "Caine," he addressed him.

"Saar," Caine responded. There was still a hint of underlying tension in their tone.

"It is time for her to go."

Cara stood. Caine reached out and grabbed her hand, pulling her close to his side.

"Will I be able to see her go?"

"You can be there," Saar agreed. "I do have some things I need to discuss with you further."

Caine let out a sigh of relief. "Thank you, Turcan." He meant it. After years of brewing animosity, Saar had no obligation to allow Caine to witness Cara's departure. The fact that Saar was so willing to allow him to be there meant there was hope for them to repair their relationship.

Saar summoned an officer. "Cara, please follow Officer Uan. Caine, this way."

Cara was led away as Saar walked off in the opposite direction with Caine. What tale would Saar try to spin with him? Would he say the same things he said to her? Tell him there was no chance they'd ever be together and to let her go without a fight?

"Where are you taking me?" she asked the officer, glancing back at Caine and Saar over her shoulder.

"I will be bringing you back to the Caelum until further arrangements are made." His formal tone was like a splash of cold water.

"Cara, wait!" Than jogged up. She instantly burst into tears. He wrapped her up in his arms. "Shh. Hey now, it's going to be okay." He looked up at Officer Uan. "Can you give us a moment, please?" Uan backed away a short distance, allowing them some privacy.

"I'm happy to see you on your feet again." Than wiped away a tear on her cheek with his thumb.

"If Caine hadn't shown up, I wouldn't be." Cara stopped. How had Caine been there? He had been taken away by the Council Guards. How would he have been able to stop Yugato?

"How did Caine figure out Yugato was behind it all and not Shiro?" she asked.

"I'd like to take a little credit for that," Than smiled. "Caine had me bring all the files to his brother."

"Tirio?" Cara was surprised Tirio hadn't mentioned anything to her about it in the hospital. She recalled Caine handing Than the folder when they had first arrived at the Caelum.

"Caine wanted him to take a look at the evidence, knowing there would be a bigger investigation needed to prove Shiro's involvement. Once Tirio started digging, it wasn't long before he figured out someone was setting Shiro up. Tirio came directly to the Caelum, just in time, it seems."

"I'm leaving," she sniffed.

He pulled away, looking down at her. "When?" he asked.

He knew she meant she was being sent home, not just leaving the scene.

"Tonight."

He sucked in a big breath. "I didn't realize they were able to figure out a way to do it already."

"No one did."

"What did Caine have to say about it?"

"He isn't happy about it."

"That isn't surprising. He isn't happy about anything ever." He winked, lightening the mood. "Don't worry. You'll be back.".

Cara frowned. "What do you mean?" She didn't understand what he was saying.

"There's a theory. It's a lot of fancy science, but the basic explanation is two particles can be linked to each other even if separated by billions of light-years of space."

Cara raised an eyebrow. "I still don't get it."

Than laughed. "Stay with me here. It's called quantum entanglement. Two atoms might collide; meet and interact somewhere, anywhere, in space or time, and eventually separate once again. Yet, they remain connected, no matter how far they travel. They could end up on opposite ends of the universe, but they have been bonded to each other."

He looked over at Caine, working in the distance. Cara followed his gaze and understood. He was saying she and Caine were entangled.

Despite the logical, scientific evidence pointing to the opposite, Cara found herself believing Than's theory. They had been drawn together in a strange, unexplainable way since the moment she landed on his ship. Call it fate, destiny, or merely the cells in their bodies finding their way together. She couldn't deny the appeal in believing she and Caine were inextricably connected.

"Time's up. We need to go," Officer Uan interrupted.

"One more minute," Than brushed off the request.

"We have to get back-"

"Back off, Uan. She can have one more minute to say goodbye." Than turned back to Cara while Uan stepped away to nurse his wounded ego.

"But I don't even understand how I got here. Once I'm home, how would I get back?" She needed more time. She needed answers.

"I'm not sure. All I know is you two were drawn to each other. Unexplainable forces brought you together. I don't think you'll be kept apart for long. So maybe we say goodbye for now, but I'll be seeing you again. Take care of yourself." Than squeezed her hand one last time and waved Officer Uan back over.

"This way," Uan instructed, pointing to the pod. Cara boarded. The metal ramp clanged shut with resounding finality.

Her time here was over.

Chapter Fifty

Saar gently led Caine away by his shoulder as Cara was taken back to the Caelum. Caine looked at the man next to him, once an enemy, now an ally, while the man he had once considered his greatest ally had been the one who ultimately betrayed him. How could Yugato have committed such treacherous acts? He had not only been Caine's biggest advocate; he was a friend. The betrayal stung.

"Caine, I have known you for a long time. I have watched you achieve incredible things," Saar paused. It was unusual for him not to get right to the point. He wasn't one to drag out a conversation with superfluous words.

"What does this have to do with Cara being sent home?" Caine demanded, knowing where the conversation was heading.

Saar sighed. "Our scientists believe they have come up with a way to send her back to her time. They believe the massive electromagnetic burst the EMP emitted pulled her forward in time. After reverse-engineering some of the components, we think we can push her back across. Unfortunately, they think it will work only once, and using it could destroy it beyond repair after, but they are confident it will work to get her home. The Council has talked and discussed it. This will happen. Cara will be sent home. Her arrival sent us down this path, which led to the death of a Council member at your hands."

"Yugato was a traitor. Cara didn't cause this!"

Saar put up a hand to quiet his outburst. "I never said Yugato did not get what he deserved, and I never implied this was Cara's fault. Whether we would have ended up in this same spot without her here, we will never know, but here we sit. You have murder charges against you - the murder of a Council member. The trial will eventually prove you innocent, but it will be at a cost to you, your crew, and the Council. You will not walk away from this unchanged. I will not be on the Council forever. You are the one who will be chosen to step in and fill Yugato's seat. You have a mission, things you have yet to accomplish, and none of it will happen with Cara around. It cannot. She will never be sanctioned to be with you. We both know the laws will never be changed. Not for an Esper. She will struggle if she stays here as a citizen. Let her go home. We have all been through enough. It is time things return to normal."

As much as Caine didn't want to admit it, he could. When he didn't argue, Saar knew Caine understood.

"I am sure you can see this from the Council's perspective. I will see you at the Caelum this evening."

Saar left Caine to his work. There was still so much work to be done to clean up the wreckage from the Archon. Massive repairs were already underway.

Caine thought about how much he would miss Cara if she ever left. He had always known from the beginning; this would always be the outcome. He had never thought about a future with her, but now, knowing it would never happen, he was curious about it. He pondered if they would have been able to be together, but now, it was an impossibility.

Yugato once told him someday he would be the most logical choice to be elected to the Council. It was the next step in his career, but an unexpected sadness gnawed at his insides. He was feeling grief for a life he lost even though it was never his to lose in the first place. He had mourned over losing Phoebe, but this was different. He loved Cara.

It wasn't long after dark when four officers came to escort him to the Caelum. They flanked him, taking him to the room where Cara was waiting.

"Can I have a minute?" he asked. The officer hesitated but agreed.

Cara was sitting on a chair, her eyes red from hours of crying. She stood when he entered. He crossed the room in three long strides, pulled her to him, and kissed her. He fisted his hands in her hair. He kissed her hard, hoping it would never end but knowing it would all too soon. He pulled back.

"Cara, I have to tell you..."

She shook her head. "Don't say it. Please," she begged him. "Don't do this now,"

He took her face in his hands. "Cara, this is not easy, but this is for the best. I cannot, will not, let you leave without you knowing. You changed me; you changed my life for the better. You have made me better in so many ways. You opened my heart back up; you are in my heart, and you always will be." He wiped away falling tears. "Look at me." She did. "Let me in," he whispered into her ear. Her brows furrowed in confusion. "We don't have a lot of time, and they are watching - let me in," he said, his voice slightly muffled as he pressed his lips against her forehead.

He drew back and looked at her and pushed into her mind. She didn't resist. He was standing in front of the walls, and instead of solid walls, there was a large wooden door. He approached, and it opened. He searched for a special memory and quickly found on that worked. It was her favorite place, a large green space with people strolling around, some running, and others walking dogs. His attention was drawn to one particular spot that had a faint glow; A green metal bench sat next to a large tree, its roots breaking through the earth and stretching out in all directions, large branches overhead casting dancing shadows as they swayed in the breeze.

All her memories of this time would be erased from her mind. There was a chance he could circumvent that by concealing duplicates of them in a memory from her past.

He worked quickly, making copies of all her memories and molding them into a small, transparent orb. He pressed the orb against the tree, and it vanished into it, leaving behind a dark spot on the bark. He ran his fingers over the black mark, sealing the contents. If she ever recalled this particular memory after she was home, hopefully, it would unlock what he had hidden away there, and she would remember everything. He pulled out. She was looking at him, unsure of what he had done. He gave her a hopeful smile but couldn't tell her what he had done in case another Esper discovered her memory of it when erasing hers.

Caine held Cara's hand, and they walked together down the long hallway. The door at the end opened, revealing a large room with high ceilings. People milled around through machinery and tables full of blinking and beeping computer equipment. The room was not brightly lit. Illuminated in the center was a large round glass chamber on a small, raised platform.

"It is time," Saar said.

Caine kissed Cara's forehead.

"We are going to have an Esper erase all your memories of this." Saar gestured to a man standing off to the side.

She wouldn't even be allowed to remember? She took a few steps back as the man approached. He had vivid blue eyes and seven little stars on his collar. An Esper. Powerful, but nothing like Caine. He stopped in front of her. She wanted to run, to fight, to be allowed to keep her memories, but they would force her if they had to. She turned to Caine; he could see the fear and devastation in her eyes.

"I love you," he ground out between his teeth, the words tearing him apart.

The sudden admission broke Cara's heart. "I love you too," she responded.

The man gave a curt nod of respect to Caine and reached out to touch Cara's temples.

"It's okay. You need to let him in," Caine said softly next to her. The Council wouldn't let Caine do it himself, obviously not trusting him to do the job impartially. It was a suspicion they were wise to have had.

The man pushed into Cara's head. His presence was slick, almost greasy, and thick, nothing like Caine. She didn't like it, but she didn't force him out. He twisted through her mind like an oily snake. The squeezing pressure made her squirm. She wanted it to be over.

Finally, he pulled out of her head. Dizzy, she wobbled, but strong hands grabbed onto her waist and held her steady. Everything was hazy. She couldn't remember what was going on or why she was there. She was gently led up some steps and into a large cylindrical glass chamber.

The door slid shut, and the machine whirred to life. She didn't like this. Something was wrong.

Caine stepped away from the chamber. There was a soft light. At first, it was a dim glow. It started to flow around her as it got brighter. It was like a vivid, liquid blue, swirling around her arms and legs.

"No, no," she breathed, not sure what was going on, why this was happening to her. "Wait!" She banged on the door, trying to pry it open. "What's happening? Please get me out!" She looked at all the people in the room standing there watching this happen. Why wasn't anyone helping her?

Caine's stomach churned as Cara clawed at the glass. He turned to Saar. "Stop this!"

"It is too late now. Don't throw it all away for her."

Caine swore. "Stop it now!" He rushed to the platform and tried to find where the door would open. His fingers clawed at the glass.

The air crackled and swirled, rushing around Cara like a tornado. All her hair on her arms stood on end. Her hair lifted away from her neck. It was electric and terrifying. There was immense pressure building around her and squeezing down on her. A man ran up the steps to her. Cara placed her hand on the glass, she couldn't speak, but she hoped the man would understand and help her get out of whatever kind of machine this was.

Caine raised his hand to the other side of the glass, covering where her palm was placed. Tears streamed down her face.

There was an explosion of bright, white light and crushing pressure. A streak of blue light followed a deafening crack, and everything went black.

Caine covered his face with his arm and stumbled back a few steps, shielding himself from the blinding light that exploded out of the chamber. The light faded, and he looked up at the chamber. Empty.

"How do we know if she made it back?"

Saar looked at him, no humor or mirth in his eyes. "We don't."

Caine knew it was time. He reached for the small device in his back pocket. "We can't let this technology continue." If this technology made it into the wrong hands, it could be catastrophic. Time-traveling was best left in the realm of fiction, not reality. Saar looked momentarily surprised when he noticed the remote in Caine's hand as he pulled it from his pocket, but he squared his gaze on Caine and nodded.

"As far as I am concerned, today never happened," Saar said.

Caine cleared his throat and caught the attention of the people in the room. It didn't take him long to erase their memories of anything and everything related to Cara and this machine.

"Leave and speak of this to no one," he commanded.

Everyone filed out of the room. Saar took one last look around and followed them out. Caine turned in the doorway.

"Goodbye, Cara," he whispered and pressed the button.

It triggered a small blast in the back corner of the room. He knew he would have time to get out before the growing fire destroyed the lab area. He walked outside, and smoke was pouring from the building. Fire crews rushed past him as he exited. Than was waiting for him on the corner. He walked over to him as Than shook his head.

"Did you have to set the Caelum on fire?" he asked with a half-smile.

"Do you want to risk this kind of technology getting into the hands of someone who would use it for the wrong reason?"

"I'm pretty sure you just wanted to set it on fire," Than accused. He searched Caine's face. "Kuso. You did." He widened his eyes, a look of mock horror on his face. "You're actually enjoying this."

Caine chuckled and pulled his friend along. "Let's go."

Chapter Fifty-One

Cara opened her eyes. She felt like she had been run through a blender, and the millions of pieces had been flattened by a steamroller and glued back together. Every cell had been ripped apart, shredded, and stitched back together. She struggled to her feet. She was an alleyway of some sort. She stood and stumbled out towards the streets but didn't recognize where she was. She was freezing. Her ears were ringing, and all the sounds were muffled. Cara tried to remember what had just happened to her and how she got there, but everything was fuzzy, hazy: as if she was trying to see something through frosted glass. She wanted to remember something, but she couldn't remember what. She was overcome with an overwhelming feeling of loss. She was forgetting something important. What had she forgotten?

She wasn't sure why she was standing in the alley. How had she gotten here? Why was she crying? She stepped forward out of the alley and slipped. She landed on something cold. Her hands had vanished into a coating of snow covering the edge of the sidewalk. Where had that come from? She tried to push herself up, but she was shaky and wobbly, and she slipped on the slick snow. She couldn't get her feet underneath her to stand. Blue light filled her vision, then red. She looked up.

A police car.

"Ma'am, are you alright," a deep voice asked. Her vision was blurry. She looked up at the police officer, and he gasped. He spoke into his radio. "I need an ambulance to my location immediately. I found the missing woman. I found Cara DeLeon."

The words struck her as odd. Missing, the officer had said. She had been missing. Since when? How long had she been gone? Where had she gone? She was missing? What had happened? Cara sat on the edge of the sidewalk listening as sirens wailed in the distance, getting closer and closer.

***

In an apartment across town, a phone rang. A hand reached out for the phone, and a voice husky with sleep answered.

"Hello?"

"Is this David Goldschmidt? You filed the missing person's report for Cara DeLeon?" a lady asked crisply.

"Yes," the voice answered, more urgent now, more awake. The light next to the bed came on. He sat up in bed.

"We need you to come to Manhattan General Hospital. We found your fiancé," the lady said.

"I'm on my way." David flew out of bed and drove recklessly fast to the hospital. "Cara DeLeon's room," he asked at the nurse's station.

"Down the hall, take a left, and it will be the third door on the right," the nurse informed him.

***

David walked up to Cara's mother sitting in a chair outside the hospital room. She sobbed and hugged him. "They won't let me in to see her yet," she sniffed. "Craig's in Denver for work. He couldn't get a flight out. He lands in the morning."

David knew Cara would want to see her father when he came in. "I can get him from the airport."

"No, thank you, David. You don't need to do that. You need to be here for-."

The door to the hospital room opened, and a doctor came out.

"Susan DeLeon?" he asked, looking down at his file.

"Yes," she responded.

"Your daughter is sleeping. You can go in to see her, but I wanted to ask you a few questions first." He looked down at the charts again. "You have no idea where she has been all this time?"

"No. I heard from her the night before she went missing."

"She has some fairly serious injuries which have healed: several broken bones and other various lacerations. They could all be a result of the subway accident, but it is highly unlikely these injuries would have healed on their own without significant medical care."

"What does that mean?" David asked.

"It's possible she was at another hospital all this time, but we have inquired at all the ones in the surrounding area. There are no reports of her being admitted anywhere locally. She could have been taken somewhere further away, but it means she would have been transported there, and it would not have been by any of our local emergency services. It is also strange her injuries are already so far along in the healing process. Some of her breaks were significant. They can easily take over three to four months in a cast to heal, but you reported her missing about three months ago. She didn't have any of these injuries before she went missing?"

"What? No. Of course, she didn't," David shot back defensively.

The doctor looked uncomfortable. "There is something else. I do have to warn you. This might be a little upsetting to look at."

Susan wrung her hands, looking pale and worried. "There is a symbol cut into her skin near her collarbone. It looks like someone carved it into her," the doctor explained as he produced a picture from his folder, revealing the image of an elaborately carved 'S' scarred up on her chest.

"What do you mean? Somebody cut this into her skin?"

David was furious. "Jesus," he breathed while Susan burst into tears again. "What the hell happened to her?"

"We don't know yet. We haven't talked to her, but the police will want to question her when she wakes up. I can assure you; she is in good hands now." The doctor tried to sound as sympathetic as possible.

"Will she be okay?" Susan asked.

"She is in remarkably good health. She isn't dehydrated or malnourished, which is what we would expect to see in a typical abduction case."

"Abduction? You think she was taken?" David asked.

"I'm no detective, but I can say there is no way she cut that onto her chest herself. Who did though-"

"That is what I am going to find out," a voice finished from behind them. David and Susan turned to see a tall, dark-haired man approaching. Despite his casual dress, he held out a badge. "Detective Pierce, I've been the one-"

"Yes, yes, we have been in touch. Thank you so much for coming," David firmly shook his hand.

"She's waking up," a nurse said as she emerged from the room.

"You can go see her. She may be tired and disoriented, so be patient," the doctor warned.

Detective Pierce gestured for everyone to enter. The trio walked in with one goal in mind. It was time to get answers.

Cara opened her eyes when the door opened and looked around her. "Mom?" she asked, confused, and looking around the hospital room. Her mother rushed to her side, tears in her eyes. David was there too.

"Cara," Susan cried, kissing her forehead.

"What happened?" she asked. She struggled to remember how she got to the hospital, but she just couldn't remember.

A doctor entered the room. "Cara," he addressed her. "I am glad to see you are awake," he walked over to some monitors, checking them. "How are you feeling?"

Cara shrugged. "I feel okay. Just a little tired." She wiped her eyes. "What happened to me? How did I get here?" she asked.

"We were hoping you could tell us," a voice responded. She looked up at the man in the doorway. "My name is Detective Pierce," he said. "I have been the one working your case."

"Case?"

"You don't remember anything?" Detective Pierce asked.

"Leaving for work and then..." she trailed off. "Why can't I remember anything after?" she asked.

Detective Pierce shrugged and looked at the doctor. "Amnesia may explain why she didn't come back. If she lost short-term memories, she might have been confused."

"Come back where? What happened?" Cara was annoyed. No one was giving her clear answers.

"Honey, you've been missing for three months," her mother said.

"After the train accident, we thought you were dead," David said.

"Accident?" She vaguely recalled, but the details were fuzzy and hard to remember clearly.

"The day you went missing, a subway train slid off the tracks. Sixteen people died. We have video footage of you getting on the subway, but we never located you after."

Cara tried to process the information. "So, what happened? I just vanished?"

"We don't know. Where did you go?" David asked.

"I have no idea." She pressed her hands to her face. "I'm so tired."

"All right, I think that is enough for now," the doctor said.

Cara watched everyone leave. What had happened to her?

The trio convened in the hall.

"How does she not remember?" David asked.

"Amnesia isn't uncommon after a trauma. Her brain is trying to repress the memories of whatever happened to her."

Detective Pierce held up his hands. "How long until she gets it back?"

The doctor shrugged. "There is no telling. Each case is unique. It could be days or months. Some patients never get the memories back."

Detective Pierce smacked his file folder against his palm, frustrated.

"We will be running every test we can to make sure she is okay, but right now, it does appear she is in good health," the doctor explained.

"When will she be able to come home?" Susan asked.

"If everything looks good and she feels like she is ready for it, she may be able to go home in just a few days. In the meantime, we will do everything possible to get you more answers. Right now, though, the best thing you can do for her is just to go home and get some rest and let her rest too."

Cara was discharged from the hospital two days later after she was deemed to be in good enough health. A host of doctors had come to see her: psychologists, psychiatrists, trauma therapists, neurologists, and more. They had questioned her, quizzed her, and tested her in a dozen different ways, but no answers were revealed. Every television station and newspaper seemed to have sent reporters to get the inside scoop, but Cara didn't want to talk to them. She didn't want to be a spectacle for people's amusement.

As Cara exited the elevator flanked by her mother and David, there was a high-pitched shriek. Startled, Cara latched onto her mother's arm. Olivia rushed to her, holding onto the strings of half a dozen bouncing pink balloons. She threw her arms around her, wrapping her in a huge hug.

"I am so happy to see you!" she squealed. "We are going for pizza!" Olivia laced her fingers with Cara's, pulling her out to the car. Not long after, Cara found herself sitting in a booth surrounded by the people she knew best, yet they seemed like strangers. Maybe it wasn't her friends who had become strangers; maybe it was her.

After lunch, David brought her back to her apartment. He tried to come in, but she turned in the doorway, keeping him from entering.

"I'm really tired." She pressed a hand against his chest.

David looked hurt but nodded. "Are you sure you're going to be okay?" he asked.

"I'm sure. I promise. If I need anything, I will call you."

She needed some space. She was suffocating. At least at the hospital, the doctors kept strict visiting hours, giving her plenty of time to herself to rest

"Okay," David leaned in to kiss her, but she tipped her head just enough so he got her cheek instead.

"See you later." She closed the door and looked around her apartment. Nothing was out of place. Everything was just as she had left it. Coffee mug on the counter, scarf by the door. Yet, it all felt wrong, but it didn't matter now. She was home and tired. She slipped her shoes off and made her way to her room. She crawled into bed and was asleep before she had even pulled the blanket up.

Olivia met Cara at her apartment the next morning. "I wanted to make sure you got off to work okay." Olivia gave her a quick hug as she walked through the door.

Cara took a deep breath and smiled. "Thanks, I could use a friend right now." She tried to sound like she meant it.

"Are you sure you're ready for this?" Olivia asked. Everyone had tried to persuade Cara to take more time to recover before going back to work, but it was the only way to get back to as normal a life as possible.

"Yes. The bills aren't going to pay themselves," Cara joked.

Olivia rolled her eyes. "That is not true at all. David can pay your bills."

"I refuse to be one of those women who just sits at home while someone pays for all my stuff." Cara refused to allow herself to believe she could rely on David. It would be good for her to get out and about and be around people. One of the therapists at the hospital said that isolating herself was the worst thing she could do while recovering.

"I guess," Olivia shrugged, handing her a paper cup and a small brown bag. "Coffee and a bagel."

Cara took the coffee. She sucked it down like it was the last coffee she was ever going to have. It tasted better than she remembered.

"Woah, girl. Slow down. You're going to have a stroke."

Cara smiled. "Sorry." She opened the bag and took out the bagel. "Want some?" She ripped off a chunk and held it out to Olivia.

"No, I ate mine on the way over. Let's go. Don't want you to be fired for being late on your first day back."

They made their way outside and down the road, Olivia guiding the light conversation, not broaching the subject of Cara's disappearance. Olivia looked back when Cara stopped in her tracks.

"What's wrong?" Olivia frowned, looking back and forth between Cara and the subway station.

"Let's take a taxi."

"But it will take at least an extra 20 minutes."

"I don't want to take the subway," Cara said more forcefully.

"Okay, we'll take a taxi." Olivia hailed one from the curb.

Cara hated how she was still so afraid, but she couldn't bring herself to take the subway. Olivia was looking at her, obviously concerned, but Cara forced a smile and hoped she wouldn't pry.

"I am so glad you're home," Olivia said as she was climbing into the taxi.

"So am I," Cara answered. She wanted to mean it, but she just didn't feel it in her heart.

Chapter Fifty-Two

Work dragged. When she got home, Cara sat on the floor in the middle of her apartment. She looked around. Scanning. Surveying. This should be home. She recognized it, but the familiarity of it was gone. It didn't feel like home. She didn't belong here. This overwhelming feeling inside of her was growing each day, and she didn't know why.

Cara still had no more answers about what had happened to her while she had been gone. She was stuck living someone else's life. She found herself searching travel destinations on her computer at work, dozens of tabs open to the furthest locations she could find. She was trapped here in the city. She couldn't even talk to anyone about it because she was afraid of what they would think about her mental status. Everyone would try to reason with her, tell her she was just feeling this way because of her disappearance, but she knew there was more to it than that. What kind of sane person would ever wish they were back where they had been held captive? Whatever had happened to her while she was gone had changed her so profoundly, she wasn't the same person who had climbed aboard the subway that fateful day.

Sleep didn't come easy. When it did, she was plagued with strange dreams. Not quite nightmares, but they weren't exactly pleasant. She would wake up trying to remember them, hoping there would be clues to what had happened to her, but she could never remember a single detail, no matter how hard she tried.

She would stand in front of the mirror, looking at the strange scar on her chest. How could she not remember something like that happening to her? The doctors had all said it was normal for memories to be blurry and for things to come back in snippets over time, but nothing was coming back to her. She often found herself feeling the puckered skin under her shirt, randomly at work, as if touching it would remind her how it had gotten there in the first place.

Before she knew it, she had been home a week already, then a month. Quickly, she found herself sliding back into the routine of her life. She came up with every reason in the book to cancel dates with David and plans with Olivia. Olivia saw right through her excuses, catching on quickly. David, on the other hand, was completely clueless.

She hadn't ventured out at all, not even to get groceries. She didn't have much of an appetite. Grief could do that to a person, but grief about what? What had she lost that she was mourning? She was starting to believe she would never feel normal again.

She was staring out the window at Central Park after work when there was a knock on her door. She opened it to find Detective Pierce standing there.

"I was hoping to have a word?"

"Please, come in." Cara gestured for him to enter. "I haven't had a chance to go to the store yet. All I have is water." She blushed, embarrassed by the admission.

Detective Pierce smiled, but she could tell he was making mental notes. She would have to be careful with what she said to prevent his mental alarms from going off.

"Water is just fine." He looked around as he walked through her living room. He sat down in one of the armchairs, and Cara brought him a glass of water and sat on the couch.

"How are you doing?"

"I'm doing okay. I've been back to work for a few weeks already, and I have a follow up at the hospital on Tuesday," she explained.

The detective nodded as she spoke. "I was wondering if I could ask you a few questions?"

Cara sighed. "I told you everything I know. I don't remember anything - the subway and then the hospital. Everything between is gone. No matter how hard I think, it just comes up blank."

Detective Pierce pulled out a photo from his folder. It was a scarred open wound in the shape of an elaborate 'S.' She unconsciously raised her hand to touch the spot on her chest where the scar was. "You have no idea what this means or how you got it?"

She shook her head; she was just as frustrated as the Detective was. "You know, Detective, I want answers just as much as you do, but I don't remember."

Pierce slipped the photo away. "I'm sorry to pry, but there are just so many unanswered questions. You were wearing the same clothes the night you were found that you wore the day you vanished. But they had been cleaned."

Frustration bubbled. "I don't know," she said sharply. "I want to remember. I do. I try, and I try and nothing." Her voice cracked.

"I'm sorry. I didn't mean to upset you." Pierce stood. "I do appreciate your time Cara. If you remember anything that can help us with your case, please let us know."

On his way out of the apartment building, his phone rang. "Pierce," he answered.

"Hey, Vince," his friend and colleague Henry Stevens spoke. "I got those test results you wanted, but they don't make any sense."

Pierce's grip tightened on the phone in anticipation. He had sent Cara's clothes off to the science lab at NYU to see if there were any contaminants that could pinpoint her location during the time she was missing.

"Like you said, her clothes were mostly clean, but I couldn't pinpoint the chemicals used to clean them. None of the major brands we tested matched. But we found some unusually odd particles on her pants."

"Odd how?" Pierce asked.

"There were traces of particles that don't match any of the elements found here on Earth."

"I don't understand," Pierce was confused, trying to put the pieces together.

"Technetium is an element not found naturally on Earth. It's been found on meteorites that fall to Earth, but there are no natural sources of it here."

"So, what does that mean? Are you saying she was in space?" Pierce still didn't understand.

"Well, unless she was taken to a science museum or one of NASA's laboratories, it appears to be the only other plausible explanation, but I'd start the search a little closer to home. Maybe check out the Goddard Institute for Space Studies at Columbia."

Pierce hung up. It wasn't much to go on, but it was a start.

That evening, Cara was sitting across from David at the little Italian place. He was eating, talking about work. She couldn't bring herself to eat a bite.

"David, when did we get engaged?" she asked. David looked away, uncomfortable.

"Well, actually." He hesitated. "It was the only way I could stay involved with the investigation. I had to be family. So, I told them we were engaged."

"You lied?" she asked, surprised and confused. "You lied to my family? To me?"

He turned red. "I was planning on it anyway. It would have happened soon, but then you vanished, and I couldn't sit in the dark the whole time, not knowing anything."

"You assumed I would have said yes?"

"Well," he paused. "I mean, wasn't that the plan?" He was floundering, struggling to find the right words.

"Maybe it was before, but now…" She pulled off the ring. "This belongs to you." She slid it to him and stood. It took him a moment to find his voice as she was leaving.

"Cara, please." He grabbed her arm as she was pulling on her coat. She pulled her arm out of his grasp and left, pushing through the front door and out into the chilly night. "Cara, wait," he called after her.

She quickened her pace, not turning around. She wasn't running from him. She was running towards something. She just couldn't say yet what that was.

The End

Thank You

Dear Reader,

Thank you so much for going on this journey with me. I am so honored you chose my book, and I hope you enjoyed reading it as much as I did writing it. Publishing a book has been an experience I will never forget, just as I hope you will not forget the story of Caine and Cara. Look for their story to continue in the sequel!

About Daniel Kasper

Daniele Kasper's travels have taken her around the world and back again, but her favorite adventures will always be found between the covers of a good book. From rescuing dolphins in the Florida Keys, to getting chased by grizzly bears in Alaska, Daniele has taken her adventures and used them as inspiration for her writing. Eventually, she married a horse trainer and settled down in central Michigan. She is now a farm girl with her husband, The Cowboy. They have four rescue dogs, a multitude of cats and chickens and a couple of cowponies. Daniele loves reading and writing fantasy and science fiction. She also loves all things Outlander and Disney, can't grow a garden to save her life and occasionally moonlights as an elementary teacher.

Social Media

Website: www.danielekasper.com

Facebook: https://www.facebook.com/danielekasperauthor

Instagram:
https://www.instagram.com/danielekasperauthor/
@danielekasperauthor

Twitter: https://twitter.com/DanieleKasper @danielekasper

Acknowledgements

For my friends, who still choose to put up with me while I talk endlessly about time travel, research the operational specs of spaceships, and hide away in dark corners scribbling in notebooks for hours on end. The fact that you still want to hang out with me after all these years shows how truly amazing you are.

For my poor family, who have no choice.

For my husband, who had no idea what he was getting into.

And for the two brightest stars in the sky, Saige and Pascal.